Dance
Upon the Air

Nora Roberts

HOT ICE

SACRED SINS

BRAZEN VIRTUE

SWEET REVENGE

PUBLIC SECRETS

GENUINE LIES

CARNAL INNOCENCE

HONEST ILLUSIONS

DIVINE EVIL

PRIVATE SCANDALS

HIDDEN RICHES

TRUE BETRAYALS

MONTANA SKY

SANCTUARY

HOMEPORT

THE REEF

RIVER'S END

CAROLINA MOON

THE VILLA

MIDNIGHT BAYOU

THREE FATES

BIRTHRIGHT

NORTHERN LIGHTS

BLUE SMOKE

ANGELS FALL

HIGH NOON

TRIBUTE

BLACK HILLS

THE SEARCH

CHASING FIRE

THE WITNESS

WHISKEY BEACH

THE COLLECTOR

TONIGHT AND ALWAYS

THE LIAR

THE OBSESSION

Series

Irish Born Trilogy
BORN IN FIRE
BORN IN ICE
BORN IN SHAME

Dream Trilogy
DARING TO DREAM
HOLDING THE DREAM
FINDING THE DREAM

Chesapeake Bay Saga
SEA SWEPT
RISING TIDES
INNER HARBOR
CHESAPEAKE BLUE

Gallaghers of Ardmore Trilogy
JEWELS OF THE SUN
TEARS OF THE MOON
HEART OF THE SEA

Three Sisters Island Trilogy
DANCE UPON THE AIR
HEAVEN AND EARTH
FACE THE FIRE

Key Trilogy
KEY OF LIGHT
KEY OF KNOWLEDGE
KEY OF VALOR

In the Garden Trilogy
BLUE DAHLIA
BLACK ROSE
RED LILY

Circle Trilogy
MORRIGAN'S CROSS
DANCE OF THE GODS
VALLEY OF SILENCE

Sign of Seven Trilogy
BLOOD BROTHERS
THE HOLLOW
THE PAGAN STONE

Bride Quartet
VISION IN WHITE
BED OF ROSES
SAVOR THE MOMENT
HAPPY EVER AFTER

The Inn BoonsBoro Trilogy
THE NEXT ALWAYS
THE LAST BOYFRIEND
THE PERFECT HOPE

The Cousins O'Dwyer Trilogy
DARK WITCH
SHADOW SPELL
BLOOD MAGICK

The Guardians Trilogy
STARS OF FORTUNE
BAY OF SIGHS
ISLAND OF GLASS

Ebooks by Nora Roberts

Cordina's Royal Family

AFFAIRE ROYALE
COMMAND PERFORMANCE
THE PLAYBOY PRINCE
CORDINA'S CROWN JEWEL

The Donovan Legacy

CAPTIVATED
ENTRANCED
CHARMED
ENCHANTED

The O'Hurleys

THE LAST HONEST WOMAN
DANCE TO THE PIPER
SKIN DEEP
WITHOUT A TRACE

Night Tales

NIGHT SHIFT
NIGHT SHADOW
NIGHTSHADE
NIGHT SMOKE
NIGHT SHIELD

The MacGregors

PLAYING THE ODDS
TEMPTING FATE
ALL THE POSSIBILITIES
ONE MAN'S ART
FOR NOW, FOREVER
REBELLION/IN FROM THE COLD
THE MACGREGOR BRIDES
THE WINNING HAND
THE MACGREGOR GROOMS
THE PERFECT NEIGHBOR

The Calhouns

COURTING CATHERINE
A MAN FOR AMANDA
FOR THE LOVE OF LILAH
SUZANNA'S SURRENDER
MEGAN'S MATE

Irish Legacy

IRISH THOROUGHBRED
IRISH ROSE
IRISH REBEL

LOVING JACK
BEST LAID PLANS
LAWLESS

BLITHE IMAGES
SONG OF THE WEST
SEARCH FOR LOVE
ISLAND OF FLOWERS
THE HEART'S VICTORY
FROM THIS DAY
HER MOTHER'S KEEPER
ONCE MORE WITH FEELING
REFLECTIONS
DANCE OF DREAMS
UNTAMED
THIS MAGIC MOMENT
ENDINGS AND BEGINNINGS
STORM WARNING
SULLIVAN'S WOMAN
FIRST IMPRESSIONS
A MATTER OF CHOICE

LESS OF A STRANGER
THE LAW IS A LADY
RULES OF THE GAME
OPPOSITES ATTRACT
THE RIGHT PATH
PARTNERS
BOUNDARY LINES
DUAL IMAGE
TEMPTATION
LOCAL HERO
THE NAME OF THE GAME
GABRIEL'S ANGEL
THE WELCOMING
TIME WAS
TIMES CHANGE
SUMMER LOVE
HOLIDAY WISHES

Anthologies

FROM THE HEART
A LITTLE MAGIC
A LITTLE FATE

MOON SHADOWS
(with Jill Gregory, Ruth Ryan Langan, and Marianne Willman)

The Once Upon Series
(with Jill Gregory, Ruth Ryan Langan, and Marianne Willman)

ONCE UPON A CASTLE   ONCE UPON A ROSE
ONCE UPON A STAR   ONCE UPON A KISS
ONCE UPON A DREAM   ONCE UPON A MIDNIGHT

SILENT NIGHT
(with Susan Plunkett, Dee Holmes, and Claire Cross)

OUT OF THIS WORLD
(with Laurell K. Hamilton, Susan Krinard, and Maggie Shayne)

BUMP IN THE NIGHT
(with Mary Blayney, Ruth Ryan Langan, and Mary Kay McComas)

DEAD OF NIGHT
(with Mary Blayney, Ruth Ryan Langan, and Mary Kay McComas)

THREE IN DEATH

SUITE 606
(with Mary Blayney, Ruth Ryan Langan, and Mary Kay McComas)

IN DEATH

THE LOST
(with Patricia Gaffney, Mary Blayney, and Ruth Ryan Langan)

THE OTHER SIDE
(with Mary Blayney, Patricia Gaffney, Ruth Ryan Langan, and Mary Kay McComas)

TIME OF DEATH

THE UNQUIET
(with Mary Blayney, Patricia Gaffney, Ruth Ryan Langan, and Mary Kay McComas)

MIRROR, MIRROR
(with Mary Blayney, Elaine Fox, Mary Kay McComas, and R. C. Ryan)

DOWN THE RABBIT HOLE
(with Mary Blayney, Elaine Fox, Mary Kay McComas, and R. C. Ryan)

Also available . . .

THE OFFICIAL NORA ROBERTS COMPANION
(edited by Denise Little and Laura Hayden)

Dance Upon the Air

NORA ROBERTS

BERKLEY

NEW YORK

BERKLEY
An imprint of Penguin Random House LLC
penguinrandomhouse.com

Copyright © 2001 by Nora Roberts
Excerpt from *Heaven and Earth* copyright © 2001 by Nora Roberts

ISBN: 9780593437698

The Library of Congress has cataloged the previous edition of this book as follows:

Roberts, Nora.
Dance upon the air / Nora Roberts.
pages cm.—(Three Sisters Island trilogy ; #1)
ISBN 9780425278147 (pbk.)
1. Women—Massachusetts—Fiction. 2. Secrets—Fiction. 3. Witches—Fiction.
4. Islands—Fiction. 5. Love stories. I. Title.
PS3568.O243D367 2014
813'.54—dc23
2014022538

Jove mass-market edition / June 2001
First Berkley trade paperback edition / January 2015
Second Berkley trade paperback edition / April 2021

Printed in the United States of America

1st Printing

Text design by Laura K. Corless.

To the Broads, the Brats, the Brawn, and the Babes,
For the fun and the friendships

It is sweet to dance to violins
When Love and Life are Fair:
To dance to flutes, to dance to lutes
Is delicate and rare:
But it is not sweet with nimble feet
To dance upon the air!

—OSCAR WILDE

Dance
Upon the Air

Prologue

In the dark green shadows of the deep woods, an hour before moon-rise, they met in secret. Soon the longest day would become the shortest night of the solstice.

There would be no celebration, no rite of thanksgiving for the light, the warmth, on this Sabbat of Litha. This midsummer was a time of ignorance, and of death.

The three who met, met in fear.

"Have we all we need?" The one known here as Air pulled her hood closer so that not a single pale lock of hair could be seen in the light of the dying day.

"What we have shall do." Earth laid her parcel on the ground. The part of her that wanted to weep and to rage over what had been done, over what was to come, was buried deep. With her head bent, her thick brown hair fell forward free.

"Is there no other way for us?" Air touched a hand to Earth's shoulder, and both looked at the third.

She stood, slim and straight. There was sorrow in her eyes, but behind it lived a firm purpose. She who was Fire threw back her hood in a gesture of defiance. Curling waves of red spilled out.

"It is because of our way there is no other. They will hunt us down like thieves and brigands, murder us, as they have already murdered a poor innocent."

"Bridget Bishop was not a witch." Earth spoke bitterly as she rose to her feet.

"No, and so she told the court of oyer and terminer. So she swore. Yet they hanged her. Murdered over the lies of a few young girls and the ravings of the fanatics who smell brimstone in every breath of air."

"But there have been petitions." Air linked her fingers together like a woman preparing to pray. Or plead. "Not everyone supports the court, or this terrible persecution."

"Too little," Earth murmured. "And far too late."

"It will not end with one death. I have seen it." Fire closed her eyes, saw again the horrors to come. "Our protection cannot outlast the hunt. They will find us, and they will destroy us."

"We have done nothing." Air dropped her hands to her sides. "No harm."

"What harm did Bridget Bishop do?" Fire countered. "What harm have any of the others accused and waiting trial done to the people of Salem Town? Sarah Osborne died in a Boston prison. For what crime?"

Temper lanced through her, hot and keen, and was ruthlessly rejected. Even now she refused to let power be stained by anger and hate.

"The blood is up in these Puritans," she continued. "These *pioneers*. Fanatics they are, and they will bring a wave of death before sanity returns."

"If we could help."

"We cannot stop it, sister."

"No." Fire nodded at Earth. "All we can do is survive. So we leave this place, the home we made here, the lives we might have led here. And make another."

Gently, she cupped Air's face in her hands. "Grieve not for what can never be, but celebrate what can. We are the Three, and we will not be vanquished in this place."

"We will be lonely."

"We will be together."

And in that last flicker of the day they cast the circle—one by two by three. Fire ringed around the earth, and the wind lifted the flames high.

Inside the magic circle they formed another, joining hands.

Accepting now, Air lifted her face to the sky. "As night takes the day, we offer this light. We are true to the Way and stand for the right. Truth here is done, a circle of one."

Earth, defiant, raised her voice. "This hour is our last upon this ground. Present, future, past, we will not be found. Strength not rue, a circle of two."

"We offered our craft with harm to none, but the hunt for our blood has already begun. We will make our place away from here." Fire lifted joined hands high. "Away from death, away from fear. Power lives free, a circle of three."

The wind kicked, the earth trembled. And the magic fire speared through the night. Three voices rose, in unison.

"Away from hate let this land be torn. Lift it from fear, from death and scorn. Carve rock, carve tree, carve hill and stream. Carry us with it on midsummer moonbeam. Out past the cliff and out past the shore, to be severed from this land forever more. We take our island out to the sea. As we will, so mote it be."

And a great roar sounded in the forest, a swirling torrent of wind, a wild leap of fire. While those who hunted what they never under-stood slept in their righteous beds, an island rose up toward sky, circled madly toward sea.

Settled safe and serene on quiet waves. And took its first breath of life on that shortest night.

One

THREE SISTERS ISLAND

JUNE 2001

She kept staring straight ahead as the knuckle of land, bumpy and green with distance, began revealing its secrets. The lighthouse, of course. What was an offshore New England island without its stalwart spear? This one, pure and dazzling white, rose on a craggy cliff. Just as it should, Nell thought.

There was a stone house near it, fog-gray in the sharp summer sunlight, with peaked roofs and gables and what she hoped was a widow's walk circling the top story.

She'd seen paintings of the Light of the Sisters and the house that stood so strong and firm beside it. It was the one she'd seen in the little shop on the mainland, the one that had sent her impulsively to the car ferry.

She'd been following impulse and instinct for six months, just two months after her meticulous and hard-worked plan had freed her.

Every moment of those first two months had been terror. Then, gradually, terror had eased to anxiety, and a different kind of fear, almost like a hunger, that she would lose what she had found again.

She had died so she could live.

Now she was tired of running, of hiding, of losing herself in crowded cities. She wanted a home. Wasn't that what she'd always wanted? A home, roots, family, friends. The familiar that never judged too harshly.

Maybe she would find some part of that here, on this spit of land cradled by the sea. Surely she could get no farther away from Los Angeles than this pretty little island—not unless she left the country altogether.

If she couldn't find work on the island, she could still take a few days there. A kind of vacation from flight, she decided. She would enjoy the rocky beaches, the little village, she would climb the cliffs and roam the thick wedge of forest.

She'd learned how to celebrate and cherish every moment of being. It was something she would never, ever forget again.

Delighted with the scatter of clapboard cottages tucked back from the dock, she leaned on the rail of the ferry, let the wind blow through her hair. It was back to its natural sun-drenched blond. When she'd run, she'd hacked it short as a boy's, gleefully snipping off the long, tumbling curls, then dyeing it deep brown. Over the past months, she'd changed the color periodically—bright red, coal black, a soft sable brown. She still kept it fairly short and very straight.

It said something, didn't it, that she'd finally been able to let it be. Something about reclaiming herself, she thought.

Evan had liked it long, with a riot of curls. At times he had dragged her by it, across the floor, down the stairs. Using it like chains.

No, she would never wear it long again.

A shudder ran through her, and she glanced quickly over her shoulder, scanning the cars, the people. Her mouth went dry, her throat hot as she searched for a tall, slim man with gilded hair and eyes as pale and hard as glass.

He wasn't there, of course. He was three thousand miles away. She was dead to him. Hadn't he told her a hundred times that the only way she would be free of him was in death?

Helen Remington had died so Nell Channing could live.

Furious with herself for going back, even for a moment in her mind, Nell tried to calm herself. She breathed in slowly. Salt air, water. Freedom.

As her shoulders relaxed again, a tentative smile played around her mouth. She stayed at the rail, a small woman with short, sunny hair that danced cheerfully around a delicate face. Her mouth, unpainted and soft, curved up and teased out the hint of dimples in her cheeks. Pleasure brought a rosy glow to her skin.

She wore no makeup, another deliberate act. There was a part of her that was still hiding, still hunted, and she did whatever she could to pass unnoticed.

Once she had been considered a beauty, and had groomed herself accordingly. She'd dressed as she'd been told to dress, wearing sleek, sexy, sophisticated clothes selected by a man who claimed to love her above all things. She'd known the feel of silk against her skin, what it was to casually clasp diamonds around her throat. Helen Remington had known all the privileges of great wealth.

And for three years had lived in fear and misery.

Nell wore a simple cotton shirt over faded jeans. Her feet were comfortable in cheap white sneakers. Her only jewelry was an antique locket that had been her mother's.

Some things were too precious to leave behind.

As the ferry slowed to dock, she walked back to her car. She would arrive on Three Sisters with one small bag of belongings, a rusted secondhand Buick, and $208 to her name.

She couldn't have been happier.

Nothing, she thought as she parked the car near the docks and began to wander on foot, could have been farther from the pleasure palaces and glitz of Beverly Hills. And nothing, she realized, had ever called more truly to her soul than this little postcard village. Houses and shops were both tidy and prim with their colors faded by sea salt and sun. Cobblestone streets were curvy and whistle-clean as they climbed the hilly terrain or arrowed back to the docks.

Gardens were lovingly tended, as if weeds were illegal. Dogs barked behind picket fences and children rode bikes of cherry red and electric blue.

The docks themselves were a study in industry. Boats and nets and ruddy-cheeked men in tall rubber boots. She could smell fish and sweat.

She hiked up the hill from the docks and turned to look back. From there she could see the tour boats plugging along in the bay, and the little sickle slash of sand beach where people spread out on towels or bobbed in the energetic surf. A little red tram with white letters that read THREE SISTERS TOURS was rapidly filling up with day-trippers and their cameras.

Fishing and tourism, she supposed, were what kept the island afloat. But that was economics. It stood against sea, storms, and time, surviving and flourishing at its own pace. That, she thought, was courage.

It had taken her too long to find her own.

High Street speared across the hill. Shops and restaurants and what she supposed were island businesses lined it. One of the restaurants should be her first stop, she thought. It was possible she could hook a job as a waitress or short-order cook, at least for the summer season. If she could find work, she could hunt up a room.

She could stay.

In a few months, people would know her. They'd wave as she

walked by, or call out her name. She was so tired of being a stranger, of having no one to talk to. No one who cared.

She stopped to study the hotel. Unlike the other buildings it was stone instead of wood. Its three stories with elaborate gingerbread, iron balconies, and peaked roofs were undeniably romantic. The name suited it, she decided. The Magick Inn.

It was a good bet that she'd find work there. Waitressing in the dining room, or as part of the housekeeping staff. A job was the first order of business.

But she couldn't make herself go inside, deal with it. She wanted time first, a little time before she settled down to the practical.

Flighty, Evan would have said. You're much too flighty and foolish for your own good, Helen. Thank God you have me to take care of you.

Because his voice played all too clearly in her ears, because the words nipped at the confidence she'd slowly rebuilt, she turned deliberately away and walked in the opposite direction.

She would get a damn job when she was ready to, but for now she was going to wander, to play tourist, to explore. When she was finished roaming High Street, she'd go back to her car and drive all over the island. She wouldn't even stop at the Island Tourist Board to get a map.

Following her nose, she hitched up her backpack and crossed the street. She passed craft shops, gift shops, loitered at the windows. She enjoyed pretty things that sat on shelves without purpose. One day, when she settled again, she'd make a home just as she pleased, full of clutter and fun and color.

An ice cream shop made her smile. There were round glass tables and white iron chairs. A family of four sat at one, laughing as they spooned up whipped cream and confetti-colored sprinkles. A boy wearing a white cap and apron stood behind the counter, and a girl in snug cutoff jeans flirted with him as she considered her choices.

Nell sketched the picture in her mind and walked on.

The bookstore stopped her, made her sigh. Her home would be full of books, too, but not rare first editions never meant to be opened and read. She'd have old, scarred books, shiny new paperbacks all in a jumble of stories. In fact, that was one thing she could start now. A paperback novel wouldn't add much weight to her pack if she had to move on.

She looked up from the display in the window to the Gothic lettering spilling across the glass. Café Book. Well, that was perfect. She would hunt through the stacks, find something fun to read, and look through it over a cup of coffee.

She stepped inside to air that was fragrant with flowers and spice, and heard music played on pipes and harps. Not only the hotel was magic, Nell thought the minute she crossed the threshold.

Books, in a banquet of colors and shapes, lined deep blue shelves. Overhead, tiny pricks of light showered down from the ceiling like stars. The checkout counter was an old oak cabinet, deeply carved with winged faeries and crescent moons.

A woman with dark, choppy hair sat on a high stool behind it, idly paging through a book. She glanced up and adjusted silver-framed reading glasses.

"Morning. Can I help you?"

"I'm just going to look around, if that's all right."

"Enjoy. Let me know if I can help you find anything."

As the clerk went back to her book, Nell roamed. Across the room two generous chairs faced a stone hearth. On the table between stood a lamp fashioned from a figurine of a robed woman with her arms lifted high. Other shelves held trinkets, statues of colored stone, crystal eggs, dragons. She wandered through, passing books on one side, rows of candles on the other.

At the rear, stairs curved to the second floor. She climbed and found more books, more trinkets, and the café.

Half a dozen tables of glossy wood were arranged near the front window. Along the side was a glass display and counter boasting an impressive array of pastries, sandwiches, and a kettle of that day's soup. The prices were on the high side, but not unreasonable. Nell thought she might have some soup to go with her coffee.

Moving closer, she heard the voices from the open door behind the counter.

"Jane, this is ridiculous, and totally irresponsible."

"It is not. It's Tim's big chance, and it's a way off this damn island. We're taking it."

"The possibility of an audition for a play that may or may not be produced Off Broadway is *not* a big chance. Neither one of you will have a job. You won't—"

"We're going, Mia. I told you I'd work till noon today, and I worked till noon."

"You told me that less than twenty-four hours ago."

There was impatience in the voice—a low, lovely voice. Unable to help herself, Nell edged closer.

"How the hell am I going to keep the café up without anyone to cook?"

"It's all about you, isn't it? You can't even wish us luck."

"Jane, I'll wish you a miracle, because that's what it's going to take. No, wait—don't go off in a huff."

Nell caught movement in the doorway and stepped to the side. But she didn't move out of earshot.

"Be careful. Be happy. Oh, damn it. Blessed be, Jane."

"Okay." There was a loud sniffle. "I'm sorry, really, I'm sorry for leaving you in the lurch this way. But Tim needs to do this, and I need to be with Tim. So . . . I'll miss you, Mia. I'll write."

Nell managed to duck behind shelves just as a weeping woman raced out of the back and ran down the stairs.

"Well, isn't this just fine."

Nell peeked out, blinked in automatic admiration.

The woman who stood in the doorway was a vision. Nell couldn't think of another word for her. She had a mass of hair the color of autumn leaves. Reds and golds spilled over the shoulders of a long blue dress that left her arms bare to the silver bracelets that winked bright on each wrist. Her eyes, sparking with temper, were gray as smoke and dominated a flawless face. Slashing cheekbones, a full, wide mouth painted siren red. Skin like . . . Nell had heard skin compared to alabaster, but this was the first time she'd seen it.

She was tall, willow-slim, and perfect.

Nell glanced toward the café tables to see if any of the customers who loitered there were as awestruck as she herself. But no one seemed to notice the woman or the temper swirling around her like water on the boil.

She inched out to get a better look, and those gray eyes shifted. Pinned her.

"Hello. Can I help you?"

"I was . . . I thought . . . I'd like a cup of cappuccino and a bowl of soup. Please."

Annoyance flashed in Mia's eyes and nearly sent Nell back behind the shelves. "I can handle the soup. We have lobster bisque today. I'm afraid the espresso machine is beyond my current capabilities."

Nell looked at the beautiful copper-and-brass machine, felt a little tingle. "I could make it myself."

"You know how to work this thing?"

"Yes, actually, I do."

Considering, Mia gestured and Nell scurried behind the counter.

"I could make you one while I'm at it."

"Why not?" Brave little rabbit, Mia mused, as she watched Nell take over the machine. "Just what sent you to my door? Backpacking?"

"No. Oh." Nell flushed, remembering her pack. "No, just exploring a little. I'm looking for a job, and a room."

"Ah."

"Excuse me, I know it was rude, but I overheard your . . . conversation. If I understand it correctly, you're in a bit of a jam. I can cook."

Mia watched the steam rise, listened to the hiss. "Can you?"

"I'm a very good cook." Nell offered Mia the frothing coffee. "I've done catering, I've worked in a bakery, and I've waitressed. I know how to prepare food and how to serve it."

"How old are you?"

"Twenty-eight."

"Do you have a criminal record?"

A giggle nearly burst out of Nell's throat. For a moment it danced lively in her eyes. "No. I'm tediously honest, a dependable worker, and a creative cook."

Don't babble, don't babble! she ordered herself, but she couldn't seem to stop. "I need the job because I'd like to live on the island. I'd like a job here because I enjoy books and I liked the, well, the feel of your shop as soon as I walked in."

Intrigued, Mia angled her head. "And what did you feel?"

"Possibilities."

Excellent answer, Mia mused. "Do you believe in possibilities?"

Nell considered. "Yes. I've had to."

"Excuse me?" A couple stepped up to the counter. "We'd like to have two iced mochas and two of those éclairs."

"Of course. Just a moment." Mia turned back to Nell. "You're hired. Apron's in the back. We'll work out the details later today." She sipped her cappuccino. "Well done," she added and stepped out of the way. "Oh—what's your name?"

"I'm Nell. Nell Channing."

"Welcome to Three Sisters, Nell Channing."

Mia Devlin ran Café Book the way she ran her life. With a style born out of instinct, and largely for her personal amusement. She was a crafty businesswoman who enjoyed making a profit. But always on her own terms.

What bored her, she ignored. What intrigued her, she pursued.

At the moment, Nell Channing intrigued her.

If Nell had been exaggerating her skills, Mia would have fired her as quickly as she'd hired her, and with no regret. She may have, if the spirit moved her, helped Nell secure a job elsewhere. But that wouldn't have taken much time, or interfered with her business.

She'd have taken that step only because something about Nell had tugged at her the instant those big blue eyes met hers.

Injured innocence. That had been Mia's first impression, and she trusted her first impressions implicitly. Competence as well, Mia thought, though the confidence was a little shaky.

Still, once Nell had suited up and started work at the café, she'd steadied in that area, too.

Mia observed her through the afternoon, noted that she handled the food orders, the customers, the cash register, and the baffling mystery of the espresso machine smoothly.

They'd need to spruce her up a bit, Mia decided. They were casual on the island, but the ancient jeans were a bit too laid-back for Mia's personal taste.

Satisfied for the moment, Mia walked back into the café kitchen. It impressed her that the counters and appliances were clean. Jane had never managed to be a tidy cook, even though most of the baked goods had been prepared by her off-site.

"Nell?"

Taken by surprise, Nell jolted and spun around from the stove, where she'd been scrubbing burners. Her cheeks flushed as she looked at Mia and the young woman beside her.

"Didn't mean to startle you. This is Peg. She works the counter from two to seven."

"Oh. Hello."

"Hi. Jeez, I can't believe Jane and Tim are just *leaving*. New York City!" Peg sounded a bit envious. She was little and perky, with a mop of curly hair bleached nearly white. "Jane made awesome blueberry muffins."

"Yes, well, Jane and her muffins aren't here anymore. I need to talk to Nell now, so you're in charge of the café."

"No problem. Catch you later, Nell."

"Why don't we use my office? We'll get to those details. We're open from ten to seven, summer hours. In the winter we cut back and close at five. Peg prefers the afternoon shift. She likes to party and isn't a morning person. In any case, since we start serving at ten, I'll need you here in the morning."

"That's okay with me." She followed Mia up another flight of steps. She hadn't paid attention, Nell realized. She hadn't known the shop had three floors. A few months before, she would never have missed that detail. She'd have checked out the space, the exits.

Relaxing didn't mean getting sloppy, she reminded herself. She had to be ready, at any time, to run again.

They passed a large storeroom, lined with bookshelves and stacked with boxes, then went through a doorway into Mia's office.

The antique cherry desk suited her, Nell thought. She imagined Mia surrounded by the rich and the beautiful. There were flowers here, and thriving plants, little bits of crystal and polished rocks in bowls. Along with the stylish furnishings were a top-of-the-line computer, a fax, filing cabinets, and shelves for publishers' catalogs. Mia gestured to a chair and took the one behind the desk for herself.

"You had a few hours in the café, so you've seen the type of fare we offer. There's a specialty sandwich each day, the day's soup, a small selection of alternate sandwiches. Two or three varieties of cold salads. Pastries, cookies, muffins, biscotti. In the past I left the menu choices up to the cook. Are you comfortable with that?"

"Yes, ma'am."

"Please, I'm barely a year older than you. It's Mia. Until we're sure this is going to work, I'd prefer you make up the next day's menu for my approval." She took a legal pad out of the drawer, passed it across the desk. "Why don't you write down what you have in mind for tomorrow?"

Panic wanted to crawl through her, tremble in her fingers. Nell took a deep breath, waited until her mind was blank and clear, then began to write. "This time of year, I think we should keep the soups light. Herbed consommé. Tortellini salad, a white bean, and a shrimp. I'd do a spiced-chicken pita for the sandwich, and a vegetarian selection, but I'd have to see what's in season. I can make you tarts, again depending on what looks good fruit-wise. The éclairs are popular— I can duplicate those. A six-layer chocolate-and-cream torte. Awesome blueberry muffins, as well as walnut. You're low on hazelnut biscotti. Cookies? Chocolate chip is never wrong. Macadamia. Instead of a third cookie, I'd offer brownies. I make an irresistible triple-fudge brownie."

"How much can you prepare on-site?"

"All of it, I guess. But if you're going to serve the pastries and muffins starting at ten, I'll need to start about six."

"If you had your own kitchen?"

"Oh, well." What a lovely fantasy that was. "I'd prep some of the menu the night before, bake fresh in the morning."

"Um-hmm. How much money do you have, Nell Channing?"

"Enough."

"Don't be prickly," Mia advised breezily. "I can advance you a hundred dollars. Going against a salary, to start, of seven an hour. You'll log your shopping, cooking hours daily. You'll charge what you need, food-wise, to the store's account. I'll want the receipts, again daily."

When Nell opened her mouth to speak, Mia simply lifted one slim, coral-tipped finger. "Wait. You'll be expected to serve and to clear tables when there's a rush, and to assist customers in the book section on your level during lulls. You get two half-hour breaks, Sundays off, and a fifteen percent employee discount on purchases, not including food or drink—which unless you turn out to be a glutton, will be part of your perks. With me so far?"

"Yes, but I—"

"Good. I'm here every day. If you have a question or problem you can't handle, get me. If I'm not available, go to Lulu. She's usually at the counter on the main floor, and she knows everything. You look quick enough to catch on; if you don't know an answer, don't be afraid to ask. Now, you're looking for a place to stay."

"Yes." It was like being swept away by a fast, unexpected wind. "I hope to—"

"Come with me." Mia pulled a set of keys out of a drawer, pushed away from the desk and clipped out—she wore gorgeous, needle-thin heels, Nell noted.

Once they were on the main level, she walked straight toward a rear door. "Lulu!" she called out. "Back in ten."

Feeling clumsy and foolish, Nell followed her through the back exit and into a small garden paved with stepping-stones. A huge black cat sunned itself on one of them and blinked open one luminous gold eye as Mia stepped nimbly over.

"That's Isis. She won't trouble you."

"She's beautiful. Is the garden your work?"

"Yes. No place is a home without flowers. Oh, I didn't ask—do you have transportation?"

"Yes, I have a car. It can loosely be called transportation."

"That's handy. You won't have far to go, but it'd be troublesome to cart your goods on foot every day." At the edge of the lot she turned left, kept up her brisk pace, passed the backs of shops, across from neatly kept houses.

"Ms.— I'm sorry, I don't know your last name."

"It's Devlin, but I told you to call me Mia."

"Mia, I'm grateful for the job. For the chance. And I can promise you, you won't be sorry. But . . . can I ask where we're going?"

"You need a place." She turned a corner, stopped and gestured. "That should do it."

Across the narrow side street sat a little yellow house, like a cheerful sunbeam at the edge of a tiny grove of stunted trees. The shutters were white, as was the narrow strip of porch. There were flowers there, too, in a happy dance of bright summer colors.

It sat back from the road on a neat square of lawn with trees tucking it into shade and dappled sunlight.

"Is this your house?" Nell asked.

"Yes. For the moment." Jingling the keys, Mia walked up the flagstone path. "I bought it last spring."

Had been compelled to, Mia remembered. An investment, she'd told herself. Though she, a businesswoman down to the bone, had done nothing so far about renting it out. She'd waited, just as, she understood, the house had waited.

She unlocked the front door, stepped back. "It's been blessed."

"Excuse me?"

Mia only nodded. "Welcome."

The furnishings were sparse. A simple sofa that desperately needed re-covering, a deep-cushioned chair, a scatter of tables.

"Bedrooms on either side, though the one to the left is more suited to an office or study. The bathroom's minute, but charming, and the kitchen's been modernized and should do very well. It's straight back. I've worked on the gardens, but they need more care. There's no AC, but the furnace works. Still, you'll be glad the fireplace works as well come January."

"It's wonderful." Unable to resist, Nell wandered, poking her head in the main bedroom where a pretty bed with a white iron headboard stood. "Like a fairy cottage. You must love living here."

"I don't live here. You do."

Nell turned back, slowly. There was Mia, in the center of the little room, her hands cupped together with the keys in her palm. Light beamed through the two front windows and seemed to set her hair to flame.

"I don't understand."

"You need a place, I have a place. I live on the cliffs. I prefer it there. This is your place, for now. Don't you feel it?"

She only knew she felt happy, and full of nerves at the same time. And that the moment she'd stepped into the house, she'd wanted to stretch and settle, very much like the cat in the sunshine.

"I can stay here?"

"Life's been hard, hasn't it?" Mia murmured. "That you'd tremble at good fortune. You'll pay rent, for nothing that comes free holds its value. We'll work the terms out of your salary. Settle in. You'll have to come back and sign forms and so on. But that can wait for the morning. Island Market is your best source for the ingredients you'll need for tomorrow's menu. I'll let them know you're coming, so you can charge to the store account. Any pots, pans, whatever are your expense, but I'll float that until the end of the month. I expect to see you, and your creations, by nine thirty sharp."

She stepped over and dropped the keys into Nell's limp hand. "Any questions?"

"Too many to know where to begin. I don't know how to thank you."

"Don't waste your tears, little sister," Mia replied. "They're too precious. You'll work hard for what you make here."

"I can't wait to get started." Nell held out her hand. "Thank you, Mia."

Their hands touched, clasped. A spark snapped out, blue as flame and quickly gone. With a half laugh, Nell jerked back. "Must be a lot of static, or something, in the air."

"Or something. Well, welcome home, Nell." Turning, Mia started for the door.

"Mia." Emotion gathered in her throat, ached there. "I said this was like a fairy cottage. You must be my fairy godmother."

Mia's smile was dazzling, and her laughter low and rich as warmed cream. "You'll find out soon enough I'm far from it. I'm just a practical witch. Don't forget to bring me the receipts," she added and quietly closed the door behind her.

Two

The village, Nell decided, was a bit like Brigadoon as seen by Nathaniel Hawthorne. She'd taken some time to explore before she'd gone to the market. For months she'd told herself she was safe. She was free. But for the first time, wandering the pretty streets with their quaint houses, breathing in the sea air, listening to the sharp New England voices, she *felt* safe. And free.

No one knew her, but they would. They would know Nell Channing, the clever cook who lived in the little cottage in the wood. She would make friends here, and a life. A future. Nothing from the past would touch her here.

One day she would be as much a part of the island as the narrow post office with its faded gray wood or the tourist center cobbled together by old clinker bricks, and the long, sturdy dock where fishermen brought their daily catch.

To celebrate she bought a wind chime fashioned of stars that she saw in a shop window. It was her first purchase for pleasure in nearly a year.

She spent her first night on the island in the lovely bed, hugging her happiness to her as she listened to the stars ring and the sea breathe.

She was up before sunrise, eager to begin. While the day's soup simmered, she rolled out pastry dough. She'd spent every penny she had, including most of the advance and a good portion of her next month's salary, on kitchen tools. It didn't matter. She would have the best and produce the best. Mia Devlin, her benefactor, would never have cause to regret taking her on.

Everything in the kitchen was precisely as she wanted it. Not as she'd been told it must be. When she had time, she would make a run to the island's garden center for herbs. Some she would plant outside the windowsill. All cluttered together the way she liked things to be. Nothing, absolutely nothing, in her home would be uniform and precise and stylishly sleek. She wouldn't have acres of marble or seas of glass or towering urns of terrifyingly exotic flowers without warmth or scent. There wouldn't be . . .

She stopped herself. It was time to stop reminding herself of what wouldn't be, and plan what would be. Yesterday would hound her until she firmly closed the door on it and shot the bolt.

While the sun came up, turning the east-facing windows to flame, she slid the first batch of tarts into the oven. She remembered the rosy-cheeked woman who had helped her at the market. Dorcas Burmingham—such a fine Yankee name, Nell thought. And full of welcome and curiosity. The curiosity would have shut Nell down once, turned her inward. But she'd been able to chat, to answer some questions breezily and avoid others.

Tarts cooled on the rack and muffins went into the oven. As the kitchen filled with light, Nell sang to welcome the day.

☙

L ulu folded her arms over her skinny chest. It was, Mia knew, her way of trying to look intimidating. As Lulu barely inched up to five feet, weighed ninety pounds soaking wet, and had the face of a woeful pixie, it took work for her to look intimidating.

"You don't know anything about her."

"I know she's alone, looking for work, and in the right place at the right time."

"She's a stranger. You don't just hire a stranger, *and* lend her money, give her a house, without at least doing a background check. Not one reference, Mia. Not one. For all you know, she's a psychopath running from the law."

"You've been reading true crime books again, haven't you?"

Lulu scowled, an expression that on her harmless face approximated a pained smile. "There are bad people in the world."

"Yes, there are." Mia printed out the mail-order requests that had come through her computer. "Without them we'd have no balance, no challenge. She's running from something, Lu, but not the law. And fate pointed her here. It brought her to me."

"And sometimes fate's a backstabber."

"I'm well aware of that." With the printouts in hand, Mia walked out of the office, Lulu on her heels. Only the fact that Lulu Cabot had essentially raised her prevented Mia from telling her to mind her own business. "And you should know I can protect myself."

"You take in strays, your guard goes down."

"She's not a stray, she's a seeker. There's a difference. I felt something from her," Mia added as she started downstairs to fill the orders. "When she's more comfortable I'll look closer."

"At least get a reference."

Mia lifted a brow as she heard the back door open. "I just got one. She's prompt. Don't poke at her, Lulu," Mia ordered as she handed the printouts over. "She's also tender yet. Well, good morning, Nell."

"Good morning." Arms full of covered trays, Nell breezed in. "I pulled my car around back. That's all right, isn't it?"

"That's just fine. Need a hand?"

"Oh, no, thanks. I have everything stacked in the car."

"Lulu, this is Nell. You can get acquainted later."

"Nice to meet you, Lulu. I'll just start setting things up."

"You go right ahead." Mia waited until Nell climbed the stairs. "Looks dangerous, doesn't she?"

Lulu set her jaw. "Looks can be deceiving."

Moments later Nell jogged downstairs again. She wore a plain white T-shirt tucked into her jeans. The little gold locket lay against it like a charm. "I started a first pot of coffee. I'll bring some down next trip, but I don't know how you like it."

"Black for me, sweet and light for Lu. Thanks."

"Um . . . would you mind not going up to the café until I've finished? I'd really like you to see the whole presentation. So just . . ." She backed toward the door, face flushed, as she spoke. "Wait. Okay?"

"Eager to please," Mia commented as she and Lulu filled the orders. "Eager to work. Yes, definite psychopathic tendencies. Call the cops."

"Shut up."

Twenty minutes later, breathless, jangled with pleasure and nerves, Nell came downstairs again. "Can you come up now? I still have time to change things around if it doesn't suit you. Oh, could you come, too, Lulu? Mia said you know everything about the shop, so you'd know if it doesn't look the way it should."

"Hmph." Grudgingly Lulu stopped ringing up the mail orders. "Café's not my department." But with a shrug, she followed Mia and Nell upstairs.

The display case was brimming with glossy pastries, wide-topped muffins and scones popping with golden currants. A tall torte gleamed under a sleek chocolate frosting and laces of whipped cream. Cookies as big as a man's palm covered two delicate white sheets of baker's paper. Wafting out of the kitchen was the scent of soup simmering.

On the chalkboard, written in a fine and careful hand, were the day's specials. The glass had been polished to a gleam, the coffee was irresistibly fragrant, and a pale blue canning jar filled with cinnamon sticks stood on the counter.

Mia walked up and down the display, like a general inspecting troops, while Nell stood struggling not to wring her hands.

"I didn't put the salads and the soup out yet. I thought if I waited till around eleven for that, people would be more apt to go for the pastries. There're more tarts in the back, and the brownies. I didn't put them out because, well, I think people want them more if it doesn't look as if you're oversupplied. And the brownies are more lunch and afternoon items. I put the torte out now, hoping customers might think about it and end up coming back into the shop again later for a slice. But I can rearrange things if you'd rather—"

She broke off when Mia lifted a finger. "Let's sample one of those tarts."

"Oh. Sure. Just let me get one from the back." She darted into the kitchen, then back out again with a tart in a little paper doily.

Saying nothing, Mia broke it in two, handed half to Lulu. As she took the first bite, her lips curved. "How's that for a reference?" she murmured, then turned back to Nell. "If you keep looking so nervous, customers are going to think something's wrong with the food. Then they won't order it, and they'll miss something very special. You have a gift, Nell."

"You like it?" Nell let out a relieved sigh. "I sampled one of everything this morning. I'm half sick," she said as she pressed a hand to her stomach. "I wanted everything to be just right."

"And so it is. Now relax, because once word gets out we've got a genius in the kitchen, you're going to be very busy."

&

Nell didn't know if word got out, but she was soon too busy for nerves. By ten thirty she was brewing another pot of coffee and resupplying trays. Every time her cash register rang, it was a separate little thrill. And when she bagged up a half a dozen muffins for a customer who claimed she'd never tasted better, Nell had to order herself not to spring into a dance.

"Thanks. Come back soon." Beaming, she turned to the next customer.

That was Zack's first impression of her. A pretty blonde wearing a white apron and a mile-wide smile with winking dimples. It gave him a quick and pleasant little jolt, and his own grin flashed in response.

"I heard about the muffins, but I didn't hear about the smile."

"Smile's free. The muffins'll cost you."

"I'll take one. Blueberry. And a large black coffee to go. I'm Zack. Zack Todd."

"Nell." She scooped up one of the to-go cups. She didn't have to shoot him a sidelong glance. Experience had taught her to read a face fast and remember it. His was still in her mind as she filled the cup.

Tanned, with faint lines fanning out from sharp green eyes. A firm jaw with an intriguing diagonal scar scoring it. Brown hair, a little long, with a bit of curl that was already sun-streaked in June. A narrow face with a long, straight nose, a mouth that smiled easily and showed a slightly crooked incisor.

It struck her as an honest face. Easygoing, friendly. She set the coffee on the counter, casting him another glance as she plucked a muffin from the tray.

He had broad shoulders and good arms. His shirt was rolled up at the sleeves and faded from sun and water. The hand that curled around the coffee cup was big and wide. She tended to trust big hands on a man. It was the slender, manicured ones that could strike so lethally.

"Just one?" she said as she bagged his muffin.

"One'll do me for now. Word is you just got to the island yesterday."

"Good timing for me." She rang up his order, pleased when he opened the bag and sniffed.

"Good timing all around if this tastes as good as it smells. Where'd you come in from?"

"Boston."

He cocked his head. "Doesn't sound like Boston. Your accent," he explained when she simply stared at him.

"Oh." She took his money with a steady hand, made change. "Not originally. A little town in the Midwest—outside of Columbus. I moved around a lot, though." Her smile stayed in place as she handed him his change and receipt. "I guess that's why I don't sound like I'm from anywhere in particular."

"Guess so."

"Hey, Sheriff."

Zack glanced over his shoulder, nodded. "Morning, Miz Macey."

"You get 'round to talking to Pete Stahr about that dog of his?"

"Heading that way now."

"Dog as soon roll in dead fish as he would in roses. Then what's he do but run right through my hanging wash. Had to do the lot of it again. I like dogs same as the next."

"Yes, ma'am."

"But Pete's got to keep that hound on a leash."

"I'll have a word with him this morning. You ought to get yourself one of these muffins, Miz Macey."

"I just came in for a book." But she looked at the display, her lips pursing in her wide face. "Do look tasty, don't they? You'd be the new girl."

"Yes." Nell's throat was raw and hot. She feared her voice sounded the same. "I'm Nell. Can I get you anything?"

"Maybe I'll just have a sit-down with a cup of tea and one of those tarts. I've got a weak spot for a good fruit tart. None of those fancy teas, mind. Give me good orange pekoe. You tell that Pete to keep his dog out of my wash," she added to Zack. "Else he'll be doing my laundry."

"Yes, ma'am." He smiled at Nell again, kept his eyes on her face deliberately as he'd noted how quickly it had paled when Gladys Macey had called him sheriff. "Nice meeting you, Nell."

She gave him a little nod. Kept her hands busy, he noticed, but not quite steady.

Just what, he wondered, would a pretty young woman like that have to fear from the law? Then again, he thought as he walked downstairs, some people were just naturally skittish when it came to cops.

He scanned the main level, spotted Mia stocking shelves in the mystery section. Either way, Zack decided, it wouldn't hurt to ask a few casual questions.

"Busy in here today."

"Mmm." She slid paperbacks into slots without looking around. "I expect it to get busier. Season's just underway, and I have my new secret weapon in the café."

"Just met her. You're renting her the yellow cottage."

"That's right."

"You check her employment record, references?"

"Now, Zack." Mia did turn now. In her heels she was nearly eye to eye with him, and she gave his cheek a sassy pat. "We've been friends a long time. Long enough for me to tell you to mind your own business. I don't want you going up to my café and interrogating my staff."

"Okay, I'll just haul her down to the station house and get out my rubber hose."

She chuckled, then leaned over and gave him a peck on the cheek. "You brute. Don't worry about Nell. She isn't looking for trouble."

"Got twitchy when she found out I was sheriff."

"Honey, you're so handsome you make all the girls twitchy."

"Never worked on you," he countered.

"A lot you know. Now go away, let me run my business."

"I'm going. Have to do my sworn duty and scold Pete Stahr over his smelly dog."

"Sheriff Todd, you're so brave." She batted her lashes. "What would we islanders do without you and your stalwart sister protecting us?"

"Ha-ha. Ripley's due in on the noon ferry. Any sooner, I'd stick her with dog detail."

"Is a week up already?" Mia grimaced and went back to shelving. "Oh, well, nothing good lasts forever."

"I'm not getting in the middle of you two again. I'd sooner deal with Pete's dog."

She laughed at him, but once he'd gone she looked toward the steps, thought of Nell, and wondered.

She made it a point to go upstairs late in the morning. Nell had already put out the salads and the soup, subtly shifting the mode toward the lunch crowd. The salads, Mia noted, looked fresh and appealing, and the scent of the soup was going to tempt anyone who walked into the store.

"How's it going?"

"Fine. We've finally hit a little lull." Nell wiped her hands on her apron. "Brisk business this morning. The muffins won the race, but the tarts came in a close second."

"You're officially on break," Mia told her. "I'll take care of anyone who comes in, unless they want something that requires the use of that monster machine."

In the kitchen, Mia slid onto a stool, crossed her legs. "Stop by my office after your shift. We'll get the employment forms signed."

"Okay. I've been thinking about tomorrow's menu."

"We'll discuss that then, too. Why don't you get yourself a cup of coffee and relax?"

"I'm already hyped enough." But Nell did open the fridge, removed a small bottle of water. "I'll stick with this."

"You've settled into the house all right?"

"It was easy. I can't remember ever sleeping better, or waking better. With the windows open, I can just hear the surf. It's like a lullaby. And did you see the sunrise this morning? Spectacular."

"I'll take your word for it. I tend to avoid sunrise. It insists on coming so early in the day." She held out her hand and surprised Nell into passing the bottle of water to her for a sip. "I heard you met Zack Todd."

"Did I?" Nell immediately picked up a cloth, began buffing the stove. "Oh. Sheriff Todd. Yes, he had coffee, black, and a blueberry muffin to go."

"There's been a Todd on the island for centuries, and Zachariah's one of the best of the lot. Kind," Mia said deliberately. "Caring, and decent without being a pain in the ass about it."

"Is he your . . ." The word *boyfriend* just didn't seem to apply with a woman like Mia. "Are you and he involved?"

"Romantically? No." Mia held the bottle back out to Nell. "He's entirely too good for me. Though I did have a mild crush on him when I was fifteen or sixteen. After all, he's a prime specimen. You must have noticed."

"I'm not interested in men."

"I see. Is that what you're running from? A man?" When Nell

didn't respond, Mia slid to her feet. "Well, if and when you're inclined to talk about it, I'm an excellent listener, with a sympathetic ear."

"I appreciate all you've done for me, Mia. I just want to do my job."

"Fair enough." The bell dinged, signaling someone had come to the counter. "No, you're on break," Mia reminded her before Nell could hurry out of the kitchen. "I'll take the counter for a while. And don't look so sad, little sister. You've no one to answer to now but yourself."

Oddly soothed, Nell stayed where she was. She could hear the low ripple of Mia's voice as she spoke to the customers. The store music was flutes now and something fluid. She could close her eyes and imagine herself here, just here, the next day. The next year. Comfortable and comforted. Productive and happy.

There was no reason to be sad or afraid, no cause to be concerned about the sheriff. He'd have no purpose in paying attention to her, looking into her background. And if he did, what would he find? She'd been careful. She'd been thorough.

No, she was no longer running away. She'd run to. And she was staying.

She finished off her water, started out of the kitchen just as Mia turned around. The clock in the square began to bong the noon hour, in slow, ponderous tones.

The floor beneath her feet seemed to tremble, and the light went brilliant and bright. Music swelled inside her head, like a thousand harp strings plucked in unison. The wind—she could have sworn she felt a hot wind flow over her face and lift her hair. She smelled candle wax and fresh earth.

The world shuddered and spun, then righted itself in a blink of time, as if it had never moved. She shook her head to clear it and found herself staring into Mia's deep gray eyes.

"What was that? An earthquake?" Even as she said it, Nell saw that no one else in the store looked concerned. People milled, sat, chatted, sipped. "I thought . . . I felt . . ."

"Yes, I know." Though Mia's voice was quiet, there was an edge to it Nell hadn't heard before. "Well, that explains it."

"Explains what?" Shaken, Nell gripped Mia's wrist. And felt something like power rocket up her arm.

"We'll talk about it. Later. Now the noon ferry's in." And Ripley was back, she thought. They, the three, were all on-island now. "We'll be busy. Serve your soup, Nell," she said gently, and walked away.

Mia wasn't often taken by surprise, and she didn't care for it. The strength of what she'd felt and experienced along with Nell had been more intense, more intimate, than she'd expected. And that annoyed her. She should have been prepared. She of all people knew, believed, and understood what twist fate had taken so many years before. And what twist it could take now.

Still, believing in fate didn't mean a woman simply stood there and let it run her down. Actions could and would be taken. But she had to think, to sort things out.

What in the goddess's name was she supposed to do to make things right when she would be bound to a stubborn twit of a woman who consistently denied her power and a scared rabbit on the run who didn't know she had any?

She closed herself in her office, paced. She rarely turned to magic here. It was her place of business, and she deliberately kept it separate and earthbound. But there were exceptions, she told herself, to every rule.

So thinking, she took her crystal globe from the shelf, set it on

her desk. It amused her to see it there, along with her two-line phone
and computer. Still, magic respected progress, even if progress didn't
always respect magic.

Laying her hands on either side of the globe, she cleared her mind.

"Show me what I have to see. This island holds the sisters three,
and we will shape our destiny. Visions in glass come clear to me. As
I will, so mote it be."

The globe shimmered and swirled. And cleared. In its depths, like
figures in water, she saw herself, Nell, and Ripley. A circle formed in
the shadows of the woods, and a fire burning. The trees were aflame
as well, but with color struck by autumn. Light poured out from a
full moon like water shimmering.

A new shadow formed in the trees and became a man. Beautiful
and golden with eyes that burned.

The circle broke. Even as Nell ran, the man struck out. She shattered like glass, a thousand pieces scattering. And the skies opened
to lightning, blasted with thunder, and all Mia could see in the glass
was a torrent of water as the woods, and the island they lived on,
tumbled into the sea.

Mia stepped back, planted her hands on her hips. "Isn't that always
the way?" she said in disgust. "A man ruins everything. Well, we'll see
about that." She put the globe back on the shelf. "We'll just see about
that."

By the time Nell knocked on her door, Mia was just finishing up
some paperwork. "Right on time," she said as she logged off the
computer. "That's a pretty habit of yours. I need you to fill out these
forms." She gestured to the neat stack on the desk. "I've dated them
yesterday. How's the lunch crowd moving?"

"Smoothly enough." Nell sat. Her palms no longer sweated when she filled out forms. Name, date of birth, Social Security number. Those basic facts and figures were hers. She'd seen to it personally. "Peg dives right in. I made up tomorrow's menu."

"Mmm." Mia took the folded paper Nell pulled out of her pocket, read it over while Nell filled in the form. "It looks good. More adventurous than Jane's tended to be."

"Too adventurous?"

"No, just more. So . . . what will you do with the rest of your day"—Mia briefly looked at the first completed form—"Nell, no middle initial, Channing?"

"Take a walk on the beach, do some gardening. Maybe explore the woods around the cottage."

"There's a small stream where columbine grows wild this time of year, and in the deeper shade jack-in-the-pulpits and ferns. The kind that make you think the faeries hide in them."

"You don't strike me as the kind of person who looks for shy faeries."

Mia's lips curved. "We don't know each other well yet. Three Sisters is alive with legend and lore, and the woods have all manner of secrets. Do you know the story of the Three Sisters?"

"No."

"I'll tell you one day when there's time for tales and stories. But for now you should be out in the light and air."

"Mia, what happened before? At noon?"

"You tell me. What do you think happened?"

"It felt like an earth tremor, but not. The light changed, and so did the air. Like a . . . blast of energy."

It sounded foolish when she said it, but she pushed on. "You felt it too. But no one else did. No one else felt anything out of the ordinary."

"Most people expect the ordinary, and that's what they get."

"If that's a riddle, I don't know how to solve it." Impatient, Nell shoved to her feet. "You weren't surprised by it—a little irritated but not surprised."

Mia sat back, intrigued, and lifted a brow. "True enough. You read people very well."

"Survival skill."

"And sharply honed," Mia added. "What happened? I suppose you could call it a connection. What happens when three positive charges occupy the same space at the same time?"

Nell shook her head. "I have no idea."

"Neither do I. But it'll be interesting to find out. Like recognizes like, don't you think? I recognized you."

Nell's blood went cold and burned under her skin. "I don't know what you mean."

"Not who you are, or were," Mia said gently. "But what. You can trust me to respect that, and your privacy. I won't pry into your yesterdays, Nell. I'm more interested in the tomorrows."

Nell opened her mouth. She nearly, very nearly, let it pour out. Everything she'd escaped from, everything that haunted her. But to do so put her fate in the hands of another. That was something she would never do again.

"Tomorrow I'll serve a summer vegetable soup and a chicken, zucchini, and ricotta sandwich. That's as complicated as it's going to get."

"That's as good a start as any. Enjoy your afternoon." Mia waited until Nell reached the door. "Nell? As long as you're still afraid, he wins."

"I don't give a damn about winning," Nell replied. Then she stepped out quickly and closed the door behind her.

Three

Nell found the stream, and the wild columbine—like little drops of sun in the green shade. Sitting on the soft floor of the forest, listening to the stream gurgle and the birds chirp, she found her peace again.

This was her place. She was as sure of that as she'd been of any single thing in all her life. She belonged here as she'd belonged nowhere else.

Even as a child she'd felt displaced. Not by her parents, she thought, running her fingers over her locket. Never by them. But home had been wherever her father was stationed, and until his orders changed. There'd been no single place for childhood, no pretty spot for memories to take root and bloom.

Her mother had had the gift of making a home wherever they were, and for however long. But it wasn't the same as knowing you would wake up to the same view out of your bedroom window day after day.

And that was a yearning Nell had carried with her always.

Her mistake had been in believing she could soothe that yearning with Evan, when she should have known it was something she had to find for herself.

Perhaps she had, now. Here in this place.

That's what Mia had meant. *Like recognizing like.* They both belonged on the island. Maybe, in some lovely way, they belonged to it. It was as simple as that.

Still, Mia was an intuitive woman, and an oddly powerful one. She sensed secrets. Nell could only hope she was as good as her word and wouldn't pry. If anyone started digging through the layers, she would have to leave. No matter how much she belonged, she couldn't stay.

It wasn't going to happen.

Nell got to her feet, stretching up her arms to the thin sunbeams, and turned slow circles. She wouldn't *let* it happen. She was going to trust Mia. She was going to work for her and live in the little yellow cottage and wake each morning with a giddy, glorious sense of freedom.

In time, she thought as she began to walk back toward her house, she and Mia might become real friends. It would be fascinating to have a friend that vivid, that clever.

What was it like to be a woman like Mia Devlin? she wondered. To be someone so utterly beautiful, so sublimely confident? A woman like that would never have to question herself, to remake herself, to worry that whatever she did, or could do, would never be good enough.

What a marvelous thing.

Still, while a woman might be born beautiful, confidence could be learned. It could be won. And wasn't there amazing satisfaction from winning those small battles? Every time you did, you went back to war better armed.

Enough dawdling, enough introspection, she thought, and quickened her pace. She was going to blow the last of her advance at the garden center.

If that wasn't confidence, she decided, what was?

❧

They let her open an account. Another debt to Mia, Nell thought as she drove back across the island. She worked for Mia Devlin, so she was looked upon kindly, she was trusted, she was allowed to take away merchandise on the strength of her signature on a tally.

A kind of magic, she supposed, that existed only in small towns. She'd struggled not to take advantage, and had still ended up with half a dozen flats. And pots, and soil. And a silly stone gargoyle who would guard what she planted.

Eager to begin, she parked in front of the cottage and hopped out. The minute she opened the back door of the car, she was immersed in her small, fragrant jungle.

"We're going to have such fun, and I'm going to take wonderful care of all of you."

Feet planted firmly, she stretched inside to lift the first tray.

Hell of a view, Zack thought as he stopped across the street. A small, shapely female bottom in snug, faded jeans. If a man didn't spend a minute appreciating that, he was a sorry individual.

He got out of his cruiser, leaned against the door, and watched her take out a flat of pink and white petunias. "Pretty picture."

She jerked, nearly bobbled the tray. He noted that, just as he noted the alarm shoot into her eyes. But he straightened lazily, strolled across the street.

"Let me give you a hand."

"That's all right. I've got it."

"And a lot more. Gonna be busy." He reached past her, took out two more flats. "Where're you going with them?"

"Just around the back for now. I haven't decided where I'm putting everything yet. But really, you don't have to—"

"Smells good. What've you got here?"

"Herbs. Rosemary, basil, tarragon, and so on." The quickest way to be rid of him, she decided, was to let him cart the trays around. So she started across the yard. "I'm going to put in an herb bed outside the kitchen, maybe add a few vegetables when I have time."

"Planting flowers is planting roots, my mother always says."

"I intend to do both. Just on the stoop'll be fine. Thank you, Sheriff."

"You've got a couple more in the front seat."

"I can—"

"I'll fetch them. Did you think to get any soil?"

"Yes, in the trunk."

He smiled easily, held out his hand. "I need the keys."

"Oh. Well." Trapped, she dug in her pocket. "Thanks."

When he strolled off, she clasped her hands together. It was all right. He was just being helpful. Not every man, not every cop, was a danger. She knew better than that.

He came back loaded, and the sight of him, a huge bag of soil slung over one shoulder and a flat of pink geraniums and white impatiens in his big hands, made her laugh.

"I got too much." She took the flowers from him. "I only meant to get herbs, and before I knew it . . . I couldn't seem to stop."

"That's what they all say. I'll get your pots and tools."

"Sheriff." It had once been natural to her to repay kindness with kindness. She wanted it to be natural again. "I made some lemonade this morning. Would you like a glass?"

"I'd appreciate it."

All she had to do was remind herself to relax, to be herself. She filled two glasses with ice and poured in the tart lemonade. He was already back when she came out. Something about the way he looked, big and male, standing in the middle of pink and white flowers, gave her a quick little jolt.

Attraction. Even as she recognized the sensation, she reminded herself it wasn't anything she could or wanted to feel again.

"I appreciate the pack mule services."

"Welcome." He took the glass, draining half of it while that little jolt became a twitchy dance in her belly.

He lowered the glass. "This is the real thing. Can't think the last time I had fresh lemonade. You're a real find, aren't you?"

"I just like to fuss in the kitchen." She bent, picked up her new garden spade.

"You didn't buy any gloves."

"No, I didn't think of it."

She wanted him to drink his lemonade and scat, Zack thought, but was too polite to say so. Because he knew that, he sat on the little stoop outside the kitchen door, made himself comfortable. "Mind if I sit a minute? It's been a long day. Don't let me stop you from getting started, though. It's pleasant to watch a woman in the garden."

She'd wanted to sit on the stoop, she thought. To sit there in the sunshine and imagine what she would do with the flowers and herbs. Now all she could do was begin.

She started with the pots, reminding herself if she didn't like the results, she could always redo them.

"Did you, um, talk to the man with the dog?"

"Pete?" Zack asked, sipped at his lemonade. "I think we came to an understanding, and peace settles over our little island once more."

There was humor in the way he said it, and a lazy satisfaction as well. It was hard not to appreciate both.

"It must be interesting, being the sheriff here. Knowing everyone."

"It has its moments." She had small hands, he noticed as he watched her work. Quick, clever fingers. She kept her head bent, her eyes averted. Shyness, he decided, coupled with what seemed to him to be a rusty sense of socializing. "A lot of it's refereeing, or dealing with summer people who're vacationing too hard. Mostly it's running herd on about three thousand people. Between me and Ripley it's simple enough."

"Ripley?"

"My sister. She's the other island cop. Todds have been island cops for five generations. That's looking real nice," he said, gesturing toward her work-in-progress with his glass.

"Do you think?" She sat back on her heels. She'd mixed some of everything into the pot, stuck in some of the vinca. It didn't look haphazard as she'd feared it might. It looked cheerful. And so did her face when she lifted it. "It's my first."

"I'd say you've got a knack. Ought to wear a hat, though. Fair skin like yours is going to burn if you stay out long."

"Oh." She rubbed the back of her hand over her nose. "Probably."

"Guess you didn't have a garden in Boston."

"No." She filled the second pot with soil. "I wasn't there very long. It wasn't my place."

"I know what you mean. I've spent some time on the mainland. Never felt home. Your folks still in the Midwest?"

"My parents are dead."

"I'm sorry."

"So am I." She tucked a geranium into the new pot. "Is this conversation, Sheriff, or an inquiry?"

"Conversation." He picked up a plant that was just out of her reach and held it. A cautious woman, he decided. In his experience, cautious people usually had a reason. "Any point in me inquiring?"

"I'm not wanted for anything, never been arrested. And I'm not looking for trouble."

"That about covers it." He handed her the plant. "It's a small island, Miz Channing. Mostly friendly. Curiosity comes along with it, though."

"I suppose." She couldn't afford to alienate him, she reminded herself. She couldn't afford to alienate anyone. "Look, I've been traveling for a while now, and I'm tired of it. I came here looking for work and a quiet place to live."

"Looks like you found both." He got to his feet. "I appreciate the lemonade."

"You're welcome."

"That's a pretty job you're doing. You've got a knack for it, all right. Afternoon, Miz Channing."

"Afternoon, Sheriff."

As he walked back to his car he tallied up what he'd learned about her. She was alone in the world, wary of cops, prickly about questions. She was a woman of simple tastes and skittish nerves. And for reasons he couldn't quite fathom, she just didn't quite add up for him.

He glanced at her car as he crossed to his own, scanned the license plate. The Massachusetts tag looked brand spanking new. Wouldn't hurt to run it, he thought. Just to settle his mind.

His gut told him Nell Channing might not have been looking for trouble, but she wasn't a stranger to it.

Nell served apple turnovers and lattes to the young couple by the window and then cleared an adjoining table. A trio of women were browsing the stacks, and she suspected they'd be lured into the café section before long.

With her hands full of mugs, she loitered by the window. The ferry was arriving from the mainland, chased by gulls that circled and dived. Buoys bobbed in a sea that was soft and green today. A white pleasure boat, sails fat with wind, skimmed along the surface.

Once she'd sailed on another sea, in another life. It was one of the few pleasures she took from that time. The feel of flying over the water, rising on waves. Odd, wasn't it, that the sea had always called to her? It had changed her life. And had taken it.

Now, this new sea had given her another life.

Smiling at the thought, she turned and bumped solidly into Zack. Even as he took her arm to steady her, she was jerking back. "I'm sorry. Did I spill anything on you? I'm clumsy, I wasn't watching where—"

"No harm done." He hooked the fingers of one hand through two mug handles and, careful not to touch her again, took them from her. "I was in your way. Nice boat."

"Yes." She sidestepped, hurried back to the counter, behind it. She *hated* having anyone come up behind her. "But I'm not getting paid to watch boats. Can I get you anything?"

"Take a breath, Nell."

"What?"

"Take a breath." He said it gently as he set the mugs on the counter. "Get yourself steady again."

"I'm fine." Resentment pricked through her. She clanged mugs together as she scooped them off the counter. "I didn't expect to have anyone hulking around behind me."

His lips twitched. "That's better. I'll take one of those turnovers and a large coffee to go. Did you finish your planting?"

"Nearly." She didn't want to talk to him, so she busied herself with the coffee. She didn't want to have the island cop making friendly conversation and watching her out of those sharp green eyes.

"Maybe you can make use of this when you're finishing up and tending to your flowers." He laid a bag on the counter.

"What is it?"

"Garden tool." He counted out his money, set that on the counter as well.

She wiped her hands on her apron, scowled. But curiosity pushed her into opening the bag. Baffled humor lit her eyes as she studied the perfectly ridiculous rolled-brim straw hat. Foolish fake flowers danced around the crown.

"This is the silliest hat I've ever seen."

"Oh, there were sillier," he assured her. "But it'll keep the sun from burning your nose."

"It's very considerate of you, but you shouldn't—"

"Around here it's called being neighborly." The beeper on his belt signaled. "Well, back to work."

She managed to wait until he was halfway down the steps before she snatched the hat and dashed into the kitchen to try it on in the reflection of the stove hood.

Ripley Todd poured herself another cup of coffee and sipped it while looking out the front window of the station house. It had been a quiet morning, and that was just the way she liked it.

But there was something in the air. She was doing her best to ignore it, but *something* was in the air. It was easier to tell herself it was overstimulation from the week she'd spent in Boston.

Not that she hadn't enjoyed herself. She had. The law enforcement workshops and seminars had interested her, given her food for thought. She liked police work, the routine and detail of it. But the demands and chaos of the city wore on her, even in that short a time.

Zack would've said it was simply that she didn't like people overmuch. Ripley would've been the last one to argue with him about that.

She caught sight of him now, heading down the street. It would, she estimated, take him a good ten minutes to make the half block. People stopped him, always had a word to say.

More, she thought, people just liked being around him. He had a kind of . . . she didn't want to use the word *aura*. It was too Mia-like. Air, she decided. Zack just had the kind of air about him that made people feel better about things. They knew if they took their troubles to him, he'd have the answer, or take the time to find it.

Zack was a sociable creature, Ripley mused. Affable and patient and consistently fair. No one would accuse her of being any of those things.

Maybe that was why they made a good team.

Since he was heading in, she opened the front door to the summer air and street sounds, the way he liked it best. She brewed a fresh pot of coffee and was just pouring him a cup when he finally arrived.

"Frank and Alice Purdue had a baby girl—eight pounds, five ounces, at nine this morning. Calling her Belinda. The younger boy, Robbie, fell out of a tree, broke his arm. Missy Hachin's cousin in Bangor bought a brand-new Chevrolet sedan."

As he spoke, Zack took the offered coffee, sat at his desk, propped up his feet. And grinned. The ceiling fan was squeaking again. He'd really meant to see to that.

"So, what's new with you?"

"Speeder on the north coast road," Ripley told him. "Don't know where they thought they were going in such a hurry. I explained that the cliffs and the light and so on had been in place for a few centuries and weren't likely to move away in an afternoon." She plucked a fax out of his in-box. "And this came in for you. Nell Channing. That's the new cook at Mia's place, right?"

"Umm-hmm." He scanned the motor vehicle report. No traffic violations. She still carried an Ohio driver's license, due for renewal in just over two years. The car was registered in her name. He'd been right about the new tags. She'd had them less than a week. Before that, the car had carried Texas tags.

Interesting.

Ripley scooted onto the corner of the desk they shared and sampled his coffee since he wasn't drinking it. "Why'd you run her?"

"Curious. She's a curious woman."

"Curious how?"

He started to answer, then shook his head. "Why don't you drop into the café for lunch, check her out yourself. I'd be interested in your impression."

"Maybe I will." Frowning, Ripley glanced at the open door. "I think a storm's coming in."

"It's clear as glass out there, honey."

"Something's coming," she said half to herself, then grabbed her baseball cap. "I'll take a walk around, maybe stop in the café and take a look at our newest resident."

"Take your time. I'll do the afternoon beach patrol."

"You're welcome to it." Ripley slid on her sunglasses and strode out.

She liked her village, the order of it. As far as Ripley was concerned, everything had a place and that's just where it should stay. She didn't mind the vagaries of sea and weather—that was just another natural order of things.

June meant a fresh influx of tourists and summer people, temperatures moving from warm to hot, beach bonfires and smoking grills.

It also meant excess partying, the routine drunk and disorderly, the occasional lost child, and the inevitable lovers' spats. But the tourists who celebrated, drank, wandered, and squabbled brought summer dollars to the island that kept it afloat during the frigid gales of winter.

She would cheerfully—well, perhaps not too cheerfully—suffer the problems of strangers for a few months in order to preserve Three Sisters.

This nine square miles of rock and sand and soil was all the world she needed.

Overbaked people were staggering up from the beach toward the village for lunch. She could never figure out what possessed a human being to flop itself down and broil like a trout in the sun. Besides the discomfort, the sheer boredom of it would have driven her wild inside an hour.

Ripley wasn't one to lie down if she could stand.

Not that she didn't enjoy the beach. She jogged along the surf every morning, summer and winter. When weather permitted, she finished off her run with a swim. When it didn't, she often ducked into the hotel and took advantage of its indoor pool.

But she preferred the sea.

As a result she had a tight, athletic body that was most often clad in khakis and T-shirts. Her skin was tanned like her brother's, her eyes the same vivid green. She wore her straight brown hair long and most often pulled through the back of her baseball cap.

Her features were an odd mix—a wide, slightly top-heavy mouth, a small nose, and dark, arching brows. Her looks had made her feel awkward as a child, but Ripley liked to think she'd grown into them, and grown out of worrying about them.

She strolled into Café Book, waved at Lulu, and headed for the stairs. With luck, she could get a look at this Nell Channing and avoid Mia altogether.

She was still three steps from the café level when she saw her luck wasn't going to hold.

Mia was behind the counter, looking slick as always in some floaty floral dress. Her hair was tied back and still managed to explode around her face. The woman working beside her looked tidy, nearly prim in comparison.

Ripley immediately preferred Nell.

She jammed her thumbs into her back pockets and swaggered toward the counter.

"Deputy Todd." Mia angled her head, looked down her nose. "What could possibly bring you here?"

Ignoring Mia, Ripley studied Nell. "I'll have today's special soup and sandwich."

"Nell, this is Ripley, Zack's unfortunate sister. As she's come in for lunch we can safely assume hell has frozen over."

"Kiss ass, Mia. Nice to meet you, Nell. I'll have a lemonade to go with that."

"Yes. All right." Nell shifted her gaze from face to face. "Right away," she murmured and ducked into the kitchen to put the sandwich together.

"Heard you scooped her up right off the ferry," Ripley continued.

"More or less." Mia ladled the soup. "Don't poke at her, Ripley."

"Why would I?"

"Because you're you." Mia set the soup on the counter. "Notice anything odd when you stepped off the ferry yesterday?"

"No." Ripley replied too quickly.

"Liar," Mia said quietly as Nell came back with the sandwich.

"Can I take this to a table for you, Deputy Todd?"

"Yeah, thanks." Ripley tugged money out of her pocket. "Why don't you ring me up, Mia?"

Ripley timed it, sliding into a chair just as Nell set the food down. "Looks great."

"I hope you enjoy it."

"I'm sure I will. Where'd you learn to cook?"

"Here and there. Can I get you anything else?"

Ripley held up a finger, spooned up soup and sampled. "Nope. This is great. Really. Hey, did you make all those pastries yourself?"

"Yes."

"A lot of work."

"It's what I'm paid for."

"Right. Don't let Mia work you too hard. She's pushy."

"On the contrary," Nell said in a voice that chilled. "She's incredibly generous, incredibly kind. Enjoy your lunch."

Loyal, Ripley decided as she continued to eat. She couldn't fault Nell for that. Polite, too, even if she was a bit stiff about it. As if, Ripley thought, she wasn't quite used to dealing with people.

Nervous. She'd visibly cringed at the relatively mild byplay between Ripley and Mia. Well, Ripley decided with a shrug, some people couldn't handle conflict, even when it had nothing to do with them.

All in all, she thought Nell Channing was harmless. And a hell of a good cook.

The meal put her in such a good mood that she took the time to go by the counter on her way out. It was easier to decide to do so since Mia was occupied elsewhere.

"Well, now you've done it."

Nell froze. She deliberately kept her face blank, her hands loose. "I beg your pardon?"

"Now I'm going to have to start coming in here regularly, something I've managed to avoid for years. Lunch was great."

"Oh. Good."

"You may have noticed, Mia and I aren't exactly chummy."

"It's none of my business."

"You live on the island, everybody's business is your business. But don't worry, we manage to stay out of each other's way for the most part. You won't get squeezed in the middle. I'm going to take a couple of those chocolate chip cookies for later."

"You save if you buy three."

"Twist my arm. Three, then. I'll give one to Zack and be a hero."

Relaxed now, Nell bagged the cookies, rang up the bill. But when she took the money from Ripley and their hands touched, the bright shock had her gasping.

Ripley glared, one long, frustrated stare. Snagging her cookies, she strode toward the stairs.

"Deputy—" Clenching her hand tight, Nell called after her. "You forgot your change."

"Keep it." She bit the words off as she stomped down the stairs. There was Mia at the bottom, hands folded, brow lifted. Ripley simply snarled and kept going.

A storm was coming. Though the sky stayed clear and the sea calm, a storm was coming. Its violence roared through Nell's dreams and tossed her helplessly into the past.

The huge white house sat on a verdant carpet of lawn. Inside, its edges were sharp, its surfaces hard. Colors were pale—sands and taupes and grays.

But for the roses he bought her, always bought her, that were the color of blood.

The house was empty. But it seemed to be waiting.

In sleep she turned her head away, resisted. She didn't want to go into that place. Not ever again.

But the door opened, the tall white door that opened into the long, wide foyer. White marble, white wood, and the cold, cold sparkle of crystal and chrome.

She watched herself walk in—long, pale hair sweeping past the shoulders of a sleek white dress that sent off an icy glitter. Her lips were red, like the roses.

He came in with her, close behind. Always so close behind. His hand was there, lightly on the small of her back. She could still feel it there if she let herself.

He was tall, slim. Like a prince in his evening black with his hair a gold helmet. She had fallen in love with the fairy-tale look of him, and she had believed his promises of happy-ever-after. And hadn't he taken her to this palace, this white palace in this fantasy land, and given her everything a woman could want?

How many times had he reminded her of that?

She knew what happened next. She remembered the glittery white dress, remembered how tired and relieved she was that the evening was over, and that it had gone well. She'd done nothing to upset him, to embarrass him, to annoy him.

Or so she'd thought.

Until she'd turned to say something about how nice an evening it had been, and had seen his expression.

He'd waited until they were home, until they were alone, to make the transformation. It was one of his best skills.

And she remembered the fear that had clutched her belly even as she scrambled to think of what she'd done.

Did you enjoy yourself, Helen?

Yes, it was a lovely party. But a long one. Would you like me to fix you a brandy before we go to bed?

You enjoyed the music?

Very much. Music? Had she said something inappropriate about the music? She could be so stupid about such things. Barely, she repressed a shudder as he reached out to toy with her hair. *It was wonderful to be able to dance outside, near the gardens.*

She stepped back, hoping to turn toward the stairs, but his hand fisted in her hair, held her in place. *Yes, I noticed how much you enjoyed dancing, especially with Mitchell Rawlings. Flirting with him. Flaunting yourself. Humiliating me in front of my friends, my clients.*

Evan, I wasn't flirting. I was only—

The backhanded slap sent her sprawling, the bright shock of pain blinding her. When she would have rolled into a protective ball, he dragged her across the marble floor by the hair.

How many times has he had his hands on you?

She denied, she wept, he accused. Until he grew weary of it and left her to crawl away and sob in a corner.

But this time, in this dream, she crawled off into the shadows of the forest, where the air was soft and the ground warm.

And there, where the stream gurgled over its smooth rocks, she slept.

Then awoke to the cannon-blast of thunder and the jagged rip of lightning. Awoke to terror. She was running through the woods now, her white dress a sparkling beacon. Her blood pumped, the blood of the hunted. Trees crashed behind her, and the ground heaved under her feet and boiled with mist.

Still she ran, her breath tearing out of her throat and ending in whimpers. There were screams in the wind, and not all of them hers. Fear ruled until there was nothing else inside her, no reason, no sense, no answer.

The wind slapped at her with sharp and gleeful hands, and clawing fingers of brush tore her dress to shreds.

She was climbing, scrabbling like a lizard along the rock. Through the dark the beam from the lighthouse slashed like a silver blade, and below, the wild violence of the sea churned.

She kicked and cried and climbed. But she didn't look back, couldn't force herself to look around and face what pursued her.

Instead, choosing flight over fight, she leaped from the rocks, spun and spun in the wind on her plunge toward the water. And the cliffs, the light, the trees all tumbled in after her.

Four

On her first day off, Nell rearranged the furniture—what there was of it. She watered her flowers and herbs, did the wash, and baked a loaf of brown bread.

It was still shy of nine o'clock when she cut the first slice for her breakfast.

Evan had hated her early-rising habit, and had complained that that was the reason she was dull at parties. Now, in her little cottage near the sea, there was no one to criticize, no need to creep about. She had her windows open wide, and the whole day belonged just to her.

Still munching on bread and with a heel of the loaf in the pocket of her shorts, she took herself off for a long walk on the beach.

The boats were out, bobbing and gliding over the water. The sea was a soft, dreamy blue with frisky waves that rolled up lacy on the sand. Gulls winged over it, white-breasted in their graceful dance on the air. The music of them, the long, shrill cries, pierced the low, endless rumble of the surf.

She turned in a little dance of her own. Then she tugged the bread from her pocket and tore it into small pieces, tossing it high to watch the gulls circle and dive.

Alone, she thought, lifting her face to the sky. But not lonely. She doubted she would ever be lonely again.

At the sound of church bells she turned to look back at the village, at the pretty white steeple. She glanced down at her shorts with the frayed hem, her sandy sneakers. Hardly dressed for services, she decided. But she could worship in her own way, and offer a prayer of thanksgiving.

While the bells rang and echoed, she sat near the edge of the water. Here was peace, she thought, and joy. She would never, never take either for granted. She would remember to give something back every day. Even if it was just a heel of bread for the gulls. She would tend what she planted. She would remember to be kind, and never forget to offer a helping hand.

She would keep her promises and expect nothing more than the chance to lead a good life that hurt no one.

She would earn what she'd been given, and treasure it.

She would take pleasure in the simple things, she decided. Starting right now.

Rising, she began to collect shells, tucking them in her pockets at first. When the pockets were full, she tugged off her shoes and used them. She reached the far end of the beach, where rocks jutted out of the sand and began to tumble toward the sea. Here there were palm-size stones worn cobble smooth. She picked one, then another, wondering if she could fashion an edging for her little herb bed.

A movement to her left had her wrapping her fingers tight around the stone and turning quickly. Her heart continued to beat in hard jerks as she watched Zack coming down a zigzag of wooden steps.

"Morning."

"Good morning." In automatic defense, she glanced back, uneasy to realize how far from the village proper she'd wandered. The beach was no longer empty, but the scattered people were some distance away.

"Nice day for a long walk on the beach," he commented, leaning against the handrail to study her. "You've sure had one."

He'd watched her, from her dance with the gulls. It was a shame, he thought, how quickly her face could go from radiant to guarded.

"I didn't realize how far I'd come."

"Nothing's really that far on an island this size. It's going to be a hot one," he said easily. "Beach'll be crowded before noon. It's nice to get a little time on it before it's full of towels and bodies."

"Yes, well . . ."

"Come on up."

"What?"

"Come on up. To the house. I'll give you a bag for those shells and stones."

"Oh, that's all right. I don't really need—"

"Nell—is it cops in general, men in general, or me in particular that worry you?"

"I'm not worried."

"Prove it." He stayed where he was, but held out a hand.

She kept her eyes on his. He had good eyes. Smart ones, but patient too. Slowly she stepped forward and lifted her hand to his.

"What do you plan to do with your shells?"

"Nothing." Her pulse was galloping, but she made herself climb the sandy steps with him. "Well, nothing brilliant. Just scatter them around, I suppose."

His hand held hers loosely, but even so she could tell it was hard and rough. He wore no rings, no watch on his wrist.

No pampering, she thought. No adornments.

Like her, he was barefoot, and his jeans were ripped at the knee, frayed at the hem. With his sun-streaked hair and tawny skin, he looked more beach bum than sheriff. It tamped down some of her anxiety.

At the landing they turned, walked along a gentle slope. Below, on the far side of the rocks, was a sunny inlet where a small red boat bobbed lazily at a rickety pier.

"Everything's a picture," she said quietly.

"Have you done any sailing?"

"Yes. A little," she said quickly. "Is that your boat?"

"She's mine."

There was a sudden wild splashing of water, and a sleek, dark head appeared, cruising around the rocks. As Nell stared, a huge black dog leaped onto the shore and shook herself madly.

"Her, too," Zack stated. "Mine, that is. Are you all right with dogs? Tell me now. I can hold her off and give you a fair head start."

"No, I like dogs." Then she blinked, looked back at him. "What do you mean, head start?"

He didn't bother to answer, just grinned as the dog leaped up the slope in powerful bounds. She jumped on Zack, tail wagging and spewing water, and licked his face. On two short, deep barks she bunched her muscles and would have given Nell the same treatment if Zack hadn't blocked her.

"This is Lucy. She's friendly, but mannerless. Down, Lucy."

Lucy got down, her entire body wagging now. Then, obviously unable to control her joy and affection, she leaped on Zack again.

"She's two," he explained, firmly pushing her down and shoving her butt to the ground with his hand. "Black Lab. I'm told they mellow out some when they're older."

"She's beautiful." Nell stroked Lucy's head, and at the first touch the dog collapsed on the ground and rolled over, belly up.

"No pride, either," Zack began, then looked surprised when Nell just hunkered down and sent Lucy into ecstasy by rubbing her belly with both hands.

"You don't need pride when you're beautiful, do you, Lucy? Oh, there's nothing like a big, beautiful dog, is there? I always— Oh!"

In a delirium of pleasure, Lucy rolled, scrambled, and knocked Nell flat on her back. Zack was fast, but not quite fast enough to keep her from being leaped on and licked.

"Jesus, Lucy. No! Hey, I'm sorry." Zack shoved at the dog and lifted Nell to her feet one-handed. "You okay? Did she hurt you?"

"No. I'm fine." She'd had the wind knocked out of her, but that was only part of the reason for breathlessness. He was brushing at her while the dog sat, head down, tail cautiously thumping. He was, Nell noted, frustrated and concerned. But not angry.

"You didn't hit your head, did you? Damn dog weighs almost as much as you do. Banged your elbow a little," he added, then realized she was actually giggling. "What's so funny?"

"Nothing, really. It's just sweet the way she's pretending to look ashamed. She's obviously terrified of you."

"Yeah, I take a bat to her twice a week whether she needs it or not." He ran his hands lightly up and down Nell's arms. "Sure you're okay?"

"Yes." It struck her then that they were now standing very close, almost embracing. And that his hands were on her, and her skin was much too warm from them. "Yes," she said again and took a deliberate step in retreat. "No harm done."

"You're sturdier than you look." There were long, lean muscles in those arms, he noted. He'd already admired the ones in her legs. "Come on inside," he said. "Not you," he added, pointing at the dog. "You're banished."

He scooped Nell's shoes up from the ground and walked toward a wide porch. Curious, and unable to think of an excuse not to follow, Nell went through the screened door he opened and into a big, bright, messy kitchen.

"It's the maid's decade off." Comfortable in his own clutter, he set her shoes on the floor and went to the refrigerator. "Can't offer you homemade lemonade, but we've got some iced tea."

"That's fine, thanks. It's a wonderful kitchen."

"We use it mostly for heating up takeout."

"That's a shame." There were acres of granite-toned counters, and wonderful rough-hewn cabinets with leaded-glass fronts. A generous double sink with a window over it offered a view of the inlet and the sea.

Plenty of storage and work space, she mused. With a little organization and a bit of imagination, it would be a marvelous . . .

We? He'd said "we," she realized. Was he married? She'd never thought of that, never considered the possibility. Not that it mattered, of course, but . . .

He'd flirted with her. She may have been out of practice and short on experience, but she knew when a man was flirting.

"You've got a lot of thoughts going on inside that head at one time." Zack held out a glass. "Want to share any of them?"

"No. That is, I was just thinking what a nice room this is."

"It was a lot more presentable when my mother was in charge of it. Now that it's just Ripley and me, the kitchen doesn't get a lot of attention."

"Ripley. Oh. I see."

"You were wondering if I was married, or maybe living here with someone who wasn't my sister. That's nice."

"It's none of my business."

"I didn't say it was, just said it was nice. I'd take you through the house, but it's probably in worse shape than the kitchen. And you've got a tidy soul. We'll go this way." He took her hand again, pulled her back outside.

"Where? I really should be getting back."

"It's Sunday, and we've hit our day off together. I've got something you'll like," he continued and tugged her across the porch.

It wrapped around the house, edged the side where there was a scrubby garden and a couple of gnarled trees. Weather-worn steps led up to a second-story porch that faced the sea.

He kept his hand over hers and led her up them.

Air and sun washed over her, made her think how easy it would be to stretch out in the wooden chaise and let the day rock away.

A telescope stood by the rail, along with a stone trough that had yet to be planted.

"You're right." She stepped to the rail, leaned out and breathed. "I do like it."

"You look west, you can see the mainland when it's clear enough."

"You don't have your telescope pointed west."

At the moment all his attention was on her very pretty set of legs. "I guess I don't."

"What do you look at?"

"Whatever strikes my fancy at the time."

She glanced over as she moved away. He was staring at her now—long, speculative looks, and they both knew it. "It'd be tempting to stay out here all day," she said as she turned the corner and looked out on the village. "Watch the comings and the goings."

"I watched you this morning, feeding the gulls." He leaned on the rail, a man at home, and drank his tea. "I woke up thinking, 'You know, I'm going to find a reason to drop by the yellow cottage today, get another look at Nell Channing,' then I came out here with my morning coffee, and there you were. So I didn't have to make up a reason to get another look at you."

"Sheriff—"

"It's my day off," he reminded her. He started to lift his hand to touch her hair, but when she edged back he simply slid it into his pocket. "Since it is, why don't we spend a couple hours of it on the water? We can go for a sail."

"I can't. I have to . . ."

"You don't have to hunt up excuses. Some other time."

"Yes." The knot that had formed in her belly loosened. "Some other time. I really should go. Thanks for the drink, and the view."

"Nell—" He took her hand again, kept his fingers light when hers jerked. "There's a line between making a woman a little nervous and scaring her. That's a line I wouldn't want to cross. When you get to know me a little better, you'll believe that," he added.

"Right now I'm working on getting to know myself a little better."

"Fair enough. I'll get you a bag for your shells and stones."

He made a point of going into the café every morning. A cup of coffee, a muffin, a few words. To Zack's way of thinking, she'd get used to seeing him, talking to him, and the next time he worked it around so they were alone together, she wouldn't feel compelled to check for running room.

He was perfectly aware that Nell wasn't the only one who noticed his new morning habit. Zack didn't mind the teasing comments, the sly winks and chuckles. Island life had a rhythm, and whenever anything new added a beat, everyone felt it.

He sipped Nell's truly excellent coffee while he stood on the dock listening to Carl Macey bitch about lobster poachers.

"Three blessed days this week trap's been empty, and they ain't troubling to close it after them, neither. I've got the suspicion it's them college boys renting the Boeing place. Ayah." He spat. "That's who's doing it. I catch 'em at it, I'm gonna give them rich college brats something to remember."

"Well, Carl, the fact is, it sounds like summer people, and sounds like kids on top of it. Why don't you let me have a talk with them?"

"Got no call interfering with a man's livelihood that way."

"No, but they wouldn't be thinking of it like that."

"They'd better start thinking." The weathered face went grim. "I went up to see Mia Devlin, asked her to put a spell on my traps."

Zack winced. "Now, Carl—"

"Better than me peppering their skinny white asses with buckshot now, ain't it? I swear that's next in line."

"Let me handle this."

"I'm telling you, ain't I?" Scowling, Carl bobbed his head. "No harm in covering all my bases. Besides, I got a look at the new mainlander while I was up to the bookstore." Carl's pug-homely, wrinkled face folded into a snicker. "See why you're such a regular customer there these days. Ayah. Big blue eyes like that sure start a man's day off on the right foot."

"They can't hurt. You keep your shotgun in your gun cabinet, Carl. I'll take care of things."

He headed back to the station house first, for his list of summer people. The Boeing place was an easy enough walk, but he decided to take the cruiser to make it more official.

The summer rental was a block back from the beach, with a generous screened porch on the side. Beach towels and swim trunks hung drooping from a nylon line strung inside the screen. The picnic table on the porch was heaped with beer cans and the remnants of last night's meal.

They hadn't had the sense, Zack thought with a shake of his head, to ditch the evidence. Scraped-out lobster shells lay upended on the table like giant insects. Zack dug his badge out of his pocket and pinned it on. Might as well get in their faces with it.

He knocked, and kept right on knocking until the door opened. The boy who opened the door was about twenty. Squinting against the sun, his hair a wild disarray, he wore brightly striped boxer shorts and a golden summer tan.

He said, "Ugh."

"Sheriff Todd, Island Police. Mind if I come inside?"

"Whafor? Timzit?"

Hungover, big-time, Zack decided, and translated. "To talk to you. It's about ten thirty. Your friends around?"

"Somewhere? Problem? Christ." The boy swallowed, winced, then stumbled through the living room past the breakfast counter and to the sink, where he turned the water on full. And stuck his head under the faucet.

"Some party, huh?" Zack said when he surfaced, dripping.

"Guess." He snagged paper towels, rubbed his face dry. "We get too loud?"

"No complaints. What's your name, son?"

"Josh, Josh Tanner."

"Well, Josh, why don't you rouse your pals? I don't want to take up a lot of your time."

"Yeah, well. Okay."

He waited, listened. There was some cursing, a few thuds, water running. A toilet flushed.

The three young men who trooped back in with Josh looked plenty the worse for wear. They stood, in various states of undress, until one flopped down on a chair and smirked.

"What's the deal?"

All attitude, Zack calculated. "And you'd be?"

"Steve Hickman."

Boston accent, Zack concluded. Upper-class one, almost Kennedyesque. "Okay, Steve, here's the deal. Lobster poaching carries a thousand-dollar fine. Reason for that is that while it's a kick to sneak out and empty the traps, boil up a couple, some people depend on the catch for their living. An evening's entertainment to you is money out of their pocket."

As he lectured, Zack saw the boys shift uncomfortably. The one who'd answered the door was flushing guiltily and keeping his eyes averted.

"What you had out there on the porch last night would've run you about forty down at the market. So you look up a man by the name of Carl Macey at the docks, give him forty, and that'll be the end of it."

"I don't know what you're talking about. Does this Macey put a brand on his lobsters?" Steve smirked again, scratched his belly. "You can't prove we poached anything."

"True enough." Zack glanced around the room, skimmed faces. Nerves, a little shame. "This place rents for what, about twelve hundred a week in full season, and the boat you've rented puts another two-fifty onto that. Add entertainment, food, beer. You guys're shelling out 'round about a grand apiece for a week here."

"And pumping it into the island economy," Steve said with a thin smile. "Pretty stupid to hassle us over a couple of allegedly poached lobsters."

"Maybe. Even more stupid not to come up with ten bucks each to smooth things over. You think about that. It's a small island," Zack said as he started for the door. "Word gets around."

"Is that a threat? Threatening civilians could result in a litigious action."

Zack glanced back, shook his head. "I bet you're prelaw, aren't you?" He strolled out, back to his cruiser. It wouldn't take him long to hit the right spots in the village and make his point.

☙❧

Ripley walked down High Street and met Zack in front of the Magick Inn. "Lobster Boy's credit card got hung up at the pizza place," she began. "Seems the circuits were down or whatever and he had to dig for cash to pay for lunch."

"That so?"

"Yeah. And you know, every video they wanted to rent was already out."

"Hell of a thing."

"And I hear all the jet skis were already reserved or out of order today."

"That's a shame."

"And continuing in a series of bizarre coincidences, the AC in their rental just up and died."

"And it's a hot one today, too. Supposed to be muggy tonight. Bound to be uncomfortable sleeping."

"You're a mean son of a bitch, Zachariah." Ripley rose on her toes and gave him a quick, smacking kiss on the mouth. "That's why I love you."

"I'm going to have to get meaner. That Hickman boy's a tough nut. The other three'll fold fast enough, but he'll take some more persuading." Zack swung an arm around Ripley's shoulder. "So, are you going into the café for some lunch?"

"I might be. Why?"

"I thought you could do me a little favor, since you love me and everything."

The long whip of her ponytail bobbed as she turned her head to look up at him. "If you want me to talk Nell into dating you, just forget it."

"I can get my own dates, thanks."

"Batting zero so far."

"I'm still on deck," he countered. "What I was hoping is that you'd tell Mia we're handling the lobster boys, and not to . . . do anything."

"What do you mean, 'do anything'? What does she have to do with it?" Ripley stopped, her temper flaring. "Damn it."

"Don't get riled. It's just that Carl said he'd talked to her. I'd just as soon it not get around that our resident witch is cooking up a spell. Or whatever."

To keep Ripley in check, Zack tightened his grip on her shoulders. "I'd go in myself and have a word with her, but the lobster boys should be coming along in a few minutes. I want to be standing here, looking smug and authoritative."

"I'll talk to her."

"You play nice, Rip. And remember it was Carl who went to her."

"Yeah, yeah, yeah." She shook off his arm and marched across the street.

Witches and spells. It was all a bunch of nonsense, idiotic hooey, she thought as she breezed down the sidewalk. A man like Carl Macey ought to know better. Stirring up a bunch of silliness. It was all right for the tourists to buy all the Three Sisters lore—it was one of the things that brought them over from the mainland. But it burned her butt when it was one of her own.

And Mia encouraged it, too. Just by being Mia.

Ripley swung into Café Book and scowled over at Lulu, who was ringing up a customer. "Where is she?"

"Upstairs. Pretty busy today."

"Yeah, she's a busy little bee," Ripley muttered and headed up.

She spotted Mia with a customer in the cookbook section. Ripley bared her teeth. Mia fluttered her lashes. Simmering with impatience, Ripley strode into the café, waited her turn, then snapped out an order for coffee.

"No lunch today?" Flushed with the bustle of the noon crowd, Nell poured out from a fresh pot.

"Lost my appetite."

"That's too bad," Mia cooed from behind Ripley. "The lobster salad's particularly good today."

Ripley merely jerked a thumb, then marched behind the counter and into the kitchen. She jammed her hands on her hips when Mia strolled in after her.

"Zack and I are handling the problem. I want you to stay out of it."

A bowl of top cream was less smooth than Mia's voice. "I wouldn't dream of interfering with the law of the land."

"Excuse me." Nell hesitated, cleared her throat. "Sandwiches. I need to make them up."

"Go right ahead." Mia gestured. "I imagine Deputy Fife and I are nearly done."

"Just save the smart-ass comments."

"I do. I store them up just for you."

"I don't want you doing anything, and I want you to tell Carl you didn't do anything."

"Too late." Enjoying herself, Mia smiled brilliantly. "It's already done. A very simple spell—even someone with your fumbling abilities could have managed it."

"Cancel it."

"No. Why does it concern you? You claim not to believe in the Craft."

"I don't. But I know how rumors work around here. If anything happens to those boys—"

"Don't insult me." All humor fled from Mia's voice. "You know very well I'd do nothing to harm them, or anyone. You know, that's the heart of it. That's what you're afraid of. Afraid that if you opened yourself to what's inside you again, you wouldn't be able to control it."

"I'm not afraid of anything. And you're not pulling me in that way." She pointed at Nell, who was struggling to keep very busy with sandwiches. "You've got no right pulling her in, either."

"I don't make the pattern, Ripley. I just recognize it. And so do you."

"It's a waste of time talking to you." Ripley stormed out of the kitchen.

Mia let out a little sigh, her only sign of distress. "Conversations with Ripley never seem particularly productive. You mustn't let it worry you, Nell."

"It has nothing to do with me."

"I can feel your anxiety all the way over here. People argue, often bitterly. They don't all solve the conflict with fists. Here, now." She moved behind Nell and rubbed her shoulders. "Let the worry go. Tension's bad for the digestion."

At the touch Nell felt a trickle of warmth melt away the ice that had balled in her belly. "I guess I like both of you. I hate to see you dislike each other."

"I don't dislike Ripley. She annoys me, frustrates me, but I don't dislike her. You wonder what we were talking about, but you won't ask, will you, little sister?"

"No. I don't like questions."

"I'm fascinated by them. We need to talk, you and I." Mia stepped back, waited for Nell to pick up the completed order and turn. "I have things to do this evening. Tomorrow, then. I'll buy you a drink. Let's make it early. Five at the Magick Inn. The lounge. It's called the Coven. You can leave your questions at home if you like," Mia said as she started out. "I'll bring the answers anyway."

Five

I t went pretty much as Zack had expected. The Hickman kid had to
flex his muscles. The other three had folded, and Zack expected Carl
to get his money from them the next morning. But Hickman had to prove
he was smarter, braver, and far superior to some dinky island sheriff.

From his place on the dock, Zack watched the rented boat putt
along toward the lobster traps. He was already on the wrong side of
the law, Zack mused, nibbling on sunflower seeds. Boating after dark
without running lights. That would cost him.

But it was nothing to the grand that the little defiance was going
to cost the college boy's father.

He expected the kid was going to give him some trouble when he
hauled him in. Which meant they'd both be spending a few hours
in the station house that night. One of them behind bars.

Well, lessons learned, Zack decided, lowering his binoculars and
reaching down for his flashlight as the boy began to haul up a pot.

The scream was high and girlish, and gave Zack a hell of a jolt.
He switched on his light, shot the bright beam of it across the water.

A light fog crept over the surface, so that the boat seemed to bob in smoke. The boy stood, the trap gripped in both hands, the look on his face as he stared into it one of sheer horror.

Before Zack could call out, the boy flung the trap high and wide. Even as it splashed into the water, he was tumbling in.

"Oh, well, hell," Zack muttered, peeved at the prospect of ending his workday soaking wet. He stepped to the end of the dock, scooped up a life preserver. The kid was doing more screaming than swimming, but he was making some progress toward shore.

"Here you go, Steve." Zack tossed the preserver in. "Head this way. I don't want to have to come in after you."

"Help me." The boy flailed, swallowed water, choked. But he managed to grab the flotation. "They're eating my face!"

"Almost there." Zack knelt down, held out a hand. "Come on up. You're still in one piece."

"My head! My head!" Steve slipped and slithered onto the dock, then lay there on his belly, shuddering. "I saw my head in the trap. They were eating my face!"

"Your head's still on your shoulders, son." Zack hunkered down. "Catch your breath. Had yourself a hallucination, that's all. Been drinking a bit, haven't you? That, and some guilt got to you."

"I saw . . . I saw." He sat up, laid shaking hands on his face to make certain all his parts were there, then began to shake in stupendous relief.

"Fog, dark, water. It's a tricky kind of situation, especially on a couple bottles of beer. You're going to feel a lot better when you give Carl that forty dollars. In fact, why don't we go get you cleaned up, get your wallet, and go by his place now? You'll sleep better for it."

"Yeah. Sure. Right. Okay."

"That's fine." Zack helped him to his feet. "I'll take care of getting the boat back, don't you worry."

That Mia, Zack thought as he led the unprotesting boy away from the water. You had to give her credit for creativity.

It took a while to calm the boy down, then to calm four boys down once he'd taken Steve back to the rental. Then there was Carl to deal with, and the boat. Which was probably why Zack ended up nodding off at the station house just before three A.M.

He woke two hours later, stiff as a board and annoyed with himself. Ripley, he decided as he stumbled out to his cruiser, was taking the first shift.

He meant to drive straight home, but he'd gotten into the habit of swinging past the yellow cottage at the end of his shift. Just to make sure everything was as it should be.

He made the turn before he realized it, and saw the lights in her windows. Concern as much as curiosity made him pull over and get out of the car.

Because the kitchen light was on, he went to the back door. He was lifting his hand to knock when he saw her standing on the other side of the screen, a long, smooth-bladed knife gripped in both hands.

"If I tell you I was just in the neighborhood, you won't gut me with that, will you?"

Her hands began to tremble, and her breath exploded out of her as she dropped the knife on the table with a clatter.

"I'm sorry I scared you. I saw your light as I was . . . hey, hey." When she swayed, he bolted through the door, gripping both her arms and lowering her into a chair. "Sit. Breathe. Head down. Jesus, Nell. I'm sorry." He stroked her hair, patted her back, and wondered whether she would just keel over on the floor if he jumped up to get her a glass of water.

"It's all right. I'm all right. I heard the footsteps. In the dark. It's so quiet here, you can hear everything, and I heard you coming toward the house."

She'd wanted to run like a rabbit in the other direction and keep going. She didn't remember picking up the knife, hadn't known she could.

"I'm going to get you some water."

"No, I'm all right." Mortified now, she realized, but all right. "I just wasn't expecting anyone to come to the door."

"Guess not. It's still shy of five thirty." He sat back on his heels when she lifted her head again. Color was coming back, he noted with relief. "What're you doing up?"

"I'm usually up by—" She jumped like a spring as the oven timer buzzed. "God! God!" With a half laugh she pounded a fist on her heart. "I'm going to be lucky to survive till sunrise at this rate. My muffins," she said and got up quickly to take them out of the oven, slide the next batch in.

"I didn't realize you started so early."

He could see, now that he looked around, that she'd been at it a while. There was something simmering on the stove and smelling like glory. A huge bowl of batter sat on the counter. Another bowl, covered with a cloth, was beside the stove. Still one more was on the table, where she'd obviously been mixing something before he'd scared ten years off her life.

Ingredients were lined up, as organized as a marching band.

"I didn't realize you worked so late." She calmed herself by cutting shortening into the flour for her pastry dough.

"I don't usually. I had a little project to finish up last night, and when it was all said and done, dropped off in my office chair. Nell, if you don't give me a cup of that coffee, I'm going to start crying. It'll embarrass us both."

"Oh. Sorry. Um."

"You just keep on with what you're doing there. Cups?"

"Cabinet to the right of the sink."

"Want me to top yours off?"

"I suppose."

He poured a cup, filled hers as it sat by the sink. "You know, I don't think these muffins look quite right."

With the bowl tucked in the crook of her arm, she turned. Her face was a study of alarm and insult. "What do you mean?"

"Just don't look quite the thing. Why don't you let me test one for you?" He gave her a quick, boyish grin that had her lips twitching.

"Oh, for heaven's sake. Why don't you just ask for one?"

"More fun this way. No, don't bother. I can get it myself." He plucked one out of the pan, burned the tips of his fingers. As he tossed the muffin from hand to hand to cool it, the scent told him it was going to be worth it. "I've sure got a soft spot for your blueberry muffins, Nell."

"Mr. Bigelow, Lancefort Bigelow, prefers my cream puffs. He said if I'd make them for him every day, he'd marry me and we'd move to Bimini."

Still grinning, Zack broke the muffin in half, treated himself to the fragrant steam. "That's pretty stiff competition."

Bigelow, a confirmed bachelor, was ninety.

He watched her stir the dough, form it into a ball. Then she emptied the muffin pan, set them to cool on a rack while she refilled the cups. When the timer buzzed again, she shifted trays, went back to roll out her pastry dough.

"You've got yourself a real system," he commented. "Where'd you learn to bake?"

"My mother—" She broke off, realigned her thoughts. It was too easy in the quiet kitchen, with all these homey smells, to get overly comfortable and reveal too much. "My mother liked to bake," she said. "And I picked up recipes and techniques here and there."

He didn't want her to stiffen up, so he let it pass. "Do you ever make those cinnamon rolls? You know the ones with that sticky white icing?"

"Mmm."

"I make them sometimes."

"Really." She began to cut the dough for tarts and glanced back at him. He looked so . . . male, she thought, leaning back on the counter with his ankles crossed and a mug of coffee in his hand. "I didn't know you cooked."

"Sure, now and then. You buy these tubes down at the market. Then you take them home, rap them against the counter and peel the bun things out, cook them, and squirt icing on the top. Nothing to it."

It made her laugh. "I'll have to try that sometime." She went to the refrigerator, took out her bowl of filling.

"I'll give you some pointers on it." He drained his cup, set it in the sink. "I guess I'd better get home, and get out of your way. Thanks for the coffee."

"You're welcome."

"And the muffin. It was just fine."

"That's a relief." She stood at the table, methodically spooning filling into the center of her rounds of dough. When he stepped toward her, she tensed a little, but continued to work.

"Nell?"

She looked up, and filling slopped out of her spoon when he put his hand on her cheek.

"I sure hope this doesn't put you off," he said, and leaning down, he laid his lips on hers.

She didn't move a muscle. Couldn't. Her eyes stayed open, locked on his. Watching, as a deer might watch when pinned in the cross-hairs.

His lips were warm. She registered that. And softer than they looked. He didn't touch her. She imagined she'd have leaped out of her skin if he'd laid his hands on her now.

But it was only his mouth, light and easy on hers.

He'd prepared himself for her to be annoyed, or disinterested. He hadn't expected her to be scared. That was what he felt from her, a rigid anxiety that could easily bloom into fear. So he didn't touch her as he wanted to, not even a gentle brush of fingers down her arms.

If she'd stepped back, he'd have done nothing to stop her. But her absolute stillness was its own defense. It was he who stepped back, and kept it light despite a gnawing in the gut that was more than a stir of desire for her—it was a cold fury for whoever had hurt her.

"Seems I have a soft spot for more than your muffins." He tucked his thumbs in his front pockets. "See you later."

He strolled out, hoping the kiss and the ease of his leaving would give her something to think about.

He wasn't going to get any sleep. Resigned to it, he thrilled Lucy by taking her for an early-morning swim in the inlet. The romp, and her sheer foolishness, worked off a good portion of his stiffness, and his frustration.

He watched Ripley finish her run on the beach and dive into the surf. Dependable as sunrise, he thought as she cut through the waves. Maybe he didn't always know what went on in her head, or how it got there, but he rarely had to worry about Ripley Todd.

She could handle herself.

Lucy ran out to meet her as she started back, and the two wet females had a wrestle and a race. They both joined him on the upper

porch, Lucy to flop down in delighted exhaustion, and Ripley suck-
ing on a bottle of water.

"Mom called last night." Ripley flopped down herself, on one of
the deck chairs. "They made it to the Grand Canyon. They're sending us six million pictures that Dad took with his digital. I'm afraid
to start the download."

"Sorry I missed the call."

"I told them you were on a stakeout," she said with her tongue in
her cheek. "They got a kick out of the lobster caper. Any updates?"

"Oh, yeah."

He sat on the arm of the Adirondack chair, and filled her in.

She turned her face up to the sky and hooted. "I *knew* I should've
gone with you. Idiot drunk putz. Lobster Boy, not you."

"I figured. He wasn't that drunk, Rip."

She lifted a hand, waved it at him. "Don't start that. I'm in too
good a mood for you to spoil it by mentioning Mia and her double,
double, toil and trouble routine."

"Suit yourself."

"I usually do. I'm going to get a shower. I'll take the first shift.
You must be wiped."

"I'm okay. Listen . . ." But he trailed off, trying to think how to
put what he wanted to say.

"Listening."

"I went by the yellow cottage on the way home. Nell's lights were
on, so I stopped in."

"Aha," Ripley teased.

"Gutter-face. I had a cup of coffee and a muffin."

"Gee, Zack, I'm sorry to hear that."

Normally he'd have laughed. Instead he rose, paced to the rail.
"You stop in and see her most every day. You're friendly, right?"

"I guess we're friendly enough. It's hard not to like her."

"Women tend to confide stuff to their female friends, don't they?"

"Probably. You want me to ask her if she likes you enough to go to the school dance with you?" She started to snicker, but stopped when he turned around and saw his face. "Hey, sorry. I didn't know it was serious. What's up?"

"I think she's been abused."

"Man." Ripley stared down at her water bottle. "That's tough."

"Some son of a bitch messed with her, I'm sure of it. Whether or not she's had counseling or gotten help, it seems to me she could use a . . . you know, a girlfriend. Somebody she could talk to about it."

"Zack, you know I'm no good at that kind of thing. You are."

"I've got the wrong equipment to be Nell's girlfriend, Rip. Just . . . just see if you can spend some time with her. Go out on the boat, or go shopping or . . ." He gestured vaguely. "Paint each other's toenails."

"Excuse me?"

"Give me a break. I don't know what you people do in your mysterious caves when men aren't around."

"We have pillow fights in our underwear."

He brightened because she wanted him to. "Really? I was afraid that was a myth. So, be a friend, okay?"

"Are you starting to get a thing for her?"

"Yeah. So?"

"So, I guess I'll be a friend."

Nell walked into the Coven at precisely five. It was not, as she'd feared, a dark, eerie place, but rather cozy. The light was faintly blue and added a soft tint to the white flowers in the center of each table.

The tables themselves were round, with deep chairs and small sofas circling them. At the glossy bar the glasses sparkled. Nell had no more than chosen a table when a young waitress in trim, unrelieved black set a silver bowl of mixed snacks in front of her.

"Can I get you a drink?"

"I'm waiting for someone. Maybe just a mineral water for now. Thanks."

The only other patrons were a couple poring over an Island Tours brochure while they sipped white wines and nibbled from a cheese plate. The music was low, and very like what Mia tended to play in the bookstore. Nell tried to relax in her chair, wishing she'd brought a book.

Ten minutes later, Mia breezed in, the long skirt swirling around her long legs. She carried a book, and lifted her free hand in a wave toward the bar. "A glass of Cabernet, Betsy."

"First glass is on Carl Macey." Betsy shot Mia a wink. "He gave me orders."

"Tell him I enjoyed it." She sat down across from Nell. "Did you drive over?"

"No, I walked."

"Do you drink alcoholic beverages?"

"Now and then."

"Have one now. What's your pleasure?"

"The Cabernet'll be fine. Thanks."

"Two, Betsy. Damn, I love these things." She began to pick through the snack bowl. "Especially the little cheese ones that look like Chinese symbols. So, I brought you a book. A gift." Mia nudged the book toward Nell. "I thought you'd like to read about where you've chosen to live."

"Yes, I've been meaning to. *The Three Sisters: Legends and Lore*," she said, reading the cover. "Thank you."

"You're settling in now, getting your feet under you. I should tell you first that I couldn't be happier with your work."

"I'm glad to hear it. I love working at the café, the store. I couldn't have tailor-made a job I'd like more."

"Oh, you're Nell." Catching the comment as she served the wine, Betsy beamed. "You're always gone when I get to the café. I try to zip in before I open the bar. Great cookies."

"Thanks."

"You hear from Jane, Mia?"

"Just today. Tim got his audition, and they're hopeful. They're paying the rent by working at a bakery in Chelsea."

"I hope they're happy."

"So do I."

"I'll leave you two alone. Let me know if you need anything."

"So." Mia lifted her glass, tapped it to Nell's. "*Slainte.*"

"I'm sorry?"

"A Gaelic toast. Cheers." Mia brought the glass to her lips, watching Nell over the rim. "What do you know about witches?"

"Which sort? Like Elizabeth Montgomery on *Bewitched* or the ones who wear crystals and burn candles and sell little bottles of love potion?"

Mia laughed, crossed her legs. "Actually, I wasn't thinking of Hollywood or pseudo-Wiccans."

"I didn't mean to be insulting. I know there are people who take the matter very seriously. A kind of religion. That should be respected."

"Even if they are kooks," Mia said with a hint of a smile.

"No. You're not a kook. I understand . . . Well, you mentioned it that first day, then your conversation with Ripley yesterday."

"Good. Then we've established that I'm a witch." Mia sipped again. "You're a sweet one, Nell. There you are, trying very hard to discuss this intelligently, soberly, when you're thinking I'm—let's say—eccentric. We'll table that for the moment and go back in history so I can lay some groundwork for you. You know of the witch trials in Salem."

"Sure. A few hysterical young girls, fanatical Puritans. Mob mentality. Burn the witch."

"Hang," Mia corrected. "Nineteen people—all innocents—were hanged in 1692. One was pressed to death when he refused to declare himself innocent or guilty. Others died in prison. There have been witch-hunts throughout time. Here, in Europe, in every corner of the world. Even when most stopped believing, or admitting to a belief, in witchcraft, there were hunts. Nazism, McCarthyism, the KKK, and so on. Nothing more than fanatics with power, pushing their own agendas and finding enough weak minds to do the dirty work."

And don't, Mia thought, taking a breath, get me started. "But today we're concerned with one microcosm of history."

She leaned back, tapped a finger lightly on the book. "The Puritans came here, searching, they said, for religious freedom. Of course, many of them were only looking for a place to force their beliefs and their fears on others. And in Salem, they persecuted and murdered blindly, so blindly that not one of the nineteen souls they took was the soul of a witch."

"Prejudice and fear are never clear-sighted."

"Well said. There were three among them. Women who'd chosen this place to live their lives and live their craft. Powerful women who had helped the sick and the sorry. They knew, these three, that they could no longer stay where they would, sooner or later, be accused and condemned. So the Isle of Three Sisters was created."

"Created?"

"It's said that they met in secret and cast a spell. And part of the land was torn away from the mainland. We're living on what they took from that time and that place. A sanctuary. A haven. Isn't that what you came for, Nell?"

"I came for work."

"And found it. They were known as Air and Earth and Fire. For some years they lived quietly and at peace. And alone. It was loneliness that weakened them. The one known as Air wished for love."

"We all do," Nell said quietly.

"Perhaps. She dreamed of a prince, golden and handsome, who would sweep her away to some lovely place where they would live happily and have children to comfort her. She was careless with her wish, as women can be when they yearn. He came for her, and she saw only that he was golden and handsome. She went away with him, left her haven. She tried to be a good and dutiful wife, and bore her children, loved them. But it wasn't enough for him. Under the gold, he was dark. She grew to fear him, and he fed on her fear. One night, mad with that hunger, he killed her for being what she was."

"That's a sad story." Nell's throat was dry, but she didn't lift her glass.

"There's more, but that's enough for now. Each had a sad story, and a tragic end. And each left a legacy. A child who would bear a child who would bear a child, and so on. There would come a time, it was said, when a descendant from each of the sisters would be on the island at the same time. Each would have to find a way to redeem and break the pattern set three hundred years ago. If not, the island would topple into the sea. Lost as Atlantis."

"Islands don't topple into the sea."

"Islands aren't created by three women, usually," Mia countered. "If you believe the first, the second isn't much of a stretch."

"You believe it." Nell nodded. "And that you're one of the descendants."

"Yes. As you are."

"I'm no one."

"That's him talking, not you. I'm sorry." Instantly contrite, Mia reached out and gripped Nell's hand before she could rise. "I said I wouldn't pry, and I won't. But it annoys me to hear you say you're no one. To hear you mean it. Forget all the rest for now if you must, but don't forget who and what you are. You're an intelligent woman with spine enough to make a life for herself. With a gift—magic in the kitchen. I admire you."

"I'm sorry." Struggling to settle again, Nell reached for her wine. "I'm speechless."

"You had the courage to strike out on your own. To come to a strange place and make yourself part of it."

"Courage had nothing to do with it."

"You're wrong. He didn't break you."

"He did." Despite herself, Nell's eyes filled. "I just took the pieces and ran away."

"Took the pieces, escaped and rebuilt. Can't you be proud of that?"

"I can't explain what it was like."

"You don't have to. But you will, eventually, have to recognize your own power. You'll never feel complete until you do."

"I'm only looking for a normal life."

"You can't forget the possibilities." Mia held out a hand, palm up. Waited.

Unable to resist, Nell reached out, laid her palm against Mia's. And felt the heat, a painless burn of power. "It's in you. I'll help you find it. I'll teach you," Mia stated as Nell stared dumbfounded at the shimmer of light between their palms. "When you're ready."

Ripley scanned the beach scene and saw nothing out of the ordinary. Someone's toddler was having a tantrum, and the high-pitched cranky sound of No! No! No! blasted the air.

Somebody missed his nap, she thought.

People were scattered over the sand, staking out their territory with towels, blankets, umbrellas, totes, coolers, portable stereos. Nobody just went to the beach anymore, she mused. They packed for a day on the sand the way they packed to go to Europe.

It never failed to amuse her. Every day couples and groups would haul their possessions out of their rentals and hotel rooms and set up their temporary nests on the shore. And every day they would pack everything up again and haul it, along with a good bit of sand, back again.

Holiday nomads. The Bedouins of summer.

Leaving them to it, she headed up to the village. She carried nothing but her police issue, a Swiss Army knife, and a few dollars. Life was simpler that way.

She turned on High Street, intending to spend those few dollars on a quick meal. She was off duty, as much as either she or Zack was ever off duty, and was looking forward to a cold beer and a hot pizza.

When she spotted Nell standing in front of the hotel, looking dazed, she hesitated. It was as good a time as any, she supposed, to make that friendly overture.

"Hey, Nell."

"What? Oh. Hello, Ripley."

"You look a little lost."

"No." She knew just where she was, Nell thought. At the moment, it was the only thing she was absolutely sure of. "Just a little distracted."

"Long day, huh? Listen, I'm about to grab some dinner. A little early, but I'm starved. Why don't we split a pizza? My treat."

"Oh." She continued to blink, like someone coming out of a dream.

"The Surfside makes the best pizza on the island. Well, it's the only pizza place on the island, but still . . . How're things going at the café?"

"Good." There was really nothing to do but fall into step. She couldn't think clearly and would have sworn that her fingers still tingled. "I love working there."

"You've classed up the place," Ripley commented, and angled her head to get a look at the book Nell carried. "Reading up on island voodoo?"

"Voodoo? Oh." With a nervous laugh, Nell tucked the book under her arm. "I guess if I'm living here, I ought to know . . . things."

"Sure." Ripley pulled open the door of the pizzeria. "The tourists love all that island mystique crap. When we hit the solstice, we'll be flooded with New Agers. Hey, Bart!"

Ripley gave the man behind the counter a salute and grabbed an empty booth.

It may have been early, but the place was jammed. The jukebox was blaring, and the two video games tucked back in a small alcove shot out noise and light.

"Bart and his wife, Terry, run the place." Ripley shifted, stretched her legs out on the bench. "They've got your calzones, your pasta, and yadda yadda," she said, tossing Nell a laminated menu. "But it's really all about the pizza. You up for that?"

"Sure."

"Great. Anything you don't like on it?"

Nell scanned the menu. Why couldn't she *think*? "No."

"Even better. We'll get a large, loaded. What we don't eat, I'll take home to Zack. He'll pick off the mushrooms and onions and be grateful."

She slid out of the booth again. "Want a beer?"

"No. No, thanks. Just water."

"Coming up."

Seeing no point in waiting for table service, Ripley walked up to the counter, placed the order. Nell watched the way she joked with the long, thin man behind the counter. The way she hooked her sunglasses in the collar of her shirt. The way she stretched gorgeously toned and tanned arms out for the drinks. The way her dark hair bobbed as she turned to walk back to the booth.

The noise receded, like echoes in a dream, until it was a wash of white sound under a rising roar. Like waves cresting. As Ripley sat across from her again, Nell saw her mouth moving, but heard nothing. Nothing at all.

Then, like a door flung open, it all swarmed back.

". . . right up through Labor Day," Ripley finished, and reached for her beer.

"You're the third." Nell gripped her tingling hands together on the table.

"Huh?"

"The third. You're the third sister."

Ripley opened her mouth, then closed it again in a long, thin line. "Mia." She ground the two syllables together, then gulped down half her beer. "Don't start with me."

"I don't understand."

"There's nothing *to* understand. Just drop it." She slapped the glass back on the table, leaned forward. "Here's the deal. Mia can think, believe, whatever she wants. She can behave however she wants as long as she doesn't break the law. I don't have to buy into it. If you want to, that's your business. But I'm here for pizza and a beer."

"I don't know what I buy into. It makes you angry. It just confuses me."

"Look, you strike me as a sensible woman. Sensible women don't go around claiming to be witches descended from a trio of witches who carved an island out of a chunk of Massachusetts."

"Yes, but—"

"No buts. There's reality and there's fantasy. Let's stick with reality, because anything else is going to put me off my pizza. So, are you going to go out with my brother?"

"Go . . ." Confused, Nell pushed a hand through her hair. "Could you rewind that question?"

"Zack's working up to asking you out. You interested? Before you answer, let me say he's had all his shots, practices good personal hygiene, and though he has some annoying habits, he's reasonably well adjusted. So, think about that. I'll get the pizza."

Nell blew out a breath, sat back. She had, she decided, entirely too much to think about in one short evening.

Six

Ripley was right about the solstice. Café Book was so busy Mia had taken on two part-time clerks for the shop and added another behind the café counter.

The run on the vegetarian dishes over a two-day period kept Nell in a constant state of panic.

"We're running low on eggplant and alfalfa," she said as Peg came on shift. "I thought I'd calculated . . . Hell." She yanked off her apron. "I'm going to run down to the market, get what I can. I may have to substitute, change the menu for the rest of the day."

"Hey, whatever. Don't sweat it."

Easy for you to say, Nell thought as she rushed downstairs. She'd run out of hazelnut muffins by noon, and there was no way the chocolate chunk cookies were going to last the day at the rate they were disappearing. It was her responsibility to make certain everything in the café ran as Mia expected it to run. If she made a mistake—

In her rush to the back door, she all but ran over Lulu.

"I'm sorry. I'm sorry. I'm such an idiot. Are you all right?"

"I'll live." Lulu brushed fussily at her shirt. The girl had put in a good three weeks' work, but that didn't mean Lulu was ready to trust her. "Slow down. Just because you're off shift doesn't mean you have to run out of the place like it's on fire."

"No, I'm sorry. Is Mia— Would you tell Mia I'm sorry, and that I'll be right back?"

She bolted out the door and didn't stop running until she was in the produce section of Island Market. Panic and dread churned in her stomach. How could she have been so *stupid*? Buying supplies was an essential part of her job. Hadn't she been told to expect larger crowds over the solstice weekend? A moron could have done a better job planning for it.

The pressure in her chest was making her head light, but she forced herself to think, to study her choices, to select. She filled her basket quickly, waiting in agony in the checkout line as the minutes ticked away.

Dorcas chatted at her, and Nell managed to make some responses, and all the while her brain was screaming: Hurry!

She gathered the three heavy bags and, cursing herself for not thinking to bring her car, began to carry them as quickly as she could manage back to the shop.

"Nell! Nell, wait a minute." Shaking his head when she didn't respond, Zack jogged across the street. "Let me give you a hand with those."

It amazed her she didn't jump straight out of her sneakers as he reached out, took two of the bags. "I can get them. I can do it. I'm in a hurry."

"You'll move faster if you're not weighed down. Supplies for the café?"

"Yes. Yes." She was nearly running again. She could get another salad put together. Ten minutes, fifteen tops. And prep the ingredients for sandwiches. Then she could deal with the sweets. If she could get started right away, there might not be any gap.

"I guess you're pretty busy." He didn't like the look on her face. It was so grim, so set. Like someone about to go to war.

"I should've anticipated. There's no excuse for it."

She shoved through the back door of the shop, bolted up the stairs. By the time he got to the kitchen, she was already unbagging.

"Thank you. I can take care of it now. I know what to do."

She moved like a dervish, Zack thought, her eyes glassy and face pale.

"I thought you got off at two, Nell."

"Two?" She didn't bother to look up, but continued to chop, grate, mix. "No. I made a mistake. I have to fix it. Everything's going to be all right. It's going to be fine. No one's going to be upset or inconvenienced. I should have planned better. I will next time. I promise."

"Need two sandwich specials and a veggie pita— Jeez, Nell," Peg murmured as she stepped to the doorway.

Zack put a hand on her arm. "Get Mia," he said quietly.

"Two specials and a veggie. Okay. Okay." Nell set the bean-and-cucumber salad aside, hauled out the sandwich ingredients. "I bought some more eggplant, so we'll be fine. Just fine."

"No one's upset, Nell. You don't need to worry. Why don't you sit down a minute?"

"I only need a half hour. Twenty minutes. None of the guests will be disturbed." She picked up the orders, spun around, then jerked to a halt as Mia came in. "It's all right. Really, it's all right. We'll have plenty of everything."

"I'll take those." Peg eased by, slipped the orders out of Nell's hand. "They look great."

"I'm just putting together a new salad." There were bands around her chest, around her head. Tightening, tightening. "It won't take any time at all. Then I'll take care of the rest. I'll take care of it. Don't be angry."

"No one's angry, Nell. I think you should take a break now."

"I don't need one. I'll just finish." In desperation, she grabbed a bag of nuts. "I know I should've planned better, and I'm terribly sorry, but I'll make sure everything's perfect."

He couldn't stand it, couldn't stand to see her standing there, trembling now, her face white. "Hell with this," Zack spat, and stepped toward her.

"Don't!" She stumbled back, dropping the bag, flinging her arms up as if to guard her face from a blow. The moment she did, shame smothered panic.

"Oh, baby." Zack's voice was ripe with sympathy. She could do nothing but turn away from it.

"I want you to come with me now." Mia moved to her, took her hand. "All right? Come with me now."

Miserably embarrassed, helplessly shaken, Nell let herself be led away. Zack jammed his hands in his pockets and felt useless.

I don't know what got into me." The fact was, the last hour was largely a blur.

"I'd say you had a big, whopping panic attack. Now sit down." Mia walked across her office, opened what Nell had taken to be a file drawer. Instead she saw a mini-fridge stocked with small bottles of water and juice.

"You don't have to talk to me," Mia said as she stepped over, gave Nell an opened bottle of water. "But you should think about talking to someone."

"I know." Rather than drinking, Nell rubbed the chilled bottle over her face. It was beyond ridiculous, she thought now, falling to pieces over eggplant. "I thought I was over it. That hasn't happened in a really long time. Months. We were so busy, and supplies were running low. It got bigger and bigger in my mind until I thought if I didn't get some more eggplant, the world was going to end." She drank now, deeply. "Stupid."

"Not stupid if you were used to being punished for something just that petty in the past."

Nell lowered the bottle. "He's not here. He can't hurt me."

"Can't he? Little sister, he's never stopped hurting you."

"If that's true, it's my problem. I'm not a dishrag anymore, I'm not a punching bag or a doormat."

"Good to hear."

She pressed her fingers to her temple. She had to let something out, she realized. Lift something off, or she'd break again. "We had a party once and ran out of martini olives. It was the first time he hit me."

Mia's face registered no shock, no judgment. "How long did you stay with him?"

There was no censure in the question, no slick surface of pity or underlying smugness. Because the question was asked in a brisk and practical tone, Nell responded in kind. "Three years. If he finds me, he'll kill me. I knew that when I left. He's an important man. Wealthy, connected."

"He's looking for you?"

"No, he thinks I'm dead. Nearly nine months now. I'd rather be dead than live the way I was living. That sounds melodramatic, but—"

"No, it doesn't. The employment forms you filled out for me? Are they safe?"

"Yes. My grandmother's maiden name. I broke some laws. Computer hacking, false statement, forged documents to get new identification, a driver's license, Social Security number."

"Computer hacking?" Lifting a brow, Mia smiled. "Nell, you surprise me."

"I'm good with computers. I used to—"

"You don't have to tell me."

"It's all right. I helped run a business, a catering business, with my mother a long time ago. I used a computer for records, invoices, what have you. Since I was going to keep the books, the records, I took some courses. When I started planning to run, I did a lot of research. I knew I'd only get one chance. God. I've never been able to talk to anyone about it. I never thought I could."

"Do you want to tell me the rest?"

"I'm not sure. It gets stuck somewhere. Right about here," she said, tapping a fist on her chest.

"If you decide you want to, come up to the house tonight. I'll show you my gardens. My cliffs. Meanwhile, take a breather, take a walk, take a nap."

"Mia, I'd like to finish in the café. Not because I'm upset or worried. I'd just like to finish."

"All right."

The drive up the coast was breathtaking. The curving road with its sudden, unexpected twists. The steady roar of the water, the rush of wind. The memories it brought back should have disturbed her, left her shaken. Instead as Nell pushed her poor rust-bucket of a car for speed, she felt exhilarated. As if she were leaving all her excess weight on the twisted road behind her.

Maybe it was the sight of that tall white tower against the summer sky and the broody stone house beside it. They looked like something out of a storybook. Old and sturdy and wonderfully secret.

The painting she'd seen on the mainland hadn't done them justice.

Oil and canvas hadn't been able to translate the sweep of the wind, the texture of the rocks, the gnarled humps of trees.

And, she thought as she rounded the last turn, the painting hadn't had Mia, standing between two vivid flows of flowers in a blue dress with her miles of red hair rioting in the wind.

Nell parked her sad car behind Mia's shiny silver convertible.

"I hope you don't take this the wrong way," Nell called out.

"I always take things the right way."

"I was just thinking, if I were a man, I'd promise you anything."

When Mia only laughed, Nell tipped back her head and tried to take in all the house at once—the dour stone, the fanciful gables, the romance of the widow's walk.

"It's wonderful. It suits you."

"It certainly does."

"But so far from everything, everyone. You're not lonely here?"

"I enjoy my own company. Are you afraid of heights?"

"No," Nell answered. "No, I'm not."

"Have a look at the headland. It's spectacular."

Nell walked with her, between the house and the tower, out to the rugged jag of cliffs that jutted over the ocean. Even here there were flowers, tough little blooms that fought their way through cracks or blossomed along the scruffy tufts of wild grass.

Below, the waves thrashed and fumed, hurling themselves against the base of the cliffs, rearing back to slap again. Beyond, the water turned a deep, deep blue and stretched forever.

"When I was a girl I would sit here, and wonder at all this. Sometimes I still do."

Nell turned her head, studied Mia's profile. "Did you grow up here?"

"Yes. In this house. It's always been mine. My parents were for the sea, and now they sail it. They're currently in the South Pacific, I think. We were always more a couple and a child than a family. They never quite adjusted to me, nor I to them, for that matter. Though we got along well enough."

With a little shrug, she turned away. "The light's been here nearly three hundred years, sending out its beam to guide ships and seamen. Still, there've been wrecks, and it's said—as one would expect it to be said of such places—that on some nights, when the wind is right, one can hear the desperate calls of the drowned."

"Not a comforting bedtime story."

"No. The sea isn't always kind."

Still she was drawn to it, compelled to stand and watch its whims, its charm and its violence. Fire, drawn to Water.

"The house came before," she added. "It was the first house built on the island."

"Conjured by magic in the moonlight," Nell added. "I read the book."

"Well, magic or mortar, it stands. The gardens are my joy, and I've indulged myself there." She gestured.

Nell looked back toward the house, blinked. The rear was a fantasy of blooms, shapes, arbors, paths. The juxtaposition between raw cliffs and lush fairyland almost made her dizzy.

"My God, Mia! It's amazing, spectacular. Like a painting. Do you do all the work yourself?"

"Mmm. Now and then I'll dragoon a strong back, but for the most part I can handle it. It relaxes me," she said as they walked toward the first tangle of hedges. "And gratifies me."

There seemed to be dozens of secret places, unexpected turns. An iron trellis buried under wisteria, a sudden stream of pure white blossoms curling through like a satin ribbon. A tiny pool where water lilies drifted and reeds speared up around a statue of a goddess.

There were stone fairies and fragrant lavender, marble dragons and trailing nasturtium. Cheerfully blooming herbs tumbled through a rock garden and spilled toward a cushion of moss covered with starry flowers.

"No wonder you're not lonely here."

"Exactly." Mia led the way down a crooked path to a small stone island. The table there was stone as well, and stood on the base of a laughing winged gargoyle. "We're having champagne, to celebrate the solstice."

"I've never met anyone like you."

Mia lifted the bottle out of a gleaming copper pail. "I should hope not. I insist on being unique." She poured two glasses, sat, then stretched out her legs and wiggled the painted toes of her bare feet. "Tell me how you died, Nell."

"I drove off a cliff." She took her glass, drank deep. "We lived in California. Beverly Hills and Monterey. It seemed at first like being a princess in a castle. He swept me off my feet."

She couldn't sit, so she wandered the little island and drew in the scent of the flowers. She heard the tinkle of bells and saw that Mia had the same starry wind chime she'd bought for herself on her first day.

"My father was in the military. We moved around a lot, and that was hard. But he was wonderful. So handsome, and brave and strong. I suppose he was strict, but he was never unkind. I loved being with him. He couldn't always be with us, and we missed him. I loved seeing him come back, in his uniform, and the way his face would light up when my mother and I went to meet him. He was killed in the Gulf War. I still miss him."

She drew a deep breath. "It wasn't easy for my mother, but she got through it. That's when she started the catering business. She called it A Moveable Feast. Hemingway."

"Clever," Mia acknowledged. "Classy."

"She was both. She's always been a terrific cook and loved to entertain. She taught me . . . it was something we liked doing together."

"A bond between you," Mia commented. "A lovely and strong one."

"Yes. We moved to Chicago, and she built up an impressive reputation while I went to college, took care of the books, and pitched in whenever I could manage it around classes. When I was twenty-one, I started working with her full-time. We expanded and developed an elite list of clients. That's how I met Evan, at a party in Chicago we were catering. A very important party for very important people. I was twenty-four. He was ten years older, and everything I wasn't. Sophisticated, brilliant, cultured."

Mia held up a finger. "Why do you say that? You're a traveled, educated woman with an enviable skill."

"I didn't feel like any of those things when I was with him." Nell sighed. "In any case, I didn't move in the same circles. I cooked for the rich, the high-powered, the glamorous. I didn't share the table with them. He made me feel . . . grateful that he would pay attention to me. As if it were some fabulous compliment. I just realized that." She shook her head.

"He flirted with me, and it was exciting. He sent me two dozen roses the next day. It was always red roses. He asked me out, and took me to the theater, to parties, to fabulous restaurants. He stayed in Chicago for two weeks, made it clear he was staying, reorganizing his schedule, putting off his clients, his work, his life, for me. I was meant for him," Nell whispered, rubbing arms that were suddenly chilled.

"We were meant for each other. Then, when he told me that, it was thrilling. Later, not so very much later, it was terrifying. He said things to me that seemed romantic then. We'd always be together. We'd never be apart. He would never let me go. He dazzled me, and when he asked me to marry him, I didn't think twice. My mother had reservations, asked me to give it some time, but I wouldn't listen. We eloped, and I went back to California with him. The press called it the romance of the decade."

"Ah. Yes." Mia nodded as Nell turned back. "It clicks. You looked different then. More like a pampered kitten."

"I looked the way he told me to look, and behaved the way he told me to behave. At first that seemed fine. He was older, wiser, and I was new in his world. He made it seem reasonable, just as he made it seem . . . instructional when he would tell me I was slow or dull. He knew best, so if he ordered me to change my dress for another before I was permitted to go out, he was only looking out for my interests—and our image. It was very subtle at first, those digs, those demands. And whenever I pleased him, I was given a little treat. Like a puppy being trained. Here, you performed very well for company last night, have a diamond bracelet. God, it disgusts me how easily I was manipulated."

"You were in love."

"I did love him. The man I thought he was. And he was so clever, so relentless. The first time he hit me, it was a horrible shock, but it never occurred to me that I didn't deserve it. I'd been so well trained. It got worse after that, but slowly, bit by bit. My mother was killed, hardly a year after I left. Drunk driver," Nell said, her voice thickening.

"And you were alone then. I'm so sorry."

"He was so kind, so supportive. He made all the arrangements, canceled his appointments for a week to take me to Chicago. He did everything a loving husband could do. And the day we got home, he went wild. He waited until we were home, back in that house, and he'd sent all the servants away. Then he knocked me down, he raved, and slapped. He never used his fists on me, always an open hand. I think it was somehow more degrading. He accused me of having an

affair with one of the mourners. A man who'd been a good friend of
my parents. A kind and decent man whom I thought of as an uncle.

"Well." Surprised that her glass was empty, she walked back to
the table, poured another. There were birds singing, a pretty chipper-
ing among the flowers. "We don't need a blow-by-blow account. He
abused me, I took it."

She lifted her glass, drank, steadied herself again. "I went to the
police once. He had a lot of friends on the force, a lot of influence.
They didn't take me seriously. Oh, I had some bruises, but nothing
life-threatening. He found out, and he explained to me in ways I'd
understand that if I ever humiliated him like that again, he'd kill me.
I got away once, but he found me. He told me I belonged to him, and
that he would never let me go. He told me that when his hands were
around my throat. That if I ever tried to leave him, he'd find me, and
he'd kill me. No one would ever know. And I believed him."

"But you did leave him."

"I planned it for six months, step by step, always careful not to
upset him, not to give him cause to suspect. We entertained, we
traveled, we slept together. We were the picture of the perfect affluent
couple. He still hit me. There was always something I didn't do quite
right, but I would always apologize. I pilfered cash whenever I could
and hid it in a box of tampons. Pretty safe bet he wouldn't look there.
I got a fake driver's license, and I hid that too. And then I was ready.

"He had a sister in Big Sur. She was having a lavish tea party. Very
female. I was expected to go. That morning, I complained of a headache, which, of course, annoyed him. I was just making excuses, he
said. A number of his clients would be there, and I just wanted to
embarrass him by not showing up. So I said I'd go. Naturally I'd go.
I would just take some aspirin and be fine. But I knew my reluctance
would ensure him letting me out of the house."

She'd gotten clever, too, Nell thought now. At deceit, at pretense.

"I wasn't even frightened then. He went off to play golf, and I put what I needed in the trunk of the car. I stopped on the way and put on a black wig. I picked up the secondhand bike I'd bought the week before, and put it in the trunk. I stopped again before I got to the party, hid the bike at a spot I'd picked out. I drove down Highway 1, and I went to tea."

Nell sat down, spoke calmly while Mia sat in silence. "I made sure that a number of people noted I wasn't feeling very well. Barbara, his sister, even suggested I lie down for a bit. I waited until most of the guests had left, then I thanked her for a lovely time. She was worried about me. I looked pale. I brushed her off, and I got back in the car."

Her voice was calm, almost flat. She was just a woman telling a mildly distasteful story. One that had happened to someone else.

That's what she told herself.

"It was dark now. I needed it to be. I called Evan on my cell phone to tell him I was on my way. He always insisted on that. I got to the stretch of the road where I'd hidden the bike, and there were no other cars. I knew it could be done. Had to be. I took off my seat belt. I didn't think. I'd practiced it in my head a thousand times, so I didn't let myself think. I opened the door, still driving, swerving, going faster. I aimed for the edge. If I didn't make it, well, I was no worse off. I jumped. It was like flying. The car soared over the edge, just soared like a bird, then it crashed on the rocks, horrible sound, and it tumbled and rolled and fell into the water. I ran, back to where I had the bike and the bag. I pulled off my beautiful suit and put on old jeans and a sweatshirt, the wig. I still wasn't afraid."

No, she hadn't been afraid, not then. But now, as she relived it, her voice began to hitch. It hadn't happened to someone else after all.

"I rode down the hills, and up and down. When I got to Carmel, I went into the bus station and I paid cash for a one-way ticket to Las Vegas. When I was on the bus, and it started to move out of the station, I was afraid. Afraid he would come and stop the bus. And I would lose. But he didn't. In Vegas I got on a bus for Albuquerque, and in Albuquerque I bought a paper and read about the tragic death of Helen Remington."

"Nell." Mia reached out, closed a hand over Nell's. She doubted that Nell was aware she'd been crying for the last ten minutes. "I've never met anyone like you, either."

Nell lifted her glass and, as tears spilled down her cheeks, toasted. "Thanks."

At Mia's insistence, she spent the night. It seemed sensible after several glasses of champagne and an emotional purge to let herself be led to a big four-poster. Without protest, she slipped on a borrowed silk nightshirt, climbed between soft linen sheets, and fell instantly asleep.

And woke in the moonlit dark.

It took her a moment to orient herself, to remember where she was and what had awakened her. Mia's guest room, she thought groggily. And people were singing.

No, not singing. Chanting. It was a lovely, melodious sound, just on the edges of her hearing. Drawn to it, she rose and, still logy with sleep, moved directly to the terrace doors.

She pushed them open to a warm, whipping wind and stepped out into the pearl-white light of a three-quarter moon. The scent of flowers seemed to rise up and surround her until her head spun with it as it had with wind.

The heartbeat of the sea was fast, almost a rage, and her own raced to keep pace.

Then she saw Mia, dressed in a robe that gleamed silver in the moonlight, step out of the woods where trees swayed like dancers.

She walked to the cliffs, the silver of her gown, the flame of her hair, whirling. There, high on the rocks, she faced the sea and lifted her arms to star and moon.

The air filled with voices, and the voices seemed filled with joy. With her eyes dazzled with wonder, stinging with tears she didn't understand, Nell watched as light, shimmering beams of it, slid down from the sky to brush the tips of Mia's fingers, the ends of her flying hair.

For a moment it seemed she was like a candle, straight, slim, incandescent, lighting the edge of the world.

Then there was only the sound of the surf, the pearl-white light of the waning moon, and a woman standing alone on a cliff.

Mia turned, walked back toward the house. Her head lifted, and her eyes met Nell's. Held. Held.

She smiled quietly, moved into the shadow of the house. And was gone.

Seven

It was still dark when Nell tiptoed down to Mia's kitchen. The house was huge, and took some maneuvering. Though she wasn't sure what time Mia rose for the day, she brewed a pot of coffee for her hostess and wrote a note of thanks before she left.

They would have to talk, Nell thought as she drove home in the softening light of pre-dawn. About a number of things. And they would, she decided, as soon as she could figure out where to begin.

She could almost convince herself that what she'd seen in the moonlight had been nothing more than a champagne-induced dream. Almost. But it was too clear in her mind to be a dream.

Light spilling out of stars like liquid silver. A rising wind full of song. A woman glowing like a torch.

Such things should be fantasy. But they weren't . . . if they were real and she had a part in them, she needed to know what it all meant.

For the first time in nearly four years she felt absolutely steady, absolutely calm. For now, that was enough.

ℰℬ

By noon she was too busy to think about more than the job at hand. There was a paycheck in her pocket, and a day off around the corner.

"Iced hazelnut cappuccino, large." The man who ordered leaned on the counter as Nell began to work. She judged him as mid-thirties, health-club fit, and a mainlander.

It pleased her that she could already, with very decent accuracy, spot a mainlander. And feel the slightly smug reaction of an islander.

"So, how much aphrodisiac do you put in those cookies?" he asked her.

She glanced at him. "I'm sorry?"

"Ever since I tasted your oatmeal raisin, I haven't been able to get you out of my mind."

"Really? I could've sworn I put all the aphrodisiac in the macadamia nut."

"In that case I'll take three," he said. "I'm Jim, and you've seduced me with your baked goods."

"Then you'd better stay away from my three-bean salad. It'll ruin you for all other women."

"If I buy all the three-bean salad, will you marry me and have my children?"

"Well, I would, Jim, but I've taken a sacred oath to stay free to bake for all the world." She capped his coffee, bagged it. "Do you really want those cookies?"

"You bet. How about a clambake? Some friends and I are sharing a house. We're going to do in some clams tonight."

"Tonight a clambake, tomorrow a house in the suburbs and a cocker spaniel." She rang him up, took his money with a smile. "Better safe than sorry. But thanks."

"You're breaking my heart," he said, and sighing heavily, he walked away.

"Oh, man, he is so cute." Peg craned her neck to keep him in sight until he'd gone downstairs. "You're really not interested?"

"No." Nell took off her apron, rolled her shoulders.

"Then you wouldn't mind if I gave him a shot?"

"Be my guest. There's plenty of bean salad in the fridge. Oh, and Peg? Thanks for being understanding about yesterday."

"Hey, everybody gets weird now and then. See you Monday."

See you Monday, Nell thought. It was just that simple. She was a member of the team, she had friends. She had deflected an overture from an attractive man without getting the jitters.

In fact, she enjoyed it, the way she used to enjoy such things. The day might come when she didn't feel compelled to deflect.

One day she might go to a clambake with a man and some of his friends. Talk, laugh, enjoy the companionship. Light, casual friendships. She could do that. There couldn't be any serious relationships in her future even if she could learn to handle one emotionally.

She was, after all, still legally married.

But now, just now, that fact was more of a safety net than the nightmare it had been. She was free to be whoever she wanted to be, but not free enough to be bound again, not to any man.

She decided to treat herself to an ice cream cone, and a detour to the beach. People called her by name as she passed, and that was a quiet thrill.

As she crossed the sand, she spotted Pete Stahr and his infamous dog. Both looked sheepish as Zack stood beside them, hands on hips.

He never wore a hat as he'd advised her to do when gardening. As a result his hair was lighter at the tips and almost always disordered from the ocean breeze. He rarely wore his badge either, she noted, but the gun rode in the holster at his hip almost casually.

It occurred to her that if he had stopped by the café and asked her to go to a clambake, she might not have brushed him off.

When the dog lifted his paw hopefully, Zack shook his head, pointed to the leash that Pete held. Once the leash was secured, man and dog walked off, heads hung low.

Zack turned, the sun bouncing off his dark glasses. And she knew instinctively that he was looking at her. Nell braced herself and went to him.

"Sheriff."

"Nell. Pete let his dog off the leash again. Mutt smells like a fish house. Ice cream's dripping."

"It's hot." Nell licked at the cone and decided to get it over with. "About yesterday—"

"Feeling better?"

"Yes."

"Good. Gonna share any of that?"

"What? Oh. Sure." She held out the cone, felt a little tingle in the blood when he licked just above her fingertips. Funny, she thought, she hadn't gotten any tingles from the cute guy with the clambake. "You're not going to ask?"

"Not as long as you'd rather I didn't." Yes, he'd looked at her. And had seen the deliberate squaring of her shoulders before she started toward him. "Why don't you walk with me awhile? There's a nice breeze off the water."

"I was wondering . . . what does Lucy do all day when you're out upholding the law?"

"This and that. Dog chores."

That tickled a laugh out of her. "Dog chores?"

"Sure. Some days a dog's got to hang around the house, roll in the grass, and think long thoughts. Other times, she comes on in to the office with me, when she's in the mood. Swims, chews up my shoes. I'm thinking about buying her a brother or sister."

"I was thinking about getting a cat. I'm not sure I'd be able to train a puppy. A cat would be easier. I saw a notice on the board in the market for free kittens."

"The Stubens girl's cat. They've still got one or two left, last I heard. Their place is over on Bay. White saltbox, blue shutters."

She nodded, stopped. Impulse, she reminded herself, had served her well so far. Why stop following it? "Zack, I'm going to try out a new recipe tonight. Tuna and linguini with sun-dried tomatoes and feta. I could use a guinea pig."

He lifted her hand, took another taste of her dripping ice cream. "Well, it happens I don't have any pressing plans for tonight, and as sheriff I do what I can to serve the needs of the community. What time?"

"Is seven all right with you?"

"Works for me."

"Fine, I'll see you then. Bring an appetite," she said as she hurried away.

"Count on it," he said, and tipped down his dark glasses to watch her dash back toward the village.

At seven, the appetizers were ready, and the wine was chilling. Nell had bought a secondhand table and planned to spend part of her day off scraping and painting it. But for now she covered the scarred wood and peeling green paint with a sheet.

It stood on her back lawn, along with the two old chairs she'd picked up for a song. They weren't particularly pretty at the moment, but they had potential. And they were hers.

She'd set the table with two plates, two bowls, and wineglasses—all purchases from the island thrift shop. Nothing matched, but she thought the result was cheerful and charming.

And as far from the formal china and heavy silver of her past as possible.

Her garden was coming along well, and the tomato and pepper plants, the squash and zucchini, would all be put in the following morning.

She was very close to broke again, and completely content.

"Well, now, doesn't that look sweet?"

Nell turned to see Gladys Macey standing on the edge of her lawn, gripping an enormous white purse.

"Just as pretty as a picture."

"Mrs. Macey. Hello."

"Hope you don't mind me dropping by this way. I'd've called, but you haven't got a phone."

"No, of course not. Um, can I get you something to drink?"

"No, no, don't you fuss. I've come by on business."

"Business?"

"Yes, indeed." Her tidy helmet of black hair barely moved as she gave a sharp nod. "Carl and I got our thirtieth anniversary coming up last part of July."

"Congratulations."

"You can say that again. Two people stick it out for three decades, it's saying something. Since it is, I want a party, and I just finished telling Carl he's not getting out of putting on a suit for it, either. I was wondering if you'd take care of putting the refreshments together for me."

"Oh. Well."

"I want a catered affair," Gladys said definitely. "And I want it spiffy. When my girl got married, two years ago last April, we hired a caterer from the mainland. Too snippy for my taste, and too dear for Carl's, but we didn't have much to choose from. I don't figure you're going to get snippy with me or charge me a king's ransom for a bowl of cold shrimp."

"Mrs. Macey, I appreciate you thinking of me, but I'm not set up to cater."

"Well, you got time, don't you? I've got a list here of how many people and the kind of business I'm thinking of." She pulled a file folder out of the enormous purse, pushed it into Nell's hand. "I want to have it right at my house, and I've got my mother's good china and so forth. You just look over what I've put together there, and we'll talk about it tomorrow. You come on by the house tomorrow afternoon."

"I'd certainly like to help you. Maybe I can . . ." She looked down at the folder, saw that Gladys had marked it "Thirtieth Anniversary" and had added a heart with her initials and Carl's in the center.

Touched, she tucked the folder under her arm. "I'll see what I can do."

"You're a nice girl, Nell." Gladys glanced over her shoulder at the sound of a car, lifted her eyebrows as she recognized Zack's cruiser. "And you've got good taste. You come on by tomorrow, and we'll talk this out. Have a nice dinner now."

She strolled toward her car, stopping to say a few words to Zack. She gave him a pat on the cheek, noted the flowers in his hand. By the time she was behind the wheel, she was planning who she'd call first to spread the news that Zachariah Todd was sparking the little Channing girl.

"I'm a little late. Sorry. We had a fender bender in the village. Put me behind."

"It's all right."

"I thought you might like these for your garden."

She smiled at the pot of Shasta daisies. "They're perfect. Thanks." She took them, set them beside her kitchen stoop. "I'll get the wine and the appetizers."

He walked into the kitchen behind her. "Something smells great."

"Once I got started, I tried out a couple of different recipes. You've got your work cut out for you."

"I'm up for it. Now what's this?" He crouched down, stroked a finger over the smoke-gray kitten circled on a pillow in the corner.

"That's Diego. We're living together."

The kitten mewed, stretched, then began to bat at Zack's shoelaces. "You've been busy. Cooking, buying furniture, getting a roommate." Scooping up Diego, he turned toward her. "Nobody's going to find any moss on you, Nell."

He stood there, big and handsome, with a gray kitten nuzzling at his shoulder.

He'd brought her white daisies in a plastic pot.

"Oh, damn." She set her tray of appetizers down again, took a breath. "I might as well get this over with. I don't want you to get the wrong impression about dinner, and . . . things. I'm very attracted to you, but I'm not in a place where I can act on my feelings. It's only fair to tell you that up front. There are good reasons for it, but I'm not willing to get into them. So, if you'd rather just go, no hard feelings."

He listened soberly, rubbing a finger between the kitten's silky ears. "I appreciate you spelling that out for me. Seems a shame to waste all this food, though." He plucked a stuffed olive from the tray, popped it into his mouth. "I'll just hang around, if it's all the same to you. Why don't I take the wine outside?"

He picked up the bottle and, still carrying Diego, bumped the screened door with his hip. "Oh, and in the interest of fair play, I'll tell you I'll be nudging you out of that place you're in."

With that said, he held the door open. "You want to bring those on out?"

"I'm not as easy a nudge as you might think."

"Honey, there's nothing easy about you."

She picked up the tray, sailed by him. "I take that as a compliment."

"It was meant as one. Now, why don't we have some wine, relax, and you can tell me what Gladys Macey was after."

When they were seated, she poured the wine, and he settled the kitten in his lap. "I thought, being sheriff, you'd know all there is to know about what's going on."

"Well." He leaned over the tray, selected a gnocchi. "I can deduce, seeing as I'm a trained observer. There's a file on your counter, marked with Gladys's handwriting, which leads me to believe she's planning on an anniversary party. And, as I'm sitting here, heading straight toward heaven with whatever the hell it is I just put in my mouth—and knowing Gladys is a shrewd lady—I'd suppose she's wanting you to cater it. How'd I do?"

"Dead on."

"Are you going to do it?"

"I'm going to think about it."

"You'd do a great job." He plucked another selection from the tray, examined it suspiciously. "Any mushrooms in this thing? I hate mushrooms."

"No. We're fungi-free tonight. Why would I do a good job?"

"I said great job." He popped it in his mouth. Some creamy cheese and herbs in a thin and flaky pastry. "Because you cook like a magician, you look like an angel, and you're as organized as a computer. You get things done, and you've got style. How come you're not eating any of this?"

"I want to see if you live first." When he only grinned and kept eating, she sat back and sipped her wine. "I'm a good cook. Put me in a kitchen, and I rule the world. I'm presentable, but I don't look like an angel."

"I'm the one looking at you."

"I'm organized," she continued, "because I keep my life simple."

"Which is another way of saying you're not going to complicate it with me."

"There you go, dead on again. I'm going to get the salad."

Zack waited until her back was turned before he let his amusement show. "Easy enough to ruffle her feathers," he said to Diego, "when you know where to scratch. Let me tell you something I've learned over the years about women. Keep changing the rhythm, and they'll never know what to expect next."

When Nell came back out, Zack launched into the story of the pediatrician from Washington and the stockbroker from New York who'd bumped fenders outside the pharmacy on High Street.

He made her laugh, put her gently at ease again. Before she knew it, she was telling him about various kitchen feuds in restaurants where she'd worked.

"Temperaments and sharp implements," she said. "A dangerous combination. I once had a line chef threaten me with an electric whisk."

Because dusk was falling, he lit the squat red candle she'd set on the table. "I had no idea there was so much danger and intrigue behind those swinging doors."

"And sexual tension," she added, twirling linguini onto her fork. "Smoldering looks over simmering pots of stock, broken hearts shattering in the whipping cream. It's a hotbed."

"Food's got all that sensuality. Flavor, texture, scent. This tuna's getting me pretty worked up."

"So, the dish passes the audition."

"It's great." Candlelight suited her, he thought. It put little gold lights in those deep blue pools. "Do you make this stuff up, or collect recipes, what?"

"Both, I like to experiment. When my mother . . ." She trailed off, but Zack merely picked up the wine bottle, topped off their glasses. "She liked to cook," Nell said simply. "And entertain."

"My mother—well, we'll just say the kitchen wasn't her best room. I was twenty before I realized a pork chop wasn't supposed to bounce if you dropped it. She lived on an island most of her life, but as far as she was concerned tuna came out of a can. She's hell with numbers, though."

"Numbers."

"Certified public accountant—retired now. She and my dad bought themselves one of those big tin cans on wheels and hit the great American highway about a year ago. They're having a terrific time."

"That's nice." And so was the unmistakable affection in his voice. "Do you miss them?"

"I do. I'm not going to say I miss my mother's cooking, but I miss their company. My father used to sit out on the back porch and play the banjo. I miss that."

"The banjo." It sounded so charming. "Do you play?"

"No. I never could get my fingers to cooperate."

"My father played the piano. He used to—" She stopped herself again, realigning her thoughts as she rose. "I could never get my fingers to cooperate either. Strawberry shortcake for dessert. Can you manage it?"

"I can probably choke some down, just to be polite. Let me give you a hand."

"No." She waved him down before he could rise. "I've got it. It'll just take me . . ." She glanced down as she cleared his plate, saw Diego sprawled belly-up in apparent ecstasy in his lap. "Have you been sneaking that cat food from the table?"

"Me?" All innocence, Zack picked up his wineglass. "I don't know what makes you think that."

"You'll spoil him, *and* make him sick." She started to reach down, scoop up the kitten, then realized that considering Diego's location, the move was just a tad too personal. "Put him down awhile so he can run around and work off that tuna before I take him inside."

"Yes, ma'am."

She had the coffee on and was about to slice the cake when he came through the door with the serving bowl.

"Thanks. But guests don't clear."

"They did in my house." He looked at the cake, all fluffy white and succulent red. And back at her. "Honey, I've got to tell you, that's a work of art."

"Presentation's half the battle," she said, pleased. She went still when he laid his hand over the back of hers. Nearly relaxed again when he simply moved hers to widen the size of the slice.

"I'm a big patron of the arts."

"At this rate Diego's not the only one who's going to be sick." But she cut him a piece twice the size of her own. "I'll bring the coffee."

"I should tell you something else," he began as he picked up the plates, then held the door for her again. "I plan on touching you. A lot. Maybe you could work on getting used to it."

"I don't like being handled."

"I didn't plan to start out that way." He walked to the table, set down the cake plates, and sat. "Though handling, on both sides, can have some satisfying results. I don't put marks on women, Nell. I don't use my hands that way."

"I'm not going to talk about that," she answered curtly.

"I'm not asking you to. I'm talking about me, and you, and the way things are now."

"Things aren't any way now—like that."

"They're going to be." He scooped up some cake, sampled it. "God, woman, you sell this on the open market, you'd be a millionaire inside of six months."

"I don't need to be rich."

"Got your back up again," he observed and kept right on eating. "I don't mind that. Some men look for a woman who'll buckle under, tow the line, whatever." He shrugged, speared a fat strawberry. "Now, me, I wonder why. It seems that would get boring fast for both parties involved. No spark there, if you know what I mean."

"I don't need sparks either."

"Everybody does. People who set them off each other every time they turn around, though, well, that would just wear you out." Something told her he didn't wear out—or wear down—easily.

"But if you don't light a spark now and again," he went on, "you miss the sizzle that comes with it. If you cooked without spice or seasoning, you'd come up with something you could eat, but it wouldn't satisfy."

"That's very clever. But there are some of us who stay healthier on a bland diet."

"My great-uncle Frank." Zack gestured with his fork before he dived into the cake again. "Ulcers. Some said it came from pure meanness, and it's hard to argue. He was a hardheaded, miserly Yankee. Never married. He preferred curling up in bed with his ledgers rather than a woman. Lived to be ninety-eight."

"And the moral of the story?"

"Oh, I wasn't thinking of morals. Just Great-uncle Frank. We'd go to dinner at my grandmother's the third Sunday of every month when I was a boy. She made the best damn pot roast—you know, the kind circled around with the little potatoes and carrots? My mother didn't inherit Gran's talent with a pot roast. But, anyway, Great-uncle Frank would come and eat rice pudding while the rest of us gorged. The man scared the hell out of me. I can't look at a bowl of rice pudding to this day without getting the shakes."

It must be some kind of magic, she decided, that made it so impossible not to relax around him. "I think you're making half that up."

"Not a single word. You can look him up in the registry at the Island Methodist Church. Francis Morris Bigelow. Gran, she married a Ripley, but was a Bigelow by birth and older sister to Frank. She lived to just past her hundredth birthday herself. We tend to be long-lived in my family, which is why most of us don't settle down to marriage and family until into our thirties."

"I see." Since he'd polished off his cake, Nell nudged hers toward him and wasn't the least bit surprised when he took a forkful. "I'd always thought New England Yankees were a taciturn breed. You know—ayah, nope, maybe."

"We like to talk in my family. Ripley can be short-winded, but then she isn't overly fond of people as a species. This is the best meal I've had since Sunday dinner at my gran's."

"That is the ultimate compliment."

"We'd finish it off exactly right if we were to take a walk on the beach."

She couldn't think of a reason to say no. Maybe she didn't want to.

The light was fading, going deep at the edges. A needle-thin and needle-bright swath of light swept over the horizon, and a blush of pink gleamed in the west. The tide had gone out, leaving a wide avenue of dark, damp sand that was cool underfoot. The surf teased it, foaming out in ribbons while narrow-bodied birds with legs like stilts pecked for their supper.

Others strolled the beach. Almost all couples now, Nell noted.

Hand-in-hand or arm-in-arm. As a precaution, she'd tucked her own hands in her pockets after she'd pried off her shoes and rolled up her jeans.

Here and there were stockpiles of driftwood that would be bonfires when full dark fell. She wondered what it would be like to sit by the flames with a group of friends. To laugh and talk of nothing important.

"Haven't seen you go in yet."

"In?"

"The water," Zack explained.

She didn't own a bathing suit, but saw no reason to say so. "I've waded in a couple of times."

"Don't swim?"

"Of course I can swim."

"Let's go."

He scooped her up so fast her heart stuck between her chest and her throat. She could barely manage to breathe, much less scream. Before full panic had a chance to bloom, she was in the water.

Zack was laughing, spinning her away from an oncoming wave to take the brunt of it himself. She was sliding, rolling, fighting to gain her feet when he simply nipped her at the waist and righted her.

"Can't live on Three Sisters without being baptized." Tossing his wet hair back, he pulled her farther out.

"It's freezing."

"Balmy," he corrected. "Your blood's just thin yet. Here comes a good-size one. You'd better hold on to me."

"I don't want to—" Whatever she did or didn't want, the sea had its own ideas. The wave hit, knocked her off her feet, and had her legs tangling with his.

"You idiot." But she was laughing as she surfaced. When the air hit her skin, she quickly dunked neck-deep again. "The sheriff's supposed to have more sense than to jump in the ocean fully dressed."

"I'd've stripped down, but we haven't known each other long enough." He rolled over on his back, floating lazily. "The first stars are coming out. There's nothing like it. Nothing in the world like it. Come on."

The sea rocked her, made her feel weightless as she watched the color of the sky change. As the tone deepened bit by bit, stars winked to life.

"You're right, there's nothing like it. But it's still freezing."

"You just need a winter on the island to thicken your blood up." He took her hand, a quiet connection as they drifted an armspan apart. "I've never spent more than three months at a time off-island, and that was for college. Had three years of that, and couldn't take it anymore. I knew what I wanted anyway. And that's what I've got."

The rhythm of the waves, the sweep of the sky. The quiet flow of his voice coming out of the dark.

"It's a kind of magic, isn't it?" She sighed as the cool, moist breeze whispered over her face. "To know what you want, to just know. And to get it."

"Magic doesn't hurt. Work helps. So does patience and all kinds of things."

"I know what I want now, and I'm getting it. That's magic to me."

"The island's never been short on that commodity. Comes from being founded by witches, I suppose."

Surprise tinged her voice. "Do you believe in that sort of thing?"

"Why wouldn't I? Things are, whether people believe in them or not. There were lights in the sky last night that weren't stars. A person could look the other way, but they'd still have been there."

He planted his feet again, lifting her until she stood facing him with the water fuming at waist level. Night had drifted in, and the lights of the stars sprinkled over the surface of the water.

"You can turn away from something like this." He skimmed her wet hair away from her face, left his hands resting there. "But it's still going to be there."

She pressed a hand against his shoulder as his mouth lowered to hers. She meant to turn away, told herself to turn away, to where everything was safe and ordered and simple.

But the spark he'd spoken of snapped inside her, warm and bright. She curled her fingers into his wet shirt and let herself feel.

Alive. Cold where the air whisked over her skin. Hot in the belly where desire began to build. Testing herself, she leaned into him, parted her lips under his.

He took his time, as much for himself as for her. Sampling, savoring. She tasted of the sea. Smelled of it. For a moment, in the star-drenched surf, he let himself drown.

He eased back, let his hands run over her shoulders, down her arms before he linked his fingers with hers. "Not so complicated." He kissed her again, lightly, though the lightness cost him. "I'll walk you home."

Eight

"Mia, can I talk to you?" With ten minutes until opening, Nell hurried down from the café. Lulu was already ringing up mail orders and shot her a typically suspicious look while Mia continued to put the finishing touches on a new display.

"Of course. What's on your mind?"

"Well, I . . ." The store was small enough, and empty enough, that Lulu would hear every word. "I thought we could go up to your office for a minute."

"Here's fine. Don't let Lulu's sour face put you off." Mia built a small tower out of new summer releases. "She's worried you're going to ask me for a loan, and naturally I'm such a soft touch—along with my soft head—I'll let you rob me blind so I'll die penniless and alone in some filthy gutter. Isn't that right, Lu?"

Lulu merely sniffed and jabbed keys on the cash register.

"Oh, no, it's not about money. I'd never ask for—after you've been so— Damn it." Nell fisted her hands in her hair, tugged until the pain stiffened her spine. Deliberately now, she turned to face Lulu.

"I understand you're protective of Mia, and you have no reason to trust me. I came out of nowhere, with nothing, and haven't been here a month. But I'm not a thief, and I'm not a user. I've carried my weight here, and I'm going to keep carrying it. And if Mia asked me to try serving sandwiches while standing on one foot and singing 'Yankee Doodle Dandy,' I'd give it my best shot. Because I came out of nowhere, with nothing, and she gave me a chance."

Lulu sniffed again. "Wouldn't mind seeing that myself. Likely bring in fresh trade, too. Never said you didn't carry your weight," she added. "But that doesn't mean I won't keep a watch on you."

"Fine with me. I understand."

"All this sentimental bonding." Mia dabbed at her lashes. "It's ruining my mascara." She stepped back from her display, nodded in approval. "Now what do you need to talk to me about, Nell?"

"Mrs. Macey is having an anniversary party next month. She'd like to have a fancy catered affair."

"Yes, I know." Mia turned to straighten stock on the shelves. "She'll drive you a bit crazy with changes and suggestions and questions, but you can handle it."

"I didn't agree to . . . We just discussed it yesterday. I didn't realize you'd heard she asked already. I wanted to talk to you first."

"It's a small island, word gets around. You don't need to talk to me about an outside catering job, Nell."

She made a mental note to order more ritual candles. There'd been a run on them during the solstice, and they were running unacceptably low on Passion and on Prosperity. Which just showed, she supposed, where many people's priorities lay.

"Your free time is your time," she added.

"I just wanted to tell you that if I did the job for her, it wouldn't interfere with my work here."

"I should hope not, particularly since I'm giving you a raise." She glanced at her watch. "Time to open, Lu."

"You're giving me a raise?"

"You've earned it. I hired you at a probationary salary. You're officially off probation." She unlocked the door, walked over to turn on the music system. "How was your dinner with Zack the other night?" Mia asked with amusement. "A small island, as I said."

"It was fine. It was just a friendly dinner."

"Good-looking boy," Lulu said. "Quality, too."

"I'm not trying to lure him into temptation."

"Something wrong with you, then." Lulu tipped down her silver frames and peered over them. It was a look she was particularly proud of. "If I were a few years younger, I'd be setting out lures. Got a great pair of hands on him. Bet he knows how to use them."

"No doubt," Mia said mildly. "But you're embarrassing our Nell. Now where was I? Gladys's anniversary, check. Raise, check. Dinner with Zack, check." She paused, tapped a fingertip against her lips. "Ah, yes. Nell, I wanted to ask. Do you have a religious or political objection to cosmetics or jewelry?"

She could find nothing more constructive to do than huff out her breath. "No."

"That's a relief. Here." She took off the silver dangles on her ears, handed them to Nell. "Wear these. If anyone asks where you got them, they come from All That Glitters, two doors down. We like to promote other merchants. I'll want them back at the end of your shift. Tomorrow you might try a little blush, maybe some lipstick, eyeliner."

"I don't have any."

"I'm sorry." Mia held up a hand, laid the other on her heart, and staggered to the counter for support. "I feel a little faint. Did you say you don't own *any* lipstick?"

The corner of Nell's mouth turned up and brought out a hint of dimples. "I'm afraid not."

"Lulu, we have to help this woman. It's our duty. Emergency supplies. Hurry."

Lips quivering with what might have been a smile, Lulu hauled a large cosmetics bag out from under the counter. "She's got good skin."

"A blank canvas, Lu. A blank canvas. Come with me," she ordered Nell.

"The café—the regulars will be coming in any second."

"I'm fast, and I'm good. Let's move." She grabbed Nell's hand, hauled her upstairs and into the rest room.

Ten minutes later, Nell was serving her first customers and wearing silver earrings, peach-toned lipstick, and expertly smudged slate eyeliner.

There was something, she decided, very comforting about feeling female again.

She took the catering job and crossed her fingers. When Zack asked if she'd like to go for an evening sail, she said yes and felt powerful.

When a customer asked if she could bake a cake in the shape of a ballerina for a birthday party, she said absolutely. And spent her fee on a pair of earrings.

As word spread, she found herself agreeing to provide picnic-style food for a party of twenty for July Fourth and ten box lunches for a private day sailor.

At her kitchen table, Nell spread out notes, files, menus. Somehow she was becoming her own cottage industry. Which, she thought, looking around, seemed perfectly apt.

She glanced up at the brisk knock on the door, and happily welcomed Ripley in.

"Got a minute?"

"Sure. Sit down. Do you want anything?"

"I'm fine." Ripley sat, then picked up Diego when he sniffed at her shoes. "Meal planning?"

"I've got to organize these catering jobs. If I had a computer . . . Well, eventually. I'd sell my soul for a professional blender. And both feet for a commercial-grade food processor. But for now, we make do."

"Why don't you use the computer at the bookstore?"

"Mia's already doing enough."

"Whatever. Listen, I've got this date for the Fourth. A date with potential," she added. "Casual because Zack and I are more or less on duty right through the night. Fireworks and beer sometimes make people a little too festive for their own good."

"I can't wait to see the fireworks. Everyone says they're spectacular."

"Yeah, we do a hell of a job on them. The thing is, this guy—he's a security consultant on the mainland—he's been hitting on me, and I decided to let him land one."

"Ripley, that's so romantic, I can barely catch my breath."

"He's really built, too," Ripley continued as she scratched Diego's ears, "so the after-fireworks fireworks potential is fairly high, if you get me. I've been in a downswing sex-wise. Anyway, we talked about having this night-picnic deal, and somehow I got stuck with doing the food. Since I think I'd like to jump this guy's bones, I don't want to poison him first."

"A romantic picnic for two." Nell made notes. "Vegetarian or carnivore?"

"Carnivore. Not too fancy, okay?" Ripley plucked a grape from the bowl of fruit on the table, popped it in her mouth. "I don't want him more interested in the food than me."

"Check. Pickup or delivery?"

"This is so cool." Cheerful, she popped another grape. "I can pick it up. Can we keep it under fifty?"

"Under fifty. Tell him to pick up a nice crisp white wine. Now if you had a picnic hamper . . ."

"We've got one somewhere."

"Perfect. Bring that by and we'll pack it up. You'll be set, food-wise. The bone-jumping portion of the evening is up to you."

"I can handle that. You know, if you want, I can ask around, see if anybody's got a secondhand computer they want to sell."

"That would be great. I'm glad you came by." She rose, got out two glasses. "I was afraid you were annoyed with me."

"No, not with you. That particular subject annoys me. It's a bunch of bullshit, just like . . ." She scowled through the screened door. "Well, speak of the devil."

"I try not to. Why borrow trouble?" Mia sailed in, laid a note on the counter. "Phone message for you, Nell. Gladys and her newest party brainstorm."

"I'm sorry. You don't have time to run over here this way. I'll speak to her again and I promise I'll see about getting a phone."

"Don't worry about it. I wanted a walk or I'd have left it for tomorrow. And I'll have a glass of that lemonade."

"She needs a computer," Ripley said flatly. "She won't use the one at the store because she doesn't want to hassle you."

"Ripley. Mia, I'm perfectly fine working this way."

"She can certainly use the computer at the store when it's free," Mia said to Ripley. "And she doesn't need you running interference between her and me."

"She wouldn't if you weren't trying to push your psychic hooey on her."

"'Psychic hooey' sounds like the name of a second-rate rock band and has nothing to do with what I am. But even that's better than blind, stubborn denial. Knowledge is always better than ignorance."

"You want ignorance?" Ripley said, getting to her feet.

"Stop! Stop it." Jittering inside, Nell put herself between them. "This is ridiculous. Do you two always go at each other this way?"

"Yes." Mia picked up a glass, sipped delicately. "We enjoy it, don't we, Deputy?"

"I'd enjoy popping you one more, but then I'd have to arrest myself."

"Try it." Mia angled her chin. "I promise not to press charges."

"Nobody hits anybody. Not in my house."

Instantly contrite, Mia set down her glass, rubbed a hand down Nell's arm. It was rigid as steel. "I'm sorry, little sister. Ripley and I irritate each other, a long-standing habit. But we shouldn't put you in the middle. We shouldn't put her in the middle," Mia said to Ripley. "It isn't fair."

"Something we agree on. How about this? If we run into each other here, it's a neutral zone. You know, like Romulan space. No warfare."

"Romulan Neutral Zone. I've always admired your grip on popular culture. Agreed." She even picked up the second glass, passed it to Ripley. "There. You see, Nell, you're a good influence on us already." She handed the third glass to Nell. "To positive influences."

Ripley hesitated, cleared her throat. "Okay, okay, what the hell. Positive influences."

And standing in a loose circle, they tapped glasses. They rang like a bell, one bright peal as a shower of light fountained up from that connection of secondhand kitchenware.

Mia smiled slowly as Nell let out a laughing gasp.

"Damn it," Ripley muttered, and gulped down lemonade. "I hate that."

Celebrants streamed to the island for the Fourth. Red, white, and blue flags snapped from the rails of the ferries as they chugged to the mainland and back. Banners and bunting swagged the eaves of the storefronts on High Street, waving cheerfully as tourists and islanders alike jammed the streets and beaches.

For Nell it was anything but a holiday, but that didn't prevent her celebrational mood as she delivered orders. She not only had a job she loved, she had a business she could be proud of.

Independence Day, she thought. She was going to make it hers.

For the first time in nine months, she began to plan for a future that included bank accounts, mail delivery, and personal possessions that couldn't be stuffed into a duffel or backpack at a moment's notice.

A normal, functioning life, she thought as she paused by the display window of Beach Where. The mannequin was wearing breezy summer slacks with bold blue and white stripes and a gauzy white top that scooped low at the breasts. Strappy white sandals as fun as they were impractical adorned its feet.

Nell bit her lip. Her pay was burning a hole in the pocket of her ancient jeans. That had always been her problem, she reminded herself. If she had ten dollars, she could find a way to spend nine of it.

She'd learned how to save and scrimp and resist. How to make five dollars stretch like elastic.

But she hadn't had anything new, anything pretty, in so long. And Mia had been hinting, not quite so gently of late, that she should spruce up a bit on the job.

Plus, she had to make some sort of a showing of herself for the catering sideline. If she was going to be a businesswoman, she should dress the part. On the island that meant casual. Still, casual could mean attractive.

On the other hand, it would be more practical, more sensible, to save the money and invest it in kitchen tools. She needed a food processor more than she needed sandals.

"Are you going to listen to the good angel or the bad angel?"

"Mia." Vaguely embarrassed at being caught daydreaming over a pair of shoes, Nell laughed. "You startled me."

"Great sandals. On sale, too."

"They are?"

Mia tapped the glass just below the Sale sign. "My favorite four-letter word. I smell possibilities, Nell. Let's shop."

"Oh, but I really shouldn't. I don't need anything."

"You really do need work." Mia tossed back her hair, took Nell's elbow in a firm grip, much like a mother with a stubborn child. "Shopping for shoes has nothing to do with need, and everything to do with lust. Do you know how many pair of shoes I own?"

"No."

"Neither do I," she said as she strong-armed Nell into the shop. "Isn't that wonderful? They have those slacks in a candy-cane pink. They'd look fabulous on you. Size six?"

"Yes. But I really need to save for a good food processor." Despite herself she reached out to finger the material of the slacks that Mia pulled off the rack. "They're so soft."

"Try them with this." A brief hunt turned up what Mia considered the perfect top, a clingy white halter. "Don't forget to lose the bra. You've got little feet. Six there, too?"

"Yes, actually." Nell took a discreet peek at the price tags. Even with the sale it was more than she'd spent on herself in months. She was stuttering protests as Mia shoved her behind a dressing room curtain.

"Trying doesn't mean buying," she whispered to herself over and over as she stripped down to her practical cotton panties.

Mia was right about the pink, she thought as she slipped into the slacks. The bright color was an instant mood lifter. But the halter, well, that was another matter. It felt . . . decadent to wear something so close-fitting without a bra. And the back—she turned to look over her shoulder. There basically wasn't a back.

Evan would never have allowed her to wear something so revealing and casually suggestive.

Even as the thought popped into her mind, Nell cursed herself.

"Okay, back up and erase," she ordered herself.

"How you doing in there?"

"Fine. Mia, it's an adorable outfit, but I don't think . . ."

Before she could finish, Mia whisked open the curtain and stood, the sandals in one hand while she tapped her lip with the finger of her free hand. "Perfect. Girl-next-door sexy, casual, chic. Add the shoes. I saw this little bag. Just the thing. Be right back."

It was like being marched through a campaign by a veteran general, Nell thought. And she, a mere foot soldier, couldn't seem to do anything but follow orders.

Twenty minutes later, her habitual jeans, T-shirt, and sneakers were tucked into a shopping bag. What was left of her cash was stuffed into a palm-size purse that she wore cross-body and at the hip of her new slacks, which flapped softly around her legs in the frisky breeze.

"How do you feel?"

"Guilty. Great." Unable to resist, Nell wiggled her toes in her new sandals.

"That'll do. Now, let's buy some earrings to go with it."

Nell abandoned all resistance. Independence Day, she reminded herself. She fell for the rose quartz drops the minute she saw them.

"What is it about earrings that makes you feel so confident?"

"Body adornments show that we're aware of our bodies and expect others to be aware as well. Now, let's take a walk on the beach and get some reaction."

Nell fingered the pale pink stones swinging from her ears. "Can I ask you a question?"

"Go ahead."

"I've been here a month now, and in all that time I haven't seen you with anyone. A date, I mean. A male companion."

"I'm not interested in anyone at the moment." Mia held the flat of her hand above her brow to skim the beach. "Yes, there was someone. Once. But that was another phase of my life."

"Did you love him?"

"Yes, I did. Very much."

"I'm sorry. I shouldn't pry."

"It's no secret," Mia said lightly. "And the wound's long healed. I like being on my own, in control of my destiny, and all the little day-to-day decisions and choices. Coupling requires a certain amount of unselfishness. I'm a selfish creature by nature."

"That's not true."

"Generosity has levels." Mia began to walk, lifting her face to the breeze. "And it's not synonymous with altruism. I do what suits me, which stems from self-interest. I don't find that something to apologize for."

"I've had personal acquaintance with the selfish. You may do what suits you, Mia, but you'd never deliberately hurt anyone. I've watched you with people. They trust you because they know they can."

"Not causing harm is a responsibility that comes from what I've been given. You're the same."

"I don't see how that can be. I've been powerless."

"And because of it you have empathy for those in pain and those who despair. Nothing happens to us without purpose, little sister.

What we do because of it, what we do about it, is the key to who and what we are."

Nell looked out to sea, to the boats gliding, the jet skiers racing, the swimmers gleefully riding the waves. She could turn away, she thought, from what she was being told and what would be asked of her. She could have a calm and normal life here.

Or she could have more.

"The night I stayed at your house, the night of the solstice, when I saw you on the cliffs I told myself I was dreaming."

Mia didn't turn, just continued to look calmly out over the ocean. "Is that what you want to believe?"

"I'm not entirely sure. I dreamed of this place. Even when I was a child, I had dreams. For a long time I ignored them, or blocked them out. When I saw the painting—the cliffs, the lighthouse, your house—I had to come here. It was like finally being allowed to come home."

She looked back at Mia. "I used to believe in fairy tales. Then I learned better. The hard way."

And so, Mia thought, had she. No man had ever lifted his hand to her, but there were other ways to bruise and scar. "Life isn't a fairy tale, and the gift carries a price."

A shudder raced up Nell's spine. Easier, she thought, to turn away. Safer, to run away.

A boat out to sea let off a sky rocket. The gleeful shriek of sound ended on a burst of light that showered little specks of gold as it shattered. A delighted roar went up from the beach. She heard a child call out in wonder.

"You said you would teach me."

Mia let out a breath she hadn't been aware she was holding. So much rested on this. "And so I will."

They turned together to watch the next rocket soar.

"Are you going to stay to watch the fireworks?" Nell asked her.

"No, I can see them from my cliffs. And it's less frantic. Besides, I hate being a fifth wheel."

"Fifth wheel?"

"Ladies." Zack strolled up. It was one of the rare times he had his badge pinned to his shirt. "I'm going to have to ask you to move along. Two beautiful women standing on the beach creates a safety hazard."

"Isn't he cute?" Mia reached up to cup his face and give him a noisy kiss. "When I was in third grade, I planned to marry him and live in a sand castle."

"You might've clued me in on it."

"You were sweet on Hester Burmingham."

"No, I just had lustful feelings for her shiny red Schwinn. The Christmas I turned twelve, I got one of my own from Santa, and Hester ceased to exist in my little world."

"Men are bastards."

"Maybe, but I've still got the bike, and Hester's got twin girls and a minivan. Happy ending all around."

"Hester still checks out your butt when you're walking away," Mia told him, delighted when his mouth dropped open. "And on that note, I take my leave. Enjoy the fireworks."

"That woman always manages to get the last word," Zack muttered. "By the time a man untangles his tongue, she's gone. And speaking of getting a man's tongue tangled, you look great."

"Thanks." She held her arms out to the side. "I splurged."

"In all the right places. Let me cart that for you." He slipped the shopping bag out of her hand.

"I need to take it home, and see to some things."

"I can walk in that direction for a bit. I was hoping to see you around today. I heard you've been busy, delivering potato salad all over the island."

"I must've made twenty gallons of it, and enough fried chicken to deplete the poultry population for the next three months."

"Don't suppose you've got any left."

Her dimples winked. "I might."

"It's been hard to find time to eat—traffic control, beach patrol. I had to sit on a couple of kids who thought it'd be fun to toss firecrackers in trash cans and watch them blow up. I've confiscated enough firecrackers, roman candles, and bottle rockets to start my own insurrection. And all that on two hot dogs."

"That doesn't seem fair."

"No, it doesn't. I spotted a couple of your box lunches. Looked to me like there was apple pie in there."

"You have good vision. I could probably hunt up a few drumsticks, scrape together a pint of potato salad. I might even be able to manage a slab of apple pie and donate it to a hardworking public servant."

"Might even be tax deductible. I've got to supervise the fireworks display." He stopped at the end of the street. "We usually get it started right around nine." He set her shopping bag down to run his hands up her bare arms. "Things start thinning out around nine thirty, nine forty-five. I lost the toss with Ripley, so I've got to take the last patrol, cruise around the island to make sure nobody's set their house on fire. Maybe you'd like to take a drive."

"I might."

His fingers danced up and down her back. "Do me a favor? Put your hands on my shoulders. I'd like you to have a grip on me when I kiss you this time."

"Zack—" She took two careful breaths. "I'd like you to have a grip on me this time, too."

He wrapped his arms around her. She circled his neck. For a moment they stood, lips a breath apart while her system shivered with anticipation.

Mouths brushed, retreated, brushed again. It was she who moaned, she who crushed her lips to his on a hot spurt of hunger.

She hadn't let herself want. Even when he'd stirred those dormant needs to life, she'd been careful not to want. Until now.

She wanted the strength of him, the press of that hard, male body. She wanted the ripe flavor of him and the heat.

The silky dance of tongues, the teasing nip of teeth, the edgy thrill of feeling a heart pound against her own. She let out a little gasp of pleasure when he changed the angle of the kiss.

And dived in again.

She set off aches in him that throbbed like pulse beats. Quiet sounds of need hummed in her throat and burned in his blood. Her skin was like hot satin, and the feel of it under his hands sent erotic images through his brain—desires, demands that belonged to the dark.

Dimly he heard another rocket burst, and the shouts of approval from the beach behind them.

He could have her inside her cottage in two minutes. Naked and under him in three.

"Nell." Breathless, churning toward desperate, he broke the kiss.

And she smiled at him. Her eyes were dark, filled with trust and pleasure.

"Nell," he said again, and lowered his forehead to hers. There were times when you took, he knew. And times when you waited. "I've got to make my rounds."

"All right."

He picked up her bag, handed it to her. "You'll come back?"

"Yes. I'll come back." She was floating on air as she spun around and headed for her cottage.

Nine

"Power," Mia told Nell, "carries with it responsibility, a respect for tradition. It must be tempered with compassion, hopefully intelligence, and an understanding of human flaws. It is never to be used carelessly, though there is room for humor. Above all, it must never be used to harm."

"How did you know you were . . . How did you know what you were?"

"A witch." Mia sat back on her heels. She was weeding her garden. She was wearing a shapeless dress of grass green with deep pockets in the skirt, thin floral gardening gloves, and a wide-brimmed straw hat. At the moment, she couldn't have looked less like the witch she professed to be.

"You can say the word. It's not illegal. We're not the pointed-hat-wearing, broomstick-riding cacklers that much of fiction drew us to be. We're people—housewives, plumbers, businesswomen. How we live is a personal choice."

"Covens?"

"Another personal choice. I've never been much of a joiner myself. And most who form groups or study the Craft are just looking for a pastime, or an answer. There's nothing wrong with that. Calling yourself a witch and holding rituals is one thing, being one is another."

"How do you know the difference?"

"How do I answer you, Nell?" She leaned forward again, neatly snipping off deadheads. "There's something inside you, burning. A song in your head, a whisper in your ear. You know these things as well as I do. You just didn't recognize them."

The deadhead went along with her weeds into a basket.

"When you peel an apple, haven't you ever thought if you could finish it without breaking the chain, you'd have a wish granted or gather good luck? Snapped a wishbone? Crossed your fingers? Little charms," Mia said, sitting back again, "old traditions."

"It can't be as simple as that."

"As simple as a wish, as complex as love. As dangerous, potentially, as a lightning bolt. Power is risk. It's also joy."

She picked up one of the deadheads, cupped it gently in her hands. Opening them again, she offered Nell a sunny yellow blossom.

Delighted, fascinated, Nell twirled it in her fingers. "If you can do this, why do you let any of them die?"

"There's a cycle, a natural order. It's to be respected. Change is necessary." She rose, picked up her basket of weeds and dead flowers, and carried it to a composter. "Without it there'd be no progress, no rebirth, no anticipation."

"One flower blooms off to make room for another."

"A lot of the Craft is philosophy. Would you like to try something more practical?"

"Me?"

"Yes, a simple spell. A stir of the air, I think, considering. Besides, it's a warm day, and a breeze would be welcome."

"You want me to . . ." Nell made a circling motion with her finger . . . "stir the air?"

"It's a matter of technique. You need to focus. Feel the air moving over your face, your body. See it in your mind, rippling, turning. You can hear it, the music of it."

"Mia."

"No. Put doubts aside and think of those possibilities. Focus. It's a simple goal. It's all around you. You only have to stir it. Take it in your hands," she said, lifting her own, "and say the words. 'Air is breath and breath is air. Stir it round from here to there. Spin a breeze and spin it lightly.' As you will, Nell, so mote it be. Say the words, one times three."

Mesmerized, Nell repeated them. Felt the faintest flutter across her cheek. Said them again and saw Mia's hair lift. On the third count, Mia's voice joined hers.

The wind spun around them, a private carousel of air, cool and fragrant with a happy little hum. The same hum sounded inside her as Nell turned, circling round and round, her short cap of hair dancing.

"It feels wonderful! You did it."

"I gave it the last nudge." Mia laughed as her dress billowed out. "But you got it started. Very well done for your first time. Now quiet it again. Use your mind. Visualize it going still. That's it. Good. You picture things well."

"I've always liked to draw moments in my head," Nell said, breathless now. "You know, images that appeal or that I want to remember. It's sort of like that. Wow, I'm dizzy." She sat straight down on the ground. "I felt a tingling inside, not unpleasant. Almost like you do when you're thinking—really thinking—about sex."

"Magic is sexy." Mia dropped down beside her. "Especially when you hold the power. Have you been doing a lot of thinking about sex?"

"I didn't give it a thought for eight months." Steadier now, Nell shook back her hair. "I wasn't sure I'd ever want to be with a man again. Since the Fourth, I've been doing a lot of thinking about sex. The kind of thinking that makes you very itchy."

"Well, I've been there. Why don't you do something about it? Scratch the itch?"

"I thought, I'd assumed, that after the fireworks last week, Zack and I would end up in bed. But after we drove around and he finished his patrol, he took me home. Kissed me good night at the door, the kind of kiss that lifts the top of your head off and spins it around. Then he went home."

"I don't suppose it occurred to you to drag him inside, toss him on the floor, and rip his clothes off."

The idea made Nell chuckle. "I can't do things like that."

"A minute ago you didn't think you could conjure a breeze either. You have the power, little sister. Zachariah Todd is the kind of man who's willing to put that power in your hands, to give you the choice of time and place. If there was a man like that I was attracted to, and who was attracted to me, I'd do something about that power."

She felt the tingle again, the stir inside her this time. "I wouldn't know how to begin."

"Visualize, little sister," Mia said wickedly. "Visualize."

Zack couldn't think of a better way to spend a Sunday morning than skinny-dipping with the girl he loved. The water was cool, the sun warm, and the inlet private enough to allow for such activities.

They discussed taking a sail later, and the adoration in her beautiful brown eyes told him she'd follow him anywhere. He stroked her, sent her into a wiggle of delight before they swam companionably through the crisp and quiet water.

When a man had a female so uncomplicatedly devoted, Zack figured, he had it all.

Then she gave a yip of excitement, splashed a stream of water in his face, and headed to shore. Zack watched his boon companion desert him for the woman standing on the rough bank.

Lucy bounded onto the bank and straight into Nell, knocking her back two full steps and drenching her with seawater and doggie kisses.

Zack listened to Nell's laughter, watched her scrub her hands enthusiastically over Lucy's wet fur. Maybe a man who had a pretty dog didn't have quite everything, he decided.

"Hey. How's it going?"

"It's going good." Shoulders, she thought. The man had amazing shoulders. "How's the water?"

"Close to perfect. Come on in, see for yourself."

"Thanks, but I don't have a suit with me."

"Me either." He flashed a grin. "Which is why I didn't follow Lucy's example."

"Oh." Her gaze shot down, then immediately back up to hover six inches over his head. "Well. Ha."

Visualize, Mia had told her. But this didn't seem quite the appropriate time.

"I promise not to look. You're already wet."

"All the same, I think I'll stay out here."

Lucy dived back in, retrieved a mangled rubber ball. After scrabbling back to shore again, she deposited it neatly at Nell's feet.

"Wants to play," Zack told her. And so did he.

Obliging, Nell picked up the ball and tossed it. Before it hit the surface, Lucy was leaping in pursuit.

"Pretty good arm. We've got a softball game coming up in a couple of weeks if you're interested." He drifted closer to the bank as he spoke.

Nell scooped up the ball Lucy retrieved, heaved it again. "Maybe. I was thinking about trying out another recipe."

"Is that so?"

"The catering's turning into an actual enterprise. If I want to expand on it, I need to be able to offer a variety of dishes."

"I'm a strong believer in capitalism, so anything I can do to help."

She looked down. He had such a nice face, she thought. She would just concentrate on that and wouldn't think about the rest of him. Right now. "I appreciate that, Sheriff. I've been playing it by ear so far, but I think it's time to put together an actual list, with pricing and services. If I do all that, formalize it, I have to apply for a business license."

That wouldn't be a problem, she assured herself. She was clear.

"It's going to keep you busy."

"I like being busy. There's nothing worse than not being able to do anything with your time or your interests." She shook her head. "And don't I sound dull and boring?"

No, but she had sounded grim. "How do you feel about recreation?"

"I approve of recreation." Her eyebrows lifted as he hooked a hand lightly around her ankle. "And just what is that?"

"I call it the long arm of the law."

"You're too nice to pull me in after I've come over here to offer to feed you."

"No, I'm not." He gave her foot a playful little tug. "But I'm willing to give you a chance to strip first."

"That's considerate of you."

"My mother raised me right. Come on in and play, Nell." He glanced back at Lucy, who was busy paddling around with the ball in her mouth. "We've got a chaperone."

Why not? she thought. She wanted to be with him. Even more,

she wanted to be the kind of woman who *could* be with him. A woman confident and open enough to do something fun and foolish like tossing off her clothes and diving in.

The grin she sent him was quick and careless. As she toed off her shoes, he treaded water. "I changed my mind. I'm going to watch," he warned her. "I'd tell you I wouldn't peek, but I'd be lying."

"Do you lie?"

"Not if I can help it." His gaze lowered as she gripped the hem of her T-shirt. "So I'm not going to tell you I'll keep my hands off you once you get in here. I want you wet and naked, Nell. I just plain want you."

"If I wanted you to keep your hands off me, I wouldn't be here." She took a deep breath, started to peel off her shirt.

"Sheriff Todd! Sheriff Todd!"

"There is no God," Zack grumbled as the lovely glimpse of creamy flesh vanished under Nell's hastily tugged-down shirt. "Out here," he called. "Is that you, Ricky?" To Nell, he said, "It'll only take me two, three minutes to drown him. Just stand by."

"Yes, sir, Sheriff."

A towheaded boy of about ten scrambled across the rocky slope, his freckled face pink with excitement. He gave Nell a hasty nod. "Ma'am. Sheriff, my mom said I was to come right over and tell you. The tenants in the Abbott rental are having a big fight. There's screaming and crashing and cursing and everything."

"Is that Dale Abbott's or Buster's place?"

"Buster's, Sheriff. The one right across from ours. Mom says it sounds like the man in there's beating the woman something fierce."

"I'm on my way. Go on back. Go straight home and in the house."

"Yes, sir."

Nell stayed where she was. She saw a blur of tanned, muscled body as Zack levered himself out of the water. "Sorry, Nell."

"No, you need to go. You need to help her." It felt as though there were a thin glaze over her brain as she watched him hitch on jeans. "Hurry."

"I'll be back as soon as I can."

He left her there, hated leaving her there with her hands gripping each other tightly, and bolted up the steps to get a shirt.

He was at the Abbott rental in under four minutes. A handful of people edged the street while the sounds of shouting and breaking glass poured out of the house. A man Zack didn't recognize jogged up to him as he approached the deck stairs.

"You're the sheriff. I'm Bob Delano, renting the place next door. I tried seeing what I could do, but the doors're locked. I thought about breaking one in, but they said you were on the way."

"I'll take care of it, Mr. Delano. Maybe you could keep those people back."

"Sure. I've seen that guy, Sheriff. Big sonofabitch. You want to watch yourself."

"I appreciate it. Get on back now." Zack pounded a fist on the door. Though he'd have preferred to have Ripley with him, he hadn't risked waiting for her to answer his beeper call. "This is Sheriff Todd. I want you to open the door, and open it now." Something shattered inside, and a woman began to wail. "If this door isn't open in five seconds, I'm kicking it in."

The man came to the door. Delano was right. He was one big sonofabitch. Six-four, maybe, and a good two seventy-five. He looked hungover and mad as piss.

"What the hell do you want?"

"I want you to step back, sir, and keep your hands where I can see them."

"You got no right coming in here. I'm renting this place paid in full."

"Your rental agreement doesn't give you leave to destroy property. Now back up."

"You're not coming in here without a warrant."

"Bet?" Zack said softly. His hand shot out, lightning-quick, gripped the man's wrist, and twisted. "Now, you want to take a swing at me," he continued in the same mild tone, "we'll add resisting arrest and assaulting an officer to the mix. More paperwork, but I get paid for it."

"By the time my lawyer's done, I'm going to own this fucking island."

"You're welcome to call him—from down at the station house." Zack cuffed him and looked around with relief as he heard Ripley pounding up the stairs.

"Sorry. I was all the way over on Broken Shell. What's this? Domestic dispute?"

"And then some. This is my deputy," Zack informed his prisoner. "Take my word, she can clean your clock. Put him in the back of the cruiser, Ripley. Get his particulars, read him his rights."

"What's your name, sir?"

"Fuck you."

"Okay, Mr. Fuck You, you're under arrest for . . ." She glanced back at Zack, who was already moving through the broken glass and crockery to the woman sitting on the floor, holding her face in her hands and sobbing.

"Destruction of private property, disturbing the peace, assault."

"You got that? Now unless you want me to kick your ass in front of all these nice people, we'll just walk to the cruiser and take a little drive. You have the right to remain silent," she continued, giving him a helpful shove to get him going.

"Ma'am." She was late thirties, Zack estimated. Probably pretty when her lip wasn't split and her brown eyes weren't blackened. "I need you to come with me. I'll take you to a doctor."

"I don't need a doctor." She curled into herself. Zack noted shallow cuts on her arms, gifts from flying glass. "What's going to happen to Joe?"

"We'll talk about that. Can you tell me your name?"

"Diane, Diane McCoy."

"Let me help you up, Ms. McCoy."

Diane McCoy sat hunched in a chair with an ice bag held to her left eye. She continued to refuse medical assistance. After offering her a cup of coffee, Zack pulled his own chair from behind his desk, hoping the move would put her more at ease.

"Ms. McCoy, I want to help you."

"I'm okay. We'll pay for the damages. You just have the rental agency make up a list and we'll pay for it."

"That's something we'll need to see to. I want you to tell me what happened."

"We just had a fight, that's all. People do. You didn't need to lock Joe up. If there's a fine, we'll pay it."

"Ms. McCoy, you're sitting there with your lip bleeding, your eye black, and cuts and bruises all over your arms. Your husband assaulted you."

"It wasn't like that."

"What was it like?"

"I asked for it."

Even as Ripley let out a vicious stream of air across the room, Zack leveled a warning glance. "You asked him to hit you, Ms. McCoy? To knock you down, to bloody your lip?"

"I aggravated him. He's under a lot of pressure." The words tumbled out, slurred a bit from her swollen lip. "This is supposed to be a vacation, and I shouldn't've nagged at him that way."

She must have sensed Ripley's furious disapproval as she turned her head, stared defiantly. "Joe works hard, fifty weeks a year. The least I can do is leave him alone on his vacation."

"It seems to me," Ripley countered, "the least he could do is keep from punching you in the face on your vacation."

"Ripley, get Ms. McCoy a glass of water." And shut up. He didn't have to say the last with his mouth, when his expression said it so clearly. "What started the trouble, Ms. McCoy?"

"I guess I got up on the wrong side of the bed. Joe was up late, drinking. A man's entitled to sit in front of the TV with a few beers on his vacation. He left the place a mess—beer cans, spilled chips all over the rug. It irritated me, and I started on him the minute he was awake. If I'd shut up when he told me to, none of this would've happened."

"And not shutting up when you were told gave him the right to use his fists on you, Ms. McCoy?"

She powered up. "What happens between a husband and wife is nobody's business but theirs. We shouldn't have broken things, and we'll pay for them. I'll clean the place up myself."

"Ms. McCoy, they have counseling programs back in Newark," Zack began, "and shelters for women who need them. I can make some calls, get you some information."

Her eyes might have been swollen, but they could still flash fury. "I don't need any information. You can't keep Joe locked up if I don't press charges, and I won't."

"You're wrong there. I can keep him locked up for disturbing the peace. And the property owners can press charges."

"You'll just make it worse." Tears began to fall. She took the paper cup Ripley offered her and gulped at the water. "Don't you see? You'll just make it worse. He's a good man. Joe's a good man, he's just got a short fuse is all. I said we'd pay. I'll write you a check. We don't want any trouble. I'm the one who made him mad. I threw things at him, too. You're going to have to lock me up along with him. What's the point?"

What was the point? Zack thought later. He hadn't been able to reach her, and he wasn't egotistical enough to think he was the first to try. He couldn't help when help was rejected. The McCoys were caught in a cycle that was bound to end badly.

And all he could do was remove the cycle from his island.

It took half the day to straighten out the mess. A check for two thousand satisfied the rental company. A cleaning crew was already in place by the time the McCoys had packed up. Zack waited, saying nothing as Joe McCoy loaded suitcases and coolers into the back of a late-model Grand Cherokee.

The couple got in from opposite sides. Diane wore big sunglasses to hide the damage. They both ignored Zack as he got into the cruiser and followed them to the ferry.

He stayed there, watching, until the Jeep and the people inside it were no more than a dot on their way to the mainland.

He hadn't expected that Nell would have waited for him, and decided it was just as well. He was too depressed and far too angry to talk to her. Instead he sat in the kitchen with Lucy, nursed a beer. He was considering indulging in a second when Ripley came in.

"I don't get it. I just don't *get* women like that. The guy's got a hundred fifty pounds on her, but it's *her* fault he bashed her face. And she believed it." She got out a beer for herself, jerking the bottle at him as she twisted off the cap.

"Maybe she needs to."

"Oh, like hell, Zack. Like hell." Still simmering, she dropped into the chair across from him. "She's healthy, she's got a brain. What does she gain hooking herself to a guy who uses her for a punching bag when the mood strikes him? If she'd pressed charges, we could've held him long enough for her to pack her bags and get gone. We should've held him anyway."

"She wouldn't have left. It wouldn't have made one damn bit of difference."

"Okay, you're right. I know it. It just burns me, that's all." She sipped her beer, watching him. "You're thinking about Nell. You figure it was like that for her?"

"I don't know what it was like for her. She doesn't talk about it."

"Have you asked?"

"If she wanted to tell me, she would."

"Well, don't snap my head off." Ripley propped her feet on the chair beside her. "I'm asking you because I know you, big brother. If you've got a thing for her, and the thing turns into a *big* thing, you're never going to be square with it unless you have the story. Without the story, you can't help, and when you can't help, it drives you nuts. You're brooding right now because you couldn't help—to your satisfaction—a woman you'd never seen before and won't see again. It's that Good Samaritan gene of yours."

"Isn't there someone else on the island you can go annoy?"

"No, because I love you best. Now, instead of having another beer, why don't you take Luce and go for a sail? Still plenty of daylight yet, and it'll clear your head and improve your disposition. You're just no fun to be around when you're broody."

"Maybe I will."

"Good. Go. Odds of a second crisis in one day are slim to none, but I'll take a cruise around, just in case."

"Okay." He got up and after a moment's hesitation leaned down and kissed the top of her head. "I love you best, too."

"Don't I know it." She waited until he got to the door. "You know, Zack, whatever Nell's story is, there's one key difference between her and Diane McCoy. Nell got gone."

Ten

On Monday the incident at the Abbott rental was the talk of the village. Everyone had had time to form an opinion, particularly those who hadn't witnessed the event.

"Buster said they'd busted up every blessed knickknack in the place. I'll have some of that lobster salad, Nell, honey," Dorcas Burmingham said, then went straight back to gossiping with her companion. She and Biddy Devlin, Mia's third cousin once removed and the proprietor of Surfside Treasures, had a standing lunch date at the café every Monday at twelve thirty.

"I heard Sheriff Todd had to forcibly remove the man from the premises," Biddy expounded. "At *gunpoint*."

"Oh, Biddy, no such thing. I talked to Gladys Macey, who had it straight from Anne Potter who sent for the sheriff in the first place that Zack had his gun holstered right along. Can I have an iced mocha with that salad, Nell?"

"Domestic disputes are one of the most dangerous calls for a policeman," Biddy informed her. "I read that somewhere. My, that soup smells divine, Nell. I don't believe I've ever had gazpacho before, but I'm going to have to try a cup, and one of your brownies."

"I'll bring your lunch out to you," Nell offered, "if you'd like to get a table."

"Oh, that's all right, we'll wait for it." Dorcas waved the offer away. "You've got enough to do. Anyway, I heard that even though that brute bloodied that poor woman's lip and blackened her eye, she stuck by him. Wouldn't press charges."

"It's a crying shame is what it is. Odds are her father beat on her mother, so she grew up seeing such things and thinking that's just what happens. It's a cycle. That's what the statistics say. Abuse spawns abuse. I'll wager you, if that woman had grown up in a loving home, she wouldn't be living with a man who treated her that way."

"Ladies, that'll be thirteen eighty-five." Nell's head throbbed like a bad tooth, and her nerve endings stretched thin as hair strands while the two women went through their weekly routine of whose turn it was to pay.

It was always playful, and usually it amused Nell. But now she wanted them gone. She wanted to hear no more about Diane McCoy.

What did they know about it? she thought bitterly. These two comfortable women with their comfortable lives? What did they know about fear and helplessness?

It wasn't always a cycle. She wanted to scream it. It wasn't always a pattern. She'd had a loving home, with parents who'd been devoted to each other, and to her. There had been arguments, irritation, annoyances. While voices may have been raised, fists never had.

She had never been struck in her life before Evan Remington.

She wasn't a goddamn statistic.

By the time the women headed off to a table, thin, sharp-edged bands of steel had locked themselves around Nell's temples. She turned blindly to the next customer and found Ripley studying her.

"You look a little shaky, Nell."

"Just a headache. What can I get you today?"

"Why don't you get yourself an aspirin? I'll wait."

"No, it's fine. The fruit-and-cabbage salad's good. It's a Scandinavian recipe. I've had positive feedback on it."

"Okay, I'm game. I'll take an iced tea with it. Those two," she added, nodding toward Biddy and Dorcas. "They chatter like a couple of parrots. It'd give anybody a headache. I guess everybody's been yakking about the trouble yesterday."

"Well." She wanted a dark room, an hour's quiet. "Big news."

"Zack did everything he could to help that woman. She didn't want to be helped. Not everyone does."

"Not everyone knows what to do with an offer of help, or who they can trust to give it."

"Zack can be trusted." Ripley laid her money on the counter. "Maybe he plays it low-key, that's his way. But when push comes to shove, he stands up. You ought to do something for that headache, Nell," she added, and took her lunch to a table.

She didn't have time to do more about it than swallow a couple of aspirin. Peg was late, rushing in full of apologies and with a sparkle in her eye that told Nell a man had been responsible for her tardiness.

As Nell had an appointment with Gladys Macey to—please, God—finalize the menu for the anniversary party, she had to rush home, gather her notes and files.

The headache had escalated to nightmare territory by the time she knocked on Gladys's door.

"Nell, I've told you, you don't have to knock. You just call out and walk in," Gladys said and pulled her inside. "I'm just so excited about this. I watched this program on the Home and Garden channel just the other day. Got me all sorts of ideas to talk over with you. I think we ought to string those little white lights through my trees, and put those luminaries—with little hearts on the bags—along the walk and the patio. What do you think?"

"Mrs. Macey, I think you should have whatever you want. I'm really just the caterer."

"Now, honey, I think of you as my party coordinator. Let's sit down in the living room."

The room was spotlessly clean, as if dust was a sin against nature. Every stick of furniture matched, with the pattern in the sofa picked up in the valance of the window treatments and the narrow border of wallpaper that ran just under the ceiling.

There were two identical lamps, two identical chairs, two identical end tables. The rug matched the curtains, the curtains matched the throw pillows.

All the wood was honey maple, including the cabinet of the big-screen TV, which was currently running a Hollywood gossip program.

"I've got a weakness for that kind of show. All those famous people. I love seeing what clothes they're wearing. You just sit down," Gladys ordered. "Make yourself comfortable. I'm going to get us a nice cold Coke, then we'll roll up our sleeves and dive right in."

As she had the first time she'd toured Gladys's house for pre-party plans, Nell found herself bemused. Every room was tidy as a church pew and as rigidly organized as a furniture showroom floor. Magazines were fanned precisely on the coffee table, and offset by an arrangement of silk flowers in the exact tones of mauve and blues as the upholstery.

The fact that the house managed to be friendly said more, to Nell's mind, about the occupants than the decor.

Nell sat, opened her files. She knew Gladys would bring the tea in pale green glasses that matched her everyday dishes and would set them on blue coasters.

There was, she thought, a comfort in knowing that.

She began to read over her notes, then felt her stomach hitch at the chirpy voice of the program host.

"Last night's gala brought out the glitter and the glamour. Evan Remington, power broker extraordinaire and attorney to the stars, looked as sensational as one of his own clients in Hugo Boss. Though Remington denies rumors of a romance between him and his companion for the evening, the delectable Natalie Winston—who simmered in a beaded sheath by Valentino—sources in the know say differently.

"Remington was widowed only last September when his wife, Helen, apparently lost control of her car while driving back to their home in Monterey. Her Mercedes sedan crashed over the cliffs on Highway 1. Her body, sadly, was never recovered. *Hollywood Beat* is happy to see Evan Remington back in stride after this tragic event."

Nell was on her feet, her breath short and shallow. Evan's face seemed to fill the wide screen, every handsome line, every strand of golden hair.

She could hear his voice, clear and terrifyingly calm. *Do you think I can't see you, Helen? Do you think I'll let you go?*

"I didn't mean to take so long, but I thought you might appreciate someone else's baking for a change. I just made this pound cake yesterday. Carl packed away nearly half of it. I can't think where that man puts it. Why, if I ate a fraction of what he—"

Tray in hand, Gladys stopped, her happy chatter shifting instantly to surprised concern when she saw Nell's face. "Honey, you're so pale. What's wrong?"

"I'm sorry. I'm sorry, I'm not feeling well." Panic was an icy poker jabbing through her belly. "Headache. I don't think I can do this now."

"Of course not. Poor thing. Don't you worry. I'm going to drive you home and tuck you right into bed."

"No, no. I'd rather walk. Fresh air. I'm so sorry, Mrs. Macey." Nell fumbled with her files, almost sobbing when they slipped through her trembling fingers. "I'll call you. Reschedule."

"I don't want you to think a thing of it. Nell, sweetheart, you're shaking."

"I just need to go home." With a last terrified glance at the television screen, she bolted for the door.

She forced herself not to run. When you ran, people noticed you, and they wondered. They asked questions. Fitting in, that was essential. Blending. Doing nothing to draw attention. But even as she ordered herself to breathe slow and steady, the air wheezed in her lungs, clogged there until she was gulping for it.

Do you think I'll let you go?

Sweat ran cold and clammy on her skin, and she smelled her own fear. The edges of her vision blurred as she shot a single wild look over her shoulder. The minute she was through the door of her cottage, the nausea hit, a bright bite of pain.

She stumbled to the bathroom, was hideously ill. When she was empty, she lay on the narrow floor and waited for the shaking to pass.

When she could stand again, she peeled off her clothes, leaving them in a heap as she stepped into the shower. She ran the hot water, as hot as she could bear, imagining the spray penetrating her skin until it warmed her icy bones.

Wrapped in a towel, she crawled into bed, pulled the covers over her head, and let herself slide into oblivion.

Diego climbed agilely up the bedskirt, stretched out alongside her. And lay still and silent as a sentry.

She wasn't sure how long she slept, but she woke as if from a long illness that had left her body heavy and tender and her stomach raw. She was tempted simply to roll back into sleep and stay there. But that would solve nothing.

It was doing that got her through, and always had.

She sat on the edge of the bed, like an old woman testing bone and balance. The image of Evan's face could float back into her mind if she let it. So she closed her eyes, let it form.

That, too, was a kind of test.

She could look at him, would look at him. Remember what had been, and what had changed. To deal, she reminded herself, with what had happened.

For comfort, she gathered the kitten into her lap and rocked.

She had run again. After almost a year, the sight of him on a television screen had terrorized her to the point of blind flight. Had made her ill and stripped away every bit of the hard-won armor she'd built until she'd been a quivering, quaking mass of panic.

Because she had allowed it. She let him have that hold on her. No one could change that but herself. She'd found the courage to run, Nell told herself. Now she had to find the courage to stand.

Until she could think of him, until she could say his name without fear, she wasn't free.

She held the picture of him in her mind, imagined it breaking apart, her will a hammer against glass. "Evan Remington," she whispered, "you can't touch me now. You can't hurt me. You're over, and I'm just beginning."

The effort exhausted her, but she set Diego on the floor, then pushed herself to her feet, dragged on a sweatshirt and shorts. She would go back to work, design and evaluate her menu. It was time to figure out how to set up an office of sorts in the little bedroom.

If Gladys Macey wanted a party coordinator, that's just what she was going to get.

She had dropped the file when she bolted into the cottage, and now she gathered up all the scattered notes, magazine clippings, and carefully written menu selections and carried them into the kitchen. She was mildly surprised to see that the sun still shone.

It felt as if she'd slept for hours.

The clock on the stove told her it was barely six. Time enough to reevaluate the Macey job proposal, to create a comprehensive list of menu and service selections for what she was going to call Sisters Catering.

She would take Mia up on the offer of the store computer and design a look for her handouts, her business cards. She had to calculate a budget, set up books.

No one was going to take her seriously unless she took herself seriously first.

But when she put her files down and looked around, she wondered why the prospect of putting on water for coffee seemed so far out of her scope.

The knock on the front door had her spinning around. Her first thought when she saw Zack through the screen was, not now. Not yet. She hadn't had time to gather herself back to what she needed to be.

But he was already opening the door, already studying her across the short distance from the front of the cottage to the back. "Are you all right, Nell?"

"Yes."

"You don't look all right."

She could imagine how she looked. "I wasn't feeling well earlier."

Self-conscious, she scooped a hand through her hair. "I had a head-ache, and so I took a nap. I'm fine now."

Hollow-eyed and pale, and far from fine, was Zack's judgment. He couldn't back off and leave her alone any more than he could have left a stray pup on the side of the road.

Diego gave him an opening, pouncing out of a corner to attack his shoes. Zack picked up the kitten, ruffling his fur as he walked to Nell. "You take anything?"

"Yes."

"Eat anything?"

"No. I don't need a nurse, Zack. It was just a headache."

Just a headache didn't send a woman bolting out of someone's house as if the devil were on her heels. Which was exactly how Gladys had described it. "You look pretty rough, honey, so I'm going to fix you the traditional Todd family restorer."

"I appreciate it, but I was going to work for a while."

"Go ahead." He handed her the kitten, moved past her to the refrigerator. "I'm not much in the kitchen, but I can manage this—just like my mother did when one of us wasn't feeling right. Got any jelly?"

It was right in front of his face, she thought crossly. What was it about men that struck them blind the minute they opened a refrig-erator door? "Second shelf."

"I don't— Oh, yeah. We always used grape, but strawberry should work. Go ahead and work. Don't mind me."

Nell set Diego by his dish of food. "What are you fixing?"

"Scrambled eggs and rolled-over jelly sandwiches."

"Rolled-over jelly sandwiches." Too tired to argue, she sat. "Sounds perfect. Mrs. Macey called you, didn't she?"

"No. I did run into her, though. She mentioned you were upset about something."

"I wasn't upset. I had a headache. The skillet's in the bottom cabinet, left."

"I'll find what I need. Place isn't big enough to hide much."

"Do you make scrambled eggs and rolled-over jelly sandwiches for everyone on the island when they have a headache?"

"That would depend. I'm making it for you because you tug at me, Nell. Have since I first met you. And when I walk in here and see you looking like something that's been flattened by a passing steamroller, it troubles me."

She said nothing when he cracked eggs, dumped in milk and too much salt. He was a good man, she believed. A kind and decent one. And she had no right tugging at him.

"Zack, I'm not going to be able to give you what you want, what you're looking for. I know yesterday I indicated I could—that I would. I shouldn't have."

"How do you know what I'm looking for, what I want?" He stirred the eggs in the bowl. "And whatever it is, it's my problem, isn't it?"

"It isn't fair for me to give you the impression there can be anything between us."

"I'm a big boy." He put enough butter in the skillet to make her wince. "I don't expect everything to be fair. And the fact is, there's already something between us. You pretending otherwise doesn't change it." He turned around as the butter melted. "The fact that we haven't slept together doesn't change it either. We would have yesterday, if I hadn't gotten that call."

"It would've been a mistake."

"If life wasn't full of mistakes, it'd be a mighty tedious process. If all I wanted was a roll in the sheets, I'd've gotten you there."

"You're probably right—that's my point."

"Right about the mistakes or the sex?" he asked and began slathering jelly on bread.

She decided that even if she had the answer, it wouldn't matter. Kind, decent, he was. And also stubborn as a mule. "I'll make coffee."

"Don't do coffee with this. Calls for tea. And I'll make it."

He filled the kettle, set it on the stove. Poured the eggs into the heated skillet in a sizzling rush.

"Now you're angry."

"I walked in half angry, and one look at you took care of part two. Funny thing, though, I can be pissed off at a woman and hold myself back from knocking her around. That's the kind of amazing self-control I have."

Nell drew a calming breath, folded her hands on the table. "I'm well aware that not every man deals with temper with physical violence. That's the kind of amazing intelligence I have."

"Good for us." He rooted around until he found teabags, an herbal blend he felt more suited to fancy china cups than the solid stoneware mugs she had available.

He scooped eggs onto plates, found forks, and tore off paper towels in lieu of napkins.

He'd said he wasn't much in the kitchen, Nell thought as he set a plate in front of her and went back to dunk the teabags in the mugs. But even here he had an appeal. He never wasted a move, she noted, and wondered if it came from grace or practicality.

Either way, it worked.

He sat across from her, let Diego climb adventurously up the leg of his jeans and knead his thigh. "Eat."

She forked up a bite, sampled. "They're better than they should be, considering you used a pound of salt per egg."

"I like salt."

"Don't feed the cat at the table." She sighed, ate. It was so blessedly normal, sitting like this, eating oversalted eggs and strawberry jelly squished in a piece of folded bread.

"I'm not the mess I used to be," she said. "But I still have moments. Until I don't, I'm not prepared to complicate my life, or anyone else's."

"That's sensible."

"I'm going to concentrate on my work."

"A person's got to have priorities."

"There are things I want to do, things I need to learn. For myself."

"Uh-huh." He polished off his eggs, sat back with his tea. "Ripley said you're scouting for a computer. The rental agency's looking to upgrade a couple of theirs. You could probably get a fair deal. You might want to stop by, ask for Marge. She manages the place."

"Thanks. I'll check it out tomorrow. Why aren't you mad anymore?"

"Who said I'm not?"

"I know how to read mad."

He studied her face. She had some color back now, but she looked exhausted. "I bet you do. Not much point in it." He took his plate to the sink, rinsed it off. "I might brood some later. I've got a real knack for that, according to my sister."

"I used to be a champion sulker." Satisfied that they were back on an even keel, she picked up her plate. "I might see if I can get back into that. You were right about the traditional Todd meal. It did the trick."

"Never misses. Still, grape jelly's better for it."

"I'll stock some, just in case."

"Good. I'm going to let you get back to work. In a minute."

He yanked her against him, jerked her up to her toes, covered her mouth with his in a hot, possessive kiss. The blood seemed to rush to her head, then poured out of it again, leaving her dizzy, weak, and achy.

One strangled moan escaped before she was back on the flat of her feet and gripping the edge of the counter for balance.

"Nothing sensible about that," Zack said, "but it's real. You're going to have to shuffle it into your list of priorities. Don't work too late."

He strolled out, letting the screened door slap comfortably shut behind him.

In her dream that night there was a circle. A thin line upon the earth as silver as starlight. Within that sphere there were three women, robed in white. Their voices flowed like music, though the words were strange to her. As they sang, spears of light sprang up from the circle, shimmering bars of silver against the black curtain of night.

She saw a cup, a knife with a carved handle, and sprigs of herbs as green as summer.

From the cup they drank, one by one. And she tasted wine, sweet and light, on her tongue. The dark-haired one drew symbols on the ground with the blade of the knife.

And she smelled earth, fresh and dark.

As they circled, chanted, a pure gold flame spurted in the center. The heat of it warmed her skin.

Then they rose up, above the gold of the fire, above the cool silver of the spears of light, as if they danced on the air.

And she knew the freedom and the joy as the wind kissed her cheeks.

Eleven

Closed in Mia's office, Nell sweated over facts, figures, reality, and possibilities.

She liked the possibilities best, as they included a secondhand computer with all the capabilities she required, an attractive sales kit, professional business cards, a cozy yet functional home office, and a commercial-grade food processor.

The fact was, she needed all of these things, and several more, in order to create a viable, reasonably profitable business.

Her figures proved she could make this her reality if she settled for a reality without any frills—which included food, drink, and clothing—for approximately twelve months.

As she saw it, her choices were to live like a mole for about a year, or to do without the professional tools that would help her build her business.

Living like a mole wasn't so bad, she mused. She'd done essentially that for months before she'd come to the island. If she hadn't weakened and frittered away money on wind chimes and sandals and earrings, she wouldn't have remembered how much fun it was to fritter away money in the first place.

Now it had to stop.

By her calculations she could, provided Marge at Island Realty was patient enough, scrape up the money for the computer within three weeks. She would need several hundred more, of course, for the printer, the phone line, the business license, the office supplies. Once she was set up, she could design and generate the sales kits and menus right on the desktop.

With a sigh, she sat back, combed her hands through her hair. She'd left out the uniform. She could hardly cater the Macey affair in jeans and a T-shirt, or a sexy little halter. She needed good black slacks, a crisp white shirt, sensible but classy black shoes.

She looked up when Mia walked in.

"Hi. I'll get out of your way."

"No need." Mia waved her back. "I just need to check something in the September catalog." She plucked it off a shelf, flipped through while watching Nell over the pages. "Financial worries?"

"Why do you ask?"

"Vibes."

"They're not worries so much as obstacles of varying heights. I hate admitting I'm taking on too much too fast."

"And why is that? Not hating it, but why do you say you're taking on too much?" Mia asked as she sat, stretched out like a cat on a hearth rug.

"A few side jobs, some boxed lunches, one major party, and here I am designing logos and business cards, trying to squeeze out money for a computer when I can easily keep things organized in a spiral notebook. I need to rein myself in."

"There's little that's more boring than reining in," Mia stated. "When I started this place, most people didn't think I could make it fly. A small community, a seasonal tourist trade. Bookstores and fancy coffee were for cities and snazzy suburbs. They were wrong. I knew what I wanted, and what I was capable of achieving. So do you."

"In another six months or a year," Nell agreed. "But I'm getting ahead of myself."

"Why wait? You need capital, but you can't risk going to the bank for a business loan. So many pesky questions about credit history, employment history, and so on."

Mia inclined her head when Nell sighed. She enjoyed hitting the center of the target with the first arrow. "As careful as you've been, you may have left a hole," Mia continued, "and you're too smart to take chances there."

"I thought about it," Nell admitted. "If I opened myself up that way, I'd never relax. Nell Channing doesn't have a credit history, and it'll take me time to establish one."

"Which is one of the obstacles to that capital. There are spells, of course. But I dislike doing spells for financial gain. It seems so . . . crass."

"It doesn't seem so crass when I'm trying to stretch my budget to buy basic office equipment."

Pursing her lips, Mia tapped the tips of her fingers together. "I had an acquaintance who was in a bit of a financial squeeze. She worked a spell asking that her current money worries be cleared. And won fifty thousand in the lottery the next week."

"Really?"

"Really. She was able to pay her debts and treat herself to a week at the Doral Spa in Miami. Fabulous place, by the way. When she returned, her car broke down, her roof sprang a leak, her basement flooded, and she received an audit notice from the IRS. In the end, she'd done nothing more than trade one set of worries for another, though she did get that week at the spa, which can't be discounted."

Nell acknowledged the humor in Mia's words with a small grin. "I hear you. Magic isn't a crutch to be used for convenience."

"You're a quick study, little sister. So, let's talk business." Mia toed off her pretty heels, curled up her legs. "I'm in the market for an investment."

"Mia, I can't tell you how much I appreciate that, but—"

"You want to do it yourself, and blah, blah, blah." With a flick of the wrist, Mia swatted Nell's protest aside. "Please, let's behave like grown-ups."

"Are you trying to irritate or intimidate me into accepting a loan?"

"I don't generally try to irritate or intimidate, though I've been told I'm good at both. And I didn't say anything about a loan. We're discussing an investment."

She uncurled lazily and got a bottle of water for each of them out of her mini-fridge. "I would consider a loan, I suppose, for your start-up costs. Say, ten thousand, payable over a period of sixty months at twelve percent interest."

"I don't need ten thousand," Nell said, giving the bottle cap an annoyed twist. "And twelve percent is ridiculous."

"A bank would charge less, but I'm not a bank and I wouldn't ask those pesky questions."

Mia's lips curved, red and shapely over the mouth of the bottle. "But I prefer an investment. I'm a businesswoman who likes profit. You have a skill, a marketable one, which has already proven itself of interest on the island. With working capital, you can establish a viable business, which, I feel, will enhance rather than compete with my own. I've some ideas on that, actually, but we can get into that later. I make a ten K investment, become your silent partner, for a reasonable compensation of, say, eight percent of gross profits."

"I don't need ten." It had been a very long time, Nell thought as she tapped her fingers on the desk, since she'd negotiated fees, contracts. Amazing how quickly it came back.

Ten thousand would be welcome and would eliminate the sweat and worry. But if you avoided the sweat and worry, she thought, you eliminated the glow of satisfaction that came when you succeeded.

"Five will do," she decided. "For six percent, of net."

"Five, then, for seven, net."

"Done."

"Excellent. I'll have my lawyer draw up a contract."

"I'll open an account for the business at the bank."

"Would it be less sticky if I took care of that, and the license application?"

"I'll do it. I have to take a stand sometime."

"Little sister, you took one months ago. But I leave it to you. Nell," she said as she opened the door, "we're going to kick ass."

She worked like a demon, preparing, planning, implementing. Her kitchen was a hotbed of experimentation, rejections, and successes. Her little office was the scene of hours of late-evening sessions where, on her secondhand computer and printer, she became her own desktop publisher, producing menus, flyers, business cards, invoices, and stationery, all with the inscription "Sisters Catering" and the logo she'd designed of three women standing in a circle, hands clasped.

And every one listed Nell Channing as proprietor and carried her new phone number.

When she finished putting her first sales kit together, she took it, along with the best bottle of champagne she could afford, and drove to Mia's to leave them on her doorstep.

They were in business.

On the day of the Macey party, Nell stood in Gladys's kitchen and surveyed the scene. She'd been working on-site since four, and had thirty minutes before the guests were due to arrive.

For the first time since Nell had begun the setup for the party, she finally had a moment's peace and quiet. If Gladys made it through the evening without fainting from excitement and anxiety, it would be a miracle.

Every inch of the kitchen was organized to Nell's specifications. In precisely ten minutes, she would begin setting out the appetizers. As the guest list had expanded to more than a hundred, she had used all her powers of persuasion to convince Gladys to forgo the formal, sit-down meal in favor of fun, interesting food stations set up at strategic points throughout the house and on the patio.

She'd seen to the floral arrangements herself, and had personally helped Carl deal with the fairy lights and luminaries. There were candles in rented silver holders, and paper napkins that, at Nell's suggestion, carried a heart with the happy couple's initials inside.

It still touched her the way Gladys's eyes had filled when she'd seen them.

Satisfied the kitchen was ready for the battle to come, she went out to check on the rest of the field, and her troops.

She'd hired Peg to help serve, and Betsy from the Magick Inn to tend the bar. She herself would fill in in both areas whenever she could leave the kitchen unattended.

"It looks great," she announced and moved to the patio doors. The evening promised to be clear. Both she and Gladys had suffered untold agonies over the possibility of rain.

Nell tugged down the black vest she'd added to her uniform selection. "One more time. Peg, you circulate, trying to make a complete circuit every fifteen minutes. When your tray's empty, or nearly so, you head back to the kitchen. If I'm not there to refill, you'll arrange the next selection the way I showed you."

"I practiced it a zillion times."

"I know." Nell gave her an encouraging pat on the arm. "Betsy,

I'll try to keep up with the empties and discards. If I run behind, or you're running low on anything, just give me a sign."

"Check. And everything looks great."

"So far, so good." And she was determined it would only get better. "Carl Junior's in charge of the music, so I'm not going to worry about it. Let's get this show on the road. Peg, vegetable crudites, station one."

It was more than just a party to Nell—it was a new beginning. As she lit the last of the candles, she thought of her mother, and the first official catering job they'd worked together.

"I've made a circle, Mom," she murmured. "And I'm going to make it shine." Touching the flame to wick, with her mother in her mind, Nell made that vow.

She glanced over and beamed as Gladys Macey came out of the master bedroom. "You look beautiful."

"Nervous as a bride." She fluffed at her hair. "I went into Boston for this getup. Not too fussy, is it?"

The cocktail suit was a pale mint green with a sparkle of beads glittering on the lapels and cuffs.

"It's gorgeous, and so are you. And there's nothing for you to be nervous about. All you have to do is enjoy yourself."

"Are you sure there's going to be enough cocktail shrimp?"

"I'm sure."

"I just don't know what people are going to think of that chicken in peanut sauce."

"They'll love it."

"What about—"

"Gladys, stop haranguing the girl." Scowling, dragging at the knot of his tie, Carl stepped out. "Let her do her job."

"Mr. Macey, you make a picture." Unable to resist, Nell reached over and straightened his tie herself.

"Made me buy a new suit."

"And you look very handsome in it," Nell assured him.

"Done nothing but complain about it since he got home from work."

Well used to their squabbling by now, Nell smiled. "Personally, I like a man who's not too comfortable in suits and ties. It's very sexy."

At Nell's statement Carl's face went bright pink. "Don't know why we couldn't have had a barbecue and a couple of kegs."

Before Gladys could snap back at him, Nell lifted a tray of appetizers. "I think you're going to have a wonderful time, starting right now."

Manners forced Carl to take one of the fancy salmon bites. The minute it hit his tongue, he pursed his lips. "Got a nice flavor to it," he admitted. "Guess it'd go down nice with a beer."

"You step right into the living room and Betsy will fix you up. I think I hear the first guests arriving."

"Oh, my! Oh, my goodness." Patting her hair again, Gladys shot quick looks everywhere. "I meant to see if everything was as it should be before—"

"Everything's exactly as it should be. You greet your guests, leave the rest to me."

It took less than fifteen minutes for the initial party stiffness to unbend. Music began to pump, conversation began to roll, and as Nell made her circuit with the chicken kabobs, she saw that she'd been right. People loved them.

It was fun to see the familiar island residents in their festive best, knotted into conversational groups or wandering out to the patio. She kept her ears open for comments about the food and the atmosphere, and felt a quick tingle with each positive remark. But best of all was seeing her client glow like a candle.

Within an hour the house was jammed, and she was working at top speed.

"They're going through these trays like starving hordes," Peg told her as she scrambled into the kitchen. "You'd think every one of them fasted a week before tonight."

"It'll slow down after the dancing starts." Moving quickly, Nell refilled the tray.

"Station . . . hell, I can never remember the numbers. The meatballs are about half gone. You said I should tell you."

"I'll take care of it. Is anything not going over?"

"Not that I've seen." Peg hefted the tray. "The way it's moving, I'd say this crowd would eat the paper napkins if you put sauce on them."

Amused, Nell took out the miniature egg rolls she had warming in the oven. As she arranged them on a tray, Ripley strolled in.

"Some party."

"It's great, isn't it?"

"Yeah, swank."

"You look pretty swank yourself," Nell commented.

Ripley looked down at her basic black dress. It was short, satisfactorily clingy, and had the advantage of being able to go to a party or, with a blazer, double as meeting attire.

"I got this number in black and in white. Figure that covers the bases as far as dresses go." She glanced around, saw absolute order, heard the hum of the dishwasher, smelled the scent of spice. "How do you keep everything organized in here?"

"I'm brilliant."

"Seems like." Ripley plucked up one of the egg rolls, popped it into her mouth. "Food's fabulous," she said with her mouth full. "I never told you, but that picnic deal you fixed for me was really great."

"Oh, yeah? How did that work out?"

"Just dandy, thanks," Ripley replied.

Her smug smile transformed into a scowl when Mia stepped in.

"I wanted to extend my compliments." She spotted the egg rolls.

"Ah, a new offering." She took one, bit in. "Lovely. Hello, Ripley. I barely recognized you in your girl attire. How did you decide whether to wear the black or the white this evening?"

"Up yours."

"Don't start. I haven't time to referee."

"Don't worry." Ripley snagged one more egg roll. "I can't waste the energy on Hecate here. Gladys's nephew from Cambridge just arrived and is looking just fine. I'm going to go hit on him."

"It's so comforting to know some things never change."

"Don't touch anything," Nell ordered, then hurried out with the tray.

"So . . ." Because she preferred being away from the crowd of people, but still wanted to eat, Ripley eased up the lid on a covered tray. "Nell seems okay."

"Why wouldn't she?"

"Don't play dumb, Mia. It doesn't suit that cat face of yours." Ripley helped herself to a couple of frosted, heart-shaped cookies. "I don't need a scrying mirror to see she's had a rough time. A woman like her doesn't pop up on the island with nothing to her name but a backpack and a secondhand Buick unless she's on the run. Zack figures some guy knocked her around."

When Mia said nothing, Ripley leaned back on the counter, nibbled. "Look, I like her, and my brother's gone over her. I'm not looking to hassle her, but maybe to help if she needs it."

"With or without your badge?"

"Either or both. It seems to me she's putting down stakes here, not just working for you, but starting this catering deal. She's starting a life on Three Sisters. That makes her one of mine."

"Give me one of those." Mia held out her hand, waited until Ripley gave her a cookie. "What are you asking me, Ripley?"

"If Zack's right, and if he is, if someone's going to come after her."

"Whatever Nell's told me in confidence has to be respected."

Loyalty, Ripley was forced to admit, was never a question with Mia. It was more a religion. "I'm not asking you to break a confidence."

Mia nipped into the cookie. "You just can't say it, can you?"

"Oh, kiss ass." Ripley slapped the lid back on the tray, started to storm out. But there was something about the way Nell had been, flushed and happy, as she worked in the miraculously ordered kitchen, that pulled at her.

She spun back. "Tell me what you've seen. I want to help her."

"Yes, I know." Mia finished the cookie, dusted the crumbs from her fingers. "There's a man. He hunts and he haunts her. He's the physical reality of her every fear, doubt, worry. If he comes here, if he finds her, she'll need both of us. And she'll need the courage to take her own power and use it."

"What's his name?"

"I can't tell you that. It wasn't shown to me."

"But you know it."

"What she gave to me I can't pass on to you. I can't break her trust." The worry in Mia's eyes crawled into Ripley's belly. "If I could, and did, his name would make no difference. This is her path, Ripley. We can guide and support, instruct and assist. But in the end, it'll be her choice. You know the legend as well as I."

"I'm not getting into that." Ripley pushed the subject away with a sharp gesture. "I'm talking about someone's safety. A friend's safety."

"So am I. But I'm also talking about a friend's destiny. If you really want to help her, you could start by taking responsibility for your own." With that, Mia walked out.

"Responsibility, my butt." Ripley was annoyed enough to pry up the lid for one more cookie.

She knew what her responsibilities were. She was obliged to see to the safety of the residents and visitors of Three Sisters Island. To keep order and uphold the law.

Beyond that, her responsibilities were nobody's business but hers. And it wasn't responsible to go around practicing mumbo jumbo and clinging to some stupid legend that was as much nonsense now as it had been three centuries before.

She was the island deputy, not part of some mystic trio of saviors. And she wasn't destined to mete out some nebulous psychic justice.

Now she'd lost her appetite, and her desire to hit on Gladys Macey's nephew. Served her right for wasting time with Mia Devlin.

Disgusted, she stalked out of the kitchen. The first thing she saw as she moved back toward the party was Zack. He was in the middle of things, where he always seemed to be when it came to people. They were drawn to him. But even as he stood in the middle of a group who chattered at him, she could see that his gaze and his mind were aimed elsewhere.

It was all for Nell.

Now, Ripley watched her brother as he watched Nell circulate with her fancy little egg rolls. There was no doubt about it.

The man was completely over the moon.

While she could resist and ignore Mia's talk of destinies and responsibilities when it came to herself, when it came to a newly formed and still evolving friendship, it was an entirely different matter. Especially if it involved her brother.

There was nothing she wouldn't have done for Zack, even if it meant linking hands with Mia.

She was going to have to pay close attention to the situation, reevaluate periodically. Do some hard, uncomfortable thinking.

"He's on the edge," Mia whispered in her ear. "The shimmering edge just before the breathless tumble."

"I've got eyes, don't I?"

"Do you know what happens when he falls?"

Ripley took the wineglass out of Mia's hand, drank half of it. "Why don't you tell me?"

"He'll lay down his life for her, without an instant's hesitation. He's the most admirable man I know." She took the glass back, sipped. "That, at least, is a point of absolute agreement between us."

Because she knew it, Ripley weakened. "I want a protective spell. I want you to take care of that."

"I've already done what I can. In the end, it has to be a circle of three."

"I can't think about this now. I'm not going to talk about it now."

"All right. Why don't we just stand here and watch a strong and admirable man fall in love? Moments this pure shouldn't be wasted." Mia laid a hand on Ripley's shoulder, a casual link. "She doesn't see it. Even as it passes over her like a breath of warm air, she isn't whole enough to know it."

With a sigh that may have held the barest whiff of envy, Mia looked down into her wine. "Come on. I'll buy you a drink."

Zack bided his time. He talked with the other guests, danced with the ladies, shared a celebratory beer with Carl. He listened with apparent interest to village complaints and scrutinized the alcohol intake of anyone who held car keys.

He watched Nell serve food, chat with the guests, replenish pots staying warm over little cans of sterno. What he observed, he thought, was a blooming.

He started to ask if he could lend her a hand, then realized it was laughable. Not only did he have no clue what needed to be done, but she so obviously needed no one's help.

As the crowd thinned out, he drove a few celebrants home himself, to be on the safe side. It was nearly midnight before he felt his own duties were dispatched and he could hunt Nell up in the kitchen.

Empty trays were stacked neatly on Gladys's marbled white counter. Serving bowls were nested. The sink was filled with soapy water that sent up little fingers of steam, and Nell was systematically loading the dishwasher.

"When's the last time you were off your feet?"

"I lost track." She slid plates into slots. "But the fact that they're killing me makes me incredibly happy."

"Here." He held out a glass of champagne. "I thought you deserved this."

"I certainly do." She took a quick sip before she set it aside. "All these weeks of planning, and it's done. And I have five, count them, five appointments for jobs next week. Did you know Mary Harrison's daughter is getting married next spring?"

"I heard that. To John Bigelow. Cousin of mine."

"I have a shot at catering it."

"I vote you put those meatballs of yours on the menu. They were really tasty."

"I'll make a note of it." It felt so good to be able to plan ahead. Not just a day or a week, but months ahead. "Did you see the way Gladys and Carl danced together?"

She straightened, pressing hard on the aching small of her back. "Thirty years, and they were dancing on the patio, looking at each other like it was the first time. It was the best moment of the night for me. Do you know why?"

"Why?"

She turned to him. "Because them dancing together, them looking at each other the way they were, was what this was all about. Not decorations or pretty lights or cocktail shrimp. It was about people

making a connection, and believing in it. In each other. What would
have happened if either one of them, all those years ago, had stepped
back or turned away? They'd have missed dancing on the patio, and
everything in between."

"I never got to dance with you." He reached out, skimmed his
fingers over her cheek. "Nell—"

"There you are!" Eyes damp and brilliant, Gladys rushed in. "I
was afraid you'd slipped out."

"No, indeed. I need to finish up here, then do a run-through of
the house to make sure I have everything back in order."

"You certainly do not. You've done enough, more than I expected.
I never had such a party, not in my whole life. Why, people will be
talking about it for years."

She took Nell's shoulders, kissed both her cheeks. "I was a pest,
and I know it." Then she hugged Nell breathless. "Oh, this was such
a treat, and I'm not waiting three decades to do it again. Now, I want
you to go home and get off your feet."

She pressed a crisp hundred-dollar bill into Nell's hand. "This is
for you."

"Mrs. Macey, you're not supposed to tip me. Peg and—"

"I've taken care of them. You're going to hurt my feelings if you
don't take this and go buy yourself something pretty. Now I want
you to scat. Anything else needs to be done, it'll wait until tomorrow.
Sheriff, you help our Nell out to her car with her trays."

"I'll do that."

"This was better than my wedding," Gladys said as she started to
the door. She turned back briefly, winked. "Now let's see if we can
improve on my wedding night."

"Looks like Carl's in for a surprise." Zack hefted a stack of trays.
"We'd better move along, give the young couple some privacy."

"I'm right behind you."

It took three trips between them, with Carl pushing a bottle of champagne into Nell's hands as he nudged them along.

"Here's your hat, what's your hurry?" Zack chuckled as he loaded Nell's trunk.

"Where's your car?"

"Hmm? Oh, Ripley used it to take the last couple of semi-impaired guests home. Most people walked, which helped out."

Nell let herself look at him. He was wearing a suit, but had already rid himself of the tie. She could see the faint bulge where he'd stuffed it in his pocket.

He'd opened his collar, so she could see the clean, tanned line of his throat.

There was a faint smile on his lips as he watched the lights in the Macey house wink out, one at a time. His profile wasn't perfect. His hair hadn't been styled. And the way he stood, his thumbs tucked in the front pockets of his suit pants, was relaxed rather than posed.

When the shimmer of desire came, she didn't try to close it off. Instead she took a step forward.

"I've only had half a glass of champagne. I'm unimpaired, thinking clearly, and my reflexes are perfect."

He turned his head toward her. "As sheriff, I'm glad to know it."

Still watching him, she drew her keys out of her pocket, held them dangling. "Come home with me. You drive."

The twinkle in his eyes turned to razor-sharp intensity. "I'm not going to ask if you're sure." He took the keys. "I'm just going to tell you to get in the car."

Her knees felt a bit wobbly, but she walked to the door, slid in while he got behind the wheel.

When he yanked her across the seat, ravished her mouth, she forgot all about wobbly knees and did her best to crawl into his lap.

"Hold on, just hold on. Christ Jesus." He stabbed the keys into the ignition. The engine whimpered to life, and he swung the protesting car into a tight U-turn. It shimmied in protest, making Nell giggle nervously.

"If this heap falls apart before we get there, we'll have to run for it. Zack—" She flipped off the seat belt she'd automatically snapped on, and slithered over to bite his ear. "I feel like I'm going to explode."

"Did I ever mention I'm particularly partial to women wearing little black vests?"

"No. Really?"

"I just found out tonight." Reaching out, he snagged the vest by the center vee, tugged her back against him. Understandably distracted, he took the turn too sharp and bumped the wheels over the curb.

"One more minute," he panted. "Just one more minute."

With a squeal of brakes and a violent jerk, he stopped in front of Nell's cottage. He managed, barely, to turn off the ignition before he reached for her. Dragging her across his lap, he found her mouth with his again. And let his hands do as they pleased.

Need spurted through her, hot and welcome. Riding on it, she tugged at his jacket, arched against his hands. And thrilled at the first scrape of callus over her flesh.

"Inside." He felt as randy and impatient as a teenager, and as fumbling as he fought to open the car door. "We have to get inside."

He whipped her out, his breathing already ragged as they continued to fight with each other's clothes. They stumbled, and buttons popped off his shirt. As he half carried her toward the cottage, her delighted laughter rang in his head.

"Oh! I love your hands! I want them all over me."

"I'll take care of that. Goddamn it, what's wrong with this door?" Even as he vented his frustration by rapping his hip hard against it, it flew open.

They ended up in a heap on the floor, half in, half out.

"Right here. Right here." She chanted it while her fingers worked busily at his belt.

"Wait. Just a—let me close the—" He managed to roll, scoot, and kick the door shut.

The room was all moonlight and shadows. The floor was as hard as brick. Neither of them noticed as they tore at clothes, rolled and tugged. He caught glimpses, beautiful, erotic images of pale skin, soft curves, delicate lines.

He wanted to look. He wanted to wallow.

He had to take.

When her shirt caught at her wrists by the cuffs, he gave up, gave in and lowered his mouth to her breast.

She vibrated beneath him, a volcano on the brink of erupting. Flashes of white-hot heat, curls of keen-edged longing raced through her system until she was raw and ready.

She arched under him, more demand than offer, her nails biting restlessly into his back. The world was spinning, faster and faster, as if she'd leaped upon some mad carousel and all that kept her earthbound was the glorious weight of his body on hers.

"Right now." She gripped his hips, opened for him. "Right now!"

He plunged, letting his body take over, letting his mind go. There was nothing but the relentless fury to mate. She closed around him, a hot, wet fist, and he felt her tighten, stretching like a bow beneath him before she let out a cry that rang with triumph.

Her climax ripped through him like madness.

Pleasure geysered through her, flooding senses, swamping reason. Flying free, she wrapped herself around him, clinging tight to take him with her.

And with her sheer joy, drove him over the edge.

Twelve

His ears were ringing. Or maybe it was just the sound of his heart banging against his ribs like a fist on piano keys. Either way, he couldn't get his mind clear or his body to move. He'd have worried about temporary paralysis if he could've worked up the energy to worry about anything.

"Okay," he managed and breathed in. "All right." And out again. "I guess I tripped."

"Me, too." She was flattened under him, in the perfect position to nuzzle at his throat.

"Did you get banged up anywhere?"

"No. You broke my fall." She gave the strong line of that throat a little scrape with her teeth. "Such a hero."

"Yeah. You bet."

"I rushed you. I hope you don't mind."

"It's a little hard to complain just at the moment." He found the energy to roll over, dragging her with him so she was cushioned against him. "But I'm hoping you'll give me a chance to show off my style and finesse."

She lifted her head, shook her hair back, and just grinned down at him.

"What?"

"I was just thinking how much I like your style. Every time I caught a glimpse of you tonight during the party, I just wanted to lick my lips. Big, handsome Sheriff Todd standing around in a suit he wished he didn't have to wear, nursing one lonely beer all evening so he could drive people home safe, and watching me with those patient green eyes until I was so turned on I'd have to go back to the kitchen just to calm down again."

"Is that right?" He ran his hands down her arms, amused when he hit the cuffs of her shirt. Carefully he began to unbutton them. "Do you know what I was thinking when I was watching you?"

"Not exactly."

"I was thinking how you looked like a dancer, all grace and competence. And I tried not to think what you might have on under that starched white shirt and sexy little vest."

Once he'd freed her wrists, he ran his hands back up her arms. "You've got such a fine, streamlined shape to you, Nell. It's been driving me crazy for weeks."

"I don't know how to explain how it makes me feel to know that. To feel steady enough to want that." She threw her head back, her arms up. "Oh, God! I feel so alive. I don't want it ever to stop."

She leaned down again, kissed him hard, then scrambled to her feet. "I want that champagne. I want to get drunk and make love with you all night."

"I can get behind that idea." He sat up, then his eyes widened as she pulled open the door. "What're you doing?"

"Getting the champagne out of the car."

"Let me get my pants on, and I'll get it. Nell!" Stupefied, he sprang to his feet as she raced outside, naked as a jaybird. "Well, for God's sake!" He grabbed his pants, carrying them with him to the doorway. "Get back in here before I have to haul you in for indecent exposure."

"There's nobody to see." It felt fabulous, and exactly right to stand naked in the cool night air, to feel it caress the skin so recently heated by passion. With the grass tickling her feet, she threw her arms out to the side and turned in circles. "Come on out, it's a beautiful night. Moon and stars and the sound of the sea."

She looked impossibly alluring, the gold of her hair silvered by starlight, her milky skin shimmering with it, and her face lifted to the sky.

Then her gaze met his across the little patch of lawn with a power so intense it stole his breath. For a moment he would have sworn the whole of her sparkled.

"There's something in the air here," she said, turning her hands up, palms cupped as if she could catch the breath of the night. "I feel it inside me, beating like a pulse. And when I feel that, it seems I could do anything."

With her palm still cupped, she held out her hand to him. "Will you come kiss me in the moonlight?"

He couldn't resist, and didn't try, but walked to her, took her outstretched hand. With the sky sprinkling light over them, he lowered his mouth to hers in a kiss that warmed rather than burned.

The tenderness of it crept into her heart. When he lifted her into his arms, she cradled her head on his shoulder, knowing she was safe and welcome there.

He carried her inside, through the little cottage and to the old bed that shifted quietly under their weight.

Later, he told himself as he lost himself in her, he would think about how he felt to find himself falling in love with a witch.

She awoke before dawn from one of the snatches of sleep they'd allowed each other. She felt his warmth, and his weight. The ease of it, the sheer and steady normality of him, was both comfort and arousal.

She drew his face for herself in her mind, feature by feature. When she had it complete, she held it there as she slipped out of bed to start her day.

She showered, dressed in shorts and a sleeveless shirt. Quietly, she picked up the clothes they'd scattered in the living room and all but floated into the kitchen.

She'd never experienced desire like that before, not the kind that sprang like an animal inside you and swallowed you whole.

She hoped to have the experience again.

And the tenderness that had come later, the insatiable thirst for more, the dark, breathless groping. All of it.

Nell Channing had a lover. And he was sleeping in her bed.

He wanted her, and that was a thrill. He wanted her for who she was, and not who he could mold her to be. And that was a balm.

Blissful, she brewed coffee, and while its scent perfumed the air she worked up a dough for cinnamon buns, another for bread. While she worked she sang to herself and watched the new day put roses in the sky.

Once her garden was watered, and she'd sipped at her first cup of coffee, she slid a batch of buns into the oven. With her mug in one hand, a pencil in the other, she began to toy with her menu for the coming week.

"What're you doing?"

She jumped like a rabbit at the sleep-roughened sound of his voice, and the coffee slopped over onto the paper. "Did I wake you? I'm sorry. I tried to be quiet."

He held up a hand. "Nell, don't do that. It pisses me off." His voice was thick with sleep, and despite herself dread curled in her stomach as he stepped toward her.

"There's one thing I'm going to ask you." He picked up her mug, drank to clear his mind and voice. "Don't ever mix me up with him. If you'd waked me up and it annoyed me, I would say so. But the fact is I woke up because you weren't there and I missed you."

"Some habits are hard to break, no matter how much you try."

"Well, keep trying." He said it lightly, moved over to the stove to pour a full mug for himself. "You got something baking already?" He sniffed the air. "Mother of God." He breathed it, reverently. "Cinnamon buns?"

Her dimples flickered. "And if they are?"

"I'll be your slave."

"You're so easy, Sheriff." She got a hot mitt out of the drawer. "Why don't you sit down? I'll give you breakfast, and we can discuss what I expect from my slave."

On Monday morning Nell breezed into Café Book loaded with boxes of baked goods, called out a cheery hello, and swung upstairs.

At the front counter, Lulu stopped ringing up weekend mail orders, her lips twitching as Mia turned from stocking shelves.

"Somebody," Mia said, "got lucky this weekend."

"You going up to squeeze her for details?"

"Please." Mia tucked in another book, brushed lint from her skirt. "Do dryads dance in the woods?"

Amused, Lulu cackled. "Well, don't forget to fill me in."

Mia walked into the café, and through the homey, irresistible scent of cinnamon buns. "Busy weekend," she commented, scanning the morning's offerings.

"You bet."

"And a terrific party Saturday night. Hell of a job, little sister."

"Thanks." Nell lined up her muffins before pouring the first of the morning coffee for Mia. "I've got several meetings this week with potential clients that came out of it."

"Congratulations. But . . ." Mia drew in the scent of her coffee. "I don't think future catering jobs are what has you glowing today. Let me try one of those buns there."

Casually, she walked around to the rear of the counter while Nell selected the bun. "You definitely have the look of a woman who spent her weekend doing more than baking."

"I did some gardening. My tomato plants are coming right along."

"Mmm-hmm." She brought the fragrant bun to her lips, took a neat bite. "I'm imagining Sheriff Todd was just as tasty as this. Give. We open in ten."

"I shouldn't talk about it. It's rude, isn't it?"

"Absolutely not. It's required and expected. Have a little sympathy, will you? I haven't engaged in sexual activities for a considerable time, so I'm entitled to a few vicarious thrills. You look so damn happy."

"I am. It was wonderful." Nell did a quick little dance, then grabbed a bun for herself. "Outrageous. He has such . . . stamina."

"Oh. Mmm." Mia ran her tongue over her lips. "Don't stop now."

"I think we broke several standing records."

"Now you're bragging, but that's all right. You're among friends."

"You know the best part?"

"I'm hoping you'll tell me, and all the other parts as well."

"He didn't, doesn't, treat me like I'm fragile or needy or, I don't know . . . wounded. So I don't feel fragile or needy or wounded when I'm with him. The first time, we barely made it into the house, and ended up on the floor tearing at each other's clothes. It was so *normal.*"

"We could all use a bit of that kind of normal now and then. He's a great kisser, isn't he?"

"Oh, boy, and when he . . ." Trailing off, Nell paled.

"I was fifteen," Mia explained as she bit into the cinnamon bun again. "He gave me a ride home from a party, and we satisfied our mutual curiosity with a couple of very long, very intense lip-locks. While I won't insult your intelligence and claim it was like kissing my brother, I will say we didn't suit and have chosen to be friends. But they were really fine kisses."

She licked icing off her finger. "So I have some small idea just how delightful your weekend was."

"I'm glad I didn't know that before. I might have been intimidated."

"Aren't you sweet? So, what are you going to do about Zachariah Todd?"

"Enjoy him."

"Perfect answer." For the moment. "He has really good hands, too, doesn't he?" Mia commented as she strolled away.

"Now you're going to have to shut up."

Laughing, Mia started down the steps. "I'm opening the doors."

And so, she thought, little sister, are you.

It wouldn't have surprised Mia to know that Zack was undergoing personal interrogation over coffee and buns as well.

"Didn't see you around much this weekend."

"Had stuff to do. And didn't I bring you a present?"

Ripley worked her way enthusiastically through the first bun.

"Um. Good," she managed to slur. "Guess the stuff had to do with the island's best cook, which I cleverly deduced since you've got a bag holding half a dozen buns."

"Down to four now." He enjoyed one of his own while he slogged through paperwork at his desk. "John Macey still hasn't paid these parking tickets. He needs a goose."

"I'll goose him. So, you and Nell got down to the mattress rhumba?"

Zack gave her a single withering look. "You've got such a mushy, romantic heart, Rip. I don't know how you get through life with it weighing you down."

"Avoiding the question's usually answering the question in the affirmative. Cop 101. How'd it go?"

"Do I ask you about your sex life?"

She waved a finger, signaling a pause in the conversation while she swallowed. "Yes."

"Only because I'm older and wiser."

"Yeah, right." She snagged a second bun, not only because they were incredible but because she knew it would annoy him. "If we let you slide on the older and wiser bull, then we'll agree I'm younger and more cynical. Are you going to do a deeper run on her background?"

"No." Deliberately he opened a drawer, dropped the bag of buns inside, shut it.

"If you're serious about her, and knowing you, you are, you need a handle on it, Zack. She didn't drop out of the sky onto Three Sisters."

"She took the ferry," he said coolly. "What's your problem with her? I thought you liked her."

"I do. A lot, as it happens." She eased a hip onto the corner of his desk. "But for reasons that often escape me, I like you a lot, too. You've got a soft spot for the troubled and wounded, Zack, and sometimes, through no fault of their own, the troubled and wounded can bite right through the soft parts."

"Have you ever known me not to be able to take care of myself?"

"You're in love with her." When he blinked, stared, she pushed off the desk, paced restlessly around the office area. "What, am I blind and stupid? I've known you all my life, and I know every move, every tone, every expression on that dopey face of yours. You're in love with her, and you don't even know who she is."

"She's exactly who and what I've wanted my whole life."

Ripley stopped in the act of kicking the desk, and her eyes went soft and helpless. "Aw, damn it, Zack. Why'd you have to go and say something like that?"

"Because it's true. It's the way it is for us Todds, isn't it? We go along, go alone, then *pow*, it hits and it's all over. I've been hit, and I like it."

"Okay, let's just back up a little." Determined to stand up for him whether he wanted it or not, she slapped her palms on the desk, leaned over. "She's got trouble. She's managed to break free of it, at least temporarily, but it's there. He may come after her, Zack. If I hadn't been worried about you, I'd never have asked Mia about it. Rather saw my tongue in half with a rusty kitchen knife. But I did ask her, and she's not clear on it."

"Honey, what you said before about knowing me, that's true. Now what do you think my reaction is to what you just said?"

She hissed out a breath. "If he comes after her, he'll have to get through you."

"Close enough. Shouldn't you be out on patrol, or would you rather take the paperwork portion of our day?"

"I'd rather eat lice." She put on her cap, yanked the tail of her hair through the back. "Look, I'm glad you found someone who suits you.

I'm even more glad I like her. But there's more to Nell Channing than a nice woman with a murky past who can bake like a team of angels."

"You mean she's a witch," he said easily. "Yeah, I figured that out. I've got no particular problem with it." So saying, he went back to the keyboard, chuckling to himself when Ripley slammed the door behind her.

The goddess doesn't require sacrifice," Mia said. "She's a mother. Like a mother, she requires respect, love, discipline, and wants happiness for her children."

The evening was cool. Mia could already scent the end of summer. Soon her woods would change from green and lush to wild color. She'd already seen the woolly caterpillars, watched the busy squirrel hoarding nuts. Signals, she thought, of a long, cold winter.

But for now, her roses bloomed, and the most tender of her herbs trailed fragrantly among her garden stones.

"Magic springs from the elements, and from the heart. But its rituals are best served with tools, even visual aids, if you will. Any craft depends on certain routines and implements."

She walked through her garden to her kitchen door, opened it for Nell. "I have some for you."

The room was as fragrant as the garden. Hanks of herbs dried on hooks. Pots of flowers that Mia had chosen for indoor company stood on the long line of smooth counter. What could only be described as a cauldron sat on the stove, simmering away with the strong sweetness of heliotrope.

"What are you cooking?"

"Oh, just a little charm for someone who has a job interview later in the week. She's nervous." Mia passed a hand through the steam. "Heliotrope for success, sunflower for career, a bit of hazel to assist in communication—and this and that. I'll empower some suitable crystals for her that she can carry in a pouch in her purse."

"Will she get the job?"

"That's up to her. The Craft doesn't promise us everything we desire, nor is it a crutch for weak spines to lean on. Now, your tools," she continued, gesturing to the table.

She'd selected them carefully, with an image of Nell in her mind.

"You should, once you're home, cleanse them. No one should touch them without your permission. They require your energy. The wand is made from a birch branch pruned from a living tree on the winter solstice. The crystal on its tip is clear quartz. It was a gift to me from the one who trained me."

It was lovely, slim and smooth, and felt almost silky when Nell trailed a finger over it. "You can't give me something that was a gift."

"It was meant to be passed on. You'll want to have others, too; copper is good. This is your broom," she continued, lifting a brow as Nell stifled a laugh.

"Sorry, I just never thought . . . a broom?"

"You won't be riding on it. Hang it at the door of your home for protection, use it to sweep out negative energy. A cup—again, one day you'll want to select your own, but for now this will serve. I bought it at Island Market, glassware section. Sometimes the simple works best. The pentacle is from a maple bur. It must always stand upright. The athame isn't used for physical cutting, but for directing energy."

She didn't touch it, but told Nell to do so.

"Some prefer swords, but I don't think you will," she added as Nell explored the carved handle with a fingertip. "The blade's dull, and meant to be. The bolline, on the other hand, is meant to cut in the physical. The handle's curved, which will give you a good grip for harvesting your herbs and plants, carving wands, inscribing candles, and so on. There are those, kitchen witches, who use it to cut food. The choice is yours, of course."

"Of course," Nell agreed.

"I assume you can handle the purchase and selection of your own cauldron. Cast iron's best. You can find an incense burner that appeals to you at one of the gift shops, and the incense as well—cones and sticks are more accessible locally. When you've time you can make your own incense powder. You'll need some straw baskets, some swatches of silk. Do you want to write this down?"

Nell blew out a breath. "Maybe I'd better."

"Candles," Mia continued after handing Nell a pad and pencil. "I'll explain the purpose of colors and symbols. I have some crystals for you, but you'll want more, of your own selection. A couple dozen canning jars, with lids, a mortar and pestle, sea salt. I have a Tarot deck you can borrow, and some wooden boxes, though I'll want them back as well. This will get you started."

"It's more involved than I thought. Before—the day in the garden—all I did was stand there."

"There are things you'll be able to do with your mind and heart, and others that require things—as an extension of power, and as a respect for tradition. Now that you have a computer, you'll want to keep a record of spells."

"A record of spells, on my computer?"

"Why not be practical and efficient? Nell, have you spoken to Zack about any of this?"

"No."

"Are you worried about his reaction?"

She touched the wand again, and wondered. "That's part of it, but before we even get there, I don't know how I'd begin to tell him. I haven't resolved it completely for myself."

"Fair enough. What you share or don't is your choice, just as what you give or what you take."

"With Ripley feeling the way she does, I thought he might feel the same. I guess I don't want to hit any hitches so soon."

"Who could blame you? Let's take a walk."

"I really should be getting back. It's nearly dark."

"He'll wait." Mia opened a carved box, took out her wand. The tip was a round of quartz as smoky as her eyes. "Take yours. It's time you learned how to cast a circle. We'll keep it simple," she promised, nudging Nell through the door. "And after what I have in mind, I can almost guarantee the sex will be sensational."

"It's not all sex," Nell began. "But that's a definite plus."

As they walked toward the woods, a light mist swirled to hug the ground. Long shadows spilled out of the trees, black lines over pale gray.

"The weather's changing," Mia said. "The last weeks of summer always make me melancholy. It's odd, because I love the autumn, the smells and the colors of it, that slice in the air when you step out first thing in the morning."

You're lonely. Nell nearly said it before she checked her tongue. How could such a statement help but sound smug and self-satisfied coming from a woman who'd just taken a lover?

"Maybe a holdover from childhood," she suggested. "End of summer means back to school." She followed Mia down a well-beaten path, through mist and shadow. "I always hated those first couple of weeks of school, not so much if my father had a second year on the same base, but at those times when I was the new kid and everyone else was already picked off in groups."

"How did you handle it?"

"I learned how to talk to people, to make friends even though they were transient. Lived in my own head a lot. I guess some of that made me a perfect target for Evan. He promised to love, honor, and cherish, forever. I really wanted forever with someone."

"And now?"

"Now I just want to carve out my own space, and stick."

"Something else we have in common. This is one of my spaces."

They stepped into a clearing where the mist was white from the quiet light of the rising moon. The full ball of it shimmered between the trees, teased the dark summer leaves, spilled through at the edges of a stand of three stones. From the branches that ringed the clearing hung hanks of herbs. The glitter of strung crystals rang gently together in the light wind.

And the sound of the wind, the stones, the nearby sea, was music.

There was a primitive, *essential* feel to the place.

"It's beautiful here," Nell began, "and . . . I want to say eerie, but not in a frightening way. You almost expect to see ghosts, or headless horsemen. And if you did, it would seem absolutely natural, not frightening at all."

She turned, her steps shredding the mist like gray silk, and caught the scents of verbena, rosemary, and sage carried on the breeze from the tree branches.

Caught something else as well—a quiet hum that was almost like music.

"This is where you were the night of the solstice, before you came out to stand on the cliffs."

"This ground is hallowed," Mia told her. "It's said the sisters stood here, three hundred years and more past, and worked their spell to create their haven. Whether they did or not, I've always been drawn here. We'll cast the circle together. It's a basic ritual."

Mia drew her ritual knife from her pocket and began. Fascinated, Nell repeated the words, the gestures, and found herself unsurprised when a thin ring of light glowed through the smoke of the mist.

"We call on Air, on Earth, on Water and Fire to guard our circle and grant our desire. Here protect and witness this rite. Open our minds to the magic of night."

Mia laid down her knife, her wand, nodded to Nell after her chant was repeated. "You can cast your own circle in your own way, with your own words when you're ready. I hope you don't mind, but I prefer working skyclad when weather permits."

With this Mia slipped off her dress and folded it neatly while Nell gaped. "Oh, well, I don't really—"

"It's not required." At ease with her nakedness, Mia picked up her wand again. "I generally prefer it, particularly for this ritual."

There was a tattoo—a birthmark? Nell wondered. A small pentagram shape against the milk-white skin of her thigh.

"What ritual?"

"We'll draw down the moon. Some—most—usually do this when there's serious work to be done, but I sometimes need, or like, the extra burst of energy. To begin, open yourself. Mind, breath, heart, loin. Trust yourself. Every woman is ruled by the moon, just as the sea is. Hold your wand in your right hand."

Mirroring Mia's gestures, Nell lifted her arms, slowly raising them high, then clasping her wand with both hands.

"On this night, in this hour, we call upon Luna's power. Merge with us light into light." Slowly, the wands were turned, aimed at hearts. "Woman and goddess glowing bright. Power and joy pour down from thee. As we will, so mote it be."

She felt it, cool and fluid and strong, a flood of energy and light inside her. Pulsing, as that white ball of moon seemed to pulse as it rose gracefully above the trees. She could all but see it, blue-edged silver spurts of light that spun down and into her.

With the power came a rush of joy. It came out of Nell in a laughing gasp as Mia lowered her wand.

"Sometimes it's just lovely being a girl, isn't it? We'll close the circle now. I believe, little sister, you'll find an appropriate outlet for all that fresh energy."

When she was alone, Mia put her own energy to use working a protective spell. Nell had a great deal of natural power, largely untapped. She could and would help her explore it, control it, and refine it. But there was something more immediate preying on her mind now.

Within the circle, within the woods, she'd seen something Nell had not. She'd watched the single dark cloud slide over the heart of the moon.

Thirteen

The last weeks of summer passed in a blur. Days were filled with work, with plans for the jobs she'd won and proposals for more.

Once the weather turned she would lose the summer-people aspect of her business. So she would be the clever ant, Nell decided, who carefully prepared for winter.

She'd solicit jobs for holiday parties, for Super Bowl Sunday, for cabin fever victims. The islanders were growing so accustomed to calling her for their events, small and large, it would become strange to do otherwise.

Nights were nearly always spent with Zack—taking advantage of the final burst of warmth with candlelight dinners alfresco, evening sails made brisk from the chill rising from the water, long, luxurious lovemaking in the cozy nest of her bed.

Once she lit red candles for passion. They seemed to work exceptionally well.

At least two evenings a week she worked with Mia on what she thought of as her ritual lessons.

And at dawn she was baking in her kitchen.

The life she'd always looked for was all around her, and more. She had a power inside her that ran like silver. And love that glowed warm gold.

There were times she caught him watching her, quietly, patiently. The waiting look. Each time she did, there was a tug of guilt, a ripple of unease. And each time that she took the coward's way and ignored it, she disappointed both of them.

She could rationalize it. She was happy, and entitled to a time of peace and pleasure. Only a year before, she'd risked her life, and would have forfeited it, rather than live trapped and afraid.

For so many months following, she'd been alone, constantly on the move, wary of every sound. She awakened night after night in cold sweats from dreams she couldn't face even in the dark.

If she'd locked that time in a box and buried the key, who had a better right?

It was the now that mattered, and she was giving Zack all she could of the now.

As summer slipped into fall she was convinced of it, and of the solidity of her haven on Three Sisters.

With her latest kitchen catalogs and her new subscription to *Saveur* under her arm, Nell walked out of the post office and headed down High Street toward the market. The summer people had been replaced by tourists eager to view New England foliage at its peak.

She couldn't blame them. Wedges of the island were covered with a brilliant patchwork of flaming color. Every morning she studied the changes from her own kitchen window, dreaming into her own woods as the leaves took on fire. There were times she walked the beach in the evening just to see the slow roll of fog tumble in, swallow water, cloak the buoys, and muffle the long, monotonous *bongs*.

Mornings, a fine, glassy frost might glitter on the ground only to melt under the strengthening sun until it beaded on the grass like tears on lashes.

Rains swept in, pounded the beaches, the cliffs, then swept out again until it seemed to her that the whole of the world sparkled like something under a glass dome.

She was under that dome, Nell thought. Safe and secure and away from the world that raged beyond sea and inlet.

With the brisk wind sneaking up her sweater, she waved at familiar faces, paused briefly at the crosswalk to check traffic, then jogged carelessly into the market for the pork chops she intended to make for dinner.

Pamela Stevens, on an impromptu visit to the island with her husband, Donald, gave a little cry of surprise and rolled down the window of their rented BMW sedan.

"I'm not stopping at any of these shops, Pamela, no matter how quaint they are, until I find the right place to park."

"I've just seen a ghost." Pamela dropped back on the seat, laid a hand over her heart.

"It's witches around here, Pamela, not ghosts."

"No, no, Donald. Helen Remington. Evan Remington's wife. I'd swear I've just seen her ghost."

"Don't know why in God's name she would come all the way out here to haunt anybody. Can't even find a damn parking lot."

"I'm not joking. The woman could've been her double, except for the hair and the clothes. Helen wouldn't have been caught dead in that frightful sweater." She craned her neck to try to keep the market in sight. "Pull over, Donald. I've just got to go back and get a closer look."

"As soon as I find a parking place."

"It looked just like her," Pamela repeated. "So odd, and it gave me such a jolt. Poor Helen. I was one of the last people who spoke to her before that terrible accident."

"And so you said, a hundred times for six months after she drove off the cliff."

"Something like that stays with you." Bristling, Pamela straightened in her seat, sent her nose in the air. "I was very fond of her. She and Evan were a beautiful couple. She was so young and pretty, with everything to live for. When something tragic like that happens, it reminds you that lives can change with the snap of a finger."

By the time Pamela managed to drag her husband back to the market, Nell was unpacking her single bag of groceries and trying to decide between couscous and a spicy new sauce she wanted to try out on red potato wedges.

She decided to decide later, and flipping on the portable stereo Zack had left at her cottage, she settled down with Alanis Morissette and her issue of *Saveur*.

While she crunched on an apple from the basket on her table, she pulled over her notepad and began to scribble ideas sparked from an article on artichokes.

She moved from there to a feature on Australian wines and noted the writer's opinion of the best values.

The sound of footsteps didn't jolt her now, but gave her a warm feeling as she glanced over to watch Zack come in.

"A little early for the upholder of law and order to call it a day, isn't it?"

"I swapped some time with Ripley."

"What's in the box?"

"A present."

"For me?" Shoving her notebook aside, she got up, stepped hurriedly to the counter. Her mouth fell open. Love and lust tangled and burned inside her.

"A food processor. Commercial grade, top of the line." With reverent hands, she stroked the box the way some women might stroke mink. "Oh, my God."

"According to my mother, if a man gives a woman anything that plugs into an electric socket for a gift, he'd better be fully paid up on his life insurance. But I didn't think that rule applied here."

"It's the best on the market. I've wanted it forever."

"I've seen you ogling it in the catalog a few times." He caught her when she launched herself into his arms to cover his face with kisses. "I guess I'm not going to need that life insurance."

"I love it, I love it, I *love* it." She finished with a hard, smacking kiss, then leaped down to attack the box. "But it's outrageously expensive. I shouldn't let you give me an outrageously expensive present right out of the blue. But I'm going to because I can't stand the idea of not having it."

"It's rude to turn down a gift, and anyway, it's not out of the blue. A day early, but I didn't think that mattered. Happy birthday."

"My birthday's in April, but I'm not arguing because . . ."

She caught herself. The pulse began to throb in her temples, hot and hard. Helen Remington's birthday was in April. Nell Channing's was listed clearly on all identification as September nineteenth.

"I don't know what I was thinking. Slipped my mind." Because her palms sprang with damp, she wiped them hastily on her jeans. "I've been so busy, I forgot about my birthday."

All of his pleasure of giving her the gift curdled, left a sour ball in his belly. "Don't do that. Keeping things to yourself is one thing. Lying to my face is another."

"I'm sorry." She bit down hard on her lip, tasted shame.

"So am I." Because he wanted her to look at him, he cupped her chin, lifted it.

"I keep waiting for you to take the step, Nell, but you don't. You sleep with me, and you don't hold anything back there. You talk to me about what you hope to do tomorrow, and you listen when I talk to you. But there're no yesterdays."

He'd tried not to dwell on that, tried to tell himself, as he'd told Ripley, that it wasn't important. But now, slapped in the face with it, he couldn't pretend. "You let me into your life from the day you stepped onto the island."

It was true, perfectly true. What point would there be in denying it? "For me, my life started from there. Nothing before then matters anymore."

"If it didn't, you wouldn't have to lie to me."

Panic wanted to climb into her throat. She countered it with a snap of temper. "What difference does it make if my birthday's tomorrow, or a month from now, or six months ago? Why does it have to matter?"

"What matters is you don't trust me. That's hard on me, Nell, because I'm in love with you."

"Oh, Zack, you can't—"

"I'm in love with you," he repeated, taking her arms to hold her still. "And you know it."

And of course, that was perfectly true as well. "But I don't know what to do about it. I don't know what to do with what I feel for you. Trusting that, trusting you, it's not that simple. Not for me."

"You want me to accept that, but you don't want to tell me why it's not that simple. Play fair, Nell."

"I can't." A tear spilled over, shimmered down her cheek. "I'm sorry."

"If that's the way it is, we're both fooling ourselves."

He let her go and walked away.

Knocking on Zack's front door was one of the hardest things Nell had ever done. She'd spent so much time stepping back from anger. Now she would have to face it, head on. And with little defense. This was a turmoil she'd caused, and only she could resolve it.

She walked to the front of the house because it seemed more formal than strolling across the beach and up the stairs to the back. Before she knocked, she rubbed her fingers over the turquoise stone she'd slipped into her pocket to aid her verbal communication.

Though she wasn't convinced such things worked, she didn't see how it could make her situation any worse.

She lifted her hand, cursed herself as she lowered it again. There was an old rocker on the front porch, and a pot of geraniums that were frost-burned and pathetic. She wished she'd seen them before the weather had turned so she could have urged Zack to carry them inside.

And she was stalling.

She squared her shoulders, knocked.

Was torn between relief and despair when no one answered.

Just as she'd given up and turned away, the door swung open.

Ripley stood in leggings cropped just below the knee and a T-shirt marked with a vee of sweat between her breasts. She gave Nell one long, cool stare, then leaned on the doorjamb.

"Wasn't sure I heard anyone knock. I was lifting, and had the music up."

"I was hoping to talk to Zack."

"Yeah, I figured. You pissed him off good. It takes work to do that. Me, I've had years of practice, but you must have an innate talent for it."

Nell slipped her hand in her pocket, fingered the stone. She would have to get through the shield to get to the target. "I know he's angry with me, and he has a right to be. Don't I have a right to apologize?"

"Sure, but if you do it with choking little sobs and flutters, you're going to piss me off. I'm a lot meaner than Zack."

"I don't intend to cry and flutter." Nell's own temper bubbled up as she stepped forward. "And I don't think Zack would appreciate you getting in the middle of this. I know I don't."

"Good for you." Satisfied, Ripley shifted to let Nell in. "He's up on the back deck, brooding through his telescope and drinking a beer. But before you go up and say whatever you have to say to him, I'm going to tell you something. He could've looked into your background, picked the pieces apart. I would have. But he's got standards, personal standards, so he didn't."

The guilt that had settled on her since he'd walked out her door took on more weight. "He would've considered that rude."

"Right. I don't mind being rude. So you square this with him, or deal with me."

"Understood."

"I like you, and I respect someone who takes care of business. But when you mess with a Todd, you don't get off free. Fair warning."

Ripley turned toward the stairs leading to the second floor. "Help yourself to a beer on the way through the kitchen. I've got to finish my reps."

Nell skipped the beer, though she'd have relished a tall glass of ice water to ease the burn in her throat. She walked through the comfortably untidy living room, through the equally untidy kitchen, and took the outside steps up to the deck.

He sat in a big chair faded to gray by the weather, a bottle of Sam Adams nestled between his thighs and his scope tilted starward.

He knew she was there but didn't acknowledge her. The scent of her was peaches and nerves.

"You're angry with me, and I deserve it. But you're too fair not to listen."

"I might work my way up to fair by tomorrow. You'd be smarter to wait."

"I'll risk it." She wondered if he knew how much it meant—how much he meant—that she would risk it. "I lied. I've lied often and I've lied well, and I'd do it again. The choice was between honesty and survival. For me, it still is, so I'm not going to tell you everything you need to know. Everything you deserve to know. I'm sorry."

"If two people don't trust each other, they've got no business being together."

"That's easy for you to say, Zack."

When he shifted his gaze from the stars to hers, and the heat of it scorched her, she stepped closer. Her heart throbbed. She didn't fear that he would strike her. But she did fear that he'd never want to touch her again.

"No, damn it, it is easy for you. You've got your place here. You've always had it, and you don't have to question it, or fight for it."

"If I've got a place," he said in careful, measured tones, "I've had to earn it. The same as anyone."

"That's different, because you started on a foundation, a solid one, and built from there. These past few months I've been working to earn a place here. I have earned it. But it's different."

"Okay, maybe it is. But you and I started on the same ground, Nell, when it comes to what we were making together."

Were making, she thought. Not are making. If this was his line she could stand where she was, keep on her side of it, or take the first step over.

It wasn't any harder, she decided, than driving off a cliff.

"I was with a man, for three years. I was with a man who hurt me. Not just the slaps and the shoves. Those kinds of bruises don't last. But others do."

She had to let out a little breath to ease the pressure in her chest. "He systematically chipped away at my confidence, my self-esteem, my courage and my choices, and he did it so skillfully they were gone before I realized what was happening. It's not easy to rebuild those things, and I'm still working on it. Coming here, just walking over here tonight took everything I've managed to store up. I shouldn't have gotten involved with you, and I didn't intend to. But something about being here, and about being with you, made me feel normal again."

"That's the start of a fine speech. Why don't you sit down and just talk to me."

"I did what I had to do to get away from him. I'm not going to apologize for it."

"I'm not asking you to."

"I'm not going into the details." She turned away, leaned on the rail and stared out at the night-dark sea. "I'll tell you it was like living in a pit that got deeper and deeper and colder and colder. Whenever I tried to crawl out, he was right there."

"But you found a way."

"I won't go back. Whatever I have to do, wherever I have to run, I won't go back. So I've lied, and deceived. I've broken the law. And I've hurt you." She turned back. "The only thing I'm sorry for is the last."

She said it defiantly, almost furiously as she stood with her back to the rail and her hands in white-knuckled fists.

Terror and courage, he thought, dragging at each other inside her. "Did you think I wouldn't understand?"

"Zack." She lifted her hands, dropped them. "*I* still don't understand. I wasn't a doormat when I met him, I wasn't a victim waiting to be exploited. I came from a solid, steady family, as functional as any family manages to be. I was educated, independent, helping to run a business. There'd been men in my life before, nothing really serious, but normal, healthy relationships. Then there I was, manipulated and abused. And trapped."

Oh, baby, he thought, as he had when she'd fallen to pieces in the café kitchen. "Why are you still blaming yourself for it?"

The question broke her rhythm. For a moment she could only stare at him, baffled. "I don't know." She walked over to sit in the chair beside him.

"It'd be a good next step to stop doing that." He said it easily, taking a sip of his beer. There was still temper inside him, dregs of it for Nell, but a new and ripe well of it for the man—the faceless, nameless entity—who'd scarred her.

He thought he might work that off later by pounding the hell out of Ripley's punching bag.

"Why don't you tell me about your family?" he suggested and offered her the beer. "You know my mother can't cook worth a damn and my father likes to take snapshots with his new toy. You know they grew up here on the island, got married, and had a couple of kids. And you've had personal acquaintance with my sister."

"My father was in the Army. He was a lieutenant colonel."

"An Army brat." Since she shook her head at the beer, he took another pull himself. "Saw some of the world, didn't you?"

"Yeah, we moved around a lot. He always liked getting new orders. Something new to handle, I suppose. He was a good man, very steady, with a wonderful, warm laugh. He liked old Marx Brothers movies and Reese's peanut butter cups. Oh, God."

Grief caught her by the throat, choked off her voice, dug raw wounds in her stomach.

"He's been gone so long, I don't know how it could seem like yesterday."

"When you love somebody, it's always there. I still think about my grandmother now and again." He took Nell's hand, held it loosely. "When I do, I can smell her. Lavender water and peppermint. She died when I was fourteen."

How was it he could understand, and so exactly? That, she thought, was the magic of him. "My father was killed in the Gulf War. I thought he was invincible. He'd always seemed to be. Everyone said he was a good soldier, but I remember he was a good father. He would always listen if I needed to tell him something. He was honest and fair, and had this code of honor, a personal one that meant more than all the rules and regulations. He . . . God." She turned her head to study Zack's face. "It just hit me, how much you're like him. He would have approved of you, Sheriff Todd."

"I'm sorry I never got the chance to meet him." He turned the scope toward her. "Why don't you take a look, see what you can find up there?"

She lowered her head toward the viewer, scanned the stars. "You've forgiven me."

"Let's say we've made some progress."

"Good thing for me. Otherwise Ripley was going to kick my ass."

"And she's a hell of an ass-kicker, too."

"She loves you. I always wanted a brother or a sister. My mother and I were tight, and I guess we got tighter after we lost my father. But I always wanted a sister. You'd've liked my mother. She was tough and smart and full of fun. Started her own business from the ground up after she was widowed. And she made it work."

"Sounds like someone else I know."

Her lips curved. "My father always said I took after her. Zack, who I am now is who I was before. The three years between, they were the aberration. You wouldn't recognize the person I became during that lost time. I barely do."

"Maybe you had to go through it to get where you are now."

"Maybe." The light through the scope haloed as her eyes misted. "I feel like I was always headed here. All those moves when I was growing up. I'd look around and think: No, this isn't it. Not yet. The day I crossed over on the ferry, and I saw the island floating on the water, I knew. This is my place."

He lifted their joined hands, kissed the back of hers. "The day I saw you behind the counter in the café, I knew."

The thrill rocketed up her arm, and straight into her heart. "I've got baggage, Zack. I've got complications. More than I can tell you. You matter to me more than I thought anyone ever could. I don't want to mess up your life with my problems."

"From where I'm sitting, Nell, it's too late to worry about that. I'm in love with you."

Another long thrill rippled through her. "There's so much you don't know, and any one piece of it could change your mind."

"You don't think much of my wherewithal."

"Oh, yes, I do. Okay." She pulled her hand away, rose. She faced crises better on her feet. "There's something else I can tell you, and I don't expect you to understand or accept it."

"You're a kleptomaniac."

"No."

"An agent for a clandestine splinter group."

She managed to laugh. "No. Zack—"

"Wait, I get one more. You're one of those *Star Trek* addicts who can recite all the dialogue in every episode."

"No, only in the first season of the original."

"Well, that's all right, then. Okay, I give up."

"I'm a witch."

"Oh, well, I know that."

"I'm not using that as a euphemism for temperament," she said impatiently. "I mean it literally. Spells and charms and that sort of thing. A witch."

"Yeah, I got that the night you were dancing naked on your front lawn and glowing like a candle. Nell, I've lived on Three Sisters all my life. Do you expect me to be stupefied, or to do that crossed-fingers thing to ward off evil?"

Unsure if she was relieved or disappointed by his reaction, she frowned at him. "I guess I expected you to be something."

"It gave me a moment," he admitted. "But then, living with Rip sort of tones down the jolt. Of course she hasn't had anything to do with that kind of thing for years now. If you were to tell me you'd put some sort of love spell on me, I might be a little irked."

"Of course I didn't. I wouldn't even know how. I'm just . . . learning."

"An apprentice witch, then." Amused at both of them, he got to his feet. "I imagine Mia'll whip you into shape before long."

Did nothing surprise the man? "A couple of nights ago, I drew down the moon."

"What the hell does that mean? No, never mind, I don't have much of a head for the metaphysical. I'm a simple man, Nell." He ran his hands up and down her arms in the way he had that managed to arouse and soothe at the same time.

"No, you're not."

"Simple enough to know I'm standing here with a pretty woman and wasting the moonlight." He lowered his mouth to hers, drew her up and into a sumptuous kiss.

When her head fell back in surrender, and her arms wound around his neck, he circled her toward the glass door.

"I want to take you to bed. My bed. I want to love you—the Army brat who takes after her mother." He slid the door open, drew her inside. "I do love you."

Here, she thought as they lowered to the bed, was truth. And here was compassion. He would give these to her, as much as desire, as much as need. When he touched her, those thrills, those soft and fluid aches, were welcome.

The yearning she'd felt for home was satisfied.

Slow and sweet she moved with him. Freely, she opened for him, baring her heart as well as her body.

Her skin hummed under the brush of his fingers. The long, liquid pull inside her made her sigh. When her mouth met his again, she poured all she had into the kiss. What she couldn't give him in words, she could give him here, with her heart. With her body.

He skimmed his lips over her shoulder, tracing the shape of it, marveling at the firmness of muscle, the delicacy of bone. The taste of her intoxicated him, a flavor he'd come to crave as much as the next breath of air.

He found her breast, pleasured them both with lips and teeth and tongue until her heart began to beat under his mouth like the endless pulse of the sea. And as that beat quickened, she rose beneath him with a single breathless gasp.

Without hurry, he moved down her. A skim of fingers, a brush of lips. Felt her begin to tremble while his own blood pounded in sharp, anvil strikes of need.

Her hands groped, then fisted desperately in the sheets when he lifted her hips and used his mouth on her. With a kind of ruthless patience, he shot her screaming to peak.

Her breath was sobbing now, her skin slick and damp as she rolled with him over the tangled sheets. Heat spiked, seemed to throb in the air, under her skin until her body felt like a furnace stoked too high.

"Zack—"

"Not yet. Not yet."

He was wild for her, for the taste of flesh, the urgency of her hands. In the pale splash of moonlight through the glass, her body seemed unearthly, white marble erotically hot to the touch and glimmering with the healthy sweat of lust.

When he fixed his teeth on her neck, it felt like feeding. Her mouth was wild, her body plunging. Then she cried out again, shocked pleasure, when his fingers drove her relentlessly over the edge.

Beyond control, beyond reason, she moved like lightning. She would have sworn the bed spun, in fast, dizzy circles, as she straddled him. Panting, she took him, rode him, drove him as he had driven her. Curved down to him, she ravished his mouth, then flung herself back, arms bowed behind her head, and flew as power whipped through her.

He reached for her, his fingers sliding helplessly down her busy hips. His blood was a rage, his mind a torrent. For a moment, all he could see was her eyes, flame-blue and vivid as jewels.

He reared up, pressed his lips to her heart, and shattered.

Fourteen

Ripley stopped her cruiser and watched Nell unpack her car. The sun had gone down, and with the cold snap that had slapped the island with a wicked northeast punch, any tourists were snuggled into the hotel sipping hot drinks.

Most of the natives would be sensibly settled in front of the television or finishing up dinner. She was looking forward to engaging in both those activities herself.

But she hadn't managed a one-on-one with Nell since the evening she'd come to the door.

"You're either getting a very late start or a really early one," Ripley called out.

Nell hefted the box and hunched inside the fleece-lined jacket she'd mail-ordered from the mainland. "A second start. The book club that Mia runs is back from its summer break. First meeting's tonight."

"Oh, yeah." Ripley got out of the car. She was wearing an ancient and well-loved bomber jacket and hiking boots. Her summer-weight ball cap had been replaced by one of plain black wool. "Need a hand?"

"I wouldn't turn one down." Happy that she sensed no lingering animosity, Nell gestured with her elbow to the second box. "Refreshments for the meeting. Are you going?"

"Not a chance."

"Don't like to read?"

"No, I like to read, I just don't like groups. Groups are made up of members," she explained. "And members are almost always people. So there you go."

"People you know," Nell pointed out.

"Which gives my stand a firmer base. This group's a bunch of hens who'll spend as much time pecking at the latest gossip as they will discussing whatever book they used as an excuse to get out of the house for the evening."

"How do you know that if you don't belong to the club?"

"Let's just say I have a sixth sense about these things."

"All right." Nell adjusted the balance of her box as they walked toward the rear entrance. Despite the weather, Mia's salvia hung on, as red and sassy as July. "Is that why you don't accept the Craft? Because it's like joining a group?"

"That would be reason enough. Added to that, I don't like being told I have to fall in line with something that started three hundred years before I was born."

A blast of wind blew her ponytail into a thick, dark whip. She ignored it, and the cold fingers that tried to sneak under her jacket. "I figure whatever needs to be dealt with can and should be dealt with without cackling over a cauldron, and I don't like having people wondering if I'm going to come flying by on my broom wearing a pointy black hat."

"I can't argue with the first two reasons." Nell opened the door, stepped into the welcome warmth. "But the second two don't hold. I've never once heard Mia cackle, over a cauldron or otherwise, and I've never seen anyone look at her as if they expected her to jump on a broom."

"Wouldn't surprise me if she did." Ripley strode into the main store, nodded at Lulu. "Lu."

"Rip." Lulu continued setting up the folding chairs. "Joining us tonight?"

"Are they holding the Ice Capades in hell?"

"Not that I've heard." She sniffed the air. "Do I smell ginger-bread?"

"Got it in one," Nell told her. "Is there any special way you want the refreshments set up?"

"You're the expert there. Mia's upstairs yet. If she doesn't like the way you've done it, she'll tell you."

Nell carried the box to the table that was already waiting. She'd made some pricks in Lulu's shell, but had yet to crack all the way through. It was, she admitted, becoming a personal challenge.

"Do you think I can stay for some of the discussion?"

Lulu peered narrowly over the tops of her glasses. "You read the book?"

Damn. Nell took out the plate of gingerbread first, hoping the scent would sweeten her chances. "Well, no. I didn't know about the club until last week, and—"

"A person's got an hour a day that can be put to reading. I don't care how busy they are."

"Oh, stop being such a bitch, Lulu."

Nell's jaw dropped at Ripley's command, but the sidelong look she risked showed her Lulu's reaction was a happy grin.

"I can't. It goes down to the bone. You can stay if this one stays." She jerked a thumb at Ripley.

"I'm not interested in hanging out with a bunch of females chattering about a book and who's sleeping with who, who shouldn't be. Besides, I haven't had my dinner."

"Café's open another ten minutes," Lulu told her. "Split pea and ham soup was good today. And it'll do you good to spend some time with females. Explore your inner woman."

Ripley snorted. But the idea of the soup—in fact, any food that she wasn't obliged to fix herself—held tremendous appeal. "My inner woman doesn't need any exploration. She's lean and mean. But I'll check out the soup."

She sauntered toward the steps. "I might stay for the first twenty minutes," she called back. "But if I do, I want first crack at that gingerbread."

"Lulu?" Nell arranged star-shaped cookies on a glass plate.

"What?"

"I'll call you a bitch if it'll help bring us closer as people willing to explore our inner woman."

Lulu gave a snort of her own. "You've got a quick mouth on you when you want to. You carry your weight and you keep your word. That goes a way with me."

"I also make superior gingerbread."

Lulu walked over, picked up a slice. "I'll be the judge of that. See that you read October's book before the next discussion."

Nell's dimples flickered. "I will."

Upstairs, Ripley annoyed Peg by demanding a bowl of soup minutes before closing.

"I've got a date, so if you don't finish this before my time's up, you'll just have to wash the bowl yourself."

"I can dump it in the sink the same as you would, for Nell to deal with in the morning. Give me a hot chocolate to go with it. Are you still stepping out with Mick Burmingham?"

"That's right. We're snugging in and having a video festival. We're watching *Scream One*, *Two*, and *Three*."

"Very sexy. If you want to take off, I won't snitch to Mia."

Peg didn't hesitate. "Thanks." She whipped off her apron. "I'm gone."

Appreciating the fact that the café was empty, Ripley settled down to enjoy her soup in blissful solitude. Nothing could have spoiled her pleasure more quickly than hearing the click of Mia's heels on the floor barely one minute later.

"Where's Peg?"

"I cut her loose. Hot date."

"I don't appreciate you giving my employees permission to leave early. The café doesn't close for another four minutes, and it's part of her job description to clean the case, counters, and kitchen after that time."

"Well, I booted her along, so you can kick my ass instead of hers." Intrigued, Ripley continued to spoon up soup as she studied Mia.

It was a rare event to see the cool Ms. Devlin heated up, and jittery. She was twisting the chain of the amulet she wore around her neck, continued to worry it as she strode over to the display counter and hissed.

"There are health regulations about cleanliness in food services. Since you were so generous to Peg, you can damn well scrub this up yourself."

"In a pig's eye," Ripley muttered, but felt a tug of guilt that threatened to spoil her appetite. "What bug crawled up your butt?"

"I have a business to run here, and it takes more than stalking around the village looking cocky, which is your specialty."

"Oh, get fucked, Mia. It'll improve your humor."

Mia rounded back. "Unlike you, fucking isn't my answer to every whim and itch."

"You want to play the ice maiden because Sam Logan dumped you, that's your . . ." Ripley trailed off, despising herself even as the hot color in Mia's face drained. "Sorry. Out of line. Way out of line."

"Forget it."

"When I sucker punch somebody, I apologize. Even if you did come in here looking for a fight. In fact, I'll not only apologize, I'll ask you what's wrong."

"What the hell do you care?"

"Normally, I don't. But normally I don't see you spooked. What's the deal?"

They'd been friends once, and good ones. As close as any sisters. Because of that it was harder for Mia to sit, to open up, than it would have been if Ripley had been a stranger.

But the matter was more important than feuds or grudges. She sat across from Ripley, leveled her gaze. "There's blood on the moon."

"Oh, for—"

Before Ripley could finish, Mia's hand shot out, gripped her wrist. "Trouble, bad trouble is coming. A dark force. You know me well enough to be sure I wouldn't say it, wouldn't tell you, of all people, unless I was sure."

"And you know me well enough to know what I think of portents and omens." But there was a cold chill working up her spine.

"It's coming, after the leaves finish dying, before the first snow. I'm sure of that, too, but I can't see what it is, or where it comes from. Something's blocking it."

It disturbed Ripley when Mia's eyes went that deep, that dark. It seemed you could see a thousand years in them. "Any trouble comes to the island, Zack and I will handle it."

"It'll take more. Ripley, Zack loves Nell and you love him. They're at the center of this. I feel it. If you don't flex, something will break.

Something none of us can put right again. I can't do whatever needs to be done alone, and Nell isn't ready yet."

"I can't help you that way."

"Won't."

"Can't or won't comes out to the same thing."

"Yes, it does," Mia said as she got to her feet. There wasn't temper sparking her eyes; that would have been easy to fight. There was weariness. "Deny what you are, lose what you are. I sincerely hope you don't regret it."

Mia went downstairs to greet her book club and deal with the business at hand.

Alone, Ripley rested her chin on her fist. It was a guilt trip, that was all. When Mia wasn't shooting out spiteful little darts, she heaped on layers of sticky guilt. Ripley wasn't falling for it. If there was a red haze over the moon, it was due to some atmospheric quirk and had nothing to do with her.

She would leave the omens and portents to Mia since she enjoyed them so much.

She shouldn't have dropped in tonight, shouldn't have put herself in a position where Mia could try to pin her. All they did was annoy each other. It had been that way for more than a decade.

But not always.

They'd been friends, next to inseparable friends, until they'd teetered on the cusp of adulthood. Ripley remembered her mother had called them twins of the heart. They'd shared everything, and maybe that was the problem.

It was natural for interests to diverge when people grew up, natural for childhood friends to drift apart. Not that she and Mia had drifted, she admitted. It had been more like a sword slash down the center of their friendship. Abrupt and violent.

But she'd had the right to go her own way. She'd *been* right to go her own way. And she wasn't going back now just because Mia was jittery over some atmospheric hitch.

Even if Mia was right and trouble was coming, it would be dealt with through the rules and obligations of the law, and not with spell-binding.

She had put away her childish things, the toys and the tools she had no further interest in. That had been sensible, mature. When people looked at her now, they saw Ripley Todd, deputy, a dependable, responsible woman who did her job; they didn't see some flaky island priestess who would brew them a potion to beef up their sex lives.

Irritated because even her thoughts sounded defensive and nasty, she gathered up her dishes and took them into the kitchen. There was just enough guilt still pricking at her to oblige her to rinse the dishes, load them in the dishwasher, scrub out the sink.

That, she decided, paid her debt.

She could hear the voices, all female, flowing back from the front of the store where the book club gathered. She could smell the incense Mia lit, a scent for protection. Ripley snuck out the back. A fleet of steamrollers couldn't have pushed her forward and into that noisy clutch of women now.

Just outside the back door she saw the fat black candle burning, a charm to repel evil. She would have sneered at it, but her gaze was drawn up.

The waning globe of the moon was shrouded in a thin and bloody mist.

Unable to work up that sneer, she jammed her hands in her jacket pockets and stared down at her own boots as she walked to her car.

When the last of the book club members were out the door, Mia flipped the locks. Nell was already clearing plates and napkins while Lulu closed the register.

"That was fun!" Stoneware rang gaily as Nell stacked coffee cups. "And so interesting. I've never discussed a book that way. Whenever I read one, I just think, well, I liked it or I didn't, but I never talked about why. And I promise to read next month's selection so I'll have something to contribute."

"I'll see to the dishes, Nell. You must be tired."

"I'm not." Nell lifted a loaded tray. "There was so much energy in here tonight. I feel like I just lapped it up."

"Isn't Zack waiting for you?"

"Oh, not tonight. I told him I was going to crash the party."

Lulu waited until Nell was upstairs. "What's wrong?" she asked Mia.

"I'm not entirely sure." To keep her hands busy, Mia began folding the chairs. "That's what concerns me most. Something's coming, and I can't pin it down. It's all right for tonight." She glanced up the stairs as she carted chairs to the storeroom. "She's all right for tonight."

"She's the center." Lulu stored her own haul of chairs. "I guess I felt that all along, and didn't cut her much of a break. But the fact is, that's a sweet girl who works hard. Does somebody want to hurt her?"

"Someone already has, and I don't intend to let him do it again. I'll try a foretelling, but I need to prepare for it. I need to clear my mind. There's time. I can't tell how much, but it'll have to be enough."

"Will you tell her?"

"Not just yet. She'll have her own preparations, her own cleansing to do. She's in love, and that makes her strong. She'll need to be."

"What makes you strong, Mia?"

"Purpose. Love never worked for me."

"I heard he's in New York."

Mia shrugged, a deliberate gesture. She knew who Lulu meant, and it irritated her to have Sam Logan tossed at her twice in one night.

"It's a big city," she said flatly. "He'll have plenty of company. I want to finish and go home. I need sleep."

"Idiot man," Lulu muttered under her breath. There were too many idiot men in the world, to her way of thinking. And most of them ended up bumping up against stubborn women.

Spells were, Nell decided, really just a kind of recipe. And there she was on solid ground. A recipe required time, care, and quality ingredients in proper proportions for success. Add a bit of imagination and it became a personal dish.

She set aside time between jobs and book work to study the spell book Mia had lent her. She imagined Mia would be amused by the idea of viewing it as a kind of metaphysical cookbook, but she didn't think she would be offended.

Time also had to be carved out for meditation, visualization, for gathering and creating her own tools so that she'd have what she liked to consider a well-supplied witch's pantry.

But now she intended to reward herself with her first solo practice session.

"Love spells, banishing spells, protection spells," she chanted as she flipped through. "Binding spells, money spells, healing spells."

Something for everybody, she thought, and remembered Mia's warning about being careful what she wished for. A careless or selfish wish could boomerang in unpleasant, or certainly unexpected, ways.

She would keep it simple, choosing something that involved no one and couldn't inadvertently cause harm or trouble.

She used her broom first, sweeping the negative energy away, then she set it by the kitchen door to prevent any reentry. With Diego ribboning between her legs, she chose her candles, inscribed them with the appropriate symbols. Deciding that she could use all the help she could get, she selected crystals to bolster the energy. She arranged them, and the pot of frost-burned geraniums she'd taken from Zack's front porch.

Expelled a breath, drew in fresh.

She referred back to the healing spell Mia had written out on parchment in India ink and, closing her eyes, adjusted the words in her mind to suit her purpose.

"Here goes," she whispered.

"This damaged bloom I seek to heal, from its withered petals fresh beauty reveal. Um . . . its blooming time was too soon done, its color brings pleasure to all and harm to no one. Set the flower within it free. As I will, so mote it be."

She bit her lip, waited. The geranium sat stubbornly wilted in its pot. Nell bent over, looking close for some little sign of green.

She straightened again. "Shoot. I guess I'm not ready to solo."

But maybe she should try again. She needed to visualize, to *see* the plant lush and full and blooming. She needed to smell leaves and petals, channel her energy. Or was it the plant's energy? In any case, giving up after one try made her a pretty wimpy witch.

She closed her eyes again, started to process, then yelped at the brisk knock on her back door. She spun around so quickly, she booted Diego halfway across the little room, which caused him to plop down and begin to wash himself as if that was what he'd intended all along.

Chuckling, Nell opened the door to Ripley.

"I was cruising by, saw the candlelight. Are you having power trouble?" Even as she asked, she looked past Nell and saw the ritual candles on the table. "Oh."

"Practicing, and from the results, I need a lot more. Come on in."

"I don't want to interrupt." Since the night of the book club meeting she'd made a point to stop by, or at least cruise by, every evening. "Isn't that the dead plant from our front porch?"

"It's not dead yet, but it's close. I asked Zack if I could try to bring it back."

"Working spells on dead geraniums? Man, you slay me."

"I figured if I made any mistakes, it couldn't hurt anything. Do you want some tea? I brewed some just a while ago."

"Well, maybe. Zack said to let you know he'd be by when he finished up. We had a D and D—drunk and disorderly," she explained. "Underage minor. He's just about sicked up all of the six-pack he swiped from his parents' refrigerator. Zack's walking him home."

"Anyone I know?"

"The Stubens boy, the oldest. His girlfriend dumped him yesterday, so he decided to cry in his daddy's beer. Since the result was him getting sick as three dogs, I think he'll look for another way to ease his broken heart next time out. What's that smell?"

"I've got a pork loin roasting. You're welcome to stay for dinner."

"I'd just as soon not sit here and watch you two make googly eyes at each other. But I wouldn't mind you sending a doggie bag home with Zack."

"Happy to." She handed Ripley a cup of tea. "But we don't make googly eyes at each other."

"Do so."

Nell got a plate of tiny appetizers out of the fridge.

"Man, do you guys eat like this every night?" Ripley asked.

"I practice on Zack."

"Lucky bastard." Ripley helped herself to a little wedge of bruschetta. "Anything he doesn't go for, you can send on to me. I'll let you know if it's any good."

"That's generous of you. Try a stuffed mushroom. Zack won't touch them."

"Doesn't know what he's missing," Ripley announced after one bite. "The catering deal's moving along pretty well, huh?"

"It is." But Nell dreamed of a convection oven and a Sub-Zero refrigerator. Impossible and impractical in her cozy cottage kitchen, she reminded herself. And, for the moment, out of Sisters Catering's financial grasp. "I'm doing sandwiches and cake for a christening on Saturday."

"The new Burmingham baby."

"Right. And Lulu's sister and family from Baltimore are coming in next week. Lulu wants to wow them. There's some sibling rivalry there." Nell jerked a thumb toward the oven. "I'm making this pork loin, so I wanted to try it out first."

"That's going some for Lu. She squeezes a penny until Lincoln weeps."

"We worked out a deal, a barter. She's knitting me a couple of sweaters. I can use them with winter coming."

"We've got a warm spell coming. We'll snag a bit of Indian summer before it hits."

"I hope you're right."

"So . . ." Ripley bent down, picked up Diego. "How's Mia doing?"

"She's fine. She seems a little distracted lately." Nell lifted her eyebrows. "Why do you ask?"

"No reason. I guess she's busy making plans for Halloween. She really gets into it."

"We're going to decorate the store the week of the first. I'm warned that every kid on the island hits Café Book for trick or treat."

"Who can resist candy from the witch? I'd better go." She gave Diego a quick scratch as she set him down. "Zack'll be along any minute. I can take that pot out of your way if you . . ." She trailed off as she glanced over.

A glory of crimson petals covered healthy green stalks. "Well, well, son of a bitch."

"I did it! It worked. Oh! Oh!" In one leap Nell was at the table, her nose buried in blooms. "I can't believe it. I mean, I wanted to believe it, but I didn't really think I could manage it. Not by myself. Isn't it lovely?"

"Yeah, it's okay."

She knew what it was like, the rush of power, that bright thrill. The pleasures, both small and huge. Ripley felt an echo of it now as Nell lifted the pot high and circled.

"It's not all flowers and moonbeams, Nell."

"What happened?" Nell lowered the pot, cradled it like a baby. "What happened to make you resent what you have?"

"I don't resent it. I just don't want it."

"I've been powerless. This is better."

"What's better isn't being able to make flowers bloom. It's being able to take care of yourself. You didn't need a spell book to figure out how to do that."

"One doesn't have to be exclusive of the other."

"Maybe not. But life's a hell of a lot easier when they are." She walked to the door, opened it. "Don't leave your candles unattended."

By the time Zack arrived, Nell had the table cleared and set. The kitchen was fragrant with her roast and the aftermath of her candles.

She liked hearing him come to the kitchen door, those long strides. The way he stopped and wiped his feet on the mat. The rush of brisk air he let in when he opened the door. And the easy smile he gave her as he kept on walking until his mouth covered hers.

"Later than I expected."

"It's all right. Ripley stopped by and told me you would be."

"Then I guess I don't need these." He took the bouquet of carnations from behind his back.

"No, but I do." She gathered them up. "Thanks. I thought we'd try this Australian wine I read about, if you want to open it."

"Fine." He turned to shrug out of his jacket and hang it on the kitchen peg. His gaze hit the pot of geraniums she'd set on the side counter. It gave him a little jolt, but after the briefest hesitation, he went on and pegged his jacket. "I don't guess you did that with fertilizer."

"No." She linked her fingers together around the carnation stems. "I didn't. Does it bother you?"

"Not bother. But talking about it, even knowing about it's different than seeing it." At home in her kitchen, he pulled open a drawer for a corkscrew. "In any case, you don't have to smooth out every ripple with me."

"I love you, Zack."

He stood, the corkscrew in one hand, the bottle of wine in the other. And suddenly couldn't move. Emotions overwhelmed him.

"It's been hard waiting for you to say that to me."

"I couldn't say it before."

"Why now?"

"Because you brought me carnations. Because I don't have to smooth out every ripple with you. Because when I hear you coming up to my door everything inside me lifts and sighs. And because love is the most vital magic. I want to give mine to you."

He set the wine and corkscrew aside carefully, stepped over to her. Gently, he stroked his hands across her cheeks, into her hair. "I've waited my whole life for you." Tenderly, he kissed her forehead, her cheeks. "I want to spend the rest of it with you."

She ignored the clutch in her belly and concentrated on the joy. "Let's give each other the now. Every minute's precious." She laid her head on his shoulder. "Every minute counts."

Fifteen

Evan Remington wandered the palatial rooms of his Monterey home. Bored, restless, he studied his possessions. Each one had been selected with care, either by him personally or by a decorator following explicit instructions.

He had always known precisely what he preferred, and precisely what he wanted. He'd always made certain to obtain it. Whatever the cost, whatever the effort.

Everything that surrounded him reflected his taste, a taste admired by associates, peers, and those whose goal it was to fall into either category.

And everything dissatisfied him.

He considered an auction. He could find some currently trendy charity and generate some nice press while he disposed of items he no longer wanted. He could let it leak that he was disposing of those items because they held too many painful memories of his dead wife.

The lovely, lost Helen.

He even considered selling the house. The fact was, it did remind him of her. It wasn't a problem in Los Angeles. She hadn't died in Los Angeles.

Since her accident, he had seldom come to Monterey. It was rare for him to stay more than a few days, and he always came alone. He didn't consider the servants. They fell along the same lines as the furnishings to him. Necessary and efficient.

The first time he'd come back, he'd been raw with grief. He'd wept like a madman while lying across the bed he'd last shared with her, clinging to the nightgown she'd worn. Breathing in the scent of her.

His love was consuming, and his pain threatened to eat him alive. She had *belonged* to him.

When the torrent had passed, he'd wandered the house like a ghost, touching what she had touched, hearing her voice echo in his ears, catching a whiff of her scent everywhere. As if it were inside him.

He'd spent an hour in her closet, caressing her clothes. And forgetting the night he had locked her in there when she'd been late coming home.

He wallowed in her, and when he could stand the confinement of the house no longer, he'd driven to the site of her death. And had stood, a solitary figure, weeping on the cliffs.

His doctor prescribed medication and rest. His friends encircled him with sympathy.

He began to enjoy it.

Within a month, he'd forgotten he had insisted that Helen make the trip to Big Sur that day. In his mind, in the cradle of his memory, he saw himself entreating her not to attend, to stay home and rest until she was well again.

Of course, she hadn't listened. She had never listened.

Grief turned to fury, a raging flood of anger that he drowned with liquor and solitude. She'd betrayed him, going out against his wishes, insisting on attending some frivolous party rather than respecting her husband's request.

She had left him unforgivably alone.

But even rage passes. The hole it left in him he filled with a fantasy of her, of their marriage, even of himself. He heard people speak of them as a perfect couple, cruelly parted by tragedy.

He read it, thought it. Believed it.

He wore one of her earrings on a chain next to his heart and let the affectation leak to a suitable media source. It was said Gable did the same when he'd lost Lombard.

He kept her clothes in her closets, her books on the shelves, her perfumes in their bottles. He had an angel of white marble erected for her in the cemetery where no body lay. Every week, a dozen red roses were placed at its feet.

To keep himself sane, he threw himself into his work. He began to sleep again, without so many dreams in which Helen came to him. Gradually, at the urging of friends, he began to go out again socially.

But the women eager to comfort the widower didn't interest him. He dated only because it kept him in the press. He bedded a few of the women only because there would be talk otherwise, of an unflattering sort.

Sex had never driven him. Control had.

He had no wish ever to marry again. There would never be another Helen. They had been destined for each other. She'd been meant for him, meant to be molded and formed by him. If he'd had to punish her occasionally—well, discipline was part of the formation. He'd had to teach her.

Finally, in their last few weeks together, he had believed she had learned. It had been a rare thing for her to make a mistake, in public or private. She'd deferred to him as a wife was meant to defer to a husband, and had made certain that he was pleased with her.

He remembered, or convinced himself that he remembered, that he'd been about to reward her with a trip to Antigua. She had been fascinated by the ocean, his Helen. And had told him, during those first heady weeks of love and discovery, how she sometimes dreamed of living on an island.

In the end, the sea had taken her.

Because he could feel the depression rolling into him like a fog, he poured a glass of mineral water and took one of his pills.

No, he wouldn't sell the house, he decided in one of his lightning mood changes. He would open it. He would give one of the lavish, A-list parties, the kind he and Helen had hosted so often and so successfully.

It would feel as if she were there beside him, as she was meant to be.

When the phone rang, he ignored it and continued to stand, gently rubbing an etched gold hoop earring through the fine linen of his shirt.

"Sir? Ms. Reece is on the phone. She'd like to speak with you if you're available."

Saying nothing, Evan held out a hand for the portable phone. He never glanced at the uniformed maid who gave it to him, but slid open the terrace door and stepped outside in the balm of breeze to speak to his sister.

"Yes, Barbara?"

"Evan, I'm glad you were in. Deke and I were hoping you'd join us at the club this afternoon. We can have a set of tennis, lunch by the pool. I hardly see my baby brother these days."

He started to refuse. His sister's country club circle held little interest for him. But he reconsidered quickly, knowing how well Barbara planned entertainment. And how much of the annoyance of the details she would willingly take from his hands.

"I'd like that. I want to speak to you anyway." He glanced at his Rolex. "Why don't I meet you there. Eleven thirty?"

"Absolutely perfect. Prepare yourself. I've been working on my backhand."

His tennis game was off. Barbara had broken his serve yet again and was prancing around like a fool in her designer tennis skirt. Of course, *she* had time to fritter around any fucking day of the week, making time with some slick-fingered tennis pro while her asshole husband practiced his putting.

He, on the other hand, was a busy man, with a demanding business and high-powered clients who whined like babies if he didn't give them his full attention.

He didn't have time for goddamn games.

He bulleted one over the net, gritted his teeth audibly when Barbara hustled and returned it. Sweat dampened his face, ran down his back. And his mouth peeled back in a snarl as he raced over the court.

It was a look Nell would have recognized. One she would have feared.

Barbara recognized it as well and instinctively bungled a return. "You're killing me," she called out, and shook her head as she took her time going back to position.

Evan had always been temperamental, she thought. It was hard for him not to win, not to get his way. It always had been. As a child his retribution had come in one of two forms. Icy silence that could bore holes in steel. Or quick, hot violence.

You're older, her mother had said, always. *Be a good girl, be a good sister. Let the baby win.*

It was such an old and ingrained habit, she barely registered her decision to blow the next return as well. And after all, the afternoon would be so much more pleasant if he won the match. Why cause contention over a tennis game?

So, burying her own competitive spirit, she took a dive, surrendering the game.

His expression changed almost instantly.

"Good game, Evan. I never could keep up with you."

She sent him an indulgent smile as they positioned themselves for the next. Boys hate to lose to girls, she thought. It was another of her mother's homilies.

And what were men but big boys?

By the time it was over and he'd won the match, he was in a fine mood. He felt loose and limber and affectionate. He swung an arm over Barbara's shoulders, bussed her cheek. "Your backhand still needs some work."

There was a little bubble of annoyance in her throat, automatically swallowed. "Yours is lethal." She picked up her bag. "And since you humiliated me, you get to buy lunch. I'll meet you on the lounge terrace. Thirty minutes."

She kept him waiting, always a minor irritation. But it pleased him to see how attractive she was, how well presented. He detested sloppy attire or unkempt hair on a woman, and Barbara never disappointed him.

She was four years his senior, but could have passed for thirty-five. Her skin was pampered and taut, her hair sleek and glossy, and her figure trim.

She joined him under the shade of the umbrella, smelling subtly of her favored White Diamonds.

"I'm going to console myself with a champagne cocktail." She crossed legs garbed in thin raw silk. "Between that and sitting with the most handsome man in the club, my mood should immediately improve."

"And I was just thinking what a beautiful woman I have for a sister."

Her face lit up. "You always say the sweetest things."

It was true, she thought. He did. When he won. It made her all the more pleased that she'd tanked the match.

"Let's not wait for Deke," she said, still beaming at him. "Lord knows when he'll finish his game."

She ordered her cocktail and a Cobb salad, moaning dramatically when Evan selected shrimp scampi. "Oh, I hate you for your metabolism. You never gain an ounce. I'm going to have a bite of yours, then curse you when I'm tortured tomorrow by my personal trainer."

"A little more discipline, Barbara, and you'd keep your figure without paying someone to make you sweat."

"Believe me, she's worth every penny. The sadist." With a contented sigh, she sat back, careful to keep her face out of the sun. "Tell me, darling, what did you want to talk to me about?"

"I'm going to give a party, at the Monterey house. It's time to . . ."

"Yes." She leaned forward again to cover his hand with hers, squeezed. "Yes, it is time. I'm so glad to see you looking well again, Evan, to hear you making plans. You went through such a horrible time."

Tears welled, and her affection for him was such that she blinked them back thinking not of her mascara but of his sensibilities.

He detested public scenes.

"You've begun to move on in the past few months. That's healthy. Helen would have wanted that."

"You're right, of course." He eased his hand away as their drinks were served.

He didn't like being touched. Casually, of course, was one thing. In the business world, hugs and kisses were just another tool. But he detested being touched with intensity.

"I haven't entertained, not really, since it happened. Business affairs, of course, but . . . Helen and I planned every detail of our parties together. She handled so much of it—the invitations, the menu—all subject to my approval, of course. I was hoping I could impose on you to help me."

"Of course I will. You just tell me what you have in mind, and when. I went to a party just last week, very lavish and fun. I'll steal some ideas. It was Pamela and Donald. Pamela's often a pain in the neck, but she does know how to throw a party. Speaking of her, I feel I should tell you—and I hope it doesn't upset you. I'm afraid you'll hear it from someone else."

"What is it?"

"Pamela's been nattering, you know how she is."

Evan could barely picture the woman. "About what?"

"She and Donald took a holiday out east a couple of weeks ago. Cape Cod, primarily, though she talked him into driving about and staying at a few bed-and-breakfasts like nomads. She claims while they were out there, sightseeing in some little village or other, she saw a woman who looked just like Helen."

Evan's hand vised on his glass. "What do you mean?"

"She cornered me at her party, went on and on about it. Claimed that at first glance she thought she'd seen a ghost. In fact, she was so insistent about how this . . . apparition might have been poor Helen's double, she asked me if Helen had a sister. I told her no, of course. I imagine she caught a glimpse of some fine-boned blonde about Helen's age and enhanced the whole thing in her mind. The way she's going on about it, I didn't want you to hear some rumor that would cause you any pain."

"The woman's an idiot."

"Well, she's certainly imaginative," Barbara said. "Now that we've gotten that out of the way, tell me how many people you're planning to invite."

"Two hundred, two-fifty," he said absently. "Just where did Pamela claim to see this ghost of hers?"

"Oh, some island off the East Coast. I'm not even sure of the name, as I was busy trying to change the subject. Something about sisters. Formal or casual?"

"What?"

"The party, honey. Formal or casual?"

"Formal," he murmured, and let his sister's voice buzz in his head like bees.

L ulu lived in a saltbox two blocks back from High Street. It stood out from its more conservative neighbors with its lipstick-red shutters and porch. On that red porch was a glider splattered and streaked with a rainbow of paint in a mad pattern that rivaled a Jackson Pollock canvas.

A purple gazing ball stood on the thin swath of lawn and shaded a gargoyle who squatted, permanently sticking out his tongue at passersby.

A winged dragon of iridescent green flew on the roof as a weather vane, along with a wildly striped wind sock. In the short driveway sat a dignified late-model sedan in practical black, and Lulu's Day-Glo orange VW, circa 1971.

Love beads, from the same era, dangled from the rearview mirror.

Following instructions, Nell parked on the street one house down, then hauled her delivery to the back door. Lulu swung it open before Nell could knock.

"I'll give you prompt." And with this, Lulu grabbed Nell's arm just above the elbow and yanked her inside. "I sent the lot of them out for a walk and don't figure they'll be back for twenty minutes. More, if I'm lucky. Syl's been a pain in my butt since she was born."

"Your sister."

"My parents insist she is, but I have my doubts." Lulu poked her head in the box the minute Nell set it down on the center island. "The idea that I share blood with that pompous, narrow-minded, pissy little twerp gives me the willies. I'm eighteen months older, so we went through the sixties at close to the same pace. Difference is, she remembers them, which says it all."

"Ah." Nell tried to imagine Lulu as a freewheeling, free-loving hippie, and found it wasn't that much of a stretch. For the family dinner, she'd donned a sweatshirt that announced she was all out of estrogen and had a gun.

Fair warning, Nell decided.

"Um. Still, it's nice that you sometimes get together like this."

"She just comes out here, once every damn year, to lord it over me. According to the Gospel of Sylvia, a woman isn't a woman unless she has a husband and children, chairs some crappy committee, and knows how to make an emergency centerpiece out of twine, spit, and an empty tuna can."

"We're going to do a hell of a lot better than that." Nell busied herself by putting the roast in the oven, turning it to warm. "I made it au jus, so you just spoon that over, and serve it with the side dishes. The autumn salad goes first. Tell them to leave room for the pumpkin cheesecake."

"That'll totally amaze her." Lulu poured another glass of the wine she was tippling to get through the event. "I had a husband."

She said it so fiercely, so viciously that Nell turned to stare. "Oh?"

"Don't know what made me do it legal. I wasn't knocked up or anything. Stupid. I guess I did it to prove I could still rebel. He was no good, just as useless as he was handsome. It turned out his idea of marriage was having someplace to go after he'd finished boinking whatever floozie caught his fancy that particular night."

"I'm sorry."

"No need to be sorry. Live and learn. I kicked his ass out in 1985.

The only time it bothers me is when Syl comes around gloating about her husband, who's no more than a paper pusher, and has a spare tire you could ride on to Cleveland, her kids, who are a couple of snotty teenagers in two-hundred-dollar track shoes, and the joys of her life in the suburbs. I'd rather be shot dead than live in some cookie-cutter house in the 'burbs."

Since either the wine or the situation with Syl was making Lulu loquacious, Nell took advantage. "So, you didn't grow up here together?"

"Hell, no. We grew up in Baltimore. I took off when I was seventeen, went straight to Haight-Ashbury. I lived in a commune in Colorado for a while, traveled, experienced. When I came here, I wasn't yet twenty. I've been here over thirty-two years now. God."

The idea of that had her knocking back the wine and pouring more.

"Mia's grandmother gave me a job doing this and that for her, then when Mia came along, her mother hired me to mind her when she needed minding. Carly Devlin's a nice enough person, but the fact was she didn't have much interest in raising a child."

"So you did. I didn't realize." No wonder, Nell thought, she was so protective of Mia. "Whatever your sister thinks, you've got a daughter at the heart of it."

"Damn right." She gave a little nod, then set down her glass. "Do whatever you need to do here. I'll be right back." She started out, turned back. "If Syl the Pill comes back before I do, just tell her how you work at the bookstore and stopped in to ask me something about work."

"No problem." Keeping tabs on the time, Nell organized the meal, slipping the salad and the dressing in the refrigerator, sliding the scalloped potatoes and the herbed green beans in with the roast.

She peeked into the dining room, saw the table had yet to be set, and hunted out dishes and linens.

"First half of your payment," Lulu announced as she came back in with a wrinkled shopping bag.

"Thanks. Listen, I didn't know what dishes you wanted, but I think these'll work well. It's family, and they're casual and cheerful."

"Good thing, as that's all I've got."

Lulu waited while Nell dipped into the shopping bag, then smiled smugly at the gasp of pleasure. "Oh, oh, Lulu!"

It was a simple design, a mock turtleneck that could and would be worn with everything. But the color was a deep, rich blue and the material was as soft as a cloud.

"I never expected anything like this." Already, Nell was holding it up, rubbing her cheek against the shoulder. "It's absolutely wonderful."

"You wear too many neutrals." Pleasing herself, Lulu tugged and fussed, then stood back to admire the result. "They wash the color out of your face. This brings it in, goes with your coloring. I started on the second one, nice tunic length in a good strong red."

"I don't know how to thank you. I can't wait to try it on and—"

"They're back," Lulu hissed, and immediately began shoving Nell toward the door. "Go! Get."

"You need to toss the salad just before—"

"Yes, yes. Go!"

Nell clutched her new sweater as Lulu slammed the door in her face.

"Serving," she finished and chuckled all the way to the car.

The minute she got home she stripped off her sweatshirt and slid into the magnificent sweater. Unable to get a satisfactory view from top to bottom, she dragged a chair in front of the mirror and stood on it.

There'd been a time when she'd had dozens of sweaters—cashmere, silk, the softest cottons, the thinnest wools. None of them brought her the sheer joy of this one, handmade by a friend.

Or close enough to a friend, she thought. And payment for a job well done.

She took it off again, folded it lovingly in a drawer. She would wear it to work on Monday. For now the sweatshirt was a better choice. She had messy work to do.

Her trio of pumpkins waited on a bed of newspapers on her kitchen table. She'd already used a portion of the largest for Lulu's dessert. It only waited to be carved into the appropriate design.

She would make pumpkin bread, she thought, as she began on the second. And pie, cookies. The hulls would serve as decorations on her front porch. Big, fat, scary pumpkins to entertain the neighbors and children.

She was up to her elbows in pumpkin meat and seeds when Zack strolled in the door. "I get to do the third one." He came up behind her, wrapping his arms tight, nuzzling her neck. "I'm a jack-o'-lantern master."

"The things you learn about people."

"Want me to dump the guts for you?"

"Dump them? How would I make a pie?"

"With a can." His brow furrowed as he watched her slide chunks of pumpkin into a large bowl. "You mean you actually use that stuff?"

"Of course. Where do you think they get the stuff *in* the cans?"

"I never thought about it. Pumpkin factory." He picked up the knife to start on the third while Nell washed her hands.

"You've obviously led a very sheltered life, Sheriff Todd."

"If that's so, I can't think of anyone I'd rather have corrupt me. How about when we finish this, we take a drive to the windward side, sit in my cruiser and break a few laws."

"Love to." She came back with a Magic Marker and began to draw a hideous face on the first pumpkin. "Everything quiet in the village?"

"It tends to be on Sundays this time of year. Did you get Lulu all set?"

"I did. I didn't realize she'd been married once."

"Long time ago. Some drifter who worked on the docks for a bit, I'm told. Seems to me I heard it didn't last six months. I guess it soured her on men, because I've never known her to take up with one since."

"She worked for Mia's grandmother, then her mother."

"That's right. Lu's kept the reins on Mia as long as I can remember. In fact, thinking about it, Lu's the only one Mia's let hold the reins for very long. Mia had a thing going with Sam Logan—his family owns the hotel. It didn't work out, and he left the island, Jesus, it's been ten years, maybe more."

"Oh, I see." Sam Logan, Nell thought. The man Mia had loved once.

"Sam and I hung out together some, back when we were younger," Zack went on as he hollowed out the pumpkin. "We've lost touch. But I remember that when Sam and Mia were seeing each other, Lulu watched him like a hawk."

He grinned, remembering it, then pulled the knife out of the heart of the pumpkin.

Nell saw it gleam in the overhead light, she saw it drip. She saw, as a rushing wind filled her head, the blood that stained his shirt, his hands, and pooled like a red river on the floor at his feet.

She made no sound at all as she slid bonelessly from the chair.

H ey, hey, hey. Come on, Nell, come on back now."

His voice was dim, as if they were both underwater. Something cool slid over her face. She seemed to rise from fathoms deep, slowly toward the surface. As her eyes opened, she saw a white mist that rolled away, layer by gauzy layer, until she saw his face.

"Zack!" In terror, she grabbed at him, yanking his shirt to check for wounds. Her fingers felt fat and fumbling.

"Hold on." He might have laughed at the way she pulled at his buttons if her face hadn't been deathly white. "Lie back down, get your breath."

"Blood. So much blood."

"Shh." His first reaction when she'd fainted had been panic, and he'd dealt with it as he always did. By doing what came next. He'd picked her up, carried her to the couch, and revived her. Now the penetrating fear she exuded tied knots in his belly.

"I bet you haven't eaten enough to keep a bird alive today, have you? Somebody who cooks as much as you do should learn how to eat regular meals. I'm going to get you a glass of water, something to eat. If you're not feeling steady then, I'm calling the doctor."

"I'm not sick. I'm not hurt. You were bleeding." Her hands shook as they ran over him. "There was blood all over your shirt, your hands, the floor. The knife. I saw . . ."

"I'm not bleeding, honey. Not so much as a nick." He lifted his hands, turning them to prove it. "Just a trick of the light, that's all."

"It wasn't." She locked her arms around him, held on ferociously. "I saw it. Don't touch the knife anymore. Don't touch it."

"Okay." He kissed the top of her head, stroked her hair. "I won't. Everything's all right, Nell."

She closed her hand around her locket, ran a charm for protection through her head. "I want you to wear this." Steadier now, she eased back and slipped the chain over her head. "All the time. Don't take it off."

He looked at the carved heart at the end of the chain and had a normal man's reaction. "I appreciate that, Nell. Really I do. But that's a girl thing."

"Wear it under your shirt," she said impatiently. "No one has to see it. I want you to wear it night and day." She looped it over his head even as he grimaced. "I want you to promise me you will."

Anticipating his next protest, Nell framed his face with her hands. "It belonged to my mother. It's the only thing of hers I still have. The only thing I brought away with me. Please do this for me, Zack. Promise me you won't take it off, not for any reason."

"All right. I'll promise that if you promise me you'll eat something."

"We'll have pumpkin soup. You'll like it."

That night, while she slept, she ran wildly through the woods, unable to find her way in the dark of the moon.

The scent of blood and death chased her.

Sixteen

Nell put it all out of her mind, or tried to, and went to work. She served coffee and muffins, joked with regulars. She wore her new blue sweater and stirred the pumpkin soup she had simmering for the lunch crowd.

She replenished the stack of business cards Mia had suggested that she put beside the café's cash register.

It was all so normal, almost breezy. Except she reached for the locket she no longer wore a dozen times through the morning. Each time she did, the image of Zack covered with blood flashed through her mind.

He'd had to go to the mainland that morning, and the idea of him being off-island was one more fear. He could be attacked on the street, mugged. Left to lie bleeding and dying.

By the end of her shift she'd concluded she hadn't done enough, and needed help.

She found Mia helping a customer with a selection of children's books. She waited, mentally wringing her hands, until the choices were made and the customer headed to checkout.

"I know you're busy, but I need to talk to you."

"All right. Let me get my jacket. We'll take a walk."

She was back moments later with a suede jacket tossed over her short dress. Both were the color of butternut squash that made her hair glint like a mane of fire.

She waved at Lulu as she walked out the front door. "Taking my lunch break. Great sweater," she added as they stepped outside. "Lulu's work, isn't it?"

"Yes."

"You've jumped a hurdle. She wouldn't have made you something that fine if she hadn't decided to accept you. Congratulations."

"Thanks. I . . . did you want to get some lunch?"

"No." Mia shook her hair back, breathed deep. There were times, rare times, when she felt locked inside the bookstore. When she needed space desperately. "I want to walk."

Ripley had been right about Indian summer. The cold snap had given way to balmy days of warmth and moist breezes that carried the scents of both sea and forest. The sky was clouded up, and against that dull pewter the trees rose like flaming beacons. The ocean mirrored the sky, and its kicky waves foretold a storm brewing.

"It'll rain within the hour," Mia predicted. "And look." She gestured out to sea. Seconds later, as if she'd ordered it, a pale jag of lightning cracked the steel mirror of sky. "Storm's coming. I love a good storm. The air goes electric and the energy of it pumps into your blood. Makes me restless, though. I want my cliffs in a storm."

Mia slipped out of her lovely shoes, hooked them on her fingers, and stepped barefoot into the sand. "The beach is almost empty," she pointed out. "It's a good place to walk, and for you to tell me what's troubling you."

"I had a . . . I don't know if it was a vision. I don't know what it was. It frightens me."

Mia slid her free arm through Nell's and kept the pace easy. "Tell me."

When she finished, Mia kept walking. "Why did you give him your locket?"

"It was all I could think of. An impulse. The thing that mattered most to me, I suppose."

"You were wearing it when you died. You brought it with you into your new life. This symbol of where you came from, this connection to your mother. Your talisman. Strong magic. He'll wear it because you asked him to, and that makes it stronger yet."

"It's a locket, Mia. Something my father bought my mother for Christmas one year. It's not particularly valuable."

"You know better than that. Its value is its meaning to you, and the love you have for your parents, the love you've given to Zack."

"Is it enough? I don't see how it can be. I know what it meant, Mia." And this was the terror that stretched like a beast inside her. "In the vision his face was gray, and the blood—there was so much blood. In the vision, he was dead." She made herself say it again. "He was dead. Isn't there something you can do?"

She'd already done all she could think of, all she felt within her power. "What do you think I can do that you haven't?"

"I don't know. So much more. Was it a premonition?"

"Is that what you believe?"

"Yes. Yes." Even thinking of it stopped her breath. "It was so clear. He's going to be killed, and I don't know how."

"What we see are possibilities, potentials, Nell. Nothing is absolute. Nothing, good or bad, is guaranteed. You were given this vision, and you acted to protect."

"Isn't there a way to stop whoever will try to hurt him? A spell?"

"Spells aren't a cure for every circumstance, or shouldn't be. And remember, what you send out can come back to you or yours, three-fold. Attack one thing, unleash another."

She didn't say what went through her mind. Stop the knife, Mia thought grimly, and you may load a gun.

"A storm's coming," she repeated. "And more than the lightning is going to slash through the sky this afternoon."

"You know something."

"I *feel* something. I can't see it clearly. Perhaps it's not for me to see." That was a frustration, this barrier. And the knowledge that she, so long a solitary witch, couldn't do what needed to be done alone. "I'll help you all I can, that I can promise."

Even as she worried it wouldn't be enough, she saw Ripley standing on the edge of the sand. "Call Ripley down. She'll come for you. Tell her what you've told me."

Nell didn't have to call, only to turn and look. In her practical chinos and sensible boots, Ripley strode toward them. "You're going to get wet if you stay out here much longer."

"Thunder," Mia said, and a dull rumbling of it rolled above the sea. "Some lightning." And it burst like a firewall toward the west. "But no rain for a half hour or so."

"You forecasting the weather now, Glinda?" Ripley said pleasantly. "You ought to get yourself a job on TV."

"Don't. Not now." Nell expected the sky to break open any second, but she didn't care. "I'm worried about Zack."

"Yeah? Me, too. I've got to worry when my brother starts wearing girlie jewelry. But I have to thank you for giving me the opportunity to razz him."

"Did he tell you why he's wearing it?"

"No. And I hesitate to repeat just what he did say to me in such polite company. But it got our day off to a fine start."

"I had a vision," Nell began.

"Oh, perfect." In disgust, Ripley started to turn away, stopping when Nell gripped her arm. "I like you, Nell, but you're going to piss me off."

"Let her go, Nell. She's afraid to listen."

"I'm not afraid of anything." And it burned her butt that Mia knew exactly which button to push. "Go ahead, tell me what you saw in the crystal ball."

"I wasn't looking at a crystal ball. I was looking at Zack," Nell said, and told her.

No matter how hard she denied it, how carelessly she shrugged, Ripley was shaken down to the toes. "Zack can take care of himself." She paced away, and back again. "Look, in case you haven't noticed, he's a capable, thoroughly trained officer of the law. He carries a weapon, and knows how to use it when and if he has to. If he makes the job look easy, it's because he knows how to handle whatever comes along. I'd trust him with my life."

"I think Nell's asking if she can trust you with his."

"I've got a badge, I've got a weapon, and a solid right cross. That's how I handle things," Ripley said furiously. "If someone comes after Zack, you can bet your ass they'll have to go through me."

"One times three, Ripley." Deliberately, Mia laid a hand on her arm. "In the end, that's what it'll take."

"I'm not going to do it."

Mia nodded. They were standing in a circle under the angry sky. "You already are."

Instinctively, Ripley stepped back, broke the connection. "Don't look for me," she said. "Not this way." She turned her back on them and the rising wind and, kicking at the sand, she walked back to the village.

"She'll think about this, and struggle with it. As her head's made of granite, it's going to take longer than I like. But for the first time in years, she's wavering." Mia gave Nell a comforting pat on the shoulder. "She won't risk Zack."

They went back to the bookstore, and had no sooner stepped inside when the rain fell in a torrent.

Nell burned the candles in her trio of jack-o'-lanterns not just to decorate now, but for their original purpose. She set them on her porch to frighten away evil.

Between the knowledge gleaned from the books Mia had lent her and her own instincts, she set about making her cottage as safe a haven as she could manage.

She swept away negative energy, lit candles for tranquility and protection. She laid red jasper and small pots of sage on the window-sills and moonstones and sprigs of rosemary under the pillows on her bed.

She made a pot of chicken soup.

It simmered while the rain lashed, and her little cottage became a cozy cocoon.

But she couldn't relax in it. She paced from window to window, door to door. She looked for busywork and couldn't find it. She forced herself to sit in her office, to complete a job proposal. But after ten minutes she was up again, her concentration as fractured as the lightning-struck sky.

Giving up, she called the station house. Surely Zack was back from the mainland by now. She would speak to him, hear his voice. Then she'd feel better.

But it was Ripley who answered and told her in a voice as cold as a slap that Zack hadn't returned, that he would be back when he got back.

Now her worry doubled. The storm took on the proportions of a tempest for her. The howl of the wind was no longer musical but full of teeth and threats. The rain was a smothering curtain and the lightning a weapon hurled.

Dark pressed against the windows as if it would break the glass and burst in. The power she'd learned to accept, even to embrace, began to waver like a candle flame under hot breath.

A thousand scenarios raced through her mind, each more horrible than the last. In the end, unable to bear it, she grabbed her jacket. She would go down to the docks, wait for the ferry. Will him to come.

She wrenched open the door in a blast of lightning. In the blind dark that followed, she saw the shadow move toward her. She opened her mouth to scream, then through the scent of rain and wet earth and the sting of ozone, she caught the scent of her lover.

"Zack!" She leaped at him, nearly sending the two of them tumbling off the stoop as he caught both her and his balance. "I've been so worried."

"And now you're wet." He carried her into the house. "I picked a hell of a day to go off-island. Bitch of a ferry ride back." He set her on her feet, then stripped off his soaking jacket. "I'd've called, but I couldn't get my cell phone to connect. That'll be the last ferry coming or going tonight, in this weather."

He dragged a hand through his hair, scattered rain.

"You're soaked to the bone." And because his shirt was wet, she saw, with relief, the faint outline of the locket just above his heart. "And cold," she added when she took his hand.

"I've got to admit, I've been dreaming about a hot shower the last half hour."

And would have had one by now, he thought, if Ripley hadn't met him at the front door, interrogated him, then told him Nell had called in a panic.

"Go take one now. Then you can have a bowl of hot soup."

"Definitely the best offer I've had all day." He cupped her face in his hands. "I'm sorry you worried. You shouldn't have."

"Now I'm not. Go on, before you catch cold."

"Islanders are hardier stock than that." But he kissed her lightly on the forehead and went straight for the shower.

He left his clothes in a sopping heap on the bathroom floor, turned the spray on hot, and let out a grateful sigh when he stepped in.

The little room, and the tub in it, hadn't been designed for a man of six-one. The nozzle was aimed straight at his throat, and if he wasn't careful he rapped his elbow against the wall whenever he moved his arms.

But he'd developed a routine during the time he'd been with Nell.

Bracing his hands on the front wall, he bent over so the spray sluiced over his head and back. Since she tended to use fragrant and feminine soaps and shampoos, he'd casually placed some of his own on the ledge above the lip of the tub.

Neither of them had mentioned these additions—or the change of clothing he'd left on the shelf of her closet.

They didn't talk about the fact that they rarely spent a night apart. Other people did, he knew. He saw the winks and was becoming accustomed to having his name and hers roll off people's tongues together as if they were one word.

But they hadn't spoken of it. Maybe it was a kind of superstition, he thought, not to speak out loud what you were most afraid to lose.

Or maybe it was just another kind of cowardice.

He wasn't sure it mattered, but he was sure it was time to take another step forward.

He'd taken one himself, the biggest step he'd ever taken, on the mainland that afternoon.

He had to admit he felt good about it. He'd felt a little jittery, but that had passed quickly enough. Even the hideous ride back from the mainland hadn't managed to dampen his mood.

The sounds on the other side of the curtain surprised him enough to make him move too quickly. The rap of his elbow against the wall echoed in the little room, and was followed, viciously, by a stream of curses.

"Are you all right?" Torn between amusement and sympathy, Nell pressed her lips together tight and kept his wet bundle of clothes crammed against her chest.

He wrenched off the spray and whipped the curtain back. "This room is a hazard. I've a good mind to check the code and . . . What are you doing with those?"

"Well, I—" She broke off, baffled when he all but leaped naked out of the tub and snatched them back from her. "I was just going to toss them in the dryer."

"I'll take care of it later. I've got a change around here." He dumped them on the floor again, ignoring her wince as they hit with a wet plop behind him.

"At least hang them up. They'll just mildew lying in a pile like that."

"Okay, okay." He grabbed a towel, ran it roughly over his hair. "Did you just come in here to pick up after me?"

"Actually, yes." Now her gaze traveled down, slowly, over the damp chest where her locket glittered, the flat belly, the narrow hips he swagged in the towel. "But right at the moment, I'm not thinking tidy."

"Is that so?" One look from her did more to warm his blood than an ocean of hot water. "What are you thinking?"

"I'm thinking the very best thing to do with a man who has just come in from a storm is tuck him into bed. Come with me."

He let her take his hand and draw him through to the bedroom.

"Are we going to play doctor? Because I think I could get really sick if it was worth my while."

She chuckled, then tossed back the quilt. "In."

"Yes, ma'am."

Before he could twitch off the towel, she did it for him. But when he grabbed for her, she evaded, then gave him a nudge onto the bed.

"You may know," she began and, picking up matches, walked around the room lighting candles, "that in lore and legend witches often served as healers."

Candlelight swayed, and it shimmered. "I'm starting to feel really healthy."

"I'll be the judge of that."

"I'm counting on it."

She turned to him. "Do you know what I've never done for anyone?"

"No, but I'm riveted."

She slowly lifted the hem of her sweater. She remembered the day she'd stood, poised like this, on the sunny back of his inlet.

"I want you to watch me." Inch by inch, she peeled the sweater up her body. "And want me."

If he'd been struck blind, he would have seen her, skin glowing in delicate light.

She slipped out of her shoes in a kind of graceful dance. Her simple white bra cut low and sweet over the subtle curve of her breasts. She lifted her hand to the center clasp, watched his eyes follow the move, then she deliberately left it fastened and trailed her fingertips down her midriff to the hook of her slacks.

His pulse began to thrum as the fabric slithered over her hips, down her legs. When it pooled at her feet, she stepped out with that same fluid ease.

"Why don't you let me do the rest?"

Her lips curved and she stepped closer, but not close enough. She'd never set out to seduce a man before, and wasn't ready to surrender the power.

She could imagine his hands on her as she ran her own up her body, as his breath rushed out of his lungs.

With that faint and knowing smile on her face, she flicked open her bra, let it slide away. Her breasts already felt full, and tender. She peeled the panties over her hips, stepped free of them. She was already wet.

"I want to take you," she whispered. "Slowly. I want you to take me." She eased onto the bed on hands and knees to straddle him. "Slowly." She seemed to melt over him. "As if there'll never be an end to it."

Her lips were warm and soft on his. Seeking. The taste of him slid through her system like a drug. When he rolled to take more, to deepen it, she went with him. But not in surrender.

She ran her fingertips lightly up and down his back, finding pleasure in the ridge of muscle, the ripple of it as she aroused him.

She let herself float on sensation as he gave her, and took from her, the gradual glide she'd demanded. Candlelight shifted, then the flames ran straight and true as spears and filled the air with fragrance.

They rose together, danced on that scented air. They knelt on the bed, centered on it, torso to torso and mouth to mouth.

If it was a spell, he'd have stayed bound eternally without question, without struggle. Witch or woman, a blend of both, she was his.

He watched the way his hand looked against her skin, dark to light, rough to fragile. The way her breasts could be cupped in his palms, and how the tips hardened under the brush of his thumb.

They touched, and tasted. A brush, a sip, a lazy caress, a long, slow drink.

When at last he slipped inside her, the gentle rise and fall was like waves of silk. Magic shimmered as they watched each other, as for each, for that moment, no one else existed. Beat to beat, with an intimacy that was more than mating, that bounded past needs and outraced passion.

It welled in her heart, overflowed in a spill like gold.

Her lips curved again as he lowered his mouth to hers. Their hands joined, fingers linking as they slid off the world together.

When she lay curled to his side, her palm over the steady beat of his heart, it seemed nothing could touch them. Her haven, she thought, was safe, as they were safe inside it.

All of her fears and worries, that creeping dread, seemed foolish now.

They were simply a man and a woman in love, lying in a warm bed and listening to the last of a storm pass overhead.

"I wonder if I'll ever learn how to manipulate objects."

"Honey, you manipulate just fine," he chuckled.

"No." She gave him a playful slap. "I mean moving things from one point to another. If I could, I'd chant the proper incantation and so on, and we'd have chicken soup in bed."

"It doesn't work like that. Does it?" he asked.

"I bet it does for Mia, if she wants it enough. But for lowly students such as me, it takes getting up, going into the kitchen and doing it all the old-fashioned way."

She turned her head to give his shoulder a pecking kiss, then rolled away.

"Why don't you stay here and I'll get the soup?"

She tossed a look over her shoulder as she walked to the closet for the robe she'd finally gotten around to buying. "Clever of you to suggest that after I was already up."

"I thought so. And since you caught me, I'll throw some clothes on and come out and give you a hand."

"Fine. Bring out that wet heap in the bathroom while you're at it."

Wet heap? It took him a minute to remember, so she was already out of the room when he leaped out of bed and snatched up his sodden pants from the floor. Digging in the pocket, he let out a breath as his fingers closed around a small box.

She had a round loaf of bread on a cutting board and was ladling up wide bowls of soup when he came in. She looked so pretty, so at home in her soft pink robe, he thought, her feet bare, her hair a little mussed.

"Nell, why don't we let that cool a minute?"

"We'll need to. Do you want some wine?"

"In a minute." Odd, he thought he'd be nervous, at least a little. Instead he was rock calm. He laid his hands on her shoulders, turned her, then ran them down to her elbows. "I love you, Nell."

"I—"

It was as far as she got before his lips silenced hers.

"I thought of different ways to do this. Taking you for a drive one night, or a walk on the beach next full moon. Or for a fancy dinner at the hotel. But this is the right way for us, the right place, and the right time."

The little flutter in her stomach was a warning. But she couldn't step back. She couldn't move at all.

"I thought of different ways to ask you, what words might suit best, and how I should say them. But the only ones that come to me right now are I love you, Nell. Marry me."

The breath that she had been holding released as joy and grief waged a helpless war inside her. "Zack. We've been together such a short time."

"We can wait a while to get married if you want, though I don't see the point in it."

"Why can't we just leave things the way they are?"

Of all the reactions he'd been expecting, the hitch of fear in her voice hadn't been among them. "Because we need a place of our own, a life of our own, not pieces of yours and mine."

"Marriage is just a legality. That's all." She turned away, reached blindly into the cupboard for glasses.

"For some people." He said it quietly. "Not for you or me. We're basic, Nell. When basic people fall in love, and mean it, they get married, start a family. I want to share my life with you, make children with you, grow old with you."

Tears threatened. Everything he said was what she wanted, so deep in her heart that it was into her soul. "You're moving too fast."

"I don't think so." He took the box from his pocket. "I bought this today because we've already started our life together, Nell. It's time to see where it takes us."

Her fingers curled into her palms as she looked down. He'd bought her a sapphire, a rich, warm stone set in a simple band of gold. He'd have known she would need warmth and simplicity.

Evan had chosen a diamond, a brilliant square in platinum that had sat on her finger like ice.

"I'm sorry. Zack, I'm so sorry. I can't marry you."

He felt the slice through his heart, but he never flinched as he watched her face. "Do you love me, Nell?"

"Yes."

"Then I deserve to know why you won't make a promise to me, and take one from me."

"You're right." She struggled to steady herself. "I can't marry you, Zack, because I'm already married."

Nothing she could have said would have stunned him more. "Married? You're *married*? For God's sake, Nell, we've been together for months."

"I know." It wasn't just shock she saw now. It wasn't just anger. He stared at her as if she were a stranger. "I left him, you see. More than a year ago."

He struggled over the first hurdle. The fact that she'd been married and hadn't told him. But he couldn't make it over the second. That she was married still.

"Left him, but didn't divorce him."

"No, I couldn't. I—"

"And you let me touch you, you slept with me, let me fall in love with you, knowing you weren't free."

"Yes." It was so cold, suddenly so cold in the little kitchen that it penetrated her bones. "I don't have any excuses for it."

"I won't ask when you were planning to tell me. Obviously you weren't." He closed the box with a snap, jammed it back in his pocket. "I don't sleep with other men's wives, Nell. A word from you, one goddamn word from you, and we wouldn't have gotten to this point."

"I know. It's my fault." As his anger grew, hardened his face, she felt the strength she'd rebuilt draining away like the color in her cheeks.

"You think that makes up for it?" he shot back, as temper and misery careened inside him. "You think taking the blame for it cleans the fucking slate on this?"

"No."

"Goddamn it." He spun away from her and caught the way she flinched at the move. "I'll yell when I need to yell. You're only making me madder standing there like you're waiting for a punch. I'm not going to hit you. Not now, not ever. And it's insulting for you to stand there wondering if I will."

"You don't know what it's like."

"No, I don't, because you won't tell me." He reined himself in as much as he could, though temper was still sparking. "Or you tell me just enough to keep things running smooth until the next time."

"Maybe that's true. But I told you I couldn't tell you everything. That I wasn't going to go into the details."

"This isn't a damn detail. You're still married to the man who did this to you."

"Yes."

"Are you planning on ending the marriage?"

"No."

"Well, that's plain enough." He snatched up his boots, his jacket.

"I can't let him find out where I am. I can't let him find me."

He started to yank the door open, then stood there a moment, his hand on the knob. "Did you ever stop and think, just once did you ever stop and look at me and know I'd do whatever needed to be done for you? I'd have done it, Nell, for a stranger, because it's my job. How could you not know I'd do it for you?"

She did know, she thought as he walked away from her. It was only one of the things that frightened her. Unable to cry, she sat miserably in the house she had made safe, and empty.

Seventeen

I've lost him. I've ruined it." Nell sat in Mia's great, gorgeous cavern of a living room, in front of an ox-roasting fire sipping a cup of healing cinnamon tea. Isis stretched her lean, warm body over her lap like a cozy blanket.

None of it lifted her mood.

"Damaged it, perhaps. And nothing's lost that can be found again."

"I can't fix this, Mia. Everything he said to me is true. I didn't want to think about it, to see it, but it's true. I had no right to let things get as serious as they did."

"I don't happen to have a hair shirt handy, but I imagine we can make something up." At Nell's shocked stare, Mia lifted one shoulder elegantly. "It's not that I don't sympathize with both of you, because I do. But the fact is, Nell, you fell in love, both of you. And both of you dealt with it the way you needed to deal with it. You brought each other something that not everyone is given. That's nothing to regret."

"I don't regret loving him, or being loved by him. I regret a lot of things, but not that."

"All right, then. You need to take the next step."

"There is no next step. I can't marry Zack because I'm legally tied to someone else. And even if Evan decides to divorce me in absentia or whatever, I still couldn't marry Zack. My identification is false."

"Details."

"Not to him."

"Yes, you're right." She tapped her pretty fingernails on the side of her cup as she considered. "Some things Zack would see, because he's Zack, as black and white. I'm sorry I didn't think this far ahead and warn you of that. I know him," Mia continued as she rose to stretch. "I didn't anticipate that he'd move toward legal binding so quickly. I'm jaded when it comes to love."

She poured more tea, pondered while she roamed the room and sipped.

There were two sofas, both in deep hunter green, that begged for a body to sink down and sink in. They were scattered with jewel-toned pillows, all in soft fabrics. Texture was essential to luxury, and when at leisure, Mia insisted on luxury.

The room was populated with antiques, because she preferred the old to the new unless it was in business equipment. The rugs on the wide-planked chestnut floor were satisfactorily faded. There were flowers everywhere, in priceless crystal or in cheerful colored bottles of no special value.

Some of the candles she surrounded herself with in every room were lit. The white ones, for peace.

"You've hurt him, Nell, on two levels. One by not falling into his arms in utter delight when he proposed." She stopped, lifting one brow. "I told you I was jaded in this area, but nonetheless, when a man asks a woman to marry him, he's not going to be pleased when she says 'No, thank you.'"

"I'm not a complete idiot, Mia."

"No, darling. I'm sorry." Contrite, though secretly amused at the biting tone, Mia stopped behind the sofa and stroked Nell's hair. "Of course you're not. And I should have said three levels, the second being his sense of honor. He has just discovered himself poaching on what he would consider another man's territory."

"Oh, really. I'm not a damn rabbit."

"Zack would see himself breaking a code. The third level is that he would certainly have done so anyway, *if* he'd known. If you'd told him the circumstances. He could adjust his line there, because he loves you and wants you, and because he would be relieved that you'd escaped from a horrible situation. But the fact that you didn't tell him, that you let him go into this, let him fall in love with you blind, is going to be hard for him to swallow."

"Why can't he see that my marriage to Evan means nothing? I'm not Helen Remington anymore."

"Do you want comfort or truth?" Mia asked flatly.

"I can't have both. It may as well be truth."

"You lied to him, and by lying you put him in an untenable position. More, you told him you didn't intend to end the marriage."

"I can't—"

"Wait. You won't end it, and without an end there can't be a beginning. This is purely your choice, Nell, and no one can or should take it from you. But you've blocked Zack from being able to stand for you. To stand with you or, more to his liking, I imagine, to step in front of you and face your demon. Nell."

She sat again, taking Nell's hands. "Do you think he wears a badge for amusement, for the pathetic pay, for the power?"

"No. But he doesn't understand what Evan can do, what he's capable of. Mia, there's a madness inside him. A kind of cold, deliberate madness that I can't begin to explain."

"People tend to think the word *evil* is overdramatic," Mia said, "when actually, it's extremely simple."

"Yes." A few knots untangled. She should have known by now that she didn't have to explain to Mia. "And he doesn't understand that I can't bear the idea of seeing Evan again, of hearing his voice. I think I'd break this time. I think it would shatter me."

"You're stronger than that."

Nell shook her head. "He . . . shrinks me. I don't know if you can understand what I mean."

"Yes, I do. Do you want a spell, a charm, to bolster yourself? To shield yourself from one man so you can have the other?" Mia reached over, stroked Isis along her sleek back. The cat raised her head, exchanged what seemed to be a telling look with her mistress, then curled up.

"There are things that can be done," Mia said, briskly now. "To protect, to center yourself, to enhance your own energies. But beneath it all, Nell, the power's inside you. For now . . ."

She slipped the silver chain and its silver disk over her head. "You gave Zack your talisman, so I'll give you one of mine. It was my great-grandmother's."

"I can't take it from you."

"On lend," Mia said, slipping the chain over Nell's head. "She was a very canny witch, my great-grandmama. Married well. Made a killing on the stock market, and kept it, for which I continue to be grateful. I wouldn't like being poor. She acted as doctor on the island before we had one with a medical degree living here. She treated warts, delivered babies, stitched up gashes, and nursed half the population through a dangerous run of influenza among other things."

"It's lovely. What does the carving mean?"

"It's an old language, similar to what was written on the ogham stones in ancient Ireland. It means courage. And now that you're wearing my courage, I'll give you my advice. Sleep. Let him wrestle with his feelings while you examine your own. When you go to him—and as much as he loves you he won't come back to you—be clear in your mind what it is you want, and what you're willing to do for it."

"You're being an asshole, Zack."

"Okay. Now will you shut up?"

Ripley considered never shutting up a sister's privilege. "Listen, I know she screwed up. But don't you want to know why?" She slapped her hands on his desk, leaning down so she could get in his face in a satisfactory manner. "Don't you want to push, dig, maneuver until she tells you why she's still married?"

"She had plenty of time to tell me if she wanted to." Zack concentrated on his computer. His business on the mainland hadn't just been buying a ring; he had also testified in a court case. Now that it was done, he could update his file.

Ripley made a sound somewhere between a groan and a scream. "You make me crazy. I don't know how you don't make yourself crazy. You're in love with a married woman."

He spared her a withering glance. "That fact is very clear in my mind right about now. Go do your patrol."

"Look, it's obvious she doesn't want the other guy. She ditched him. Also obvious is that she's moony about you and vice versa. Nell's been here, what, five months? And from all appearances she's digging in for the duration. Whatever came before is over."

"She's legally married. That doesn't spell over for me."

"Yeah, yeah, Dudley Do-Right." The fact that she admired his code of honor didn't mean it couldn't exasperate her. "So let it ride for a while. Just let things go as they've been going. Why the hell do you have to marry her, anyway? Oh, wait, I forgot who I'm talking to. But if you want my advice—"

"I don't. I really don't."

"Fine. Stew in your own juice, then." She grabbed her jacket, then immediately tossed it down again. "I'm sorry. I can't stand to see you hurting."

Because he knew that, he gave up on pretending to update files, rubbed his hands over his face. "I can't make a life with someone who has another life that she hasn't finished. I can't take a woman to bed who's legally married to another man. And I can't love someone the way I love Nell and not want, not expect, marriage, home, and children. I can't do those things, Rip."

"No, you can't." She came to him then, wrapping her arms around his neck from the back, resting her chin on top of his head. "Maybe I could." Though she couldn't imagine loving anyone enough to make the choice. "But I understand you can't. What I don't understand is why if you love her, and you want her, you can't sit her down and make her explain it. You deserve to know."

"I'm not going to make her do anything, not only because I don't work that way but because I have a feeling the man she's married to did plenty of making her."

"Zack." Ripley turned her head so that her cheek rested on his hair. "Did it ever occur to you that she's afraid to divorce him?"

"Yeah." His stomach did a quick, nasty pitch. "I came around to that about three o'clock in the morning. If it's true, I've got plenty of feelings to punch into that bag. But it doesn't change what is. She's married, she didn't tell me. She doesn't trust me enough to be there for her, whatever it takes."

He reached up, closed his hand around hers.

That's how Nell saw them when she opened the door, holding on to each other. And she saw the beam of blame shoot out of Ripley's eyes even as the shutters came down on Zack's.

"I need to speak with you. Alone. Please."

Instinctively Ripley tightened her grip, but Zack gave her hand a squeeze. "Ripley was just heading out on patrol."

"Yeah, sure, toss me out just when it's getting good." She was shrugging into her jacket, contemplating that *this* was what it felt like when people said you could cut the tension with a knife, when Betsy poked her head in the door.

"Sheriff— Hi, Nell, Ripley. Sheriff, Bill and Ed Sutter are starting to mix it up out in front of the hotel. It looks like it could get messy."

"I'll take care of it."

"No." Zack got up at Ripley's statement. "We'll take care of it."

The Sutter brothers vacillated between staunch family loyalty and hating each other like poison. Since they were both bullheaded and built like the same animal, he thought it best not to let Ripley get into a two-on-one situation. He gave Nell a brief glance as he walked outside. "You'll have to wait."

So cold, she thought, rubbing her arms. It was hard to accept ice from a man who had such warmth. He wasn't going to make this easy. Oddly enough, even after the worst of it the evening before, she'd convinced herself that he would.

He would let her talk. He would sympathize, understand, hold her.

Standing alone in the station house, Nell watched that little fantasy crack in two and disappear.

Here she was, swallowing her pride, risking her peace of mind and well-being, and all he could do was spare her a single icy look.

Well, then, maybe she should just let bad enough alone.

Stung, she pulled open the door. Two steps out and she could not only see the commotion up the street, she could hear it. Freezing in place, she hugged herself and watched it play out.

One big man with short-cropped hair belly-slammed another big man with short-cropped hair. Curses were flying. An interested crowd was gathering at a safe distance, and some of them appeared to be taking sides by hooting and calling out names.

Zack and Ripley were already wading in, muscling the men apart. Nell couldn't hear what they were saying, but while it quieted the crowd, it didn't appear to have much impact on the Sutter brothers.

They were all but snapping at each other's faces.

Nell cringed, closed in when she saw the first fist strike. There was a lot of shouting now, and she heard it like the pounding of the surf. A lot of motion that seemed lost in a fast blur.

Zack had one man's arm, Ripley the other's. Both had their hand-cuffs out. Bumping, shoving. Curses and clipped warnings.

Then one brother swung viciously at the other, missed his mark and plowed his fist into Zack's face.

She watched Zack's head snap back, heard the crowd gasp as one voice. Everyone went so still, it seemed like a film stopped in a freeze-frame.

She was already rushing across the street as motion and voices started again.

"Well, goddamn it, Ed, you're under arrest." Zack snapped the cuffs in place as Ripley did the same. "And for good measure, the same goes for you, Bill. Couple of hotheaded peckerbrains. You people go on about your business now," he ordered as he muscled Ed around.

He caught sight of Nell, standing on the sidewalk like a deer caught in the headlights, and cursed again.

"Come on, Sheriff, you know I wasn't aiming at you."

"Doesn't matter a damn to me who you were aiming at." Not when he tasted blood in his mouth. "You just assaulted an officer."

"He started it."

"Like hell," Bill shot back as Ripley walked him briskly along. "But I'm sure as hell going to finish it when I get the chance."

"You and what army?"

"Just shut up," Ripley ordered. "Couple of forty-year-old delinquents."

"Ed's the one who punched him. What're you hauling me in for?"

"You're a damn public nuisance. If the two of you want to butt heads, do it in the privacy of one of your homes and keep it off the streets."

"You're not going to put us in jail." Calmer now as he saw his fate, Ed turned his head to appeal. "Come on now, Zack, you know my wife'll skin me if you lock me up. It was just family business, after all."

"Not when it's on my street, and not when it involves my goddamn face." His jaw throbbed like a bitch. He marched Ed straight into the station house and back to one of the two tiny holding cells. "You're going to have some time to cool off before I get around to calling your wife. Whether she cares enough to come down and make your bail is up to her."

"Same goes," Ripley told Bill cheerfully as she uncuffed him and nudged him into a cell.

Once the cell doors were shut and locked, she dusted her hands. "I'll write up the report. I type slower than you do. I'll call the wives, too, though I suspect they'll hear about this before I even start on the paperwork."

"Yeah." Disgusted, Zack swiped the back of his hand over his mouth and smeared blood.

"You're going to want some ice on that jaw. Lip, too. Ed Sutter's got a fist the size of Idaho. Hey, Nell, why don't you take our hero to your place and give him some ice?"

Unaware that she'd come in, Zack turned slowly and stared at Nell as she stood in the open doorway.

"Yes. All right."

"There's ice in the back. I can take care of it."

"You'd be better off putting some distance between yourself and Ed," Ripley advised. "Until you're sure you're not going to unlock that cell and punch him back."

"Maybe."

His eyes weren't cold anymore, Nell noted. They were hot green glass. She moistened her lips. "Ice'll help keep the swelling down. And . . . some rosemary tea might help the ache."

"Fine. Great." His head was already ringing, why not finish it off? "Two-hundred-and-fifty-dollar fine, for both of them," he snapped at Ripley. "Or twenty days. They don't like the sound of that, fill out a formal arrest warrant, and they can deal with the court."

"Yes, sir." Ripley beamed as Zack stalked out. Wasn't this great? she thought. The whole thing had really brightened her mood.

They walked to the cottage in silence. Nell no longer knew what to say or how to say it. This furiously angry man was every bit as much a stranger as the icy cold one had been. There was no doubt in her mind that he didn't particularly want to deal with her right now. She knew just how long it could take to regain equilibrium after a blow to the face.

Still, he'd taken a fist at short range, and other than the head, and temper snap, he'd had little reaction.

People were always saying someone was tougher than he looked. It seemed to be true about Zachariah Todd.

She opened the cottage door and, still saying nothing, walked back to the kitchen and began to make an ice pack out of a plastic bag wrapped in a thin cloth.

"Appreciate it. I'll get the dishcloth back to you."

She'd already lifted the kettle to make tea. She blinked at him. "Where are you going?"

"To walk off what I can of this mad."

Seeing no choice, she set the kettle down again. "I'll go with you."

"You don't want to be with me right now, and I don't want to be with you."

It was quite a discovery to learn that there were times a slap was preferable to words. "That can't be helped. We have things to talk about, and the longer it's put off the harder it'll be."

She opened the kitchen door, waited. "Let's try the woods. We can consider it neutral territory."

He hadn't bothered with a jacket, and the rain that had swept in the night before had left cool temperatures in its wake. He didn't seem to mind. She glanced up at him as they headed into her little wedge of forest.

"That ice isn't going to do any good if you don't use it."

He pressed it to his aching jaw and felt mildly ridiculous.

"In the summer when I came here I wondered what it would be like to walk through the trees in autumn, with all the color and the first bites of cold. I'd missed the cold, the change of seasons, when I lived in California."

She let out a little breath, drew one in. "I lived in California for three years. Los Angeles primarily, though we spent a lot of time in the house in Monterey. I preferred it there, but I learned not to let him know that or he'd have found ways to cancel trips north. He liked to find little ways to punish me."

"You married him."

"I did. He was handsome and romantic and clever and rich. I thought, Why, here comes my prince and we'll live happily ever after. I was dazzled and flattered and in love. He worked very hard to make me fall in love with him. There's no point in going into all the details. You've guessed some of them anyway. He was cruel, in little ways, in big ones. He made me feel small. Small, smaller, smallest, until I all but disappeared. When he hit me . . . the first time it was a shock. No one had ever hit me before. I should've left, right that minute. Or tried. He would never have let me, but I should've tried. But I'd only been married a few months, and somehow he made me feel I'd deserved it. For being stupid. Or clumsy. Or forgetful. For all manner of things. He trained me like a dog. I'm not proud of that."

"Did you get help?"

It was so quiet in the woods. She could hear, in that quiet, every step she and Zack took over the ground already strewn with fallen leaves.

"Not at first. I knew about abuse, intellectually. I'd read articles, stories. But that didn't apply to me. I wasn't part of that cycle. I'd come from a good, stable home. I'd married an intelligent, successful man. I lived in a big, beautiful house. I had servants."

She slipped a hand into her pocket. She'd made a magic bag for courage, and had tied it with seven careful knots. Letting her fingers worry it helped calm her nerves.

"It was just that I kept making mistakes, that was all. I thought that once I learned, everything would be fine again. But it only got worse, and I couldn't keep deluding myself. One night he dragged me upstairs by my hair. I had long hair then," she explained. "I thought he would kill me. I thought he would beat me and rape me, then kill me. He didn't. He didn't do any of those things. But I realized he could have, and I wouldn't have been able to stop him. I went to the police, but he's an influential man. He has connections. I had a few bruises, but nothing major. They didn't do anything."

Knowing that burned a hole through him. "They should have. They should've taken you to a shelter."

"As far as they were concerned, I was a rich, spoiled trophy wife causing trouble. It doesn't matter," she said wearily. "They could have taken me anywhere. He'd have found me. I ran once, and he found me. And I paid for it. He made it clear to me, he made sure I understood one vital point: I belonged to him, and I would never get away. Wherever I went, he'd find me. He loved me."

It sent a violent chill through her to say it. She stopped, turned to face Zack. "His version of love, beyond rules, beyond bounds. Selfish, cold and obsessive and powerful. He would see me dead before he'd let me go. That's not an exaggeration."

"I believe you. But you got away."

"Because he thinks I'm dead." She told him, her voice clear and empty of emotion, what she had done to break the chains.

"Jesus Christ, Nell." He threw the ice bag to the ground. "It's a miracle you didn't kill yourself."

"Either way, I was getting away. I was coming here. I believe, completely believe, that the minute that car went over the cliff, I started coming here. And to you."

Because he wanted, too strongly, to touch her and wasn't yet sure if it would be a caress or a furious shake, he jammed his hands in his pockets. "I had a right to know, when things changed between us. I had a right to know."

"I didn't expect things to change between us."

"But they damn well did. And if you didn't know where we were heading, then you *are* stupid."

"I'm not stupid." Her voice took on an edge. "Maybe I was wrong, but I'm not stupid. I didn't expect to fall in love with you, I didn't *want* to fall in love with you, or even get involved with you. You pursued me."

"It doesn't make any difference how it happened. The fact is, it did. You know where you stood and why, but you didn't let me know."

"I'm a liar," she said evenly. "I'm a cheat, I'm a bitch. But don't you ever call me stupid again."

"Jesus Christ." At his wits' end, he stalked away, lifted his gaze to the sky.

"I won't be demeaned, not by anyone. Not ever again. I won't be belittled, and I won't be brushed aside until it's convenient for you to pay attention again."

Curious, he turned his head, stared at her. "Is that what you think this is?"

"I'm *telling* you how it is. I did a lot of thinking since you walked out of the house yesterday. I'm not going to whimper and slide into the corner just because you're annoyed with me. That insults both of us."

"Well, three cheers."

"Oh, go to hell."

He turned completely around and stepped toward her. The dread curled in her stomach, her palms went clammy, but she stood her ground.

"It's a hell of a time to pick a fight with me, especially when you're wrong."

"I'm only wrong if I'm standing where you are. Standing here, I did what I had to do. I wish I hadn't hurt you, but I can't go back and change that."

"No, you can't. So we go from here. Did you leave out anything else I should know?"

"The woman who drove off that cliff was named Helen Remington. Mrs. Evan Remington. I don't answer to that name anymore. It's not who I am."

"Remington." He said it softly. She could all but see him flipping through some mental data file. "Hollywood type."

"That's right."

"You got about as far away from that as you could manage."

"That's right, too. I'll never go back. I've found the life I want here."

"With or without me?"

For the first time since she'd begun her story, her stomach clutched. "That's up to you."

"No, it's not. You already know what I want. Now it's what you want."

"I want you. You know that."

"Then you have to finish what you started. You have to end it. File for divorce."

"I can't. Haven't you heard anything I've said?"

"Every word, and more that you didn't say." Part of him wanted to soothe her, to draw her close, shelter her. To tell her none of it mattered now.

But it did.

"You can't live your whole life wondering, looking over your shoulder, or pretending three years away. Neither can I. For one thing, it's going to start eating at you, and for another, the world's a small place. You'll never be sure he won't find you. If he does, or if you're afraid he has, are you going to run again?"

"It's been more than a year since I left. He can't find me if he thinks I'm dead."

"You'll never be sure. You have to end it, but you don't have to end it alone. I won't let him touch you. This isn't his turf," he said, lifting her face with a finger under her chin. "It's mine."

"You're underestimating him."

"I don't think so. I know I'm not underestimating myself, or Ripley, or Mia. Or a lot of people on the island who would go out of their way for you."

"I don't know if I can do what you're asking. For more than a year I've focused on doing everything I could to make certain he doesn't find out I'm alive, he doesn't find out where I am. I don't know if I've got it in me to step out again. I need to think. I need you to give me time to think."

"All right. Tell me what you decide." He stooped to get the ice bag. The ice was mostly melted. As he didn't care a great deal about the pain in his jaw, he opened it, spilled out the contents. "If you don't want to marry me, Nell, I'll accept that. But after you think all this through, I need you to tell me what you decide there, too."

"I love you. I don't have to think that through."

He stared at her, standing in the quiet woods where the leaves rioted color and the air still carried the faintest scent of yesterday's rain.

He held out a hand for hers. "I'll walk you home."

Eighteen

Ripley gave Zack her most pitiful look. And whined. She saved up her whines to add to the impact when she whipped one out.

"But I don't wanna go to Mia's."

Living with her for nearly thirty years made him immune to such tactics. Though he had to give her big points for delivery.

"When you were a kid you practically lived at Mia's."

"Then, now. See the difference? Why can't you go?"

"Because I have a penis. I'll restrain myself and not ask if you see the difference. Be a pal, Rip."

She spun in a circle, her version of drumming her heels on the floor. "If Nell's going to be hanging out at Mia's tonight, then Mia can keep an eye on her. Jesus, Zack, don't be such a mommy. The asshole in L.A. doesn't even know she's alive yet."

"If I'm being overprotective we'll just all have to live with it. I don't want her driving to the cliffs alone at night." The thought of her car flying over cliffs three thousand miles away left a ball of ice in his gut. "Until this thing is resolved, I want to keep an eye on her."

"So keep *your* eye on her. You're the ones trying to decide if you're going to be long-suffering, star-crossed lovers, or Ward and June Cleaver."

He let the insult pass, as it was her way of starting a pissing match so she could storm out and get out of doing what he asked. "I'll never figure how it is I know more about women than you do, when you're of the same species."

"Watch it, slick."

He supposed he hadn't let the insult pass after all. "She doesn't need me hovering over her. She doesn't need a man, even such a sterling example of manhood as myself, crowding her. She's got tough decisions to make. I'm trying to keep a little distance, without making an issue of keeping a little distance, until she's made them."

"Gee, you sure do think a lot."

The simple fact was, he was putting her in a hell of a pinch. He wanted her to keep an eye on Nell, and Ripley wanted to keep an eye on Zack. She hadn't had an easy moment in the two days since he'd told her Nell's story.

Blood on the moon, she thought. Nell's vision of Zack covered with blood. A sociopathic, potentially homicidal husband, and Ripley's own disturbing dreams. She hated knowing she was dipping into omen territory, but . . . hell, it didn't bode well.

"What are you going to be doing while I'm babysitting the love of your life at Witch Central?"

There was something else he'd learned in nearly thirty years of knowing her. He could always count on Ripley. "Taking both our evening patrols, buying some takeout, and going home to a lonely dinner."

"If you think that makes me feel sorry for you, think again. I'd trade places with you in a heartbeat." She walked to the door. "I'll go by Nell's, tell her I want to tag along tonight. I want you to watch your back."

"Excuse me?"

"I don't want to talk about it. I'm just saying."

"I'll watch my back."

"And buy some beer. You drank the last bottle."

She slammed the door because . . . just because.

Mia set out fresh charms. Every day, it seemed, the air got a little heavier. As if something was dragging it down. She glanced outside. It was already dark. There was so much night at the end of October, so many hours until dawn.

There were things it wasn't wise to speak of at night, or even think. Night could be an open window.

She burned incense of sage to counter negativity, fastened on earrings of amethyst to strengthen her intuition. She'd been tempted to slip some rosemary under her pillow, to help chase away her troubled dreams. But she needed to see, needed to look.

She added jasper to the chain around her neck, a strengthener of energy, a reliever of stress.

It was the first time in years she could recall being so constantly hounded by stress.

Tonight wasn't the time for it, she reminded herself. She was going to take Nell to the next step, and such things should be joyful.

She fingered the magic bag in her pocket, filled with crystals and herbs, and, as she'd taught Nell, tied with seven knots. She detested being so edgy, as if waiting and waiting for disaster to strike.

Foolish, really, when she'd been preparing for disaster, and how to divert it, all her life.

She heard the car, saw the streak of lights slash across her front windows. As she walked to the door, she visualized pouring the stress into a small silver box, locking it.

So she appeared to be her usual calm self as she opened the door. Until she saw Ripley.

"Slumming, Deputy?"

"Didn't have anything better to do." She was surprised to see Mia in a long black dress. Mia rarely wore black. The one thing Ripley had to admit, the woman wasn't often obvious. "Special occasion?"

"As it happens. I don't have any objections to you being here, if Nell wants you. But don't interfere."

"You don't interest me enough to interfere."

"Is this argument going to take long?" Nell asked pleasantly. "I was hoping for a glass of wine."

"I think we're done. Come in, and welcome. We'll take the wine with us."

"With us? Where are we going?"

"To the circle. You've brought what I told you?"

"Yes." Nell patted the large leather pouch she wore.

"Good. I'll get what I need, then we'll go."

Ripley wandered around freely enough while Mia got ready. She had always liked the cliff house. Loved it. The big, crowded rooms, the odd corners, the thick carved doors and glossy floors.

She'd have gotten by happily enough with one room and a cot, but she had to admit Mia's place had style. And class. As far as atmosphere went, you couldn't top it.

Class, style, and atmosphere aside, it was always comfortable. A place where you knew you could sink into a chair and put your feet up.

A place, she recalled, where she had once run as free and as welcome as a pet puppy. It was a hell of a note to realize, all at once, how much she'd missed it. Missed it all.

"You still use the gable room?" Ripley asked casually while Mia selected a red wine from the rack.

When Mia glanced back their eyes met. Shared memories. "Yes.

Some of your things are still there," she said as she wrapped three glasses in white linen.

"I don't want them."

"They're still there, in any case. Since you're here, you can carry this bag." She gestured, then picked up the second that held the wine and glasses.

She opened the back door, and Isis streaked through. It surprised Nell, as the cat generally couldn't be bothered to join them.

"It's a special night." Mia threw up the hood of the cloak she swirled over her shoulders. Black again, with a lining of deep wine-red. "She knows it. It's nearly Samhain. Nell needs to practice lighting the balefire."

Ripley's head snapped up. "Moving a little fast, aren't you?"

Mia merely studied the moon as they walked. It was down to a thumbnail and would soon be full dark. Around that sliver of white she could see a haze blacker, thicker than the sky.

"No."

Annoyed that Mia had made her uneasy yet again, Ripley shrugged. "Halloween. Lifting the dead. The night boils with evil spirits and only the brave or foolish walk in the dark."

"Nonsense," Mia said lightly. "And there's no point in taking that route to try to scare Nell."

"The end of the third and last harvest of the year." Nell breathed deep of the night. "A time for remembering the dead, for celebrating the eternal cycle. Also the night when the veil between life and death is said to be its thinnest. Hardly a negative time, but one of reaffirmation and fun. And, of course, Mia's birthday."

"The big three-oh this time, too," said Ripley.

"Don't be so smug." There was a little bite in Mia's voice, a not entirely playful nip. "You'll be hitting it yourself in six weeks."

"Yeah, but you'll always be older than me."

Isis was already in the clearing, sitting still as a sphinx in the center.

"We have some candles for working light. You can put them on the stones, Ripley, and light them."

"No." She shoved her hands, very deliberately, into the pockets of her bomber jacket. "Carting your bag of tricks is one thing. I won't participate."

"Oh, for pity's sake. You'll hardly spoil your magic celibacy by lighting one or two candles." But Mia snatched the bag from her and stalked to the stones.

"I'll do it," Nell insisted. "There's no point in either of you being angry, when you're each doing what you want."

"Why are you so angry?" Ripley kept her voice down, crouched as Mia came back to select what she needed from her bags. "I usually have to work a lot harder to get under your skin."

"Maybe my skin's thinner these days."

"You look tired."

"I am tired. Something's coming. It's pushing, and pushing closer. I don't know how much longer I can hold it back, or even if I'm meant to. There'll be blood."

She gripped Ripley's wrist, held her still. "And pain. Terror and grief. And I'm afraid that without the circle there'll be death."

"If you're so sure of this, afraid of this, why haven't you sent for someone? You know others."

"It's not for others, and you know it." She glanced back toward Nell. "Maybe she's strong enough."

Mia straightened, tossed back her hood. "Nell. We'll cast the circle."

Whatever she'd expected to feel, Ripley hadn't expected the yearning that ribboned through her as she watched the basic ritual, as the familiar words echoed in her head.

She'd given it up, she reminded herself. She'd set it aside.

She watched wand and athame glimmer. She had always preferred the sword.

Her mouth pursed in consideration as Mia lit candles with a wooden match. Even as she opened her mouth to speak, to question, Mia sent her a quieting look.

Fine, your way as usual, Ripley thought, and kept her comments to herself.

"Earth, wind, fire, water—elements, hear this call from your daughters. While the moon above does ride, within the magic circle rise."

With her head thrown back and her arms raised, Mia waited. And the wind lifted, all but sang, the candle flames speared, ruler-straight despite the swirl of humming air. Under her feet, the earth trembled lightly, and in her cauldron, fragrant liquid began to bubble.

As Mia lowered her arms again, each subsided.

Nell had yet to get her breath back. Over the past months, she'd seen and done and been told the fantastic. But until tonight she hadn't been treated to such a vivid display.

"Power awaits," Mia told her, and held out a hand.

When Nell clasped it, she found Mia's skin warm, nearly hot.

"It waits in you. Your link is air, and calling to it comes most easily to you. But there are four. Tonight, you'll make fire."

"The balefire, yes. But we didn't bring wood."

With a little chuckle, Mia stepped back. "We won't need it. Center yourself. Clear your mind. This fire does not burn. This fire does no harm. It lights the dark and glows from charm. When you make its golden tower, you will know your strength and power. And once begun, bring harm to none."

"It's too soon for her," Ripley said from outside the circle.

"Quiet. You're not to interfere. Look at me, Nell. You can trust me, and yourself. Watch. And see."

"Hold on to your hats," Ripley muttered, and stepped a bit farther back, just in case.

Mia opened her hands, empty hands. Spread her fingers. Turning them over, she held her arms out as if reaching.

There was a spark, electric blue. Then another, then a dozen, then too many to count. They sizzled, like fire on water, turned the air within the circle to deep sapphire.

And there, where the bare ground had been, rose a bright and gilded pillar of flame.

Nell's legs simply folded until her butt hit the ground with a solid thump. Nothing that was going through her mind, had she been able to capture any of the scattered pieces of her thoughts, could have made its way out of her mouth.

"Told you." Ripley sighed, shook her head.

"Quiet!" Mia spun away from the fire, held out a hand to help Nell to her feet. "You've seen me do magic before, little sister. You've done magic yourself."

"Not like that."

"It's a basic skill."

"Basic? Mia, really. You made *fire*. Out of nothing."

"What she means is it's along the lines of losing your virginity. It's kind of a jolt," Ripley said helpfully. "It might be less pleasurable than you expect the first time around, but after a while, you get better at it."

"Close enough." Mia agreed. "Now center yourself, Nell. You know how. Clear your mind. Visualize, gather the power. Make your fire."

"I can't possibly—"

Mia cut her off with a lifted hand. "How do you know unless you try? Concentrate." She stepped behind Nell, laid her hands on Nell's shoulders. "There's light inside you, and heat, energy. You know it.

Bring it together. Feel it. It's like a tingling in the belly, and it rises toward the heart. It spreads up, fills you."

Gently, she put her hands under Nell's arms, lifting them. "It runs under your skin, like a river, flows down your arms, to your fingertips. Let it come. It's time."

While they worked, Ripley watched. There was something lovely about it in a strange way. Something like watching Mia balance Nell on her first two-wheeler, offering encouragement, keeping pace, building confidence.

The first time wasn't easy on student or teacher, she knew. Nell's face was sheened with the sweat of effort. The muscles in her arms trembled.

The clearing, never completely silent, seemed to vibrate. The air here, never completely still, sighed.

There was a faint and fitful spark. When Nell would have leaped back, Mia was there, holding her in place, her quiet and steady encouragement like a chant.

Another spark, stronger.

Ripley watched Mia step back, leaving her little sister wobbling on two wheels, solo. Despising the weakness, Ripley felt tears, pure sentiment, gather in her eyes. And a little spurt of pride as Nell's fire shimmered to life.

For the first time since she'd begun, Nell felt the beat of her own heart, the rise and fall of her own chest. Power, bright as silver, pumped through her blood.

"It's better than losing your virginity. It's beautiful, and bright," she whispered. "Nothing will ever be the same for me again."

She turned, full of joy. But Mia was no longer looking at her, but at Ripley.

"We need three."

Furious, Ripley refused to let the tears fall. "You won't get the third from me."

Mia had seen the tears, and understood them. She also understood Ripley. "Very well." To Nell she said, "She probably can't do it anymore."

"Don't tell me what I can't do," Ripley piped up.

"It'd be hard for her to find that out, especially after watching you do so well, after such a short time."

"And stop talking like I'm not here. I hate that."

"Why *are* you here?" Mia asked with annoyance. "Nell and I can make the third together." Which had been Mia's plan before she'd seen Ripley at the door. "We certainly don't need you and your pathetic, rusty attempts. She was never as good as me," she said to Nell. "It always infuriated her that what came so easily to me was such an effort for her."

"I was every bit as good as you."

"Hardly."

"Better."

Ah, Mia thought. Ripley never could turn down a challenge. "Prove it."

Weakened by sentiment, stirred by longing, and bristling with the dare, Ripley stepped into the circle.

No, Nell thought. She swaggered.

She didn't hold out her arms as Mia had, but seemed to throw them, and the fire that burst from their tips, onto the ground.

The minute she did, she hissed like a snake. "You did that on purpose."

"Perhaps, but so did you. And look here, the sky did not fall. You made the choice, Ripley. I couldn't have pushed you into it unless you'd wanted it."

"This doesn't change anything. It's one time only."

"If you say so, but you might as well have some wine while you're here." Mia studied the trio of flames as she picked up the bottle. Ripley's was bigger than hers, a result of temper. But not, Mia thought with satisfaction, nearly as elegant.

And, pouring the wine, she felt a fire inside herself. That was hope.

They had another glass when they returned to Mia's house. Restless now, Ripley wandered from window to window. Jingling the change in her pocket. Mia ignored her. For as long as she'd known her, Ripley had never been a quiet soul. And at the moment, Mia understood there was a considerably testy war going on inside her.

"Have you decided how you're going to handle your situation with Zack?"

Nell glanced up at her. She sat on the floor, mesmerized by the fire. "No. Part of me hopes that Evan will divorce me, take it out of my hands. And the rest of me knows that's not the core of the problem."

"If you don't stand up to bullies, they tromp all over you."

Nell admired Ripley. Strong, wiry, and ready, she thought. "Knowing that and acting on it are two different things. Evan would never have taken a piece out of someone like you."

Ripley lifted a shoulder. "So, take it back."

"She will when she's ready," Mia countered. "You of all people should know that it's impossible to push one person's beliefs, ideas, or standards on another. Or to erase someone else's fear."

"She's upset with me because I hurt Zack. I can't blame you."

"He's a big boy." Ripley shrugged, then sat on the arm of the couch. "What are you going to do about him—Zack, that is—in the meantime?"

"Do?"

"Yeah, do. Are you just going to let him slide through his brooding phase—which is what comes after the pissed-off phase with him and, let me tell you, is a lot harder to live with. I figure we've gotten to be pals, more or less, since you've been here. Do a pal a favor and snap him out of it before I have to smother him in his sleep."

"We've talked."

"I don't mean talk. I mean action. Is she really that much of a sweetie?" Ripley asked Mia.

"Apparently. Ripley, in her own delicate way, is suggesting that you lure Zack back to bed and soothe away your troubles with a bout or two of hot jungle sex. Which is her answer to all manner of pesky annoyances, including hangnails."

"Bite me. Mia's given up sex, which explains why she's such a bitch."

"I haven't given it up, I'm simply more selective than a cat in heat."

"It isn't about sex." Making the statement, making it firm and fast, was Nell's only solution to fending off another argument.

Ripley snorted. "Yeah, sure, right."

Mia sighed. "It pains me, more than I can say, to agree with Ripley. Even partially. Certainly your relationship with Zack isn't, as all of Ripley's are, based on sex. But it's a vital part of it, an expression of your feelings, a celebration of them, and your intimacy."

"You can put flowers on it, it's still sex." Ripley gestured with her glass. "However high-minded Zack is, he's still a guy. Being around you and not getting laid—"

"Ripley, please."

"Not having intimacy," she said in a prissy tone after Mia's reprimand, "is going to make him edgy. If he's going to deal with your L.A. asshole, he should be in top form."

"He's been very careful to keep me at a distance, in that area."

"Then close the distance in that area," Ripley said simply. "Here's what we do. You drop me off at your place. I'll bunk there tonight. You go over to the house and take care of business. You've been hanging out with him long enough to know what buttons to push."

"That's sneaky, deceitful, and manipulative."

Ripley cocked her head at Nell. "What's your point?"

Despite herself, Nell laughed. "Maybe I will go over. To *talk*," she added.

"Whatever you want to call it." Ripley polished off her wine. "Maybe you could take these glasses and things back into the kitchen, get your stuff together."

"Sure." She rose, began to gather the glasses. "I'll just be a minute."

"Take your time."

Mia waited until Nell was out of the room. "It won't take her long, so say what you didn't want to say in front of her."

"What I did tonight doesn't change anything."

"That's redundant."

"Just shut up." She paced again. She'd opened herself—only for a short time, but that's all that had been needed. She'd felt that heaviness in the air, the pressure. "Okay, trouble's coming. I'm not going to pretend I don't feel it, and I'm not going to pretend I haven't tried to figure a way to deal with it. Maybe I could, but I won't bet Zack on it. I'm going to sign up for this, Mia." She turned back. "But just for this."

Mia didn't rub it in. In fact, it didn't occur to her to do so. "We'll light the balefires at midnight on Samhain eve. We'll meet at ten on the Sabbat. Zack already wears Nell's talisman, but I'd protect your house if I were you. Do you remember how?"

"I know what to do," Ripley snapped. "Once this passes, things go back the way they were. This is—"

"Yes, I know," Mia retorted. "A one-time-only."

ᴇꜰᴏ

Zack had given up on paperwork, given up on his telescope, and pretty much given up on the idea that he could will himself to sleep. He was trying to bore himself to sleep now, by reading one of Ripley's gun magazines.

Lucy was sprawled beside the bed in a deep sleep that he envied. Every now and then her legs would twitch as she chased dream gulls or swam in her dream inlet. But she lifted her head, one sharp motion, let out a soft, warning woof seconds before Zack heard the front door open.

"Relax, girl. It's just Ripley."

At the sound of the name, Lucy was up and scrambling for the door, where she stood wagging her entire body.

"Forget it. It's too late to play."

The knock on the bedroom door had Lucy barking joyfully and Zack cursing. "What?"

Lucy whipped herself into happy circles as the door opened, then she leaped enthusiastically on Nell.

Zack shot up in bed. "Lucy, down! Sorry. I thought it was Rip." He nearly threw back the covers, then remembered he was buck naked. "Is something wrong?"

"No. Nothing." She bent over to pet Lucy, wondering which of them was more embarrassed, and decided it was a tie. "I just wanted to see you. Talk to you."

He peeked at the clock, noted it was coming onto midnight. "Why don't you go downstairs? I'll be right there."

"No." He wasn't going to treat her like a guest. "This is fine." She came over, sat on the side of the bed. He still wore the locket, and that meant something. "I made fire tonight."

He studied her face. "Okay."

"No." She laughed a little, and scratched Lucy's head. "I made it. Not with wood and a match. With magic."

"Oh." There was a tickling inside his chest. "I don't know what I'm supposed to say to that. Congratulations? Or . . . wow?"

"It made me feel strong, and excited. And . . . complete. I wanted to tell you. It made me feel something like I do when I'm with you. When you touch me. You don't want to touch me because I have a legal tie to someone else."

"It doesn't stop the want, Nell."

She nodded, let the relief of that come. "You won't touch me because I have a legal tie to someone else. But the fact is, Zack, the only man I have a real tie to is you. When I ran, I told myself I would never tie myself to another man. Never risk that again. Then there was you. I have magic in me." She lifted a hand, fisted, to her heart. "And it's amazing and thrilling and sweet. Still, it's nothing—nothing, Zack—to what I have in me for you."

Any defense, any rational reason he may have had quite simply crumbled. "Nell."

"I miss you. Just being with you. I'm not asking you to make love with me. I was going to. I was going to try to seduce you."

He skimmed his fingers through her hair. "What changed your mind?"

"I don't want to ever lie to you again, even in a harmless way. And I won't use one set of your feelings against another set. I just want to be with you, Zack, just be. Don't tell me to go."

He drew her down until her head was cradled on his shoulder, and he felt her long, long sigh of contentment echo his own.

Nineteen

It wasn't easy for an important, successful man to get away by himself for a few days. It was a complicated and tedious business to reschedule meetings, postpone appointments, inform clients, alert staff.

There was a whole world of people dependent upon him.

More tedious yet was making travel arrangements personally rather than using the services of an assistant.

But after careful thought, Evan decided there was nothing else to be done. No one was to know where he was, or what he was doing. Not his staff, not his clients, not the press. Naturally, he could be reached via cell phone if there was a crisis of any sort. Otherwise, until he'd done what he set out to do, he would remain incommunicado.

He had to know.

He hadn't been able to get the information his sister had so casually passed on to him out of his mind.

Helen's double. Helen's ghost.

Helen.

He would wake up at night in a cold sweat from images of Helen, *his* Helen, walking along some picturesque beach. Alive. Laughing at him. Giving herself to any man who crooked his finger.

It couldn't be borne.

The terrible grief he'd felt upon her death was turning slowly, inexorably, into a cold and killing rage.

Had she tricked him? Had she somehow planned and executed the faking of her own death?

He hadn't thought her smart enough, certainly not brave enough, to try to leave him, much less succeed. She *knew* the consequences. He had made them perfectly clear.

Till death do us part.

Obviously she couldn't have done so alone. She'd had help. A man, a lover. A woman, especially a woman like Helen, could never have devised such a scheme on her own. How many times had she sneaked off to lie with some wife-stealing bastard, working out the details of her deception?

Laughing and fucking, plotting and planning.

Oh, there would be payment made.

He could calm himself again, continue about his business and his life without an outward ripple. He could nearly convince himself again that Pamela's claims were nonsense. She was, after all, a woman. And women, by nature, were given to flights of fancy and foolishness.

Ghosts didn't exist. And there was only one Helen Remington. The Helen who had been meant for him.

But at times in that big, glamorous house in Beverly Hills, he thought he heard ghosts whispering, or caught the bright sound of his dead wife's taunting laughter.

What if she wasn't dead?

He had to know. He had to be careful, and clever.

"Ferry's loading."

His eyes, pale as water, blinked. "I beg your pardon?"

The ferry worker stopped blowing on his take-out cup of coffee and instinctively stepped back from that blank stare. It was, he would think later, like staring into an empty sea.

"Ferry's loading," he repeated. "You're going to Three Sisters, ain't ya?"

"Yes." The smile that spread over the handsome face was worse than the eyes. "Yes, I am."

According to legend, the one known as Air had left her island to go with the man who promised to love her, to care for her. And when he'd broken those promises and turned her life into a misery she had done nothing. She'd borne children in sorrow, raised them in fear. Had bowed, and had broken.

Had died.

Her last act had been to send her children back to the Sisters for protection. But she had done nothing, even with her powers, to protect or save herself.

So the first link in the chain of a curse was forged.

Nell thought of the story again. Of the choices and mistakes, and of destiny. She kept it clear in her head as she walked down the street of what had become her home. What she intended to keep as her home.

When she walked in, Zack was delivering a blistering lecture to a young boy she didn't recognize. Automatically, she started to step out again, but Zack merely held up a finger and never broke rhythm.

"You're not only going straight over to Mrs. Demeara's and clean up every last scrap of pumpkin guts and apologize for being a moron, but you're going to pay a fine for possession of illegal explosives and willful destruction of property—five hundred dollars."

"Five hundred dollars!" The boy, thirteen at the outside, Nell calculated, lifted a head that had been sunk low. "Jeez, Sheriff Todd, I ain't got five hundred dollars. My mom's going to kill me as it is."

Zack merely raised his eyebrows and looked merciless. "Did I say I was finished?"

"No, sir," the boy mumbled, and went back to looking so hangdog that Nell wanted to go pat his head.

"You can work off the fine by cleaning the station house. Twice a week, three dollars an hour."

"Three? But it'll take me . . ." The boy had smartened up enough to shut up. "Yes, sir. You weren't finished."

His lips wanted to twitch, but Zack kept them in a firm, hard line. "I've got some odd chores around my place, too. Saturdays."

And oh, Zack thought, that one stung. There was no crueler fate than being imprisoned by chores on a Saturday.

"Same rate. You can start there this Saturday, and in here Monday after school. If I hear you're in any more trouble like this, your mother's going to have to stand in line to skin you. Clear?"

"Yes, Uncle Zack . . . um, I mean, yes, sir, Sheriff."

"Beat it."

He beat it, nearly spinning the air into a funnel as he raced past Nell.

"Uncle Zack?"

"Second cousins, really. It's an honorary term."

"What did he do to earn the hard labor?"

"Stuck an ash can, that's a firecracker, in his history teacher's pumpkin. It was a damn big pumpkin, too. Blew that shit all over hell and back again."

"Now you're sounding proud of him."

He pokered up, as best he could. "You're mistaken. Idiot boy could've blown his fingers off, which is what I nearly did at about the same age when I blew my science teacher's pumpkin to hell and back. Which is beside the point, especially when we'll be in for similar Halloween pranks tomorrow if I don't make an example now."

"I think you did the job." She walked over, sat down. "Have you got time for another matter, Sheriff?"

"I could probably carve out time." It surprised him that she hadn't leaned over to kiss him, and that she sat so straight, so still, so solemn. "What's the matter?"

"I'm going to need some help, and some advice. On the law, I suppose. I've generated false identification, and I've put false information on official forms, signing them with a name that isn't legally mine. I think faking my own death is illegal, too. At least there must be something about life insurance fraud. There were probably policies."

He didn't take his eyes off hers. "I think a lawyer would be able to handle that for you, and that when all facts are known, there'll be no charges brought. What are you telling me, Nell?"

"I want to marry you. I want to live my life with you, and make those children with you. To do that, I have to end this, so I will. I need to know what I'm going to have to do, and if I'll have to go to jail."

"You're not going to jail. Do you think I'd let that happen?"

"It's not up to you, Zack."

"The false papers and so on aren't going to put anyone's sense of justice up. The fact is . . ." He'd given this angle a great deal of thought. "The fact is, Nell, once you tell the story you're going to be a hero."

"No. I'm no one's hero."

"Do you know the statistics on spousal abuse?" He pulled open his bottom drawer, took out a file, and dropped it on his desk. "I've put some data together on it. You might want to have a look at it sometime."

"It was different for me."

"It's different for everybody, every time. The fact that you came from a good home and you lived in a big, fancy house doesn't change anything. A lot of people who think it's different for them or that there's nothing they can do to change their situation are going to look at you, hear what you did. Some of them might take a step they might not have taken because of you. That makes you a hero."

"Diane McCoy. It still bothers you that you couldn't help her. That she wouldn't let you help her."

"There are a lot of Diane McCoys out there."

She nodded. "All right. But even if public sentiment falls on my side, there are still legalities."

"We'll handle them, one at a time. As far as the insurance, they'll get their money back. We'll pay it back if we have to. We'll do what we have to do together."

When she heard that, a weight lifted. "I don't know where to start."

He rose, came around to her, crouched at her feet. "I want you to do this for me. That's selfish, but I can't help it. But I want you to do it for yourself, too. Be sure."

"I'll be Nell Todd. I'll have a name I want."

She saw his expression alter, the deepening of emotion in his gaze, and knew she had never been more sure of anything. "I'm afraid of him, and I can't help that either. But I think I realize I'll never stop until this is done. I want to live with you. I want to sit out on the porch at night and look at the stars. I want that beautiful ring you bought me on my finger. I want so many things with you I thought I'd never have. I'm scared, and I want to stop being scared."

"I know a lawyer in Boston. We'll call him, and we'll start."

"Okay." She let out a breath. "Okay."

"There's one thing I can take care of right now." He straightened, walked over and opened a drawer in his desk. Her heart gave a lovely little flutter when she saw the box in his hand. "I've been carting this around with me, putting it in here, or in my dresser at home. Let's put it where it belongs."

She got to her feet, held out her hand. "Yes, let's."

Her stomach was jumping when she left to walk back to the bookstore. But there was anticipation tangled with the nerves. And every time she looked down at the deep blue stone on her finger, anticipation won.

She walked in, sent a wave to Lulu, and practically floated upstairs to Mia's office.

"I need to tell you."

Mia turned from her keyboard. "All right. I could spoil your moment by saying congratulations and I know you'll be very happy together, but I won't."

"You saw my ring."

"Little sister, I saw your face." However jaded she considered herself about love, the sight of it warmed her heart. "But I want to see the ring." She leaped up, snatched Nell's left hand. "A sapphire." She couldn't stop the sigh. "It's a love gift. As a ring it sends out healing, and can also be used as protection against evil. Beyond all that, it's a doozy." She kissed Nell on either cheek. "I'm happy for you."

"We talked to a lawyer, someone Zack knows in Boston. My lawyer now. He's going to help me with the complications, and with the divorce. He's going to file a restraining order against Evan. I know it's only a piece of paper."

"It's a symbol. There's power in that."

"Yeah. In a day or two, once he's got everything in place, he'll contact Evan. So he'll know. With or without a restraining order, he'll come, Mia. I know he will."

"You may be right." Was this what she'd been feeling, the dread, the building of pressure?

The last leaves had died, and the first snow had yet to fall.

"But you're prepared, and you're not alone. Zack and Ripley will meet every ferry that comes here after he's been contacted. If you don't plan to move in with Zack right away, then you'll stay with me. Tomorrow's the Sabbat. Ripley's agreed to participate. When the circle's joined, he can't break it. That I can promise you."

She intended to tell Ripley next, if she could find her. But the minute Nell stepped outside, she was stricken with a wave of nausea that rolled thick and greasy through her belly. She staggered a little, sweat popping out on her skin. With no choice, she leaned back against the wall of the building and waited for it to pass.

When the worst of it eased, she regulated her breathing. The jitters, she told herself. Everything was going to start happening now, and happening very fast. There'd be no turning back. There would be questions, and press, and stares, murmurs even from people she'd come to know.

It was natural to be a little queasy.

She looked down at her ring again, the hopeful glint of it, and the lingering dregs of sickness passed.

She would find Ripley later, she decided. Right now she was going to buy a bottle of champagne and the makings for a good Yankee pot roast.

ে৯

Evan drove off the ferry and onto Three Sisters as Nell leaned weakly against the wall of the bookstore. He surveyed the docks, disinterested. The beach, unimpressed. Following the instructions he'd been given, he drove to High Street and pulled up in front of the Magick Inn.

A hole-in-the-wall in a town suitable for middle-class Currier and Ives buffs, he judged. He got out of the car, studied the street, just as Nell turned the corner into the market.

He walked inside, and checked in.

He'd booked a suite, but found no charm in the coffered ceilings, the lovingly preserved antiques. He detested the fussiness of such rooms, preferring the streamlined, the modern. The art, if one could call it that, ran to misty watercolors and seascapes. The mini-bar didn't hold his favored brand of mineral water.

And the view? He could see nothing but beach and water, noisy gulls and what he supposed were fishing boats run by locals.

Dissatisfied, he walked to the parlor. From there he could see the curve of the land and the sudden sharp jut of cliffs where the lighthouse stood. He noted the stone house as well and wondered what type of idiot would choose to live in such an isolated spot.

Then he found himself squinting. There seemed to be some sort of light dappling through the trees. A trick of the eye, he decided, already bored.

In any case, he had hardly come for the scenery, thank the Lord. He'd come to look for Helen or to satisfy himself that what was left of her was still at the bottom of the Pacific. On an island this size, he was sure he could get the task done in a day.

He unpacked, meticulously hanging his clothes so that each garment was aligned precisely one inch from the next. He set out his toiletries, including his triple-milled soap. He never used the amenities offered in hotels. Even the idea of it revolted him.

And last, he set the framed photograph of his wife on the bureau. He leaned over, kissed the curved bow of her mouth through the glass.

"If you're here, darling Helen, I'll find you."

On his way out, he made a reservation for dinner. The only meal he found acceptable to eat in a hotel room was breakfast.

He stepped out, turned left, just as Nell, with her two bags of groceries, swung around the end of the block to the right, toward home.

It was, Nell was sure, the happiest morning of her life. The sky was silver, with sweeps and rises of rose and gold and deep red. Her lawn was carpeted with leaves that would crunch merrily underfoot and had left the trees bare and spooky. Which was perfect for an island Halloween.

She had a man sleeping in her bed who had shown his appreciation for a good pot roast in a very satisfactory way.

Muffins were baking, the wind was shivering, and she was prepared to face her demons.

She would be leaving her little cottage behind soon, and that she would miss. But the idea of setting up housekeeping with Zack made up for it.

They would spend Christmas together, she thought. Maybe even be married by then if all the legal tangles could be unraveled.

She wanted to be married outside, in the air. It was impractical, but it was what she wanted. She would wear a long dress, of velvet. Blue velvet. And carry a spray of white flowers. The people she had come to know would all be there to bear witness.

While she daydreamed, the cat meowed piteously.

"Diego." She bent down, stroked him. He was no kitten now but a sleek young cat. "I forgot to feed you. I'm very scattered of brain today," she told him. "I'm in love, and I'm getting married. You'll come to live with us in our house by the sea, and make friends with Lucy."

She got out his kibble, filling his bowl while he wound excitedly through her legs.

"A woman who talks to her cat could be considered strange."

Nell didn't jump, which pleased both of them. Instead she rose and walked to Zack, who stood in the doorway. "He might be my familiar. But I'm told that'll be up to him. Good morning, Sheriff Todd."

"Good morning, Ms. Channing. Can I buy a cup of coffee and a muffin?"

"Payment first."

He came to her, wrapped her up in a long, deep kiss. "That do it?"

"Oh, yeah. Just let me give you your change." She drew him down again, lingered over the taste of him. "I'm so happy."

At precisely eight thirty, Evan sat down to a breakfast of sweetened coffee, fresh orange juice, an egg-white omelette, and two slices of whole wheat toast.

He'd already made use of the hotel health club, such as it was. He had only glanced at the pool. He disliked using public swimming pools, but had considered it until he'd seen it was already being used. A long, lean brunette was streaking through the water. As if she were in a race, he'd thought.

He'd only caught glimpses of her face as she turned it rhythmically in and out of the water in time with her strokes.

And he didn't see, as he dismissed her and walked away, her sudden loss of pace. The way she pulled up in the water as if gathering for attack. How she shoved her goggles, treading water as she looked around for what had felt like an enemy.

He'd showered in his room, dressed in a pale gray sweater and dark slacks. He glanced at his watch, ready to be annoyed if his meal should be above one minute late.

But it arrived, just as requested. He didn't chat with the waiter. He never did such foolish things. The man was paid to deliver food, not to fraternize with guests.

He enjoyed his breakfast, surprised that he could find no fault with it, as he read the morning paper and listened to the news on the parlor television.

He considered how best to do what he'd come to do. Walking through the village as he'd done yesterday, driving around the island as he planned to do today, might not be enough. Still, it wouldn't do to ask people if they knew anyone of Helen's description. People never minded their own business, and there would be questions. Speculation. Attention.

If, by some chance, Helen was alive and here, the less attention paid to him, the better.

If she were, what would she do? She had no skills. How could she earn a living without him to provide for her? Unless, of course, she'd used her body to entice yet another man. Women were, at the center, whores.

He had to sit back and wait for the fury to pass. It was difficult to think in logical steps through anger. However justified.

He would find her, he reassured himself. If she was alive, he would find her. He would simply know. And that took him to what would be done when and if he did.

There was no question that she would have to be punished. For distressing him, for deceiving him, for attempting to break free of the promises she'd made to him. The inconvenience, the embarrassment of it all couldn't be calculated.

He would take her back to California, of course, but not right away. They would need to go somewhere quiet, somewhere private first, so he could remind her of those promises. So he could remind her who was in charge.

They would say she'd been thrown from the car. That she'd struck her head or some such thing. She'd had amnesia and had wandered away from the scene of the accident.

The press would love it, Evan decided. They would eat it up.

They would work out the details of the story once they were settled in that private, quiet place.

If none of that was possible, if she tried to refuse him, to run again, to go crying to the police as she'd done before, he would have to kill her.

He made the decision as coolly as he had decided what to have for breakfast.

Her choices were just as simple, in his opinion. Live—or die.

At the knock on his door, Evan folded the paper precisely, walked over to answer.

"Good morning, sir," the young maid said cheerfully. "You requested housekeeping service between nine and ten."

"That's right." He checked his watch, noted it was nine thirty. He had lingered over his thoughts longer than he'd planned.

"I hope you're enjoying your stay. Would you like me to start in the bedroom?"

"Yes."

He sat with his last cup of coffee, watched a report on a fresh hot spot in Eastern Europe that couldn't have interested him less. It was too early to call the coast and see if there was anything he needed to know. But he could call New York. He had a deal cooking there, and it wouldn't hurt to stir the pot.

He went into the bedroom to retrieve his memo book and found the maid, her arms full of fresh linen, staring at the framed photograph of Helen.

"Is there a problem?"

"What?" She flushed. "No, sir. I'm sorry."

She moved quickly to make the bed.

"You were looking at this photograph very intently. Why is that?"

"She's a lovely woman." His voice was sending skitters up her spine. She wanted to get the suite clean and get out.

"Yes, she is. My wife, Helen. The way you looked at the photograph, I thought perhaps you might have met her at some time or other."

"Oh, no, sir, I doubt it. It's just that she reminded me of someone."

He had to consciously stop his teeth from grinding. "Oh?"

"She really looks a lot like Nell—except Nell doesn't have all that beautiful hair or that look of . . . I don't know, polish, I guess you'd say."

"Really?" His blood began to sizzle, but he kept his voice mild now, almost friendly. "That's interesting. My wife would be fascinated to know there's a woman who looks that much like her."

Nell. Helen's mother had called her Nell. A simple, inelegant name. He had always disliked it.

"Does she live on the island, this Nell?"

"Oh, sure. She's lived here since early summer, in the yellow cottage. Runs the café at the bookstore—does catering, too. Cooks like a dream. You should try the café for lunch. There's a soup-and-sandwich special every day, and you can't beat it."

"I might do that," he said, very softly.

☙

Nell strolled through the back door of Café Book, called out a casual greeting to Lulu, then continued upstairs.

Once she was there, she moved like lightning.

Just under two minutes later, she called down in a voice she tried to infuse with frustrated apology. "Mia, I'm sorry, but could you come up here a minute?"

"Ought to be able to set up on her own by now," Lulu mumbled and earned a slanted look from the boss.

"You ought to be able to give her a break by now," Mia returned and started upstairs.

Nell stood by one of the café tables, where a pretty frosted cake glittered under the lighted birthday candles. Also on the table were a small wrapped box and three flutes frothy with mimosas.

"Happy birthday."

The sweetness of the gesture made up for being caught off guard, as she rarely was. Mia's smile bloomed—absolute delight. "Thank you. Cake?" She lifted a brow as she picked up a flute. "Mimosas *and* presents. It almost makes it worth turning thirty."

"Thirty." Coming up behind her, Lulu snorted. "Still a baby. When you hit fifty, we'll talk." She held out another wrapped box, a larger one. "Happy birthday."

"Thanks. Well, what first?"

"Wish first," Nell ordered, "and blow out the candles."

It had been a long time since she'd made anything as simple as a wish, but she did so now, then swept her breath over the candles.

"You have to cut the first piece." Nell handed her a cake knife.

"All right. Then I want my presents." Mia cut, then picked up the large box and tore in.

The throw was soft as water, the color of midnight sky. Scattered over it were the symbols of the zodiac. "Oh, Lu, it's fabulous!"

"Keep you warm."

"It's beautiful." Nell stroked the throw. "I tried to imagine it when Lulu described it, but it's so much more."

"Thank you." Mia turned, rubbed her cheek over Lulu's before kissing it.

Though pleased color pinched Lulu's cheeks, she waved Mia away. "Go on, open Nell's before she bursts."

"It's just that they made me think of you," Nell began as Mia set the throw aside to open the little box. Inside were earrings, a dangle of silver stars twinkling against tiny globes of moonstone.

"They're wonderful." Mia held them up to the light before she kissed Nell. "And perfect, particularly today," she added, holding out her arms.

She was wearing black again, but the sleek sweep of the dress was picked out in tiny silver stars and moons. "I couldn't resist it for Halloween, and now these . . ." She made quick work of slipping off the earrings she'd put on that morning and replacing them with Nell's. "Just top it off."

"Okay, then." Lulu raised her glass. "To hitting the big three-oh."

"Oh, Lulu, don't spoil it." But Mia laughed as she clicked glasses. "I want cake." She lifted her little silver watch that dangled from one of her chains. "We're going to open just a few minutes late today."

It wasn't difficult to find the yellow cottage. Evan drove past it, slowing his car to study the small house tucked among the trees. Little better than a shack, was his opinion, and the insult of it nearly choked him.

She would live in that hovel rather than in the beautiful homes he'd provided for her.

He had to fight the urge to go to the café, to drag her out and into the street. Public scenes, he reminded himself, were not the way to deal with a deceitful wife.

Such things required privacy.

He drove back to the village, parked his car, then went back on foot. His blood was already bubbling. Careful study showed him that none of the neighboring houses were close enough to worry him. Still, he strolled into the trees first, circled around. Stood in their shadows watching the house.

When nothing moved, nothing stirred, he crossed to the back door.

There was a wave of something—something strong and fretful. It seemed to push against him, as if to bar him from the door. For a moment it laid what might have been fear over his skin, and he actually found himself stepping back, off the stoop.

Fury bubbled, burned away that fear. While the stars hanging from the eaves chimed madly in a sudden gust of wind, he shoved through what seemed like a wall of solid air and gripped the doorknob.

She didn't even lock the house, he thought in disgust as he let himself in. See how careless she was, how foolish?

He saw the cat and nearly snarled. He detested animals. Filthy creatures. They stared at each other for one long moment, then Diego streaked away.

Evan scanned the kitchen, then began to walk through the cottage. He wanted to see how his dead wife had been living this past year.

He could hardly wait to see her again.

Twenty

She started to head home half a dozen times that afternoon, but there was so much fun in the village. Most of the merchants had decked themselves out in costumes to celebrate the day. There were demons selling hardware and fairies ringing up produce.

She had a late lunch with Ripley, and an impromptu meeting with Dorcas about catering a Christmas party.

And it seemed that every second person she passed stopped her to congratulate her on her engagement.

She belonged. To the village, she thought. To Zack. And finally, finally, she belonged to herself.

She swung by the station house to make a date with Zack to hand out the goody bags she'd already made up for the ghosts and goblins expected at dusk.

"I might be a little late. Have to run herd on some of the older kids," Zack told her. "I've already dealt with a couple of teenagers who tried to convince me the twelve rolls of toilet paper they were buying were for their mothers."

"How did you get the toilet paper for rolling houses when you were a kid?"

"I stole it out of the bathroom closet at home, like anyone with half a brain."

Her dimples deepened. "Any more exploding pumpkins?"

"No, I think the word got out on that." He cocked his head. "You sure look chipper today."

"I am chipper today." She stepped forward, wrapped her arms around his neck.

He'd just gotten his arms around her when his phone rang. "Hold that thought," he told her, and answered.

"Sheriff's office. Yeah, Mrs. Stubens. Hmm?" He stopped lowering his hip to the corner of the desk and stood straight again. "Is anybody hurt? Good. No, just stay right there, I'm on my way. Nancy Stubens," he told Nell as he strode over to the coat rack for his jacket. "Teaching her boy how to drive. He ran straight into the Bigelows' parked Honda Civic."

"But is he all right?"

"Yeah, I'll just go sort things out for them. It might take a while. That Honda was brand-new."

"You know where to find me."

She walked out with him, felt a nice steady glow when he leaned down to kiss her good-bye. Then they walked in opposite directions.

She'd gone half a block when Gladys Macey hailed her.

"Nell! Hold on." Puffing a little at the effort to catch up, Gladys patted her heart. "Let me see that ring I'm hearing so much about."

Before Nell could offer her hand, Gladys was grabbing it, bending over close to get a good, long look. "Should have known that Todd boy would do a good job." She gave a nod of approval, then looked up at Nell. "You got a winner there, and I don't mean the ring."

"I know it."

"I watched him grow up. Once he got some man on him, if you know what I mean, I used to wonder what sort of woman would catch his fancy. I like knowing it's you. I've got a fondness for you."

"Mrs. Macey." Undone, Nell hugged her. "Thank you."

"You'll be good for him." She patted Nell's back. "And he'll be good for you. I know you've had some troubles." She simply nodded as Nell drew back. "You had something in your eyes when you came here. It's not there much anymore."

"I left all that behind. I'm happy."

"It shows. Have you set the date?"

"No, not yet." Nell thought of lawyers, of conflict. Of Evan. She would deal with it, she told herself. With all of it. "As soon as we can."

"I want a front-row seat at the wedding."

"You'll have one. And all the champagne you can drink at our thirtieth anniversary party."

"I'll hold you to it. Well, I've got to get on. Monsters'll come knocking at the door before long, and I don't want my windows soaped. You tell that man of yours I said he did well."

"I will." That man of hers, Nell thought as she began to walk again. What a wonderful phrase.

She quickened her steps. She was going to have to hurry to beat dusk.

She went to the front of the cottage, glancing around a bit self-consciously. Secure that she was alone in the lowering light, she held her arms out toward her jack-o'-lanterns, breathed in, focused.

It took some work, a hard slap of effort, and a match would certainly have been quicker. But it wouldn't have given her the same rush as watching the candles spurt flame and the pumpkins glow from the fire in her mind.

Boy! She let out her breath on a quick laugh. Boy, oh boy, that was so *cool*.

It wasn't just the magic, she decided. It was the knowing—who and what she was. It was finding her strength, her purpose, and her heart. Taking back control so that she could share it with a man who believed in her.

Whatever happened tomorrow, or a year from tomorrow, she was now and always Nell.

She danced up the steps and in through the front door.

"Diego! I'm home. You wouldn't believe the day I've had. Absolutely the best day."

She twirled into the kitchen, flipping on the light. She put on the kettle for tea before beginning to fill a big wicker basket with her goody bags.

"I hope we get a lot of kids. It's been years since I've done trick or treat. I can't wait." She opened a cupboard. "Oh, for heaven's sake! I left my car at the bookstore. What was I thinking?"

"You always were absentminded."

The mug she reached for slipped like water out of her hand, smashed on the counter, shattered on the floor. A roaring filled her ears as she turned.

"Hello, Helen." Evan walked slowly toward her. "It's so good to see you."

She couldn't say his name, could make no sound at all. She prayed it was another vision, a hallucination. But he reached out, and those slender fingers brushed her cheek.

She went cold to the marrow.

"I've missed you. Did you think I wouldn't come?" Those fingers slid around the back of her neck now and brought on a hideous wave of nausea. "Wouldn't find you? Haven't I told you, Helen, so many times, that nothing would ever keep us apart?"

She only closed her eyes when he bent, brushed his mouth over hers. "What have you done to your hair?" His hand fisted it, tugged viciously. "You know how I love your hair. Did you cut it off to displease me?"

A tear slithered down her cheek as she shook her head. His voice, his touch, seemed to drain everything she was away and leave her as she'd been.

She felt Nell fading away.

"It does displease me, Helen. You've caused me a great deal of trouble. A great deal. You've stolen a year of our lives."

His fingers tightened, went biting cruel as he jerked her chin up. "Look at me, you stupid little bitch. Look at me when I speak to you."

Her eyes opened and all she could see were his, those clear, empty pools.

"You'll have to pay for it, you know that. More than a year erased. And all the while you've been living in this miserable little shack, laughing at me, working as a waitress, serving people. Trying to start your pitiful little business, kitchen business. Humiliating me."

His hand slid from her cheek to her throat, squeezed. "I'm going to forgive you after a time, Helen. After a time, because I know you're slow, and just a bit stupid. Have you nothing to say to me, my love? Nothing to say after this long separation?"

Her lips were cold, felt as if they might crack. "How did you find me?"

He smiled then, and made her shudder. "I told you I'd always find you, wherever you went, whatever you did." He gave her a hard shove that jammed her back into the counter. The pain registered in kind of an absent way, like a memory.

"Do you know what I found here, in your little nest, Helen? Helen, my whore? Men's clothing. How many men have you slept with, slut?"

The kettle began to shriek, but neither of them heard.

"Did you find yourself some strapping local fisherman, let him put his fumbling, workingman's hands all over you? All over what belongs to me?"

Zack. It was her first clear thought. Clear enough that her swimming eyes registered bright fear.

"There's no fisherman," she said and barely cried out when he slapped her.

"Liar. You know how I detest liars."

"There's no—" The tears escaped at the next slap. But it snapped her back to who she was. She was Nell Channing, and she would fight. "Keep away from me. Keep away." She grabbed for the knife block, but he was quicker. He'd always been quicker.

"Is this what you want?" He drew the long, jagged-edged blade free, turned it in the light an inch from her nose. She braced herself. She thought: So, he'll kill me after all.

Instead he reared back, smashing the side of her face with a vicious backhanded slap that sent her flying. She crashed into the table, striking her head against the edge of the thick wood. The world went bright, went dark.

She didn't feel her body hit the floor.

Mia treated a young space explorer. The bookstore was one of the most popular spots on Halloween. She had dancing skeletons, grinning pumpkins, flying ghosts, and, of course, a coven of witches. Her usual store music had been replaced with howls and shrieks and rattling chains.

She was having the time of her life.

She served a cowboy ghoul a cup of punch from a cauldron as the dry ice packed beneath it sent out curls of smoke.

His eyes were huge as he watched her. "Are you gonna ride on your broomstick tonight?"

"Of course." She bent down. "What kind of a witch would I be otherwise?"

"The witch who chased Dorothy was a bad witch."

"She was a very bad witch," Mia agreed. "I happen to be a very good one."

"She was ug-ly, and had a green face. You're pretty," he giggled and slurped his punch.

"Thank you very much. You, on the other hand, are very scary." She handed him a bag of candy. "I hope you won't trick me."

"Huh-uh. Thanks, lady." He dropped the bag in his begging sack, then ran off to find his mother.

Amused, Mia started to straighten. The pain came fast, bright, like a spear of light through the temple. She saw a man with pale eyes and bright hair, and the gleam of the blade.

"Call Zack." She rushed to the door, calling out to a startled Lulu. "There's trouble. Nell's in trouble. Call Zack."

She raced into the street, swung around a group of costumed children and nearly plowed into Ripley. "Nell."

"I know it." Ripley's head was still ringing. "We have to hurry."

She came to slowly, her vision fractured, her head screaming. There was absolute silence. She rolled, moaning, and managed to get to her hands and knees. Nausea sent her curling into a ball again.

The kitchen was dark now, lit only by the faint glow of a candle in the center of the table.

He sat there, in one of her kitchen chairs. She could see his shoes, the gleam of them, the perfect crease in his slacks, and she wanted to weep.

"Why do you make me punish you, Helen? I can only think you must enjoy it." He nudged her with his shoe. "Is that it?"

She started to crawl away. Just a moment, she prayed. Give me one moment to breathe, and I can find my strength again.

He simply pressed his foot into her back.

"We're going to go somewhere where we can be alone. Where we can discuss all this foolishness, all this trouble you've caused me."

He frowned a little. How was he to get her away? He hadn't meant to put marks on her, not where they could be noticed. She had pushed him to it.

"We'll walk to my car," he decided. "You'll wait there for me while I pack and check out."

She shook her head. She knew it was useless, but she shook her head, then began to cry quietly when she felt Diego brush against her legs.

"You'll do exactly as I say." He tapped the tip of the knife against the table. "If you don't, you'll leave me no choice. People already believe you're dead, Helen. Beliefs can easily become reality."

His head snapped up as he heard a sound outside the door. "Perhaps the fisherman's come calling," he whispered, and rose, turning the knife in his hand.

Zack opened the door, hesitating, cursing as the phone on his belt rang. The break in stride saved his life.

He caught a blur of movement, a glimpse of the blade hacking down. He twisted, going for his weapon with a cross-body draw. The knife ripped through his shoulder instead of burying itself in his heart.

Nell screamed, gained her feet, only to have her head spin and send her staggering. In the dark kitchen, she could see the two silhouettes struggle. A weapon, she thought, biting her lip to keep from passing out again.

The bastard would *not* take what was hers. He would *not* harm what she loved.

She stumbled for the knife block, but it was gone.

She turned back, prepared to leap, to use teeth and nails. And saw Evan standing over Zack's body, the knife dripping in his hand.

"Oh, my God, no! No!"

"Your knight in shining armor, Helen? Is this the man you've been fucking behind my back? He's not dead yet. I have a right to kill him for trying to steal my wife."

"Don't." She drew in a breath, released it. Struggled to gather herself and find her core of strength. "I'll go with you. I'll do anything you want."

"You will, anyway," Evan commanded.

"He doesn't matter." She began to edge around the counter, saw Diego crouched, teeth bared. "He doesn't matter to either of us. It's me you want, isn't it? You came all this way for me."

He would go after her. If she could get out the door, he'd go after her and leave Zack. It took all her will to keep herself from throwing herself down over Zack, to shield him. If she did, if she so much as looked at him now, they were both dead.

"I knew you would," she continued, every muscle trembling as she watched Evan lower the knife to his side. "I always knew."

Evan took one step toward her, and the cat leaped like a tiger on his back. With his howl of rage in her ears, Nell ran.

She veered toward the street, toward the village, but even as she glanced back, he was coming through the door. She would never make it.

So, it would be the two of them, after all. Putting her faith in the fates, she dived into the trees.

Zack pulled himself to his knees as Evan bolted out the door. The pain was like hot teeth gnawing at his shoulder. Blood dripped from his fingers as he got to his feet.

Then he thought of Nell and forgot the pain.

He was flying out the door just as the trees swallowed her and the man who pursued her.

"Zack!"

He paused only to flick a terrified glance at his sister and Mia. "He's after her. He's got a knife, and she doesn't have much lead."

Ripley bit down on the worry. His shirt was soaked with blood. She nodded, drew her weapon as he did. "Whatever you've got," she said to Mia, "we use."

She plunged into the woods behind her brother.

In the dark of the moon, the night was blind. She ran like a wild thing, tearing through brush, leaping over fallen branches. If she could lose him, get him deep enough in and lose him, she could circle back to Zack.

She prayed with every beat of her heart that he was alive.

She could hear Evan behind her, close, too close. Her breath was coming in gasps, tattered by fear, but his was a steady determined beat.

Dizziness swept over her, urged her to drop to her knees. She fought it off, nearly stumbled. She would not lose now.

Then his body slammed into hers and sent her sprawling.

She rolled, kicked, her only thought to get free of him. Then froze when he yanked her head back by her short cap of hair and pressed the knife tip to her throat.

Her body emptied, went limp as a doll's. "Why don't you just do it," she said wearily. "Just end it."

"You ran from me." There was as much bafflement as rage in his voice. "You ran."

"And I'll keep running. Until you kill me, I'll keep running. I'd rather be dead than live with you. I've already died once, so do it. I've stopped being afraid of you."

She felt the blade bite. At the sound of running feet, he dragged her up.

Even with a knife at her throat, she felt joy when she saw Zack.

Alive. The dark stain on his shirt glimmered in the faint starlight. But he was alive, and nothing mattered more.

"Let her go." Zack took his stance, supporting his gun hand with his weak one. "Drop the knife and step away from her."

"I'll slit her throat. She's mine, and I won't hesitate." Evan's eyes passed from Zack's to Ripley's to Mia's as they stood in a half circle.

"Hurt her, and you're dead. You won't walk away from here."

"You've no right to interfere between a husband and wife." There was something almost reasonable in his voice, something sane under the madness. "Helen is my wife. Legally, morally, eternally." He jerked her head back another inch with the blade. "Throw your guns down and walk away. This is my business."

"I can't get a clear shot," Ripley said under her breath. "Not enough light to be sure."

"It's not the way. Put the gun down, Ripley." Mia stretched out her hand.

"The hell with that." Her finger itched on the trigger. The bastard, was all she could think as she saw Nell's exposed throat, smelled her brother's blood.

"Ripley," Mia said again, soft, insistent under the sharp, clipped orders from Zack to drop the knife. To step away.

"Damn it, damn it. You better be right."

Zack didn't hear them. They'd ceased to exist for him. His only reality was Nell.

"I'll do more than kill you." Zack held the gun rock steady and his voice was calm as a lake. "If you cut her, so much as nick her, I'll take you apart, piece by piece. I'll put bullets in your knees, in your balls, in your gut. I'll stand over you and watch while you bleed out."

The color that rage brought to Evan's face drained away. He believed what he saw in Zack's eyes. Believed the pain and death he saw there, and was afraid. His hands trembled on the handle of the knife, but he didn't move. "She belongs to me."

Ripley's hand gripped Mia's. Nell felt the punch of energy they created, felt the hot waves of love and terror that rolled off Zack as he stood bleeding for her.

And felt, as she had never felt, fear from the man who gripped her.

Her name was Nell Channing, now and always. And the man behind her was less than nothing.

She closed her hand over the pendant Mia had given her. It vibrated. "I belong to myself." Power trickled back into her, a slow pool. "I belong to me." And faster. "And to you," she said, her eyes locked on Zack's. "He's done hurting me now."

She lifted her other hand, laid it on Evan's wrist, lightly. "Let me go, Evan, and you'll walk away. We'll put all of this behind us. It's your chance. The last chance."

His breath hissed at her ear. "You stupid bitch. Do you think I'll ever let you go?"

"And your choice." There was pity in her voice. "Your last."

The chant was in her head, rising, as if it had only been waiting for her to free it.

She wondered how she could have been so afraid of him.

"What you've done to all and me, turns back to you, one times three. From you this night I'll forever be free. As I will, so mote it be."

Her skin glowed like sunlight, her pupils dark as stars. The knife trembled, whispered along her skin, away, then fell. She heard the choking gasp, the high whine that couldn't reach a scream as Evan collapsed behind her.

She didn't spare him a glance.

"Don't shoot him," she said quietly to Zack. "Don't kill him like this. It wouldn't be good for you."

Because she could see the intent, she walked to Zack as Evan began to moan. "It wouldn't be good for us. He's nothing now." She laid a hand over Zack's heart, felt its wild beat. "He's what he made himself."

Evan lay on the ground, twitching as if something vile slithered under his skin. His face was bone white.

Zack lowered the gun, wrapped his good arm around Nell. He held her there a moment as she reached out, clasping hands with Mia, and linking them all.

"Stay with them," Zack told her. "I'll deal with him. I won't kill him. He'll suffer more if he lives."

Ripley watched her brother walk toward the writhing man, take out his handcuffs. He needed to do this last thing, she thought, and she needed to let him. "He gets two minutes to secure and Mirandize that smear of slime, then I want him taken to the clinic. I don't know how bad he's hurt."

"I'll take him." Nell looked down at the blood, Zack's blood, on her hand, curled her fist over it, and felt life pump. "I'll stay with him."

"Courage"—Mia reached out, touched the pendant—"breaks the spell. Love weaves another." She pulled Nell into her arms for a fierce hug. "You did well, little sister." She turned toward Ripley. "And you found your fate."

Early on the Feast of the Saints, long after the balefires were charmed away, before dawn broke the sky, Nell sat in the kitchen of the yellow cottage, her hand resting loosely in Zack's.

She needed to come back, to be there, to tidy away what had

happened and what might have happened. She'd swept away the negative forces that had lingered and had lit candles and incense.

"I wish you'd stayed overnight at the clinic."

She turned her hand under Zack's, squeezed. "I could say the same."

"I've got a few stitches, you've got the concussion."

"Mild," she reminded him, "and twenty-three stitches is more than a few."

Twenty-three stitches, he thought. A long, nasty gash. The doctor had called it a miracle that no muscle or tendons had been severed.

Zack called it magic. Nell's magic.

She reached out to touch the fresh white bandage, then trailed her fingers over the gold locket. "You didn't take it off."

"You asked me not to. It got hot," he told her, and brought her gaze back to his. "An instant before he cut me. I could see, in my head, in that quick blur, the blade going toward my heart, then being deflected. As if it hit a shield. I thought I imagined it. But I didn't."

"We were stronger than he was." Nell brought their joined hands to her cheek. "I was afraid, drowning in fear from the minute I heard his voice. It took away everything I'd built, everything I'd learned about myself. He paralyzed me, sucked out my will. That was his power over me. But it began to come back, and when he hurt you, it flooded back. But I couldn't think, not clearly. Hitting my head was part of it, I suppose."

"You ran to save me."

"And you followed to save me. We're a couple of heroes."

He touched her face, gently. There were bruises on it that he felt throb in his own. "He's never going to hurt you again. I'll go in and relieve Ripley at dawn, and contact the prosecutor's office on the mainland. A couple of attempted-murder charges will keep him locked up, no matter how fancy his lawyers are."

"I'm not afraid of him anymore. He looked pathetic in the end, eaten up by his own cruelty. Terrified of it. His madness is staring back at him now. He'll never be able to hide it again."

He could still see Evan Remington's colorless eyes, wide and wild in a face white as bone. "A padded room's as good as a cell."

She got to her feet to pour more tea. But when she came back to the table, Zack wrapped an arm around her, pressed his face into her body.

"It's going to take a while for me to get the picture of you with a knife to your throat out of my head."

She stroked his hair. "We have a lifetime to put others in its place. I want to marry you, Sheriff Todd. I want to start that lifetime very soon."

She slid into his lap, sighing as she rested her head on his good shoulder. Through the window she could see the first streaks of color announcing dawn, the pale burn across the sky.

Laying a hand on his heart, she timed its beats to her own. And knew the truest magic was there.

KEEP READING FOR AN EXCERPT FROM THE
SECOND NOVEL IN THE THREE SISTERS ISLAND TRILOGY
BY NORA ROBERTS

Heaven and Earth

NOW AVAILABLE FROM JOVE BOOKS

THREE SISTERS ISLAND

JANUARY 2002

Sand, frosted with cold, crunched under her feet as she ran along the curving shore. Incoming waves left froth and bubbles lying on the crusted surface like tattered lace. Overhead, the gulls called, relentlessly.

Her muscles had warmed, and moved fluid as oiled gears in the second mile of her morning run. Her pace was a fast and disciplined jog, and her breath rushed out in white plumes. And rushed in, sharp and cold as shards of ice.

She felt fabulous.

The wintry beach held no footprints but her own, and hers were stamped, new over old, as she jogged back and forth across the gentle sweep of winter beach.

If she'd chosen to do her three miles in one straight line, she could have crossed Three Sisters from side to side at its widest point.

The idea of that always pleased her.

The little clump of land off the coast of Massachusetts was hers, every hill, every street, every cliff and inlet. Deputy Ripley Todd felt more than affection for Three Sisters, its village, its residents, its well-being. She felt responsibility.

She could see the rising sun glint against the windows of store-fronts on High Street. In a couple of hours, the shops would open, people would walk along the streets going about the day's business.

There wasn't much of a tourist trade in January, but some would come over from the mainland on the ferry, poke about in the shops, drive up to the cliffs, buy some fresh fish right off the docks. For the most part, though, the winter was for islanders.

She loved the winter best.

At the end of the beach, where it bumped the edge of the seawall just below the village, she pivoted and headed back across the sand. Fishing boats plied an ocean that was the color of pale blue ice. It would change as the light strengthened, as the sky deepened. It never failed to fascinate her how many colors water could hold.

She saw Carl Macey's boat, and a figure, tiny as a toy in the stern, raised a hand. She saluted back, kept running. With under three thousand islanders year-round, it wasn't hard to know who was who.

She slowed her pace a bit, not only to cool down but to prolong the solitude. She often took her morning runs with her brother's dog, Lucy, but this morning she had slipped out alone.

Alone was another thing she liked best.

And she'd wanted to clear her mind. There was a great deal to think about. Some of which she preferred not to, so she tucked those annoyances and problems away for now. What had to be dealt with wasn't precisely a problem. You couldn't call something that made you happy a problem.

Her brother was just back from his honeymoon, and nothing could have pleased her more than to see how happy he and Nell were together. After all they'd been through, and what it had nearly cost, seeing them cozied up together in the house where she and Zack had grown up was pure satisfaction.

And over the past months, since summer, when Nell had ended her flight from fear on the island, they'd become real friends. It was a pleasure to see the way Nell had bloomed, and toughened.

But all that mushy stuff aside, Ripley thought, there was one little blight on the rose. And its name was Ripley Karen Todd.

Newlyweds didn't need to share their love nest with the groom's sister.

She hadn't given the matter a thought before the wedding, and even after, when she'd waved them both off for a week in Bermuda, she hadn't seen the whole picture.

But when they'd returned, all snuggling and flushed with a honeymoon haze, it couldn't have been more clear.

Just-marrieds needed privacy. They could hardly have hot, spontaneous sex on the living room floor if she might stroll into the house any time of the day or night.

Not that either of them had said anything about it. But they wouldn't. The pair of them might as well wear we're-nice-people merit badges plastered on their chests. And that, Ripley thought, was something she would never be pinning on her own shirt.

She stopped, used the outcropping of rocks at the far end of the beach for support as she stretched out calves, hamstrings, quadriceps.

Her body was as lean and toned as a young tiger's. She took pride in it, in her control over it. As she bent from the waist, the ski cap that she'd tugged on fell to the sand and her hair, the color of varnished oak, tumbled free.

She wore it long because it didn't require regular trims and styling that way. It was just another type of control.

Her eyes were a sharp bottle green. When she was in the mood she might fuss with mascara and eyeliner. After considerable debate, she'd decided her eyes were the best part of a face made up of mismatched features and angular lines.

She had a slight overbite because she'd despised her retainer. And she had the wide forehead and nearly horizontal dark eyebrows of the Ripley side of the family.

No one would have accused her of being pretty. It was too soft a word—and would have insulted her in any case. She preferred knowing it was a strong and sexy face. The kind that could attract men. When she was in the mood for one.

Which she hadn't been, she mused, for several months.

Part of that was wedding plans, holiday plans, the time she'd spent helping Zack and Nell unwind legal tangles so they could be married. And another part, she was forced to admit, was her own sense of annoyance and unease that lingered from Halloween, when she'd ripped open pockets in herself that she had purposely sewn shut years before.

Couldn't be helped, she thought now. She'd done what needed to be done. And had no intention of a repeat performance. No matter how many cool, smirky glances Mia Devlin shot her way.

The thought of Mia brought Ripley back full circle.

Mia had an empty cottage. Nell had rented it, then moved out when she married Zack. As much as Ripley hated the idea of having any sort of dealings, even straight business, with Mia, the yellow cottage was the perfect solution.

It was small, private, simple.

It just made sense, Ripley decided and started up the worn wooden steps that zagged from the beach toward the house. It was irritating, but it was practical. Still, maybe it wouldn't hurt if she took a few days, let the word out that she was looking for a place to rent. Something—something that didn't belong to Mia—might drop in her lap.

Cheered by the possibility, Ripley bounded up the steps, jogged to the back porch.

Nell would already be baking, she knew, just as she knew the kitchen would smell like heaven. The biggest advantage was that she wouldn't have to hunt up breakfast. It would just be there. Delicious, delightful, and on demand.

As she reached for the doorknob, she saw, through the glass, Zack and Nell. They were wrapped around each other, she thought, like ivy on a flagpole. Wrapped around each other *and* wrapped up in each other.

"Oh, man."

Hissing out a breath, she backtracked, then came back up on the porch stomping like a horse and whistling. It would give them time to peel themselves off each other. At least, she hoped it would.

But it didn't solve her other problem. She was going to have to deal with Mia, after all.

She was going to keep it casual. To Ripley's way of thinking, if Mia knew she really wanted the yellow cottage, she would refuse to rent it.

The woman was so damn contrary.

Of course, the very best way to lock in the deal would be to ask Nell to run interference. Mia had a soft spot for Nell. But the idea of using anyone to clear the path was galling. She would just casually drop in at Mia's bookstore, the way she had almost every day since Nell had taken over the cooking and baking for the café section.

That way she could cop a righteous lunch and new digs all in one swipe.

She walked briskly along High Street, more because she wanted the business over and done than because the wind was up and blowing.

It tugged playfully at the long, straight tail of hair that she habitually yanked through the opening in the back of her cap.

When she reached Café Book she paused, pursed her lips.

Mia had redone the display window. A little tasseled footstool, a soft throw of deep red, and a pair of tall candlestands with fat red candles were arranged with seemingly haphazard piles of books. Because she knew Mia never did anything in a haphazard fashion, Ripley had to admit the whole tone was one of homey warmth and welcome. And subtly—very subtly—sexy.

It's cold out, the window announced. Come on in and buy some books to take home and snuggle up with.

Whatever else Ripley could say about Mia—and she could say plenty—the woman knew her business.

She stepped inside into warmth, automatically unwinding her neck scarf. The deep-blue shelves were lined with books, parlor-tidy. Glass displays held pretty trinkets and intriguing dust catchers. The fireplace was simmering with a low golden flame, and another throw, blue this time, was tossed artfully over one of the deep, sink-into-me chairs.

Yeah, she thought, Mia knew her stuff.

There was more. Other shelves held candles of various shapes and sizes. Deep bowls were filled with tumbling stones and crystals. Colorful boxes of Tarot cards and runes were tucked here and there.

All very subtle again, Ripley noted with a frown. Mia didn't advertise that the place was owned by a witch, but she didn't hide it either. Ripley imagined the curiosity factor—both tourist and local— accounted for a healthy chunk of the store's annual profits.

None of her business.

From behind the big carved counter, Mia's head clerk, Lulu, finished ringing up a customer's purchases, then tipped down her silver-framed glasses to peer at Ripley over the top of them.

"Looking for something for your mind as well as your belly today?"

"No. I've got plenty to occupy my mind."

"Read more, know more."

Ripley grinned. "I already know everything."

"Always thought you did, anyway. Got a novelty book in this week's shipment that's right up your alley. *101 Pick-Up Lines*—unisex."

"Lu." Ripley gave her a cocky grin as she strolled to the stairs leading to the shop's second level. "I wrote the book."

Lulu cackled. "Haven't seen you keeping company just recently," she called out.

"I haven't felt like company just recently."

There were more books on the second floor, and more browsers poking through them. But here, the café was the big draw. Already Ripley could scent the soup of the day, something rich and spicy.

The early crowd, which would have snagged Nell's muffins and turnovers or whatever treat she'd dreamed up for the day, had shifted to the lunch crowd. On a day like this, Ripley imagined they'd be looking for something hot and hearty, before they treated themselves to one of Nell's sinful desserts.

She scanned the display and sighed. Cream puffs. Nobody in their right mind walked away from cream puffs, even if the other choices were equally tempting éclairs, tarts, cookies, and what looked to be a cake made up of many layers of pure gooey sin.

The artist behind the temptations rang up an order. Her eyes were a deep and clear blue, her hair a short gold halo around a face that glowed with health and well-being. Dimples flashed in her cheeks as she smiled and waved her customer off to one of the café tables arranged by the window.

Marriage, Ripley thought, agreed with some people. Nell Channing Todd was one of them.

"You look pretty bouncy today," Ripley commented.

"Feel great. The day's just flying by. Soup of the day's minestrone, sandwich is—"

"I'm just doing soup," Ripley interrupted. "Because I need one of the cream puffs to ensure my happiness. I'll take coffee with it."

"Coming up. I'm baking a ham for dinner tonight," she added. "So no grabbing pizza before you come home."

"Yeah, okay. Sure." It reminded Ripley of the second stage of business. She shifted her feet, gave the room another sweeping glance. "I didn't see Mia around anywhere."

"Working in her office." Nell ladled up soup, added a crusty roll baked fresh that morning. "I expect she'll breeze through shortly. You were in and out of the house so fast this morning I didn't get to talk to you. Something up?"

"No, not up." Maybe it was rude to arrange for alternate living arrangements without saying something first. Ripley wondered if this fell into the area of social skills, a tricky business for her.

"Will I be in your way if I chow down in the kitchen?" she asked Nell. "That way I can talk to you while you work."

"Sure. Come on back."

Nell carried the food over to her worktable. "Are you sure nothing's wrong?"

"Not a thing," Ripley assured her. "Bitchy cold out. I bet you and Zack are sorry you didn't stay south until spring."

"The honeymoon was perfect." Even thinking of it brought on a warm, satisfied glow. "But it's better being home." Nell opened the refrigerator for the container holding one of the day's salads. "Everything I want is here. Zack, family, friends, a home of my own. A year ago I'd never have believed I'd be standing here like this, knowing that in an hour or so I'd be going home."

"You earned it."

"I did." Nell's eyes darkened, and in them Ripley could see the core of strength—a core that everyone, including Nell, had under-estimated. "But I didn't do it alone." The bright *ding* of the counter bell warned her she had a customer waiting. "Don't let your soup get cold."

She slipped out, her voice lifting in greeting.

Ripley spooned up soup and sighed with contentment at the first taste. She would just concentrate on her lunch and think about the rest later.

But she'd barely made a dent in the bowl when she heard Nell call Mia's name.

"Ripley's in the kitchen. I think she wanted to see you."

Shit, shit, *shit*! Ripley scowled into her soup and got busy filling her mouth.

"Well, well, make yourself at home."

Mia Devlin, her gypsy mane of red hair tumbling over the shoul-ders of a long dress of forest green, leaned gracefully against the doorjamb. Her face was a miracle formed of high, ice-edged cheek-bones; a full, sculpted mouth painted as boldly red as her hair; skin smooth as cream; and eyes gray as witch-smoke.

Those eyes looked Ripley over lazily, one brow lifted in a perfect and derisive arch.

"I am." Ripley continued to eat. "I figure it's Nell's kitchen this time of day. If I thought otherwise, I'd be searching my soup for wool of bat or dragon's teeth."

"And it's so hard to come by dragon's teeth this time of year. What can I do for you, Deputy?"

"Not a thing. But I did give some passing thought to doing some-thing for you."

"Now I'm all agog." Tall and slim, she moved to the table and sat. She was wearing those needle-thin heels she was so fond of, Ripley noticed. She could never figure out why anyone would put her innocent feet in such torture chambers without a gun being held to her head.

She broke off another piece of her roll, munched. "You lost yourself a tenant when Nell and Zack tied the knot. I figured you hadn't gotten around to doing anything about renting out the yellow cottage, and since I'm thinking about getting my own place, maybe I can help you out."

"Do tell." Intrigued, Mia broke off a bite of Ripley's roll for herself.

"Hey, I'm paying for that."

Ignoring her, Mia nibbled. "A little too crowded for you at the homestead?"

"It's a big house." Ripley gave a careless shrug, then moved the rest of her roll out of reach. "But you happen to have one going empty. It's a pretty dinky place, but I don't need much. I'd be willing to negotiate a lease on it."

"A lease on what?" Nell swung back in, straight to the fridge to get out the makings for a sandwich order.

"The yellow cottage," Mia told her. "Ripley's looking for a place of her own."

"Oh, but—" Nell turned. "You have a place of your own. With us."

"Let's not make this sticky." It was too late to regret she hadn't arranged to speak to Mia privately. "I was just thinking it'd be cool to have a little place to myself, and since Mia's got one going begging—"

"On the contrary," Mia said smoothly. "Neither I nor my possessions need to beg."

"You don't want me to do you a favor?" Ripley lifted a shoulder. "No skin off mine."

"It's so considerate of you to think of me." Mia's tone was candy-sweet. Always a bad sign. "But as it happens I just signed with a tenant for the cottage not ten minutes ago."

"Bullshit. You were just up in your office, and Nell didn't say you were with anyone."

"On the phone," Mia continued. "With a gentleman from New York. A doctor. We've signed a three-month lease for the cottage via fax. I hope that relieves your mind."

Ripley wasn't quite quick enough to mask her annoyance. "Like I said, no skin off mine. What the hell's a doctor going to do for three months on Three Sisters? We've got a doctor on-island."

"He's not a medical doctor. He's a Ph.D.—and as you're so interested, he's coming here to work. Dr. Booke is a paranormal researcher, and he's eager to spend some time on an island conjured by witches."

"Fucking A."

"Always so succinct." Amused, Mia got to her feet. "Well, my work here is done. I must go see if I can bring joy into someone else's life now." She strolled to the door, waited a beat before she turned. "Oh, he'll be here tomorrow. I'm sure he'd love to meet you, Ripley."

"Keep your weirdo spook hunters away from me. Damn it." Ripley bit into her cream puff. "She's eating this up."

"Don't go anywhere." Nell lifted her order. "Peg comes on in five. I want to talk to you."

"I've got patrol."

"You just wait."

"Damn near ruined my appetite," Ripley complained, but managed to devour the cream puff.

I n fifteen minutes she was stalking outside again, Nell glued to her side.

"We need to talk about this."

"Look, Nell, it's no big deal. I was just thinking—"

"Yes, you were thinking." Nell yanked her wool cap down over her ears. "And you didn't say anything to me, or to Zack. I want to know why you feel you can't stay in your own home."

"Okay, okay." Ripley put on her sunglasses, hunched her shoulders as they started down High toward the station house. "It just seems to me that when people get married, they need privacy."

"It's a big house. We're not in each other's way. If you were the domestic type, I could see you feeling displaced because I have to spend so much of my time in the kitchen."

"That's the least of my worries."

"Exactly. You don't cook. I hope you don't think I resent cooking for you."

"No, I don't think that. And I appreciate it, Nell, I really do."

"Is it because I get up so early?"

"No."

"Because I took one of the spare bedrooms for an office for Sisters Catering?"

"No. Jeez, nobody was using it." Ripley felt as though she was being systematically pounded with a velvet bat. "Look, look, it's not about cooking or spare rooms or your baffling habit of getting out of bed before the sun rises. It's about sex."

"Excuse me?"

"You and Zack have sex."

Nell stopped, cocked her head as she studied Ripley's face. "Yes, we do. I don't deny it. In fact, we have quite a lot of sex."

"There you are."

"Ripley, before I officially moved into the house, Zack and I often had sex there. It never seemed to be a problem for you."

"That was different. That was regular sex. Now you're having married sex."

"I see. Well, I can assure you the process works in almost exactly the same way."

"Har-har." Nell had come a long way, Ripley mused. There'd been a time when even the hint of a confrontation would have had her backing down.

Those days were over.

"It's just weird, okay? You and Zack are into the mister and missus thing and you've got me hanging around. What if you wanted to do the horizontal tango on the living room rug, or just have dinner naked some night?"

"We've actually done the first, but now I'll give some serious consideration to the second. Ripley." Nell touched Ripley's arm, rubbed lightly. "I don't want you to move out."

"Jesus, Nell, it's a small island. It's not like I'd be hard to reach wherever I landed."

"I don't want you to move," she said again. "I'm speaking for myself, not for Zack. You can talk to him separately if you want and get his feelings about it. Ripley . . . I've never had a sister before."

"Oh, man." She cringed, scanning the area from behind her dark glasses. "Don't get mushy, not right out on the street like this."

"I can't help it. I like knowing you're there, that I can talk to you whenever. I only had a few days with your parents when they came back for the wedding, but knowing them now and having you, I have a family again. Can't we just leave things the way they are, for now, anyway?"

"Does Zack ever say no to you once you turn those big blue headlights on him?"

"Not when he knows it's really important to me. And if you stay, I'll promise that when Zack and I have sex, we'll pretend we're not married."

"It might help. Anyway, since some jerk from New York snagged the cottage right out from under my nose, I'll have to let things ride." She let out a pained sigh. "Paranormal researcher, my butt. Ph.D." She sneered and felt marginally cheered. "Mia probably rented the place to him just to piss me off."

"I doubt it, but I'm sure she's enjoying that side benefit. I wish the two of you wouldn't jab at each other so much. I'd really hoped, after . . . after what happened on Halloween you would be friends again."

Instantly, Ripley closed in. "Everybody did what had to be done. Now it's over. Nothing's changed for me."

"Only one phase is over," Nell corrected. "If the legend—"

"The legend is hooey." Even thinking of it blighted Ripley's mood. "What we are isn't. What's inside us isn't."

"And what I do with what's inside me is my business. Don't go there, Nell."

"All right." But Nell squeezed Ripley's hand and even through the gloves that both women wore, there was a spark of energy. "I'll see you at dinner."

Ripley balled her hand as Nell walked away. Her skin still hummed from the contact. Sneaky little witch, Ripley thought.

She had to admire that.

Dreams came late in the night, when her mind was open and her will at rest. She could deny by day, close herself off, stand by the choice she'd made more than a decade before.

But sleep was a power of its own, and seduced the dreaming.

In dreams, she stood on the beach, where the waves rose like terror. They pounded, black and bitter, on the shore, a thousand mad heartbeats, under a blind sky.

The only light was the snake-whips of lightning that slashed each time she raised her arms. And the light that came from her was a furious gold edged with murderous red.

The wind roared.

The violence of it, the sheer, unharnessed *power* of it, thrilled her in some deep and secret place. She was beyond now, beyond right, beyond rules.

Beyond hope.

And part of her, still flickering, wept grievous tears for the loss.

She had done what she had done, and now wrongs were avenged. Death to death to death. A circle formed by hate. One times three.

She cried out in triumph as the dark smoke of black magic streamed inside her, smearing and choking out what she had been, what she had vowed. What she had believed.

This, she thought as her cupped hands trembled at the force and the greed, was better. What had come before was pale and weak, a soft belly, compared to the strength and muscle of what was now.

She could do all and any. She could take and could rule. There was nothing and no one to stop her.

In a mad dance she spun across the sand, above it, her arms spread like wings, her hair falling in coils like snakes. She could taste the death of her sister's murderer, the bright copper flavor of blood she'd spilled, and knew she had never supped so well.

Her laughter shot out like bolts, cracked the black bowl of the sky. A torrent of dark rain fell and hissed on the sand like acid.

He called her.

Somewhere through the wild night and her own fury she heard his voice. The faint glow of what had been inside her struggled to burn brighter.

She saw him, just a shadow fighting through the wind and rain to reach her. Love warred and wept in a heart gone cold.

"Go back!" she shouted at him, and her voice thundered, shook the world.

But still he came on, his hands reaching toward her—to gather

her in, to bring her back. And she saw, just for an instant, the gleam of his eyes against the night, that was love, and fear.

Out of the sky came a lance of fire. Even as she screamed, as that light inside her leaped, it speared through him.

She felt his death inside her. The pain and horror of what she'd sent out springing back, times three.

And the light inside her winked out. Left her cold, cold, cold.